Once Upon a Day

Also by Lisa Tucker

The Song Reader

Shout Down the Moon

Once Upon a Day

A NOVEL

LISA TUCKER

ATRIA BOOKS
New York London Toronto Sydney

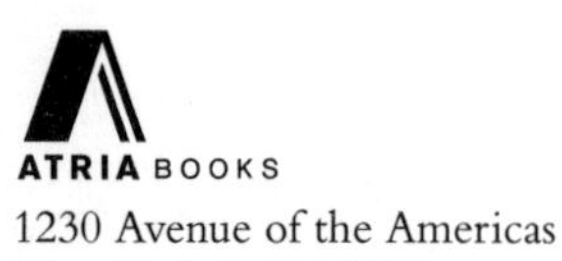

1230 Avenue of the Americas
New York, NY 10020

This book is a work of fiction. Names, characters, places and incidents are products of the author's imagination or are used fictitiously. Any resemblance to actual events or locales or persons, living or dead, is entirely coincidental.

For information address Atria Books, 1230 Avenue of the Americas, New York, NY 10020

Library of Congress Cataloging-in-Publication Data

Tucker, Lisa.
Once upon a day : a novel / Lisa Tucker.—1st Atria Books hardcover ed.
p. cm.
1. Motion picture producers and directors—Family relationships—Fiction. 2. Brothers and sisters—Fiction. 3. Missing persons—Fiction. 4. Young women—Fiction. 5. Ranch life—Fiction. 6. New Mexico—Fiction. I. Title.

PS3620.U3O53 2006
813'.6—dc22 2005053628

ISBN-13: 978-0-7434-9277-5
ISBN-10: 0-7434-9277-3

First Atria Books hardcover edition April 2006

10 9 8 7 6 5 4 3 2 1

Manufactured in the United States of America

This book is dedicated to Miles Tucker,
my beautiful son, who taught me how to imagine
and gave me back my life.

Dame Fortune once upon a day
To me was bountiful and kind;
But all things change; she changed her mind,
And what she gave she took away.
O Fortune, long I've sued to thee;
The gifts thou gavest me restore,
For, trust me, I would ask no more,
Could 'was' become an 'is' for me.

—CERVANTES, *Don Quixote*

Once Upon
a Day

PART ONE

The Charming Coincidence

one

STEPHEN SPAULDING was very happy, and you can't say that about most people. He hadn't sought happiness, but he recognized it. This was his gift: to know what he had.

When it was gone, of course he knew that too. He changed from a man who could smile at strangers first thing in the morning to a man who wouldn't look anybody in the eye. He'd lost his family in a freak accident, and the rest he let go of as easily as opening his hand and releasing a string of balloons. Good-bye to the family practice he had just started with two friends from his residency. Good-bye to the Victorian house he and Ellen had gone deeply into debt to buy when she got pregnant during his internship. Good-bye to the cradle and the tricycle and the pink and purple birthday party dress Lizzie never had a chance to wear.

More than a year later, he still hadn't adjusted to the way time itself had been altered. Before there was never enough time, and the list of things he and Ellen had not gotten around to doing was one of many things that still tortured him. The untaken trip to Paris bothered him less than the movies they'd talked about renting. Why hadn't they watched them? Ellen's entire list could be watched in a weekend. He knew this because he had done it, several times. He watched the movies his wife had wanted him to, and thought about what she would say if she were there. This was back in the early months, when he was trying to give her gifts, as though she could come back if only he worked harder to make her want this life.

After the accident, there was too much time. Each day stretched before him like a flat Kansas highway, the only landmarks the meals he forced himself to choke down, the few chores he performed, and the occasional walks he took, rarely noticing anything or anyone on his path. He finally bought the old green and white Checker cab not because he needed the income—his compensation from the city would support him forever, especially since he had no desires, nothing he wanted now—but because he could drive it as little or as much as he liked, sixteen hours a day, more if his insomnia was bad.

He wouldn't have sued, but the city gave him an enormous sum anyway. The newspaper headline called it a "regrettable tragedy." It was a Sunday in late July; the police were chasing a teenager who had stolen a rusted-out '84 Toyota from a neighbor's driveway. The car was worth less than five hundred dollars, but the patrol car that slammed into his family at the intersection had been going over eighty miles an hour. He was driving; Lizzie was in her booster seat in the back, behind Ellen. The teenage thief turned himself in when he heard what had happened. The policeman who was driving took early retirement.

And Stephen, the barely thirty-year-old family practice doc, became a cabbie. What difference did it make? His knowledge of how to heal bodies had done nothing for him anyway. His wife and four-year-old daughter had still died right in front of his eyes.

Now he was learning the quickest way to the airport from any street in St. Louis. How to slide around a bus, and when to change lanes so his customer would feel they were making progress. What times the restaurants and bars closed, and which of his regulars would be likely to drink one too many and need a ride on a Saturday night.

People often mentioned what a safe driver he was. The safest cab driver they'd ever ridden with. He nodded, but he didn't respond. He never drove without the radio playing. Talk show, pop music, news channel, it didn't matter. The radio was his excuse not to talk.

The only time he would answer was when a customer asked about the amusement park tickets. They didn't ask often, even though he'd had the tickets laminated and kept them displayed above the visor, right next to his license. Stephen wasn't surprised. He knew most people aren't interested in their cab drivers.

He wasn't surprised; still, he longed for the question. He longed for another opportunity to tell the whole story of that perfect July day at the amusement park: riding the water slides and the Ferris wheel and the child's roller coaster; eating hot dogs and ice cream—mint chocolate chip, Ellen's favorite; trying to win a giant stuffed panda bear, and when he couldn't make the ring toss (a setup, he was sure), buying the bear for his daughter anyway.

Every time he told the story, he added a few more details. As the months went by, the story often filled the entire drive; sometimes he would still be talking while his customer was trying to hand him money and get away.

He knew he was going too far, but he couldn't help himself. Back at his apartment whenever he tried to think of that day he drew a blank. It was only in the cab, talking to strangers, that he seemed to be able to bring it all to life: the feel of the sun on the back of his hands and the bright drips of green falling off their cones onto the hot pavement and how awkward and adorable Lizzie looked that night, lugging the giant panda to their car.

He didn't realize how he'd begun to live for these discussions until a rainy morning in April, when they suddenly came to an end.

He'd picked up a girl at the bus station downtown. One of the weirdos, though this one wasn't pierced or tattooed or obviously strung out, but even more bizarre, naturally pale as a made-up Goth, but dressed like a throwback to the fifties: long flared black skirt, fluffy pink sweater, even the white ankle socks and saddle oxford shoes. Her hair was in a thick braid, twisted like some kind of tight crown on top of her head, and she was sitting up so straight she looked uncomfortable, eyes unblinking, small white hands folded carefully in her lap. Stephen had already put her out of his mind when she mentioned the tickets about ten minutes into the ride. But before he could tell her about the slides or the food or even the perfect weather that day, she noticed what no one else had: that the tickets weren't stubs.

"What happened?" she said. "Why didn't you ever use those?"

He flushed with a confusion that quickly turned to anger. It had taken him nearly a year to perfect the story of the amusement park—for chrissakes, couldn't he have even this? He wasn't asking for all the days and hours and minutes he would have had with Ellen and Lizzie, he was just asking for one more day.

Stephen had been taking his family to the park when their car was broadsided. Lizzie had wanted to go all summer, and that day they had the tickets: they were really, finally going. All he had done in his story was change "were going" to "had gone." A mere verb shift, and yet it changed everything.

And now this strange girl in his cab was forcing him to change it back.

Her voice was entirely innocent. She had no idea what she'd taken from him. But then again, he had no idea what she was about to give.

two

WE HAD A FATHER who loved us. Even as my brother Jimmy turned his back on the Sanctuary, I knew he had to still believe this, deep in his soul.

In my earliest memory, Father was holding Jimmy and me on his lap, telling us how important we were to him. More important than all his money, more important than the Sanctuary, more important than the stars in the sky or the ground below. The most important thing in the known world, the most important thing imaginable. "I want you two to be happy here forever," he said, his voice as tender as his arms around us. "Whatever you want you can have, as long as it won't hurt you."

As long as it won't hurt you. Too bad Father had such an active imagination. When I was eight years old, I read a story about a girl on a tire swing, with long flowing hair glittering in the sun as she moved back and forth. I asked for a swing of my own, but Father couldn't do it. "Swings can wrap themselves around your neck and choke you, Dorothea," he said. "You can fly out of a swing and sever your spine." When Jimmy wanted paints—not watercolors, like we already had, but real rich colors, thick—so he could try to copy the encyclopedia picture of a Roman centurion onto his bedroom wall, Father wanted to give them to him, I know he did. He was shaking his head sadly when he told Jimmy, "Those paints are poison. The toxins could seep into your skin."

From pets that might bite to bicycles that could crash, our father had to protect us. He couldn't bear the idea of a plastic swimming pool, no matter how shallow, because a child can drown in only a few inches of water. Climbing trees was a sure way to break your arm, or worse. There were dozens of trees on our property, but none of them had limbs lower than twenty feet, thanks to Father and the chain saw he kept locked in the storage shed. From my bedroom window, the trees looked like a clump of upright celery stalks.

I was weaker than my brother; perhaps this was why it was easier for me to sympathize with Father's worries. I was only two years old when I developed what Grandma called my "nervous breathing," and what the doctor called an anxiety disorder. My heart would pound at a hundred and eighty beats per minute or more, and my breath would develop a frantic rhythm to match. Father taught me how to control it, so I wouldn't lose consciousness, but still, the horrible feelings of dizziness and panic were something I could never entirely forget, and they lurked in even my happiest moments, like snakes poised to strike.

We lived on thirty-five acres that straddled the border of Colorado and New Mexico, more than twenty miles from the nearest town. The four of us—Father, Grandma, Jimmy and me—were survivalists. That's what the local preacher said anyway, when he came for a visit to see what we were up to, and went away convinced, without ever stepping foot inside, that our father knew what he was about.

After he left, Father laughed. Each month, we ordered nearly everything we needed from Colorado Springs: three freezerfuls of food that arrived on the first Tuesday in a clean white truck. "Survivalists?" he said. "We wouldn't survive twenty-four hours without the delivery man."

Father could joke and laugh, but the grown-up Jimmy had forgotten all about that side of him. "He's a nut," my brother would say, and I would sigh. This was about a year before Jimmy left, for good as it turned out, though only Father suspected he wouldn't be returning. I thought he would come running back as soon as he realized what the world was like; I even tried to convince him in my letters that he was putting himself in danger, though of course I had no proof of this, and he laughed off all my fears. He wrote that he was surrounded by normal people doing normal things, like working and falling in love, things he himself was planning to do now that he had finally "escaped" from the Sanctuary at the ripe old age of twenty-three.

The Sanctuary was Father's name for our home.

We'd lived there as long as I could remember, though Jimmy claimed that he vividly remembered the time before, in California, when our mother was still alive. I was four when we left, he was six; maybe he did remember. Maybe everything he said was true: that we'd lived near the ocean in a house on a hill with a whole room just to watch movies in; that he'd gone to first grade with other children, and watched cartoons on television, and flown in airplanes to other countries, and rode at the front of a parade on Thanksgiving Day. He even got to stay outside until he was sunburned, he said, because a sunburn wasn't a big deal to our mother. She said a sunburn gave you rosy cheeks and little freckles across your nose and all you had to do was put on spray and it didn't hurt anymore.

Father would never allow us to stay outside for more than twenty minutes at a time. He would sit on our wide porch with his watch in his hand. "Sunburns can give you skin cancer," he said. "I'm sorry, children, but we have to be on the safe side."

Jimmy's first rebellion was pretending to be sick during lessons and then climbing out of his bedroom window so he could stand in the sun all morning. At first, Father thought Jimmy's redness was due to a terrible fever from his flu. When he realized the truth, he was so surprised he collapsed in the chair by Jimmy's bed, head in hands. Then Jimmy was sorry. He was only eleven years old; he still wanted to please our father.

Grandma said this rebellion would pass, but it didn't, obviously. As he grew to be a teenager, the things we'd accepted all our lives were suddenly unacceptable. Why hadn't we gone to school like normal children? Why did the doctor always come to our place? Why didn't we have a television like everyone else in the world? Why did we have to learn everything from old textbooks and an ancient set of encyclopedias? Why had we never left this stupid Sanctuary? Father got to go to town sometimes—he had a Land Rover just for such trips—why wouldn't he take us with him? What was wrong with him anyway?

It shocked me to hear my brother talk like this. Father had taken such good care of us for so long, and personally, I felt sorry for him, having to do it all with only Grandma to help. I often thought if only our mother was there, everything would have been much better, though the truth was the only thing I really remembered about her was her hair: long and fiery red, like Jimmy's. There were no pictures of her in the house; Grandma said it was because Father couldn't bear to see them. Neither Father nor Grandma would tell us how she died. Jimmy didn't remember either, but he said it must have been really awful, or why else did our father become so strange?

"He's no stranger than the Amish," I retorted during one of these arguments, sticking an encyclopedia volume in Jimmy's face, already open to a page on the Amish people of Pennsylvania. I was thirteen and I was ready. "At least we have electric lights!"

Jimmy frowned. "We don't have a religion."

I wasn't sure about this. Father said we were "lapsed Catholics," but Jimmy said that meant no longer Catholic, which meant no longer anything.

"So?" I said.

"The reason the Amish live like that is they believe it's what God wants. That's not what Father thinks at all. He thinks the people in town are evil monsters we have to stay away from."

"He never said that."

"Oh come on, Thea. You know how he talks about how corrupt the world is. What do you think he means? The dogs and cats and horses?"

Jimmy was rolling his eyes like I was a fool. Perhaps I was, but Father was not, of this I was certain. If he said the world was corrupt, then it had to be true. No matter how innocent the dusty road to town appeared, there was something out there, something unspeakably terrible and cruel. There had to be, or why would Father work so hard to keep us away from it?

It helped that Grandma took my side. She'd lived in California her entire life, but she never missed it. She said the world was a bad place that had made me sick and nearly destroyed our father. "You're lucky he bought this Sanctuary for you," Grandma said. She was in the kitchen, cooking as usual. We had Mrs. Rosa, our housekeeper, for weekly cleaning, but Grandma herself prepared all our meals. She never let me help her. Father didn't want me to get cut or burned; he thought it might bring on one of my attacks. "I hate to think what would have happened if he hadn't," Grandma concluded, and I nodded.

The unknown was always more frightening than the familiar, and the Sanctuary was familiar. Why didn't Jimmy see this too? The Sanctuary was a safe place for us all. We had very good books, old though they may have been. We had a beautiful piano, and a record player with hundreds of records, also old, but many great songs. We had fields of flowers to gaze at (but not walk through, in case of bees). We had a father who loved us more than life itself, and who had taught us algebra and geometry, Shakespeare and Spenser, the history of the world (up until 1960, when Father said the culture became so decadent that even learning about it could harm a child's spirits), biology and physics and geography.

Our own nearest town, Tuma, New Mexico, we knew only by the address on our mail. It was too small to be on any of the maps in Father's library. Too small to be interesting, I told Jimmy, when he complained about wanting to go and see it for himself.

Part of me did understand Jimmy's longings, especially when I found myself wondering how I would ever fall in love. I'd never known a boy, never had a kiss, never even had a crush, though sometimes my stomach would do a strange flip when I saw a picture of a handsome man in our encyclopedia. My favorites were John Keats, F. Scott Fitzgerald and an unnamed Civil War soldier with the most mournful expression. When I was about fourteen, I made up a story about the soldier, ending with his arrival at our front door to ask for my hand in marriage. It was a silly daydream, but it cheered me. Father said I had an optimistic temperament, and maybe it was true. Certainly I never gave up hope that the man of my future would arrive when the time was right, though how that would happen, I couldn't say.

To Jimmy, my optimism was just annoying.

"You're so conservative," he told me once. He was older then: eighteen, nineteen. I was older too, but I hadn't changed, which of course was the point.

"Conservative means to hold on to what you have." My voice was firm. "I see nothing wrong with that."

I didn't realize Father was standing right behind me until I heard his quiet laugh, but I was glad I could give this to him. Nearly every day, he had to listen to Jimmy's complaints. He'd been a patient teacher throughout our childhood and he was patient now, almost to a fault. He'd let Jimmy yell at him, yet he never raised his own voice. And he always apologized to Jimmy. He said he'd done the best he could, but maybe it wasn't enough. All he'd wanted was to protect us, and that's all he still wanted.

"I hope you understand," Father would say softly. He was a tall man with well-defined features and thick eyebrows over deep blue-gray eyes framed by his ever-present black glasses; I'd always thought he was as distinguished as any of the presidents in our encyclopedia. But lately, he'd begun to look tired: his eyes haunted and his shoulders stooped with what I knew was the weight of his only son's rebellion.

Half the time Jimmy said—or shouted—"No, I don't understand," and ended the conversation by stomping out of the room.

If Grandma hadn't gotten sick, Jimmy probably would have left even sooner. He was twenty-one, of legal age to do as he wished, as he liked to say (constantly); maybe he was just waiting for the right moment. On the other hand, maybe he would have made his peace with Father if Grandma hadn't gotten sick and suddenly decided that Father had been wrong for taking us away from California, after all.

I turned against her then, I have to confess. Not that she ever knew. I remained kind to Grandma until the end, and it wasn't hard because I did love her. But I loved Father a thousand times more, and I quickly decided that Grandma's sick-bed revelations were no different from the ramblings of a lunatic.

Even Dr. Humphrey, the town's doctor, said Grandma's mind was going faster than her body. The diagnosis, inoperable cancer, had been confirmed by tests at the hospital in Pueblo. She left in an ambulance, and returned the same way, a week later, to die at home with her family. She was eighty-six years old, and they predicted she wouldn't last more than a month or two, but she lingered for over a year. During that year, she spent most of her time talking about the past.

Jimmy listened eagerly as she transformed California from a terribly corrupt place from which we were lucky to have escaped to a gorgeous land of sandy beaches and palm trees and sunsets reflecting gold and purple on the water. And oh, Grandma said, such fun things there were to do! Strolling the pier at Santa Monica and riding on the huge Ferris wheel. Driving in the canyon with all the twists and turns and beautiful views. Sipping a glass of wine by the side of the pool. Watching the filming of a movie on the studio lot. Taking the kids to Disneyland.

"Remember that, Fred?" Grandma would say to Father, after she'd sung the praises of another wonderful thing about the place she was now calling our "home." He would sit on the side of her bed and take her hand—and I would look at Jimmy and raise my eyebrows. Our father's name was Charles. If Grandma couldn't remember her own son's name, why should anything else she said be taken seriously?

One night Jimmy had the nerve to suggest that maybe Charles wasn't his name. I pointed out that Grandma had always called Father Charles, but Jimmy wasn't persuaded. "Maybe Grandma was in on it too," Jimmy said. "Maybe now she's finally telling the truth."

We were standing outside on the porch. It was a cold night in January, so naturally I had on my coat and hat and gloves and warmest boots. Jimmy, on the other hand, was wearing only his light sweater and blue denim pants. He had decided Father's rule about dressing warmly was as pointless as all his other rules.

"You realize that you're calling him a liar," I whispered. My heart was racing a little, but I was taking deep breaths and reminding myself that Jimmy could not possibly mean this. It was just his rebellion talking.

Jimmy was rubbing his hands together vigorously, stomping his feet, shivering a little. But he would not concede he needed his coat.

"I don't want to believe it either," he said. But then he added, "What makes you so sure he's not?"

I could have given him a hundred reasons, yet in the end, I knew it came down to trust. I had trusted our father for my entire life. He had never done anything to make me question that trust.

"He has a driver's license," I finally said. We had both seen it, not often, but enough times to know it said "Charles O'Brien."

This was what it took to convince my brother that our father hadn't lied about his own name. It struck me as very sad.

During Grandma's last few months she became even more incoherent. She would talk of her own childhood as though it were happening now, even calling out in the most heartbroken voice for her mother and father. I felt so sorry for her, but Jimmy persisted in believing that somewhere in her talk he would find the key to understanding all the mysteries of our family. He even tried asking Grandma how our mother died (when Father was holed up in his study, doing his monthly accounting), but poor Grandma took the question as another opportunity to cry over all the people she'd lost over her long life. Whether she was crying about Mother too wasn't clear. Jimmy swore she said Helena, our mother's name, but I thought he only imagined it.

Actually, the only time I heard her talk about our mother, Jimmy wasn't there. He was downstairs helping Father haul wood; I was reading to Grandma when, out of the blue, she patted my hand and said, "You know, your mother would be very proud of what a fine woman you're turning out to be."

I admit I took this a bit more seriously than the rest of Grandma's talk. In fact, a few minutes later, when Grandma started crying again, I found myself crying along with her, thinking about my mother, this red-haired Helena whom I could barely remember. The idea that she would be proud of me was so wonderful, and yet, I didn't think it was true. I had read of heroic women in the encyclopedia: women like Florence Nightingale, Joan of Arc, Harriet Tubman. My accomplishments so far were limited to keeping myself from any injuries beyond the rare paper cut, reading most of the books in Father's small library and playing the piano, not particularly well. I had never had to face adversity; I had never even had to make a conscious choice that mattered to anyone but myself. What was I then but a grown-up-size little girl?

I rarely cried at all, and never for upwards of fifteen minutes as I did that day with Grandma. Crying invariably led to an attack of my nervous breathing, and I had learned over the years to stop the feelings before the tears could begin. I expected to have an attack that day too, but instead I just kept crying until I managed to pull myself together and return to the job of reading *Jane Eyre.* I'd been reading it to Grandma since the day she came back from the hospital: partly because it had always been one of her favorite novels, but mainly because every time I asked her what book she wanted now, she'd say *Jane Eyre* as though the title had just occurred to her—even if we'd just finished it. We made it all the way through the book seven times and were halfway through the eighth when she finally passed away about a month later.

Before she died though, she managed to convince Jimmy that he should leave the Sanctuary as soon as possible. This was what he told me, only two weeks after Father and the preacher had buried her. He claimed Grandma had even told him where he should go, and it wasn't to California, like I would have expected. It was to a place that made absolutely no sense. Missouri.

When I asked him why Missouri, he refused to say. My brother, who had always told me everything, would not tell me the reason for the most important decision he'd ever made in his life.

"Because there isn't a reason," I sputtered. "Because Grandma mumbled 'misery' and you decided she must have meant Missouri."

He refused to argue. He was going to Missouri, end of discussion. He was leaving even though he knew how Father would feel about it.

"Too bad," Jimmy told me, right before he left, "if I hurt him. He hurt us more."

No doubt the anger I felt at Jimmy helped me watch him walk down that dirt road and disappear.

"I'm at the bus station," Jimmy wrote. "I've never heard so much noise! The buses, the cars, talking, screaming, laughing! I'm sitting next to a woman from town who told me she heard our father was the richest man in New Mexico. Then she asked me, 'Isn't he eccentric, like Howard Hughes?' I burst out laughing."

I wasn't sure who Howard Hughes was, but I looked him up in the appropriate volume of the encyclopedia. There wasn't enough to conclude he was eccentric. I wondered how Jimmy knew to laugh.

From the beginning, he kept his promise to write; I was relieved about that. I got mail from him almost every day: sometimes letters, sometimes postcards. When he arrived in St. Louis, he sent me a card with an aerial view of the city. He talked about how excited he was, ending with, "I had to run in front of traffic to get a cab. Poor old man would shit if he knew."

I winced at Jimmy's crude language; I'd never heard him use a curse word before. The sad part was Father did know. He'd collected the mail himself every day for all the years we'd lived here. He read the postcard, and he saw all the return addresses on the letters as Jimmy moved from place to place, from new friend to new friend, trying to find where he belonged, he said. Find whatever it was he was looking for.

"I worry about him," Father would say, nearly every night at supper. He still wouldn't let me cook and nothing I could say would persuade him. Whenever I pressured him too hard, he would remind me of the day I was born.

"You only weighed five pounds. I could hold you in one hand." His voice would grow soft. "I vowed that day to make sure nothing ever happened to you."

One time I asked him, "What if your mother had vowed the same thing? Then how would we eat?"

He laughed a little, but he continued cooking the stew. And during the meal, he mentioned Jimmy again. Wondering how he was. Wishing he would return to us. Hoping he was all right, out there all alone in the world.

I was worried about Jimmy too, but I was also worried about Father. What Jimmy had done by leaving was no less than crush his spirit, and nothing I tried seemed to be of any help. My optimism was unrelenting; I never greeted Father with anything but a smile; I mentioned every day how lucky I felt to be here in the safest of places, but still, the shadow of sadness never left him.

It wasn't even two years later when it took its inevitable toll.

Father was only sixty-one, but the disease that came over him made him seem like a very old man. For weeks I watched him struggle to get out of bed, eat almost nothing, hold his head between his thin hands and wince with a pain he wouldn't talk about. He still insisted on doing all the cooking himself, but luckily, there was much less to cook now that it was just the two of us. We could and did go months without ordering any food. I could and did eat meal after meal of what I claimed was my new favorite: bread and prepackaged slices of cheese (no cutting required), so he wouldn't have to prepare anything.

I knew it was bad when he asked me to call Dr. Humphrey for a visit. I rushed to Father's study where he kept the only phone we had, an unusual kind, according to Jimmy—it could dial out but not ring in. Though I'd never used a phone before, I figured it out quickly and was so pleased with myself I almost forgot the urgency of my mission.

Dr. Humphrey came by that same day. He said he was concerned, but he couldn't make a precise diagnosis unless Father would come to the hospital for tests. I tried to persuade him, but all my attempts went nowhere. He wouldn't leave. He said the only thing he wanted was to see his son again.

I wrote to Jimmy. I'd been hearing from him less and less, but still, I expected a quick response given this emergency. No matter how angry he was with Father—and surprisingly, he seemed to get angrier as time went by; his recent letters were full of curses, talk of how our father had fucked him up royal and screwed up his whole life, et cetera to coarse et cetera—I couldn't imagine that he could ignore my cry for help.

Two weeks later, when I still hadn't heard anything, I snuck into Father's study again and tried to track down a phone number for Jimmy, to no avail. A week or so after that I decided there was no choice: I had to go to St. Louis and get my brother.

I called Dr. Humphrey and asked him what to do about caring for my father. Mrs. Rosa, our housekeeper, was still with us, but she barely spoke English and she was only at the house one day a week.

Dr. Humphrey sent a nurse who agreed to stay until I returned, as long as I gave her a large sum of money "up front," which she explained meant before I left. I did so, and an hour later, dressed in what Grandmother had always called my Sunday best clothes, I walked through the door.

Father was still asleep and I couldn't bring myself to say goodbye. I did leave him a long letter, in which I explained that I would be as careful and cautious as he'd raised me to be and promised to return to the Sanctuary very soon. I also told him I loved him, but I refused to let myself feel how true this was, knowing I would break down at the thought of how worried he would be when he discovered I was gone. But there was no choice. If the only thing he wanted was Jimmy, then I would just have to bring Jimmy home. Surely the two of us could convince Father to get the medical help that his life might depend on.

It was a Wednesday; my plan was to return by Saturday. It was feasible. Jimmy had told me the trip there took about a day and the trip back the same. That left me one day to find my brother, and it shouldn't take half that, I thought, since I could just give the taxi driver the return address on the most recent envelope.

I had decided not to carry a suitcase or umbrella or even a purse, so a thief couldn't come after me. I could wear the same clothes for three days; I'd always been a tidy person. My socks were the only things I would have to replace at some point. I had on three pairs of panties; I figured I would remove the inner pair each day and throw them out. I had the stack of money I took from Father's desk drawer, hundreds of dollars (in case of emergency), curled together and shoved deep in the pocket of my skirt. I had my toothbrush wrapped in plastic and stuck in my sock. I had Dr. Humphrey's phone number committed to memory, so I could call and check on Father's condition each day. The last few letters Jimmy had written, with three separate addresses, were tucked under my sweater close to my heart. And folded into the bottom of my shoe was a page from a poem, *The Faerie Queene.* I'd cut it out carefully, so the binding of the book wasn't disturbed. In the middle of the page was the line that would be my new motto: *Be bold, be bold, and every where Be Bold.*

I admit I tried not to think too much about what all this boldness might entail.

Dr. Humphrey offered me a ride in his automobile to the local bus station, and I gladly took him up on it. Jimmy had walked the dirt path all those miles, but I wasn't as healthy, nor did I have the time to waste. I took the local bus to Raton, and then the Greyhound to Denver, and then the second Greyhound to Missouri, and then I was finally in a taxicab, probably going down the same roads my brother had gone down when he first arrived in St. Louis. And he was right: the noise was the first shock. It was stunning how loud a city was: stunning and absolutely thrilling.

Everyone on the buses had been quietly pleasant. When people smiled at me, I acknowledged their smiles with one of my own, to be polite. After a while though, I was smiling more spontaneously. Nothing outside was bad. This was what Jimmy had been telling me for nearly two years, but I hadn't believed him. I expected to be afraid. I was waiting to feel the dread of other people that Father felt, that he couldn't help letting slip out now that he was too sick to keep up a brave front.

Nothing outside was bad, and so much was astonishing. The trip across Colorado, Kansas and Missouri was wonderful, but being in the city—knowing that I was in a real city, a place with thousands and thousands of fellow creatures—was almost more exciting than I could bear. I watched the crowds moving on the sidewalks. Such colorful clothes! The variety of expressions people made! The unusual songs playing on what appeared to be giant portable radios! The black people and brown people and especially all the younger people! People of my own age and Jimmy's!

I'd been in the taxicab for fifteen minutes and I was feeling very bold—bold enough to speak to a total stranger. The driver had an appealing face; perhaps that was why I decided to let him be the first person in the city I spoke to. I was also proud that I had something to say to him. Some months before, Jimmy had sent me a ticket stub from a concert he'd attended. When it fell out of the envelope, I'd studied it carefully before putting it away. I knew the difference between a ticket and a stub. I knew the tickets the taxi driver had displayed were never used.

My question was so ordinary, or so I thought, and yet the next thing I knew, the driver was not only refusing to answer, he was so angry he turned all the way around at the first stoplight to look at me with what seemed to be unmitigated hatred.

The sudden feeling of fear struck me with the force of a blow, and yet I also felt vindicated. So *this* was what Father had tried to protect us from. *This* was why he kept us from any contact with the world outside the Sanctuary: because human beings were every bit as unpredictable as a tire swing, and just as capable of harm.

Of course the fear was stronger than the vindication, and I squeezed my eyes tight and wished to be home harder than I'd ever wished for anything in my life. When I found myself still in the cab, I also found myself headed for the worst kind of nervous attack. My heart was already pounding so hard I felt like it would beat its way right out of my chest, when I began to steady my breathing and calm myself the way my father had taught me, the way I'd been doing since I was a very small child. I opened my mouth and began to sing.

three

"WHAT THE HELL? Are you all right?"

The taxicab driver's voice was loud. My breathing hadn't steadied. I closed my eyes again and started over at the beginning of the song. It was one of my favorites; Jimmy had told me that I'd been singing it even before we left California.

"'It's a marvelous night for a moon dance . . .'"

I sang louder when I realized the driver had pulled against the curb and stopped. This wasn't the address I'd given him. Why had he opened his door and gotten out? What was he doing now, opening my door?

"Don't touch me," I managed, when he reached for my arm.

"I just want to check your pulse."

"No!"

"All right," he said. "Put your head between your knees."

"Please," I gasped, holding up my hand palm out, hoping he would back away.

He did step back, but not enough that I could shut the door. He stood watching me as I sang the song again and again until my heart stopped thrashing and I could breathe normally.

At some point, I had dropped my head between my knees, but not because this taxi driver had told me to. Our doctor, the one before Dr. Humphrey, had told me the same thing. I always dropped my head between my knees when the dizziness got bad. Father used to joke that I'd sung more songs looking down at my shoes than anyone in the country.

When I sat up straight, the driver finally shut my door and walked around to the front of the cab. He was back in the driver's seat when I told him I was getting out now.

"Here?"

"How much do I owe?" I said.

"You don't want to get out here."

This road wasn't full of colors and music and people like the streets near the bus station. It was as deserted as the land around our house, but instead of hills and trees, there were tall, ugly brown brick buildings, one after another, sitting on concrete slabs.

Still, I was more afraid of this taxicab driver and his unpredictable anger.

"Yes, I do," I told him. "Please tell me the fare."

"Who lives here?" he said, holding up the empty envelope I'd given him with Jimmy's most recent return address. "Who are you visiting?"

I'd promised myself that I would say nothing about my life or plans to anyone. I remembered Father had always deflected questions about our family, whether those questions were asked by the doctor or the preacher or one of the delivery truck drivers. "It's none of their business," Father would say. "People are always looking for the weakness in others. It's one of the darker traits of human nature."

"I can't talk about it," I said to the driver.

"Fine," he muttered, running one hand through his thick brown hair.

"Because it's none of your business."

"Whatever."

Whatever? I'd already given him a reason, but thinking he'd misunderstood, I repeated it.

"All right, all right," he said. "Do you think I really care who you're seeing?"

If his voice had been angry, I would have jumped out of his cab right then, even though I hadn't paid the fare. The words were angry, true, but his tone was as exhausted as Father's now that he was sick.

"Look," he said, "I'm trying to keep you from walking around in that strange outfit in a bad neighborhood." He turned around to face me. "You're what? Eighteen? But if you insist on being a fool, be—"

"I'm twenty-two, almost twenty-three." The words escaped my lips before I remembered my promise, but even when I did, I couldn't stop myself. "And my clothes are not strange. They're very well made, the finest of their kind."

"That isn't a costume?" He wasn't smiling, but his tone was clearly amused. "You're actually wearing that?"

"Of course I'm wearing it. I see nothing funny here." I paused and took a long, untroubled breath. This was a topic I knew well: Father had been talking about it as far back as I could remember. "Why must everything be modern? People think that just because something is new it's automatically better. My clothes are modeled after a style from the fifties, but the fifties was a time of enormous hope in our country, a time when the family was the center of many people's lives, a time—"

"When we weren't even born."

"So?" I said, because I really didn't see what that had to do with it.

He didn't say anything for what felt like a long minute. He was still facing my direction, staring out the back window. I took this opportunity to look at him.

He was a little unkempt: brown hair that needed a trim, stubble on his face that Father would have called a "five o'clock shadow" (and yet it wasn't even ten in the morning), a button-down blue shirt that could have used an iron. Still, there was something about his face that I couldn't help finding appealing. I wanted to call his expression "caring," though there was certainly no reason to think he was a caring person. If anything, he kept making a point of how little he cared: first about who I was visiting (though he himself had asked the question), and now about what I was wearing and what he called my "theory of the fifties."

"I just want to take you where you need to be," he said, and exhaled. "Is that all right?"

"Fine," I said. He turned around and started the cab. After he pulled on to the street, though, I had to ask him something.

"Why did you call it my 'theory'?"

"What?"

I sat forward a little. " 'Theory' is from the Latin word *theoria*. It means the principles of a body of knowledge, as in a *theory* of art."

He glanced at me in the mirror. "It can also mean an assumption that hasn't been proved."

"True," I said, thinking, the man knows his *Webster's* unabridged. "But that's the way it's used in science. I don't see how it applies to what I was saying."

When he didn't respond, I was confused, but I said, "Want to know what word I would use instead of 'theory'?"

"Sure, I'll bite."

"Bite what?"

"It's just an expression."

"But what does it mean?"

"You've never heard that before?" he said, raising his eyebrows. "Where did you grow up, Mars?"

He had nice eyebrows. They were a lighter color than his hair, and not too arched. I liked looking at him in the mirror, especially as he wasn't looking back at me. I could study him, as if the black frame of the mirror were a picture frame, and he were just a photograph of a man, as in my encyclopedias, but breathing and alive.

"No," I said, smiling. "And that's no to both questions. No, I've never heard your expression, and no, I didn't grow up on Mars."

I almost added, "because Mars isn't inhabited," but luckily I'd stopped myself. Father had mentioned something about moon travel in the sixties. What if there had been Mars travel in the eighties and Mars colonies now?

He inhaled. " 'I'll bite' is like saying 'I'll take the bait.' "

"As in fishing?" I'd never done it, but of course I knew what it was.

He nodded.

"But hold on. If what I said was the bait, and you were the fish taking it, then . . ." I was having trouble finishing the idea. It made no sense. "You thought hearing my answer was going to harm you in some way?"

"Are you serious?" He ran his hand through his hair, making it even messier.

"Wouldn't that be the only conclusion? Unless you mean it's a temptation. I suppose bait can be looked at that way too, but since it's on the end of a hook, and its purpose isn't to feed the fish, but to trick—"

"Look, I think I have to pay attention to the road now. I'm sorry."

"Oh, I understand," I said happily. I was starting to really like his voice, especially the way he'd said "I'm sorry." I'd never heard anything like it. The tone reminded me of a cello. "The road is the most important thing when you're driving. Even I know that."

He turned a black knob then and music came on. A car radio. Father had one in the Land Rover too, and once Jimmy had taken his keys and snuck into the Rover to listen to it. He got caught when he forgot to remove the key and the car battery died. But "dead" for batteries turned out to mean something very different from the usual meaning of "dead." Father was able to bring it back to life with the help of red and black wires connected to the battery of one of the delivery trucks. My brother didn't get punished of course; he never did.

When I asked Jimmy what he'd heard on the radio, he told me he was trying to find the news and see if anything important was happening in the world. The only thing he'd heard about, he said, was a smashing pumpkin drummer who was arrested. We both thought it was strange that someone would even want to smash pumpkins, whether or not they could be arrested.

I sat back and watched as we drove down street after street. We were still in the concrete part of the city: no trees, no flowers, lots of buildings with gaping holes where the window glass should have been. The music on the radio seemed to fit because it wasn't at all pretty either. It sounded more like screaming than singing, but I realized that might just be me. No one can ever know what something really sounds like or looks like or even is; I learned that when Father taught us modern physics and relativity.

"Einstein!" I said, louder than I'd intended to, and I startled Stephen Spaulding. That was his name; I could see it on his taxi license. It sounded like the name of a poet.

"Dammit," he said.

"I'm sorry," I said, but my voice didn't sound like a cello. It sounded a little out of breath, more like a squeaky violin. I wished I could ask Mr. Spaulding not to curse. Cursing made me nervous, always had.

"It's all right," he said, and shook his head.

I waited a bit. "Would you like to know why I said Einstein?"

"What the hell," he said, but he smiled. His first smile. "If I say no, you'll tell me anyway."

"Actually, I wouldn't," I said, grinning. He had a really beautiful smile, this Mr. Spaulding. White teeth in rows as perfect as piano keys. No overbite, like I had. Mine was a slight overbite, but still. "However, I think you'll find it interesting. I was thinking of Einstein's theory of relativity, and then I realized there it was again! Theory!"

"Like the *Sesame Street* Word of the Day."

"Sesame Street?"

"Yeah." He turned left, and his voice grew quieter. "I never watched the show much myself, but I knew a little girl who loved all the videos."

"Video, meaning the picture on television, rather than the sound?"

"You really expect me to believe you don't know what a video is? That you're an American in 2003 and you've never been in a Blockbuster?"

He was angry again, but just like before, I heard that tired sadness in his voice that I knew so well from listening to Father. Even before he got sick, even before Jimmy left, Father sometimes sounded like this no matter how happy he claimed to be. I never understood why, and I didn't understand now either.

I sat up straighter and looked out the window. After a moment, Mr. Spaulding told me we were almost there.

"Thank you," I said quietly.

He nodded. Neither of us said anything until he pulled in front of one of the ugliest buildings on the block. It was at the top of maybe fifteen concrete steps. All the windows had bars and I shuddered at the thought that it was some type of prison.

"All right," he said, turning off the cab. "Are you sure this is where you want to go?"

"It was on the envelope," I said, gulping. My boldness was at a low point right then, but if Jimmy was in there, what choice did I have?

He waited a minute before he turned around and glanced at me. "You want me to go in with you?"

"Oh, that would be nice." I exhaled. "Very, very nice, actually."

He nodded, and then he was out of the cab and opening my door.

I stepped out right into a puddle, splashing my socks and soaking my shoes. I told him I hadn't realized the rain collected on the sides of streets. He raised those interesting eyebrows again, and I smiled. "I should have worn my rain boots, but at least my toothbrush is wrapped in plastic." I took it out of my sock to show it to him, and that's when I remembered. "Oh no, my poem!"

I sat down on the first step and slipped off my right shoe. But the page was fine. It wasn't even damp. The shoe had protected it.

"Thick leather," I said proudly. "These are handmade in Scotland, but my father says all shoes were like this in the fifties."

He smiled, only a half smile, but still very pleasant to look at. It struck me as odd that he so rarely smiled since his lips looked more comfortable that way.

I was still staring up at him when he said, "Are you going to put your shoe back on?"

"Of course I am." I crammed it on my foot and began to tie the soggy laces. "What kind of oddball goes around without shoes?"

"I can't imagine," he said, and let out a short soft laugh.

At some point during that day, it did cross my mind that I was breaking my word to Father. I'd said I would be careful and cautious, and here I was with this taxicab driver, a stranger and a fairly incomprehensible one at that. I had no reason to trust Mr. Spaulding, and yet I kept finding myself not only willing to take him into my confidence, but eager to. I would like to say it was part of my new boldness, but unfortunately it was the opposite. Many of the places I saw that day terrified me, and I increasingly relied on Mr. Spaulding to give me the courage to continue the search.

Jimmy was not at the first address we tried, or the second one, or the third. It was the middle of the afternoon; the taxi cost had grown to almost three hundred dollars when he said he was going to turn the fare machine off.

"Why?"

"So you won't have to keep paying. I'm sure you don't have this kind of money."

"I do, actually." I was leaning back against the seat with my eyes closed. I'd barely slept on the all-night bus from Denver, and now the disappointment had left me completely worn-out. "I took almost two thousand dollars from my father before I left."

"I think you need to eat," he said.

I mumbled something, maybe it was yes, though I was already floating away, telling myself it was all right to rest for a minute or two. My breath was steady, but I was sicker at heart than I'd ever been in my life.

My poor brother. How could I have been so wrong about his condition?

For all those months that Father had been worrying about Jimmy, I had been secretly angry with him for not coming home. Even though I'd never admitted it, even to myself—how could I admit it, when the world outside the Sanctuary was bad?—I had let all those postcards and letters convince me that he was out there somewhere having a wonderful time. Maybe he even wanted me to believe that. Certainly he never said anything about his real situation. He never gave me the smallest hint that he was living in hovels as squalid as in any Dickens novel.

The three places we'd been were uglier than anything I'd ever imagined. The rooms were small and dirty and inhabited by people who seemed as unlike my brother as if Jimmy really had been a Martian. No one could tell us where he'd gone, but they all knew who I was looking for as soon as Mr. Spaulding described him. (I was afraid to even talk to these people. Luckily, Mr. Spaulding graciously relayed everything I whispered to him: that we were looking for Jimmy O'Brien, a tall, thin boy with red hair and pale skin like mine.)

"Oh, Crazy Jimmy," they'd say. Or "that crazy white boy." Or "Crazy Joe," as if his name didn't even matter.

Each time when we got back in the cab, Mr. Spaulding told me not to take it too seriously. "They're strung out," he'd say. "They were on something." I didn't understand what he was talking about, but I was too disheartened to ask.

They had all called my sweet brother "crazy." And they'd said other things too. "Crazy Jimmy, he couldn't get no job." "He freaked everybody out." "He used to scream for hours at night, wake up the whole building." "He stared and stared, and that's just weird, man." "You say she's his sister? That's funny, 'cause Crazy Joe said his family was all dead."

If it wasn't for my fear of having a breathing attack, I would have cried at that last part. Not that Jimmy said we were dead, but that he'd acted like it was true, even when we could have helped him. Father had told me over and over to offer Jimmy money and I'd done it nearly every time I wrote to him. But Jimmy always said no.

"He'd buy paints instead of food, Crazy Jimmy would. He painted the weirdest-ass pictures you ever seen. He left some of 'em behind, wanna look?"

Ever since the days when Jimmy penciled the Roman centurion on his wall, he'd wanted to be a painter. He'd always had a knack for drawing. Even when we were young, he could draw an apple and it looked like an apple, where my apples looked like circles with commas on top.

I was eager to see the pictures Jimmy left behind, and once I had seen them, I would have paid nearly every dime I had to have them, but Mr. Spaulding negotiated for me and I only had to pay a dollar a piece since they were, after all, my own brother's property.

I would have paid every dime, even though I found the pictures so revolting I was glad when I first laid eyes on them that I hadn't eaten all morning. Even Mr. Spaulding winced, though as we were loading them into the trunk of the cab, he told me they were quite good. "Your brother is a real artist, Dorothea."

Of course I'd told him my name. If he was going to know Jimmy's name, he might as well know mine. He'd also told me to call him Stephen rather than Mr. Spaulding, but I hadn't been able to do it.

I nodded just to be polite, and because I couldn't trust myself to say anything without crying.

The pictures were all of death. One had a small beautiful dove that was being eaten alive by a lion. Another had what looked to be the corpses of two children floating in the middle of a pool. A third had nothing but a wall splattered with blood and the curse word "bitch." The last was a man screaming and out of his mouth came a snake with its head torn off.

I had to rest after seeing these horrible images and escape from my own fear about what could have happened to my brother to change him into this. The last time I saw him he was sauntering down the dirt road, waving a happy good-bye. In his most recent letter—some weeks ago, but still—he'd said he was looking forward to spring in the city. He wanted to get outside more and take long walks. He was hoping to go to the outdoor theater. He was going to ask a girl to a movie.

I was only planning to shut my eyes until Mr. Spaulding stopped the cab, but instead I fell into a deep sleep that lasted nearly three hours. For all that time, we were parked in front of a restaurant where Mr. Spaulding had driven us. When I woke up, it was almost dark, suppertime, and I asked him why he hadn't told me we were here.

He was listening to the radio. "It didn't matter to me," he said, and shrugged. "Ready to eat now?"

I stretched and looked at him in the mirror. "Fine," I said. I was starving.

The restaurant he'd picked was called Steak 'n Shake. It looked like a clean, bright place, and I loved the idea of eating steak after so many months of eating bread and cheese at home. The steak turned out to be steak burgers, but good enough. I also ordered a chocolate milk shake. Mr. Spaulding ordered his burger with fries and a milk shake, and I realized that he hadn't eaten today either.

"Good outfit," the waitress said, and laughed. "Going to a sock hop?"

I didn't reply. I'd already heard comments all day about these clothes, most of which I didn't understand. If I could have changed into something more modern right then, I would have. Obviously,

Father's beliefs about the fifties were a lot easier to go along with when people weren't laughing at me.

The food came quickly. I ate without talking for several minutes, and then I told Mr. Spaulding how much I appreciated what he'd done for me today.

"Not a problem," he said, but he didn't look up.

I waited another moment. "I've been thinking about something all day. Do you know of any reason someone would want to come to Missouri?"

"I take it you're not impressed with our fair state?"

"No, I am, very much. It's really the most interesting place I've ever seen. It's just that my brother left home with the explicit goal of coming to Missouri, and he wouldn't tell me his reason."

"It does seem like an unusual choice. You don't have relatives here?"

I shook my head, and fell silent as I watched a family sit down in the booth across from us. The man and the woman were holding hands, and the two children, a boy and a girl, looked very young, though the boy was a bit older than the little girl. It struck me that the composition of this family was the same as ours had been, before my mother died. If only she were here right now, she could help me get Father to a hospital and help me find Jimmy. If only she were here, I thought, none of this would have even happened.

The gloom was overtaking me, but I shook it off and concentrated on what remained of my food.

"This is delicious," I said, holding up the cylinder-shaped green food I'd just taken a bite from. "I've never tasted anything like it. What's it called?"

"A pickle," Mr. Spaulding said, and laughed that soft, musical laugh of his. I'd only heard it a few times all day, but it never failed to cheer me.

"Of course," I said, smiling. "I've heard of those. I don't think my father likes them though."

We'd both finished eating when I finally admitted I had no idea what to do next. He looked at me. "Maybe you should start again tomorrow. Where are you staying? What hotel?"

"I don't know. It probably sounds foolish, but I was hoping I wouldn't need to stay the night. I thought I would have Jimmy with me and we could go back."

He took a long breath. "Do you want to keep looking? I know a few places we could try. No guarantees."

"Oh yes. Thank you so much."

"I'm not promising anything."

"Thank you," I repeated.

We got back in the cab and headed off into the early evening darkness, though it wasn't dark at all compared to home. There were streetlamps and office buildings still lit, traffic lights changing colors, stores with blinking yellow bulbs. I wondered if anyone had trouble sleeping with all this brightness, but then I remembered that I'd taken a nap in this very cab in broad daylight. At home, I never slept after sunrise, and I certainly never napped. Maybe everyone in the city was exhausted from all this light and motion.

Mr. Spaulding drove for about twenty minutes before he stopped at a building right in the heart of what I could tell was downtown from the closeness of the Arch, which he'd pointed out earlier. He told me this was a shelter.

"A shelter?" I said.

"For the homeless."

The very idea made me sad, and I was almost glad Jimmy wasn't there. But the next place Mr. Spaulding stopped was even worse. He told me it was a hospital, and I could tell it was from the horrible noise as an ambulance blared into the driveway marked "Emergency." But then we drove to the other side of the building, by the sign that read "Psychiatric."

"My brother is not crazy," I said, leaning forward, grabbing the front seat. "I know all those people called him crazy, but it isn't true! I've known him my entire life, and he's as sane as I am. He's not in the nuthouse!"

"The what?"

"The insane asylum! Isn't that what this is?"

"This is the psychiatric ward of the county hospital. No one uses the terms 'nuthouse' and 'insane asylum' anymore." His voice was incredulous as he turned around to look at me. "Jesus, where do you come up with these things?"

I felt stupider than I'd felt all day. "An old set of encyclopedias and some even older novels," I admitted, dropping my hands. "My father's library wasn't very modern."

"You were homeschooled?"

I'd never heard the word, but it fit perfectly. School at home. Homeschooled. I told him yes, but then I pointed at the hospital. "I really am very certain that Jimmy isn't in this place."

"He probably isn't," Mr. Spaulding said, but he turned around and got out of the taxicab. I followed, though I knew it was a waste of time.

But I was wrong, Jimmy was there. He'd been brought in because he was "self-destructive." This was what the doctor told Mr. Spaulding. The doctor's name was Dr. Phillips, but Mr. Spaulding called him Jay, and he called Mr. Spaulding Stephen. They talked entirely to each other in a language I couldn't follow, much less understand, until finally I coughed and reminded them in the firmest possible way that this was my brother we were talking about.

"I'm sorry, Miss O'Brien," Dr. Phillips said.

This man's "I'm sorry" wasn't appealing. He didn't sound sorry; he sounded like he thought I was too much of a nincompoop to bother talking to.

We were standing in the waiting area. Over on the left, I could see a pair of swinging doors that obviously led somewhere important because doctors and nurses kept going in and out of them. I was feeling very bold now that I knew Jimmy was here. I was about to see my brother for the first time since he left twenty-one months ago.

I waited until Dr. Phillips and Mr. Spaulding were talking again, and I made a break for those doors.

"Dorothea!" Mr. Spaulding scolded, as both men started after me. But tough toenails, as Grandma used to say. I wasn't going to stand there listening when I could be putting my arms around Jimmy. I broke into a run.

They caught up with me, but not before I'd gone by a large white board that listed Jimmy's name and his room number, and not before I managed to get down the hall to where I stood right in front of room 328.

The door was locked, but I pressed my face to the small square window and there he was, wearing the same green hospital dress I'd seen on other patients being wheeled around in the halls; so skinny, his beautiful red hair a tangled mess, but otherwise the same boy I'd always known. I started pounding on the glass and he saw me too. And then he did something I never expected from such a brave person as Jimmy, something I hadn't seen him do as far back as I could remember. He started to cry.

Still, I did not cry myself, not even when that horrible man Dr. Phillips told me I couldn't hug my brother, I couldn't even speak to him. "You are not allowed down this hall," he said, panting a little from trying to catch me. "It's a violation of hospital policy for a relative to barge in like this."

"But why?" I said.

He gave a list of reasons that seemed to make sense to Mr. Spaulding, but made no sense at all to me. I raised my hand to pound on the glass again, and Dr. Phillips grabbed it and pulled me away from the window.

"You have to tell her she can't do this," he said to Mr. Spaulding. He looked me up and down with a sneer. "I don't know who she thinks she is."

Mr. Spaulding said gently, "Dorothea, please."

"But why can't I see my brother? He's crying. He needs me."

"They're keeping him for observation. It's standard procedure in cases like these."

"Keeping him? Can they do that?"

four

STEPHEN SPAULDING was lying on his couch at 2:47 a.m., wide awake. Nothing unusual about that. He'd had insomnia nine nights out of ten since the accident. What was unusual were his thoughts, or more precisely that he was letting himself think, rather than turning on the TV or drinking himself senseless or even staring at the ceiling until his mind was perfectly blank, something he'd become an expert at in the two years since he'd lost Ellen and Lizzie. Maybe the explanation was simple: he finally had something to think about. He could, for instance, wonder if he was losing his mind. He could wonder what the hell he'd gotten himself into, bringing that woman back to his apartment.

He'd driven her all the way to the Radisson first, despite how frightened she'd looked when he suggested it. She admitted she'd never stayed in a hotel before—why wasn't he surprised? She also admitted that she'd never spent a night away from home before, except on the Greyhound bus, which really didn't count, she said, because it wasn't like night when you were traveling on a bus. You didn't have to sleep. You could hear talking at all hours. It was friendlier than she'd expected. Nothing like being alone in a room in a strange place.

"I'll help you check in," he said. "But then I really have to go."

She didn't protest, only said thank you. Yet before they were even through the Radisson front door, he heard her start with the goofy singing again. He checked her pulse and it was up to 165. Not as bad as outside the hospital, when she was at 202, but still a cause for concern.

Her reaction when he suggested she stay with him instead was just another in a seemingly endless list of weird things about her. She said, "Do you have any extra socks?"

He couldn't help laughing, but this time rather than staring at him like she'd never seen a person laugh before, she laughed too. Who knows what she would have said if he'd asked her why. In any case, it wasn't long before she was back to the vaguely sad expression she'd had all day.

Was he trying to make her happier by offering to take her to the twenty-four-hour Wal-Mart? No, he told himself, he was just passing the time. It was only nine-thirty. Too early to go to his apartment, especially as she'd spent the afternoon asleep in his cab. Maybe some part of him was thinking it would be distracting for her. Wherever she was from—and he still hadn't asked her, he hadn't wanted to pry—she'd obviously never been to a Wal-Mart.

Her first reaction was the overwhelmed shyness he'd seen every time they stopped at another dump looking for her brother. She'd actually stepped behind him when the Wal-Mart greeter came forward. "Who is that person?" she whispered. "Do you know her?" But after about ten minutes, she seemed to get comfortable, and then the rapid-fire questions began. She was curious about damn near everything: from address books to headphones, from a cappuccino maker to a shag toilet seat cover. "What is this used for? Do most people own one of these? Do you think I should buy one for my father?"

He talked her out of buying everything except a large jar of pickles and some normal clothes. "We can come back again before you leave," he told her, though he wondered later why on earth he'd suggested that. And why he'd stood outside of the dressing room—guarding the door for her, supposedly, like she'd asked—while she tried on skirts and dresses? (No pants, she said, she wasn't sure her father would approve. Stephen wondered if her dad was some kind of religious nut.)

He was dreading the idea that she would ask his opinion as she was trying things on. How could he know which looked best? With Ellen, it had always come down to two questions: Does it make me look fat? Does it make my boobs look too big? They were both ridiculous, but he'd gotten good at helping her find something she was happy with. He couldn't imagine Dorothea asking either of these questions, but even if the questions were only in his mind, it would be a problem. Hell, even that they could have been in his mind was already a problem, because wasn't he thinking about Dorothea's body even as he thought that he couldn't think about those questions?

Luckily, she came out of the dressing room after only a few minutes, ready to go. She said she'd picked two outfits, adding, "I hope they will keep Dr. Phillips from being so rude."

Stephen had already told her they would go back to the hospital tomorrow. What he hadn't told her was most of the day-shift psych attendings were decent people, not assholes like Jay Phillips. Even if they couldn't release Jimmy to her—which they just might, considering that Dorothea was a relative and Phillips had told him they'd had Jimmy for weeks at this point—they would at least let her see her brother.

But of course none of this had anything to do with her clothes. After he asked her why she thought it did, she said, "You have on a very modern outfit. I've seen several men wearing tan pants and a blue shirt, though most of them aren't as trim as you. Even your brown shoes seem to be a very popular style."

He blinked at her. "Not sure I follow."

"Dr. Phillips wasn't rude to you."

He told her it wasn't his clothes, but he didn't explain. He shoved his hands in his pockets. "Do you think I could meet you in the socks?" he said, nodding across the aisle. "It's right over there."

"Fine." Though she looked confused, she didn't ask any questions for once.

He headed outside to think—and to smoke. A bad habit from his teen years that he'd taken up again since he started driving the cab. He wasn't addicted because he could go a whole day without a cigarette, but he could also have one when he really needed one, like right now.

When he returned, he discovered that Dorothea had found a basket and loaded it up with her new clothes and jar of pickles and what appeared to be at least a dozen pairs of knee-highs. "I've always liked socks," she said, a little sheepishly.

He waited until they'd made it through the mercifully short checkout line. They were walking to the cab when he told her, "I don't want you to do this anymore."

"Do what?"

"Try to figure out why a guy like Phillips is rude. I know you come from a nicer place, but this is the real world. People can be bastards for no reason. It has nothing to do with your clothes."

"Something made him treat me like I was beneath him though. If it wasn't my clothes, then what was it?"

"You're doing it again." He exhaled. "Look, I know Phillips. I used to work with him, and he would treat anyone in your position the same way."

"And what is my position?"

"Your brother is in the county hospital. It's one of the few hospitals in the city that has to take any patient." He shifted the bag from one hand to the other, wondering if this would insult her or if she would even understand it. "What I'm saying is they mainly treat people who can't afford to pay."

She didn't respond for a moment. Then she smiled. "But this means there is a reason for the rudeness, doesn't it? It's not as incomprehensible as you said."

He gave up then, though he was still annoyed at the idea of her trying to understand that prick Phillips. Come to think of it, it bothered him how hard she was trying, period. All day, he'd watched her trying to figure things out and trying to adapt and trying not to panic and trying not to cry and trying to breathe deeply and trying to stay positive. So much trying, and for what? The world she was struggling so hard to understand was ultimately pointless, which he knew as well as anyone. There was no reason for fifty percent of what happened in life, and the other half wasn't really important.

Not that any of this was an excuse for what he said to her. He'd been an ass on the way home from Wal-Mart, and he still felt bad every time he thought about it. She was sitting in the front of the Checker, talking about a subject that was obviously very important to her: the wonderful qualities of her father. Charles O'Brien, according to his daughter anyway, was the most intelligent, humane, patient, loving, thoughtful person imaginable. He lived by the highest principles. He would never cheat or steal or deceive, not because he would get caught, but because it was immoral.

Stephen would have bet good money Charles O'Brien didn't deserve all this praise, but he didn't mind listening to it. He remembered when his own daughter, Lizzie, used to talk like her daddy was the greatest guy on earth, like there was nothing he couldn't do for her. Of course she was only four years old. He thought she'd have plenty of time to figure out she was wrong.

"Father always says the pure-hearted person would rather lose the world than lose his soul," Dorothea said. Stephen was still listening. No reaction yet. But then she continued, "He himself would rather die than violate one of his principles."

He felt so angry that he spoke before he could stop himself. The words he used were bad enough, but his tone made it even worse.

"He'd rather die?" Stephen's voice was dripping with sarcasm, but he laughed harshly. "Good for him, since I'm sure he doesn't know a damn thing about what death is like."

"But no one knows what death is like," she said, so quietly he could barely hear her.

"Some people know enough not to make idiotic statements about dying for principles." His hands tightened around the steering wheel. "Doctors, for instance. Anyone who's ever lost a person they loved. Hell, anyone who has an imagination, even if they haven't suffered themselves."

"Father has suffered though."

"I'm sure he has," Stephen said, and laughed again.

She waited for a full minute or more. Maybe she was giving him time to calm down a little. More likely, she was composing herself, gathering her courage, *trying,* as always.

"I don't think you want to laugh the way you have at me." Her voice was surprisingly steady. "It seems cruel, and you're not a cruel man."

He hit the brakes as a Pontiac cut in front of him to get in the left turn lane. "Shit," he mumbled, but he knew he wasn't cursing at the car. Finally he said, as much to himself as to her, "Maybe I am."

"No," she said firmly. "You just made a mistake. That's what Father always said to Jimmy and me when we hurt each other. He said our goodwill was a given, so what else could it be but a mistake?"

He was a little surprised. Her father sounded like an old-school moralist and "mistake" wasn't the word that kind of person would normally use for bad behavior. Maybe Charles O'Brien made excuses for his children, which would be understandable, Stephen thought. A lot more understandable than Dorothea making excuses for what Stephen himself had just done.

He told her he was sorry and took a long breath. "I'm sure your father has suffered. In any case, I had no right to talk to you that way."

"Oh, he has. He lost his wife, my mother, when Jimmy and I were small children. Grandma used to say he never completely recovered. Then Grandma herself died not even two years ago, though she was eighty-seven, and as Father said, she'd had a long, good life."

Dorothea paused for a moment before glancing at him. "But I hope you won't feel too bad about this. You've been very kind to me all day, and I know it can't have been easy for you. From the moment you picked me up at the bus station, you've seemed very tired. I think if you get some rest, you won't feel so despondent."

He had the strangest feeling then, as if he were hovering above his own life, and seeing it, for once, with something like sympathy. But of course it was her sympathy he was feeling. Her recognition of what had become for him a near perpetual state of exhaustion.

When they arrived at his apartment, she told him they both must go straight to sleep. He was expecting her to look around, to zero in on the picture of Ellen and Lizzie on his stereo and ask who they were, to force him with her curiosity to say what had happened. He was so grateful that she hadn't; he knew this was why he'd talked so much as he was changing the sheets. Dorothea stood there with her arms crossed tightly against her chest, naturally uncomfortable being with a man in his bedroom (as later, Stephen knew he should have realized), while he told her a very long story about the ridiculously expensive house Jay Phillips had purchased a few years ago because he hoped to impress the other residents, but no one liked him enough to come to any of his parties, and finally he sold it and bought a condo in Aspen instead.

She didn't interrupt, but the second the story ended she said, "Stephen?"

Her voice was a tiny squeak, and he turned to look at her. He was sitting on the freshly made bed and she was still standing. And she wasn't just blushing; her entire pale face had been transformed to bright pink.

"Of course I'll be on the couch," he said quickly, stumbling over his own feet, he jumped up so fast.

She tried to tell him she didn't want to take his room, but he wouldn't hear of it. He mumbled something about the location of the towels and toothpaste in the bathroom and then he bolted into the living room. He didn't turn on the TV or take off his shoes or let himself flop down on the couch until she came out of the bathroom and he heard the bedroom door close.

He was finally relaxing about twenty minutes later when he realized she was standing in the doorway, looking at him. He had no idea how long she'd been there. The television was on, some sitcom. He'd been flipping channels, not really watching.

"I just wanted to ask . . ."

"Yes?" he said, muting the TV and sitting up. She was still wearing her fifties skirt and sweater, but she'd changed into one of the new pairs of socks and she didn't have on her shoes. But her hair was the main difference. It was no longer twisted on top of her head, but hanging down almost to her knees. He wondered when she'd last had a haircut, if ever.

"Do you have a book I might read?"

"What kind of book?"

"It doesn't matter," she said, looking at her hands. "It's just that I'm finding it difficult to sleep."

He pointed at the set. "Would you rather watch TV? I'm sure there's something decent on."

"Oh, I'd love to. I've never done that before."

"Never?" he said, more out of habit than real curiosity. At this point, nothing she told him seemed all that surprising.

"May I?" she said, pointing at the chair by the window. He nodded and she sat down. He noticed her hair almost touched the floor. "Actually, that's not completely true. I have watched television, as Jimmy has told me so many times. He finds it very annoying that I can't remember, because you see he was six when we left California and he remembers everything. But I was four, and no memories have come to me." She paused and her voice became sad. "I suppose it was annoying."

He knew she was worrying about her brother again. He told her Jimmy would be all right, to make her feel better, but also because he believed it. Even Phillips said the Zoloft seemed to be working. Whatever had happened to cause the breakdown—and it wasn't hard to guess, given the places Jimmy had been living, that it probably had something to do with drugs—once Dorothea took him home, he could get healthy and figure out what he wanted to do next. Maybe he would avoid cities completely and just paint. He had real talent, even if his style ran a little to the macabre.

"Thank you," she said, and smiled. Her smiles were so genuine, they were nearly impossible to resist.

He smiled back, but then he looked away and picked up the remote. "Let's see what we can find."

It was eleven-thirty when they started watching television and two a.m. when he finally turned off the set, telling her they really needed to go to sleep. The entire time Dorothea's eyes barely left the screen, even during commercials. She didn't ask any questions either. He glanced at her occasionally, wondering what she was making of all this. He'd never been more aware of how crude television had become, with all the Viagra ads and toilet humor and sexual innuendos. Too bad she couldn't have started like he had with *The Brady Bunch* and "relief equals Rolaids."

"You must be tired," he said.

"Oh, I am. I've never stayed up this long in my life. And I mean never ever."

"How does it feel?"

"Great!" she said. "This was tremendously fun."

"I don't know if I should be proud of myself," he said. "I've turned a person who would talk about the meaning of the word 'theory' and casually mention Einstein into someone who can watch an hour of Jay Leno and an hour and a half of an Adam Sandler movie." He shrugged off his own comment, but he did feel a little guilty.

"Yes," she said.

"What?"

"Yes, you should be proud of yourself." She stood up, and he watched her hair fall down her back. "That's what Father told Jimmy and me and I think he would say the same thing to you. As long as you're trying your best, you have nothing else to worry about."

His own parents had said something similar when he was in medical school and overwhelmed by the work. Of course they were extremely disappointed when he gave up his practice and even more so when he told them about the cab. They said he was only driving the cab because of the car accident, and he knew they might be right; he even vaguely remembered a psych lecture on "repetition compulsion" after trauma. But he also knew it didn't make any difference. How could it matter why he was driving the cab when nothing made any difference anymore?

"And what if I'm not trying my best?" he said quietly.

"Then you will tomorrow." Her voice was matter-of-fact. She smiled. "Tomorrow *is* another day."

He knew she was probably quoting the book *Gone With the Wind,* but after she went into the bedroom, and he'd turned off the lamp and lain down on the couch, he found himself thinking about the movie. He'd watched it because it was one of those films Ellen had always wanted to watch. He couldn't say whether his wife would have liked it, but he knew she would have wanted to discuss the differences between Scarlett and Melanie and what they should and shouldn't have done. It was something he always thought was cute: the way Ellen talked about characters in movies and books as if they were real people.

When he found himself wondering if Dorothea did that too, he rolled onto his back and cursed, sure he'd be awake all night now.

The grief counselor he'd seen after the accident had told him it was normal to feel like you were betraying your spouse. "When you start a new relationship," she said, "any kind of new relationship, even if it isn't romantic, you can feel you are leaving behind the old one, and this can seem like a betrayal."

He'd been so positive this wouldn't apply in his case because he'd never have another relationship. How could he, when his own life had ended the same day he'd lost his wife and daughter? He was a walking ghost now, and ghosts don't get involved with human beings. They might drive cabs, and drive them safely, but they don't practice medicine because that too involves relationships. It was something Stephen had always believed: that being a doctor, unless you're an asshole like Phillips, requires a heart.

The irony of this day, Stephen thought, the irony of meeting Dorothea, was that she had single-handedly reminded him of both his life as a doctor and his life as a human. And by bringing her back here, to his apartment, he'd only made the situation a thousand times worse.

He'd been awake for more than an hour, but now that he'd decided that, he felt himself getting sleepy. As he drifted off, he wondered if she liked pancakes.

five

HE WOKE TO the sound of her singing. She had a sweet, clear voice and his first reaction was to close his eyes and let himself doze off for a few more minutes. But then he remembered. He jumped up and rushed down the hall.

"Are you all right?" he said, knocking on the door.

"Yes, I'm fine." She opened the door, and he saw it was true. She wasn't flushed and gasping for breath. "Oh," she said, "I'm sorry if I woke you."

When he asked how long she'd been up, she said since the sun rose. It was after ten-thirty now; incredibly, he'd slept almost eight hours. She was already fully dressed in one of her outfits from Wal-Mart: a khaki skirt and button-down blue blouse. Her hair was already knotted on top of her head—trapped, he thought, and then wondered why that word occurred to him to describe a hairstyle.

He asked her if she was hungry and she said a little. Then he thought of something. "Do you like pancakes?"

She smiled. "Yes. Actually, they're my favorite."

A half hour later, she was seated on a bar stool in his kitchen, watching his pathetic attempt to make blueberry pancakes. Maybe he was nervous, or maybe he was just out of practice, but everything seemed to go wrong. First the butter burned in the pan, then he didn't drain the blueberries enough and the batter turned blue, then he knocked a plate off the counter with his elbow and it cracked in half and, finally, he had such a hell of a time getting the syrup open that he broke the cap. He didn't realize how much he was cussing until later, after they'd eaten and after he'd showered, when he walked into his bedroom to get another shirt and found her sitting on the edge of the bed, looking at herself in the mirror, repeatedly saying the word "shit."

Every time she said it, though, she cringed. When he asked what she was up to, she told him she'd counted the number of times he'd used the word while making breakfast. Seven. "When you say it, it seems very natural," she said. "I don't understand why I can't do the same."

"It's not exactly a necessary skill." He opened the closet to replace the shirt he'd taken into the bathroom. He'd been in a hurry, and the first one turned out to be missing several buttons.

"True," she said, "but I hoped it would help me express myself to Dr. Phillips."

He let out a laugh, but then he told her it was unlikely Phillips would be there today.

She waited for a moment before admitting that she was nervous about going back to the hospital. "I have my poem in my shoe," she said. Her saddle oxford shoes were the one thing they hadn't replaced at Wal-Mart, and he was weirdly glad to see her wearing them again. "But I'm not sure it's enough. I want to be brave and help my brother, but I'm so afraid of having another attack."

He was thinking about what to do for her as he went into the bathroom to change his shirt, and then it hit him. He called her to the door and opened the medicine cabinet and took out a bottle of pills. He told her if she took one of these, she would most likely not have an attack, no matter how difficult it got.

"It sounds like a miracle," she said. "I wonder why no one has suggested this before."

The doctor in Stephen realized he should ask a few questions before he just handed her a prescription drug. He already knew she'd been diagnosed with an anxiety disorder; she'd told him yesterday. She'd also said that they'd never been able to find any heart trouble or disease.

He said, "Do they have any theory about what causes your anxiety attacks?"

"Theory!" she said, grinning. She crossed her arms. "The doctor doesn't know. Father and Grandma told me I've had them since I was two. Essentially my whole life."

Stephen knew it was very rare for a child under five to have an anxiety disorder, and he briefly wondered what could have caused it. "It's one of the lighter anti-anxiety meds," he said. "It can't hurt." As he twisted off the cap, he was sure she noticed that his own name was written on the label. The prescription was nearly two years old, but he assumed they were still potent. He handed her a paper cup from a stack on the sink. She filled it with water and took the medicine.

Even though he'd told her the pill couldn't hurt, Stephen kept a close eye on her for the next half hour or so. They were in the Checker cab, the only car Stephen owned after he'd given Ellen's Toyota to his parents, asking them to do whatever they wanted with it, as long as he didn't have to see it again. He'd felt the same way about the house. Since he'd moved to his furnished apartment, he'd never been back to the St. Charles neighborhood where he and Ellen and Lizzie had lived. The real estate company had sold it and his mother had packed up the rest of his family's things. He had no idea what she'd done with them.

When Dorothea started talking more freely, Stephen knew the pill was working. He'd seen enough patients on benzodiazepines to know that they loosened people up, and God knows, he thought,

Dorothea could use a little of that. All that trying had to be wearing her out, not to mention that she'd gone to bed at two o'clock and gotten up at sunrise, whatever time that was.

Most of her talk was about the buildings and cars and houses they passed. She was as fascinated as Lizzie had been by things he'd seen all his life, and he found himself relaxing as he listened to her. Later, he realized he was more relaxed during that drive than he'd been since the accident. Even the intersections didn't stress him out the way they usually did.

Obviously, Dorothea was a lot more relaxed as well. She kept smiling at the people trying to flag down the cab. "It must be very pleasant," she said, "having people wave at you all the time." He shook his head, but he laughed quietly.

But maybe she was too relaxed, he thought—and found himself feeling a little guilty for giving her that pill—when, not even halfway to the hospital, she suddenly announced that he was the "handsomest" man she'd ever seen.

His face grew warm, and even warmer when he realized she was staring right at him.

"Because you haven't seen many men," he said, as lightly as he could manage.

"I have seen hundreds of pictures in our encyclopedias."

It struck him as funny, but he was too nervous to smile. He mumbled that people who end up in encyclopedias aren't exactly a good sample.

"It might surprise you to hear that there are plenty of handsome men in those volumes," she said. "I counted one time and I found fifty-six."

He couldn't think of what to say to this, so he didn't say anything. After a few moments, she apologized for her bad manners. She sounded sincerely confused and more than a little embarrassed. "I honestly can't imagine why I said something so forward and impolite."

"Don't worry about it."

"But there's no excuse for making someone else uncomfortable. Especially after everything you've done for me."

"You didn't make me uncomfortable," he said, but his voice was still hoarse and strained. He wasn't convincing even to himself.

"Thank you. However, I know I had no right to make such a personal comment."

Now he was starting to feel bad. "It was a nice thing to say," he told her, because, after all, it was. He forced a smile. "I've certainly never heard anyone say those words to me before."

"Nor have I."

He thought she was saying that no one had ever complimented her before. Which bugged him because he knew it was probably true. Wherever the hell she lived—and Stephen was thinking it had to be someplace weird: maybe even a religious cult or a commune founded by her father, who was most likely a nut job—they obviously had a problem with women wearing makeup or letting their hair down or even buying clothes that weren't fifty years out of style. This morning while he was watching Dorothea stare at herself in the mirror, Stephen could tell she had no idea how attractive she was. Even at the time, he'd felt a little bad about that, a little sorry for her.

It took him a minute, but finally he said, "You're very pretty."

Her embarrassment was so obvious—she turned bright red and hunched down into the passenger seat like she was trying to disappear—that he instantly knew he'd misinterpreted her. When she'd said, "Nor have I," she'd meant it the same way she meant most things: literally. She meant she hadn't heard anyone tell a man how handsome he was. She was still upset with herself for her "forward" comment.

Unfortunately, now he had two things to feel bad about: that he'd thought a woman other than Ellen was pretty (which was more difficult to deny, now that he'd said it aloud), and that he'd made Dorothea feel bad by telling her so.

He had no idea how to deal with any of this, so he decided to turn on the radio. The first station had a talk show about sex. He quickly switched to the classic rock station.

They listened without speaking for the remaining ten minutes of the drive. He was just turning into the hospital parking lot when she shouted, "I know that song. I was just thinking about it this morning!"

It was true. They were playing "Daniel," an Elton John song she'd been singing when he woke up.

"Is this like 'theory'?" he said, relieved to be back on a topic from yesterday morning, before everything had gotten so complicated. "Except instead of the word it's the song of the day?"

"I don't know." Her tone was surprisingly serious. "Because the song is about a brother. I thought it was on my mind when I woke up because I was very worried about Jimmy. But now it's possible that it does mean more."

"Not sure I follow."

"Perhaps it's another example of the charming coincidence."

The way she said the last three words made them sound as familiar as the National Weather Service or the Holy Grail. He thought it was probably another of her father's ideas, but it turned out he was wrong.

"Father doesn't believe in the charming coincidence," Dorothea said sadly. Stephen was putting the Checker in park, taking out the key. "He thinks I only do because I'm a natural optimist, but I know there's more to it than that. For example, yesterday when I got off the bus, I walked to your taxicab first. I was attracted by the black-and-white squares along the roof and the bright green paint, but otherwise, there wasn't any reason for my choice, was there?"

"No," he said.

"Was there a reason that you were at the bus station rather than somewhere else in the city?"

"I guess not."

"This is the charming coincidence. When things in the world that are unconnected suddenly connect, and a pattern emerges."

He exhaled. "But what if the pattern wasn't what you'd call charming?"

"It's not the pattern that's charming," she said. "It's that there is a pattern at all."

He nodded, but he was thinking, for once, that her father was right. It was only her optimism that gave her this view. Otherwise she would see that a pattern of serial killings was still a pattern, to give only one example out of millions.

They were out of the cab, walking to the hospital, when she suddenly stopped. "Jimmy believes in it too. He's actually the one who came up with the phrase. He's very brilliant."

"I'm sure he is."

"He has the most beautiful red hair. It's not straight like mine; it's what Grandma called 'a riot of curls.'"

Stephen stuck his hands in his pockets, wondering why she wasn't moving on to the hospital.

"He's very funny too. I have no sense of humor, but Jimmy can make a joke whenever he likes."

He saw her hand flutter up to her heart. "Is it racing?" he said.

She took a deep breath. "No, it's fine."

He waited a minute before he asked her what was wrong.

"I called Father's doctor this morning from the telephone by your bedside, to find out how Father was. Dr. Humphrey told me he seemed a bit better."

This was the first Stephen had heard about her father being sick, but he nodded because he knew there was something else she wanted to say.

"When Dr. Humphrey asked me about Jimmy, I told him about this place, though I couldn't remember the precise name of it. He asked if I thought it would help if Father came too, and I said no. Jimmy has been so angry with Father for so long, and . . . and one of the pictures we purchased yesterday bore some resemblance to Father."

Stephen knew it had to be the man with the snake in his mouth. It was the only picture of a man.

"I think you made the right choice," he said.

"Thank you, but that isn't my question." She paused again and looked at the front door of the psych ward. "My question is how can I be sure that Dr. Phillips was wrong? I want to see Jimmy so badly, but what if my own visit harmed him in some way?"

Stephen wasn't a psychiatrist; in fact, he barely remembered his six-week med school psych rotation. But he didn't hesitate to tell her there was nothing to worry about; her visit wouldn't hurt her brother.

"I'm ready then," she said, straightening her shoulders. "Thank you."

They walked into the hospital, and as expected, Phillips wasn't there. The attending was Nancy Baker. Stephen knew her socially; she used to date one of the partners in his practice. She was a decent psychiatrist, though far from what you'd call compassionate.

Case in point: Nancy had barely said hello to Dorothea when she turned to him. "I heard about the situation last night," she said, in hushed tones. "Jay left a note on the chart. I'm really sorry, Steve. I can't believe he treated you like this. If Cummins was still here, I could complain, but he's been replaced. Don't know if you heard that. Of course it's all politics. Phillips knows how to play the game better than the rest of us. He and Lorber, the new chief, are cut from the same cloth."

Stephen let her go on like this for another minute, but then he reminded her that Dorothea was anxious about her brother.

"Yes." Dorothea stepped forward at the mention of her name. "May I see him now?"

Nancy said, "First we should talk. I can tell you a little of the history of the case."

"I would prefer to see him first," Dorothea said.

Stephen noticed her glancing at the double doors that led to the ward. He asked Nancy to give them a minute, then he led Dorothea a few feet away and told her not to bolt again or they might not get to see Jimmy.

She whispered, "My brother is not a case."

"A 'case' just means he's a patient."

"Why would I want to hear the history of anything about Jimmy from someone who has known him for a few weeks?"

"Because she's a trained specialist in psychiatric disorders."

"Which Jimmy does not have."

Nancy moved over to them. "We'll just go to my office, Dorothea. It won't take long. You can come too, Steve."

Dorothea finally agreed and they all headed down the hall with Nancy leading. At one point when Nancy was answering a page on one of the hospital phones, Dorothea whispered, "Why does she keep calling you Steve? Would you like me to tell her you prefer Stephen?"

He laughed softly. "Not necessary."

"What did I miss?" Nancy said, when she returned. "What's the joke?"

"Nothing," Stephen said, glancing at Dorothea.

The three of them sat down in chairs around a small table. The window shades were closed, and one of the fluorescent ceiling bulbs was buzzing and cracking, probably about to go out. Nancy opened Jimmy's chart and took out her pen. She said she had a few questions first.

Stephen was surprised by what she meant by a few. He felt bad for Dorothea, especially as most of the questions were the type he knew she would think of as intrusive. He was ready to jump in and help if she needed it, but she seemed to be doing all right on her own. He was glad again that she had taken the pill.

"Jimmy has repeatedly said your father is a millionaire. Is this true?"

Dorothea sat up straighter. "Father's financial affairs are his business, I'm afraid. But if you are asking if he will settle the bills here for Jimmy, the answer is yes."

A millionaire? Stephen certainly didn't expect this. He was just wondering how Dorothea's father made his money when Nancy asked the same thing.

"Do you know his occupation before he moved you to New Mexico?"

"No," Dorothea said. "I've never asked him."

"But Jimmy asked him several times, is that right?"

"Yes, and Father's response was always that he would rather not talk about the past. This seemed fair to me."

Stephen was still thinking about New Mexico. Dorothea was so pale; he'd assumed she was from somewhere much colder and gloomier.

"Do you know how your mother died?"

"No. I've never asked because I knew it would hurt Father to talk about it."

Nancy sighed, but Stephen gave Dorothea an encouraging glance. This he understood perfectly.

"Why do you think your father refused to let you leave your home?"

"Obviously he didn't refuse or Jimmy and I wouldn't both be here in your hospital."

Stephen tried not to smile.

"When you were children," Nancy said, her tone not hiding her exasperation.

"He wanted to protect us." Dorothea took a breath. "I was sickly and mother had died. Grandma used to say it was natural that Father was afraid something would happen to us."

Nancy nodded, but she was still looking down at the chart. So far, she'd made very little eye contact with Dorothea, which annoyed the hell out of Stephen. Shrinks should have better bedside manners than regular docs, not worse.

"Jimmy said your grandmother told him your mother's family lived in Missouri. Did you know this was why he came here? To try to locate them?"

"No," Dorothea said slowly. "He didn't share with me his reasons for going to Missouri."

"Has Jimmy ever intentionally hurt himself before?"

"No."

"He has very vivid nightmares. Do you remember if he had these as a child?"

"Yes."

"Did he ever tell you the content of any of these nightmares?"

It was then that Stephen saw Dorothea hesitate for the first time. He knew she was opposed to lying, but he also saw on her face a real reluctance to answer this question.

When Nancy repeated it, he told Dorothea she didn't have to say anything she didn't want to say.

"That's helpful," Nancy said to him, frowning.

"It's not a courtroom here," he said. "Go easy on her. She's a long way from home with a sick brother."

"You met this woman when you picked her up in the cab you're driving. That's what Jay said. Isn't that your only connection?"

Nancy's voice was snotty, especially when she said the word "cab." Maybe Dorothea noticed this, because she said, "He's also my friend."

"Good to know," Nancy said blandly. "Will you answer the question about your brother's dreams or not? Of course I only ask because I think it will help him."

"All right," Dorothea said. "Jimmy did have nightmares for a year or so when we were children. Our rooms were at the opposite ends of a long hall, and most of the time I wasn't disturbed. Father was up with him nearly every night though. Jimmy told me this. He said Father would sit in his room until he was able to sleep again.

"One night, when I was eight and Jimmy was ten, I did hear him screaming. It was a terrible sound, though perhaps no more terrible than the other nights I didn't hear it. I can't say. On that particular night though, I went down to his bedroom and I overheard him telling Father about the dream. I didn't hear most of the details, but I heard enough to make me frightened myself. He said he was dreaming of our mother . . . as she looked when she was dead."

Stephen was surprised how unsurprised Nancy was. Maybe Jimmy was still dreaming the same thing, which was a pretty depressing thought.

Dorothea's eyes were dilated, possibly from the memory of fear. Not from the drug. If she hadn't had that pill, she never would have made it through this. But what if making it through this would hurt her?

The thought hit Stephen with a jolt. He was still listening to Nancy, who'd finally finished her questions and was now giving Dorothea the "history of the case," as promised (which turned out to be just the facts, and very little Dorothea hadn't already heard from Phillips last night). But Stephen was also considering whether he had made a glaringly stupid mistake.

He had no idea what was causing Dorothea's anxiety, and yet he'd medicated her anyway. What if this Charles O'Brien was some kind of abusive prick? (Her idealizing her father made this more likely, not less. Kids tend to idealize parents who don't really love them, as he knew from doing pediatrics.) What if Dorothea's only escape had been to find herself unable to breathe? What if all her singing wasn't just to help her breathe more calmly and evenly, but also to calm down that father with her sweet voice? Not a bad strategy. Certainly a hell of a lot better than what her brother seemed to have come up with.

Nancy was telling Dorothea that Jimmy might say some disturbing things. "He needs you to just listen," she told Dorothea. "Can you do that?"

Dorothea said yes. And Stephen was thinking, that's all she can do is listen. No escape.

Maybe it hit him harder because of his own experience with sedatives after the accident. If they were strong enough to put him to sleep, fine, but if they just calmed him down, it was much worse. He was calm enough to think about what happened, exactly what he didn't want to do. He wanted oblivion, distraction, something, anything, other than facing what he'd been through. What in the hell was the point of facing something he could never understand or do anything to change?

Dorothea and Nancy were standing now. Stephen stood too, and quickly turned to Dorothea. "I don't think you should do this."

She blinked with confusion.

"I can bring you back tomorrow. Even later today. But I think we should have lunch first. Wait a few hours."

Nancy shook her head. "I just had them bring Jimmy to another room. He's very anxious to see his sister. I'm not going to put him through that again."

"Then let me go with you," Stephen said. His voice was urgent, and he reached out for Dorothea's arm.

She looked in his eyes. He knew she didn't understand, but he also knew she saw how important it was to him.

"Bad idea," Nancy began, but Dorothea interrupted.

"I want Stephen to accompany me."

"What about what Jimmy wants?" Nancy snapped. "He asked to speak to you alone, and I've agreed. He's not a danger to anyone but himself."

"Jimmy and I are very much the same," Dorothea said softly, still looking at Stephen. "He will feel as I do about this."

"Fine," Nancy said, grabbing her clipboard. "I have other patients to see. I'll be back in an hour." She looked at Stephen. "You know how to buzz for a nurse if you have any problems."

She led them to a standard hospital room: green walls, two beds, a curtain between them. But Jimmy was the only patient there, and he was sitting in a chair by the window.

When he saw Dorothea, he ran to her, but she was already running to him. They met in the middle of the room. Stephen stood just inside the doorway, watching what struck him as the weirdest reunion he'd ever seen.

At the same moment, they had both put their hands up, waist high, palms out. Then they reached out to each other, touching palms and aligning their fingers, while they stared into each other's eyes. Neither of them said a word, at least not with their mouths, but their eyes seemed to be communicating. Their eyes never moved from the other's face.

For easily five minutes they stayed like this: two human statues connected at the hands. After a while, Stephen found his thoughts drifting to one of his patients, a mother of twins, who'd claimed her children had a secret language. Dorothea and Jimmy weren't twins, though they did look strikingly similar, from their bright blue eyes to their unnatural paleness, their slight frames, their nearly equal height. Maybe they had developed a twin kind of closeness from living away from the normal world for so long. From living with no one but their family, Stephen now understood. Not in a religious cult or a commune or any community at all. Just two kids taken by a man to live an incredibly isolated life in the middle of nowhere.

When Dorothea and Jimmy finally broke their spell, they sat down together on the bed. They sat very close, and she put her arms around him, but loosely, obviously trying to avoid the many places she couldn't see where he'd cut himself. Jimmy was crying again like he had last night, sobbing really. Stephen would have felt uncomfortable witnessing this if Dorothea hadn't looked at him every so often, showing in her eyes that she still felt that they were connected in some kind of pattern. "The charming coincidence," as she called it, which Stephen knew wasn't real, even if there was something he liked about the idea. Or perhaps it was just that she believed it, he thought, as he watched her holding her brother so carefully that her thin arms were twitching a little with the effort.

"I can't believe you're here," Jimmy said, sniffing hard. He glanced at Stephen and lowered his voice. "Who is that? Another doctor?"

"He's a friend," she told Jimmy. "He helped me find you."

That seemed to satisfy her brother. He rambled on then for what felt like fifteen minutes or more, and Stephen took a seat on the other bed. Most of it he couldn't decipher because it was too personal, about their childhood, about their house, about their father.

He wasn't sure that Dorothea was understanding it all either, especially since she barely spoke. But then he remembered that Nancy had told Dorothea to just listen. She was doing exactly what the doctor told her to do, trying hard, for her brother's sake.

She didn't speak until Jimmy mumbled, "I hate this place."

"It's awful," Dorothea said, and she actually shuddered. Stephen wondered what she saw here that he didn't. "Don't worry though. We're going to get you out of here." She looked at Stephen. "Maybe today?"

He nodded, even as he realized what this meant. If Jimmy got out this afternoon, the two of them would probably go back to New Mexico tonight. The whole thing would be a strange incident in his life, nothing more.

"I can't leave," Jimmy said, and his eyes filled with tears again.

"Yes, you can," Dorothea said. "Stephen will convince them to let you go."

"I'll try," Stephen said, but Jimmy shook his head violently.

"No! If I leave here, it will happen again."

"What will happen?" Dorothea said.

"It hurts." Jimmy dropped his head. "It hurts so much I can't stand it. I can't fucking stand it!"

Stephen saw Dorothea flinch at the word "fucking." He wondered if she'd ever heard it before.

Jimmy started talking about his dream, and Stephen realized his hunch was right. The first thing Jimmy said was that he was still having the same dream about their mother.

"Can I tell you what I see in the dream?" he said, looking closely at his sister. "I don't want to make you nervous."

Jimmy's voice was polite now, more like Dorothea's again. Stephen imagined how he would have been if he hadn't come to the city. Or if he hadn't had the breakdown. Maybe both. Really, Stephen had no idea what was wrong with him. He could have stitched him up, but he couldn't have done a damn thing about whatever caused him to cut himself.

Dorothea said yes, of course he could tell her about his dream. She wanted to hear whatever he wanted to say.

"She's lying on the floor." Jimmy stood up and started pacing. "She's lying on the floor, and she's . . . covered in blood. Oh God, Thea, it's so fucking horrible. I can't even tell it's Mom except I know it is. I can see her hair."

Stephen glanced at Dorothea. She still looked fine.

"She has on her bathing suit. It's strange, but in the dream I always think something must have happened to her in the pool." Jimmy walked over to the window and turned back. "You heard Grandma say we used to have a pool at our house in California."

The effort it was taking for Dorothea to keep silent was evident to Stephen then. He could see her biting her lip.

"But Mom wasn't hurt in the damned pool," Jimmy said, looking away. "I don't know where it happened, but it wasn't outside."

"Are you still talking about in the dream?" Dorothea said. Her voice was so small and frightened; her pupils were twice the size they'd been in Nancy's office. Stephen wanted to curse Nancy for telling her to just listen. What was the medical foundation for this advice? Maybe it would be good for Jimmy, but how could it possibly be good for Dorothea?

"It's not just a dream," Jimmy said. "I never understood this before, but one of the doctors here told me a dream that keeps repeating has to be real. I really saw her like that. I saw our mother lying in a pool of her own blood, cut to death."

Stephen was trying to imagine why a doctor would tell Jimmy that. He was pretty sure he'd heard the opposite: that dreams were almost never literal memories. He thought about explaining this, but Jimmy was still talking.

"I was the only one there." The tears had started again. "I don't know who did it to Mom, maybe I did. Fuck, maybe that's why I only feel better now when I cut myself."

"You were six years old," Dorothea whispered. "An innocent child."

"I wasn't innocent. I'd already killed our dog."

Jesús. Stephen seriously doubted that Jimmy had killed his dog or anything else for that matter, but he could almost feel his guilt: palpable, painful, a force in the room. It struck Stephen that this guilt was what made Jimmy seem so young, though he was close to twenty-five. He'd seen little kids who thought they were responsible for everything that happened. Of course some adults thought this too, but most had discovered that the number of things they could really affect in the world was so small, it was laughable. If only they could believe that what they did mattered, for good or bad.

"You didn't kill our dog," Dorothea said.

"Ask Father," Jimmy said, and he laughed, but it was a painful, hysterical laugh. "I asked him once and you know what he told me? He told me he loved me. Like that makes a difference. He loves me so much, he built this fucking castle of lies around me."

She stood up and went to her brother. "You're a good person." She took his hand between hers. "I will never believe otherwise."

"Because you don't remember," Jimmy said. "You only want to believe that."

When Dorothea turned around, Stephen checked her eyes. The pupils were still enormous. But her voice was surprisingly confident. "Then I will remember," she said. She looked at Stephen. "It can be done, can it not?"

Shit, he had no idea. He was pretty sure the answer was no, but he heard himself saying yes. And when both Jimmy and Dorothea seemed to perk up, he blurted out something he was almost positive was crap. He told Dorothea that she could remember anything she wanted to.

Later, after Nancy had come back for Jimmy—and noticed how much calmer her patient seemed, willing to make eye contact for the first time, a really encouraging improvement—and Dorothea had agreed to return tomorrow, to help her brother again, Dorothea turned to Stephen on the way to the parking lot. First she thanked him, as always, and then she said, "So, how is this remembering accomplished?"

PART TWO

Naked Heart

six

Lucy Dobbins had a beautiful house in one of the most desirable areas of Malibu. She had Al, who was more devoted to her now than when they'd married twelve years ago. She had her health and she still had her good looks, or so people always told her. They marveled that she was so thin without working out, that her hair was still fiery red, not a strand of gray in sight. She marveled that anyone would care about such things when there were so many more important things in the world.

By more important things, Lucy meant the tragedies and losses that, for the past nineteen years, she'd defined to be the real truth of life. Her own life, yes, but everyone else's also, whether they knew it yet or not. She'd volunteered at the domestic counseling center for more than a decade, and she'd learned that there were even worse things than what had happened to her. She'd met women whose children had died, for instance. Their ability to go on was something that always amazed her. At least there was still hope in her case, no matter how much that hope had faded with each disappointment.

Whenever the sadness threatened to overtake her, Al would convince her to use Charles's money to book another trip. Bermuda, Paris, Amsterdam, Rome. Lima, Mexico City, Jerusalem, Montreal. They had been all over the world, and everywhere they went, Lucy peered into the faces of children. It wasn't completely foolish. The last few detectives had all agreed that the United States was very unlikely at this point.

Did your ex-husband ever talk about wanting to visit any foreign countries? Does he have any relatives overseas? Old friends? Colleagues?

Unfortunately, her answers were no help. Charles had traveled when he had to for a project, but he'd never mentioned any place he actually wanted to go. He had no relatives overseas or anywhere else, other than his mother, Margaret Keenan, who'd lived with them in California until she too had disappeared. Charles didn't have any friends overseas because he didn't have any friends at all. In the last two years they were together, he'd cut himself off from everyone. His colleagues had no idea what had happened to him, Lucy was sure of this, because his colleagues had been her colleagues. They'd both been in the business—he was a writer and director, she was an actress—when he disappeared.

"Disappeared" was the word Lucy had used from the first phone call to the police to the last time she'd hired a new detective, though she knew it wasn't exactly right. If someone disappears they might have been murdered or kidnapped or killed in a car accident. They don't tell you that they are leaving, the way Charles did. They certainly don't tell you that you'll never see them again.

What kind of person would say such a thing anyway?

Vindictive, immature and retributive. Someone with a black-and-white sense of morality and a grossly inflated view of himself.

This was the description from a psychologist one of the detectives had consulted to create a personality profile of Charles, to help them determine where he might have gone. Lucy never understood how her answers had generated these traits for her ex-husband, nor could she say how accurate they were anymore. None of it led them to Charles, of course. The profile was as useless as all the psychics she'd seen and all the ads she'd placed in newspapers from Maine to Seattle, from Florida to Arizona, and every place in between.

A grossly inflated view of himself? Maybe, but what struck Lucy more and more was how inflated her own view of him had become over the years. When they met, she thought he was powerful, but now he was almost godlike to her. Sometimes she even let herself give in to the urge to pray to him for mercy. Other times, she would wake up from another nightmare and go out into the garden and scream into the night sky, "Haven't I been punished enough, Charles? How can you keep doing this to me?"

That she deserved some punishment, Lucy never doubted. Her memory of the day it happened was as fresh now as it was nineteen years ago, because she'd spent so many hours, week after week, year after year reliving it all in her mind. She knew she was sticking her finger in a wound, torturing herself with feelings of blame, but what difference did it make? The therapists she'd seen were wrong. Her guilt wasn't standing in the way of her life; it was her life now.

Tragedy, loss and especially guilt: these were the real truths of the world, and Lucy knew it. God help the person who didn't understand this, she thought. God help them if they have to find out the hard way that the life they're taking for granted is as fragile as a naked heart.

seven

THEY HAD MET at a party, twenty-seven years ago. He was thirty-five, not old by any means, but a lot older than she was—and about twelve million dollars more successful. Twelve million 1976 dollars, that is. He was just coming off a series of Westerns that had done so well at the box office, he'd become known in Hollywood as the man who'd single-handedly brought the genre back to life. The party was at his house in Beverly Hills, to celebrate his latest, *A Silver Dollar and a Gun*.

Lucy was only nineteen then. (So young! Yet not young enough to forgive herself for what happened. Never young enough for that.) She'd arrived in L.A. fresh from a bad year spent in Nashville, trying to break into country, and before that, a childhood spent in a tiny town in the southeastern part of Missouri, only a few miles from the Arkansas border. A hick from the sticks, when you got right down to it. Only in L.A. for a few months when she snuck into that party with her roommate, Janice. So impressed with the heavy silverware at the famous director's home that, in the first ten minutes she was there, she slipped a spoon into her purse.

"How *Les Misérables* of you," Charles's mother had said, when she took Lucy's wrist in her hand and very softly—they were dozens of people around the table—asked her to return the spoon and follow her upstairs.

As his mother led her to one of the empty guest rooms, Lucy didn't say anything to defend herself. There was no point, she thought. Might as well save all her pleading for the police.

She was only nineteen, but in some ways, she was already very old. She'd almost starved in Nashville, and when she was reduced to eating popcorn and fried flour month after month, when she was about to be thrown into the street because she couldn't meet her rent, she'd let her landlord pay her for sex. Only a few times, but it was enough to change her view of herself forever. Back in Missouri, when her uncle would get drunk and yell at her for dressing/talking/looking like a slut, she'd had innocence on her side. She'd never even had a real boyfriend; she was saving herself for the wonderful future her mother had always talked about. As far back as she could remember, when she was so little she could barely stand, her mother would kneel down and peer into her face and tell her, "You are special, my Lucy, remember that. Mark my words, you are going to grow up and leave this town and become something great. Maybe you'll even live by the ocean someday."

Lucy never had a father, but her mother adored her. She treated Lucy like a winning lottery ticket, the glittering prize that made up for everything in her otherwise tough life working long shifts on the line at the paint factory. But when Lucy was ten, her mother got sick and died, leaving her to an aunt and uncle who'd already raised six children. Lucy was no prize to them. They didn't want another mouth to feed, and sometimes they didn't feed her for several days. They would go on trips to the Ozarks in their RV and leave Lucy to herself. Even when they were home, they only gave her attention when they were telling her what not to do—don't leave this house, don't eat that, don't use the phone—unless her uncle was drunk, when he would turn his attention to Lucy and accuse her of things she didn't even understand. It was during one of these nights, when Lucy was a junior in high school, that she ran away and hitchhiked to Nashville, to become a country singer. Everyone said she had a good voice. Even when her mother was so sick she couldn't leave the bed, she said hearing Lucy sing made her know everything would be all right.

After her failure in Nashville, she couldn't go back to Missouri, not after what she'd done. She got lucky when she ran into a group of kids heading for L.A. She loved that she'd be near the ocean, just like her mother always dreamed. Once she was there, she claimed she was an actress just like everybody did.

She got lucky again when, after four nights of sleeping on the beach alone—because the kids she'd ridden with turned out to have family or friends in the area, and places to stay—she met Janice. She'd gone into a coffee shop to use their bathroom. The manager told her no, not without buying something, but Janice felt sorry for her and snuck her in the back way. When Lucy admitted she had no place to live, Janice took her in. "You can pay me your half of the rent later, after you get a job," Janice said, and then proceeded to find Lucy work as a waitress at another Venice restaurant.

They lived in a tiny cottage about four blocks from the beach. The floors were so warped they had to put magazines under one leg of the TV stand; the kitchen sink had rusted from a constant leak, and the bathroom was home to a family of cockroaches that kept coming back even though Lucy and Janice always managed to squish at least two before the rest escaped into the crack between the tub and the wall. Janice liked to joke that they'd be moving somewhere far more glamorous as soon as they got a chance to jump on the casting couch. "I'd do it in a minute," Janice would say. "The number of lines for the part depends on the size of the director's dick. If he's over nine, then I'll go under nine, but otherwise, I need a real supporting role. I'm not a total whore, you know!"

Lucy would laugh with Janice, but inside she vowed she would never do anything like that again. Nothing was worth the awful feeling she had with Mr. Smitty—Smutty, as some of the tenants called him—in Nashville. Sometimes when she closed her eyes, she still saw him groping her and breathing on her and climbing on top of her. He seemed to like it when she cried out, which she usually did. She was skinny and small. He didn't take his time. He'd hurt her.

But now she was starting over. Her new life in L.A. Except here she was, sitting on the bed in an empty guest room, waiting for the police to haul her off to jail.

When the door suddenly opened and Charles Keenan himself walked in, she flashed to a scene in one of his movies. "I'll give you another chance, outlaw. You leave now and don't darken my door again, and I won't kill you for the cattle thief you are." What was it called? *The Last Train?*

Janice had pointed him out downstairs, but up close he looked much taller and scarier. He was wearing a suit rather than the casual California clothes everyone else at the party wore. And he had very strange eyes: blue gray, with one eye, the left one, noticeably larger than the right. The closer he came, the more she noticed it. It was ridiculous, but she felt that one eye could see right down into her soul.

He didn't speak as he came toward her. She wanted to ask him what he was doing, but she couldn't find her voice. She watched with a growing sense of horror as he sat down on the bed and started untying his shoes.

She had no idea whether Keenan was considered attractive. Probably, but even if he wasn't, he could have all the dates he wanted. Lucy herself had seen three model types hanging on him downstairs. So what was he doing up here with her?

He sat very still for a moment before slipping off the shoes. The way he placed them carefully at the side of the bed reminded her of Smitty. Something very mechanical about it. No passion like she'd seen in the movies, where a man wants a woman so much that the whereabouts of his clothes afterward is the last thing on his mind.

Finally, he twisted his body around to face her. He still hadn't spoken. The look on his face was so confident, like he had an absolute right.

"How dare you!" Lucy's voice was louder than she expected, and she realized she was furious. "This is about a lousy spoon?"

The big eye was staring at her, and she could feel herself becoming awkward in her own body. "My mother told me you were up here waiting for me."

"Well, I'm not going to do it," Lucy said, quieter now, but with a firmness that surprised herself. "I'd rather go to jail than . . . than . . ."

"What?" He took a long look at her. She felt her cheeks get warm. He sounded annoyed. "I only came up here to talk to you."

"But you took off your shoes. You're on the bed!"

"I have blisters on the bottoms of my feet. An accident I had on the last day of shooting, when I was supposed to be showing one of my actors the right way to walk across hot coals." He inhaled. "I'm on the bed because the room isn't finished. It's the only place to sit. I assume that's why you're sitting here too."

She'd already breathed a sigh of relief when he said, "Let me make sure I understand. Were you telling me that you'd rather go to jail than have sex with me?"

She sat up straighter. "Yes, yes, I was."

"And you know who I am?"

"Of course. You're Charles Keenan, the great director." Her voice grew defiant. "But do you know who *I* am?"

"Your name is Lucy."

"That's all you know? Because I'm—"

"I know you tried to steal from me. Solid silver, worth . . ." He rubbed his forehead. "I have no idea."

"Big deal. You have enough already, don't you think? My entire place isn't as big as this guest room. The spread you have on your table would feed me and my roommate for a year."

"So you think you had a right to do this?"

"Of course not! I've never done anything like this before in my life. What do you think I am, a criminal?" Her top lip was quivering a little, but she flipped her hair and forced a smirk. "Look, just tell me what you're going to do and get it over with. Call the police. Blacklist me all over town. I don't care."

He was staring at her with both eyes now. "As long as you don't have to have sex with me."

"Sex is for love. I don't care how insane that sounds to someone like you. It's the way I'm going to live. Even if you offered me a starring role in your next movie and half this house, I still wouldn't sleep with you."

He didn't say anything as he reached for his shoes, but he groaned a little when he put them on. Maybe it was true about the blisters.

When he stood up, she was struck again by how tall he was. Tall and intimidating. She stood up too, but it didn't help.

"Let's go." He waved his hand in the direction of the door.

"Where?"

"Back to the party."

"Both of us?"

He was already opening the door, and then they were in the hall, crowded with guests. His mother, Margaret, was taking them to the screening room in the west wing of the house. It was time to watch *A Silver Dollar and a Gun.*

"Would you sit with me?" he said to Lucy.

She was very surprised, but she said okay. At least she'd have a good seat, she thought, though it didn't turn out to be true. Charles always sat in the back so he could watch everyone's reactions. He said these closed preview screenings were a farce—no one ever said what they really thought—but he could tell whether the scenes were working by the way the audience breathed and moved in their seats. Too much sighing or squirming was obviously bad, but none was bad too. "If the hero is in danger," he told Lucy, "everyone *should* be uncomfortable."

Lucy was uncomfortable, no problem there. Before the movie started, at least half the room turned around to catch a glimpse of her. Later, she would discover that Charles had never had a woman sit with him during a screening. He said he'd never trusted any woman he'd been with not to distract him with false praise.

After the movie was over, he asked if she'd stay at his side while he suffered through the applause and backslapping. When her roommate, Janice, came up to ask what was going on, Lucy shrugged, but Charles said the explanation was simple.

"Lucy is not corrupt."

Janice's eyes were on her. Several other people had gathered in a circle around Charles, and they were looking at her too. One of them was the actress Belinda Holmes, who had been the female lead in several of Keenan's movies.

Lucy wondered if he'd been drinking, but then she realized she'd been with him for more than two hours. Even if he had, it would have worn off by now.

"This girl has moral values," he said, emphasizing his point with one hand slicing the air. His tone became loud, as if he were giving a speech. Which he was. The crowd around them was growing with his every word. "Too many people in this business don't even know what that means anymore. Immoral behavior has become so commonplace that they don't even call it that, they call it 'looking out for your career. Doing what you have to do.' There's no such thing as bad or good, only the next big score."

The longer Charles talked, the more Lucy thought he sounded like one of the monologues that were considered the "signatures" of his movies. Unlike old-fashioned Westerns, Keenan's films always contained at least one direct address to the audience, usually by the sheriff. Movie critics loved to talk about the meaning of these monologues, claiming they were really about Watergate, the Vietnam War, feminism, race relations, all the issues of the day. Lucy never really caught any of that. To her, the sheriff sounded like her grandpa, spinning a tale of the old days when good was good and bad was bad and people had faith in each other and the world.

Charles himself had moved back to the topic of Lucy and was spinning a dream of the little town she must have come from. Her accent gave her away, he said. It was Southern, wholesome, without a hint of sarcasm.

She winced a little at the word "wholesome." Smitty had called her "wholesome looking"—while he was laughing and pinching her butt.

She'd let herself drift into a daydream by the time Belinda Holmes suddenly said, "Tell us, Lucy, are you really such a good person?"

"You don't have to answer that," he said irritably.

"Why not let her answer?" Belinda said, tossing her head back. When she turned to Lucy, her voice was a challenge. "Unless for some reason you don't want to."

Lucy's eyes darted around the room, but she didn't see one person crack a smile. Even the group of actors who were rumored to be twenty-four-hour speed freaks looked as serious as if they were in church.

The church of Charles Keenan, she thought. She figured he was waiting for her to say yes, so his speech would make sense, but she was so nervous, she blurted out the truth. "No," she said. She looked down at the beautiful wood floor, each plank gleaming, not a speck of dust in sight. "I want to be a good person, but I don't think I am."

She looked up when Charles started clapping. A slow, steady clap, each one loud enough that she wondered it didn't hurt his hands. Soon the rest of the crowd had joined him and she realized she'd never been more confused in her life. But she wasn't angry. Maybe she really was meant to be an actress, she thought, since she liked even this bizarre applause.

Over the next hour or so, two agents slipped her their cards. One said, "You are incredible," and the other simply told her to call him tomorrow. It felt exciting, even though she knew it was only because of Charles Keenan's interest that they were interested in her. And that won't last, she thought later, sitting next to him on a white couch that had to be eighteen feet long, eating slices of the most delicious strawberries and mangoes she'd ever tasted in her life. Now that she wasn't angry, she couldn't think of a single thing to say to him. Even when he asked what she thought of his movie, she said, "Great." It was her true reaction, but how boring.

By the time the guests started leaving, she was mainly just relieved. She was dying to be back with Janice in Janice's old VW, smoking a joint and laughing, rehashing all the strange details of this very strange night.

She did manage to tell him she was going. When he asked her to come into the dining room for a moment first, she nodded and let him lead her into the deserted room.

The chandeliers were dark, but the room wasn't, thanks to the shadows of the giant floodlights outside playing on the wall. She could see a tennis court and swimming pool in back of the house, and she remembered again that this man was a millionaire many times over.

"Before you leave, I'd like to kiss you," he said. "Is that all right?"

He must have taken her silence as a sign that she didn't mind because he leaned down and put his lips on hers, surprisingly lightly and gently, as if he were kissing a newborn baby. It was so different from the way Mr. Smitty had kissed her that she felt tears spring to her eyes.

"Is something wrong?" he said. His voice had become so kind, and she felt foolish but even sadder.

"No," she whispered.

"May I kiss you again then?"

May I? she thought. Like something from one of his movies. Next thing you knew, he'd be calling her "ma'am," and she'd be wearing gingham and calico.

At that moment, the idea struck her as incredibly romantic.

She said yes, and he did kiss her, over and over until she was dizzy. But then he walked her to the front hallway and let her leave with nothing but a good-bye.

Back in the VW with Janice, riding down Wilshire Boulevard, she realized she'd lost interest in smoking a joint. She wasn't in the mood to talk about the party and she definitely didn't want to listen to Janice going on and on about Charles. Especially in her silly pirate voice, which Lucy never liked much anyway.

"Aye, matey, it was his eye, I tell you. That wicked eye. Aargh, the eye made me do it."

"Very funny."

"Aargh. Better a weird-ass eye than missin' a leg though. That's what I always say since—"

"Cut it out."

"I lost me middle leg back in 'fifty-seven. Aargh. Wonder if that big eye means a big di—"

"Shut up already, will you?"

"What's your problem?" Janice was frowning, but then she glanced at Lucy. "Wait a minute. What's going on here? Did he promise you something? Is that what this is about? Oh, you lucky dog!" She reached over and punched Lucy lightly on the arm. "Here I am out here for a year and a half with nothing but walk-ons and already you have a part in—"

"He didn't promise me anything."

"But he said he'd give you a role, didn't he? And you know what? I bet he meant it. Everybody says he's such an honest man, the most ethical person in Hollywood, the only guy in the industry with old-fashioned values, blah, blah, blah." She honked the horn and yelled out the open window. "My friend is going to have a part in a Charles Keenan movie. Dammit! You lucky, lucky dog."

"He never said anything about a part, Janice."

"Then what?" Janice said, confused. When Lucy didn't answer, she burst out, "Oh my God, don't tell me you like him? That can't be it. You like that weirdo?"

"He's not that weird."

"Come on, Lucy, he's as weird as they come, and they come pretty damn weird in this city. He lives with his mother, for Pete's sake. He's *always* lived with his mother."

"But he's had girlfriends," Lucy said, racking her brain to remember the name of the latest one, the one she read about in some tabloid. "He dated that model, Delia Beck."

" 'Dated' is the word. He's never lived with anyone, never been married. Of course girls want him. Power is the ultimate aphrodisiac, as they say. But nobody is good enough for the fabulous Charles, that's the problem."

Lucy was trying to think of a way to change the topic without admitting it bothered her, when the radio saved her. Janice's favorite song came on and before long both girls were sticking their arms out the window, screaming along at the top of their lungs. "'Welcome to the Hotel California, such a lovely place . . .'"

By the time the song was over, Janice was ready to talk about all the cool people she herself had met at the party. Lucy listened, though each person Janice mentioned was interesting to her primarily because they were at his house. Were they his friends? Did they work with him? Had he ever said one of them was "not corrupt"?

If Lucy had had a real social life or something beyond her job as a waitress on the breakfast shift of the Venice Café, she might have been able to put him out of her mind. If either of the agents she'd tried had panned out, she might have already been on the way to being a success in her own right. Lucy would turn out to be a natural as an actress, but she didn't discover that until Charles Keenan gave her her first role. The role of a lifetime, the critics would say later. The role that defined every part she would be offered for the rest of her career, even after Charles had disappeared.

Everyone said she retired early because of what happened to her family. That was part of it, but the other part was she could no longer stand the role of saint/savior that Charles had written for her and taught her how to play.

It was almost four months after the party before she saw him again. During that time, while she was scouring for news of him in *The Hollywood Reporter* and *Variety* (there was so little news! Didn't the man ever leave his house?), he was writing the script for what would turn out to be his last Western, *The Brave Horseman of El Dorado.* The cast numbered in the hundreds, as in all Keenan's films, but the star, the horse*man,* was actually a girl. It was a fascinating idea: to retell the Joan of Arc story as a Western. And the girl, the new Joan, had long red hair, according to the script. She was small, at most five-three, no more than ninety-five pounds. She had hazel eyes and tiny hands and very white skin and the lightest sprinkling of freckles across her cheeks and nose.

In other words, Lucy herself.

"What if I hadn't wanted to do this?" she asked, attempting to be playful, though she was so nervous her voice shook. He'd called out of the blue and asked where to pick her up. She'd phoned her waitress job, pretending to be sick, but they'd fired her. So what? Now she was riding with Charles Keenan in his black sports car out to a movie studio. She was flipping through a real movie script.

"I would have asked the casting people to find someone else." He was wearing sunglasses; she couldn't see his eyes. His tone was matter-of-fact, a little cold, but then he reached for her hand. Her sweaty hand, she worried—but he held it anyway all the way to the studio, and then again as they walked into the producer's office.

Talk about a sweet deal, Janice said later. At Charles's insistence, Lucy didn't have to audition or even do a screen test. "She is Joan," he said to Walter Urig, his producer, and later to the studio execs, and that was the end of the discussion.

It helped that he was willing to work with her so much during preproduction: to hire a voice coach to tone down her accent and trainers to teach her to ride a horse, hold a sword, and fire a gun; to get the best acting coach in town to help her through rehearsals.

The acting coach was the first to proclaim Lucy a budding star. He told Charles, "She seems to draw on a well of emotion that is uncanny for her age."

Lucy flushed with happiness, but Charles just nodded. Now that he'd made up his mind that she was the perfect Joan, he never second-guessed the wisdom of his decision. This confidence was part of the reason he was a good director, but it was justified, Lucy thought, by what seemed to be his extraordinary ability to see into an actor's strengths and weaknesses. That big eye, Janice joked. Lucy couldn't help laughing a little since she'd thought the same thing.

Anthony Mills, who was playing the evil landowner responsible for Joan's arrest and eventual death, was one of the most sought after dramatic actors in Hollywood. Lucy had seen him on the big screen at least a dozen times, but even he seemed eager to take Charles's advice on everything from line delivery to how to hold his arms during the trial scenes. "You're a fucking genius," he told Charles, at least twice a day. Charles never said anything. He was usually deep in thought about the next problem to be solved.

Making a movie was nothing like Lucy expected. It was so much work, especially for her because she was in almost every scene. She usually started at six a.m. and it would be eight or nine p.m., sometimes even later, before they wrapped and she could go home. Most of her day was spent standing around, waiting for lighting or costume or the art director or the DP or the script supervisor or any one of a thousand people that needed to talk to Charles before they could film. For every fifteen minutes of shooting there were ninety minutes, sometimes more, of blocking and lighting, decisions and preparations. Everybody stayed pretty focused, at least on set. There were rumors of after-hours parties with lots of drinking and casual sex, but Lucy never went to any of these parties, so she couldn't say if the rumors were true. Nor did she particularly care, because she had other things on her mind.

What on earth was going on with Charles?

He'd never kissed her again. The hand-holding had ended after the first day. He never offered to drive her home, but instead had one of the studio's drivers pick her up and take her to the day's location, and then drop her back at her house at night. He showed no response, not even with his eyes, when he heard her turn down a dinner with the handsome Anthony.

The worst part was he knew how she felt about him. He had to know because he was the one who helped her recognize how strong her own feelings had become.

It was during the shooting of the torture scene. The scene was about a third of the way through the script; Joan had already fought off the evil gangs of robbers and murderers from several towns in Mexico, and the people loved her for it. In each place she freed, she'd remove her hat and let her red hair fall down on her shoulders, and the people would gasp with surprise, then cheer for the woman who had saved them. They called her Saint Joan and begged to touch her coat for luck.

But then the evil Paolo (played by Anthony) kidnapped Joan and forced her over the border and into a jail in San Antonio. The sheriff was a churchgoing man, inclined to agree that this woman had to be in league with the devil to have such power. He gave his approval to Paolo's request to "break her down and find the truth."

The entire scene was to be done with only the sounds of whips and knives to indicate what Paolo and his men were doing to her, and Paolo's voice, horrible in its cruel simplicity, saying over and over, "Choose, Joan." The choice he was giving her was to confess or be tortured, but for Joan herself, the choice was between suffering this pain or renouncing God. It was a tight shot; the camera was never to leave her face and she was never allowed to speak. Her agony, her faith, her heartbreak, her joy in the love of God, would all have to be readable from her expression.

Charles had written the script this way, and he was insistent on it staying this way. But Lucy wasn't pulling it off. They did take after take, and though she found the pain and fear, she was failing at anything approximating joy.

Everyone in the cast and crew was even more tired than usual. They'd only been back for a few days after three hard weeks on location in Mexico. They were taking a break when Charles came over to her while she was drinking coffee.

"You're having problems with this."

"It's very hard," she admitted, hoping she didn't sound defensive. Charles didn't like working with defensive actors. He'd given them several speeches about the importance of being open to suggestion and criticism for the film's sake.

He was resting his hand on the right side of his face, a habit he had. The effect was unexpected. Though he was covering the small eye, leaving the big left one exposed, she felt less intimidated than usual. It took her a while to realize why: with the small one covered, the big eye didn't look as big.

He paused for a minute, maybe more. "I'd like to try something to bring out your more positive feelings. All right with you?"

"Sure, but what—"

He had already walked off to consult with the DP before the next take.

It was time to begin shooting, and everyone took their places. Lucy crouched on the cement floor with her arms curled under her chest, waiting for the first snap of the whip. She was also glancing around for Charles, wondering why he wasn't in his usual spot behind the camera, still wondering what he had in mind to try.

She found out not a minute into the scene, when she looked up and found Charles sitting straight across from her on the floor. He was just out of range of the camera, behind a cardboard partition. No one could see him but Lucy—and he was taking off his shoes. Wincing like he had on the day they met, when he had those blisters.

Before she could laugh, he moved his hands over his heart with an expression so sad it made her want to cry for him. But before she could give in to that sadness, he took a plastic coffee spoon from his pocket and began to wrap it in a piece of duct tape, so it would look like silver. He slowly raised it to his mouth and kissed it. Then he looked directly into her eyes until she smiled and blushed as the truth suddenly hit her.

I'm falling in love with him. The next revelation came so quickly that it felt like both ideas had arrived in her mind at the same moment. *And he knows it. This is why he's sitting here. He knows if I look at him, my face will have to show all this.*

He kept staring at her, and she couldn't look away. Paolo said, "Choose, Joan," again and again while the whip continued to crack, and she looked at Charles until she had convinced herself that he must love her too; otherwise, how would he know?

After the scene, the crew broke into applause. The other actors told her that the play of emotions on her face was truly astonishing. But Charles himself only said mildly, "Good job."

"Time to set up the next shot, people," the line producer shouted. "Let's go. We're three hours behind already."

She went home that night and told Janice that she was so confused, she wanted to jump off the roof.

"We live in a one-story," Janice said. "Knock yourself out. Break a leg."

"Ha-ha."

"See, I got you laughing already."

"I didn't know that was the point."

"Come on," Janice said, grabbing her purse. "Let's take a walk."

"I'm tired," Lucy began, but her friend took her arm and pulled her to the door. It was June, but a breeze was blowing from the ocean. Lucy shivered when they stepped outside. Janice turned left and began walking the four blocks to the beach, and Lucy caught up with her.

Ocean Front Walk was crowded with people, even though it was a Wednesday night, after ten. Janice waited until they'd walked down the path through the sand and found a bench that wasn't occupied by a homeless person.

"Okay," she said slowly, "I know you don't want to hear this, but I'm going to tell you anyway. Ever since you started working for

Keenan, you seem miserable. A hell of a lot more miserable than you ever were at the café, and that's a shit job."

"I told you I'm worn-out. We were working night and day in Mexico. It was—"

"But what about before? You haven't seemed happy the whole time you've been making this movie."

Lucy was listening to the slap of the water, peering into the darkness, trying to see the waves. What Janice was saying seemed too ridiculous to take seriously.

"Well?" Janice finally said. "Aren't you going to tell me why I'm wrong?"

"It's a chance of a lifetime. You said so yourself." Lucy paused. "Plus, there's something I haven't told you yet."

"Are you grinning?" Janice said, peering into Lucy's face. Her voice sounded a little annoyed. "I thought you were about to jump off the roof."

Lucy was grinning, though she couldn't have said why. This was what it had been like for her all day: back and forth between despair and a silly happiness that was unlike her, even as a child.

"You want to hear a secret?" she whispered, stifling back a giggle. She never giggled. What was wrong with her? She sat up straight and tried to compose herself. "I think I'm in love with him."

Janice didn't say anything for the longest time. Lucy sensed she disapproved, but she didn't care. The surge of happiness had welled up and lifted her right out of her day-to-day existence, and now she could see her life from the outside. She was sitting on a bench facing the Pacific Ocean, hundreds and hundreds of miles from her tiny town in Missouri. She was nineteen years old, and she was acting in a movie. More than acting, she was the lead.

"Well, I hope you're wrong," Janice said. "Falling in love with him would be really, really stupid."

Her voice was so sudden and harsh that Lucy felt like she'd been slapped. She turned to Janice and gasped, "Please don't."

"Lucy, he doesn't even know you! When the movie is over, you'll see. If it's a hit, he'll use you again, but if it isn't, you'll fall off the earth as far as he's concerned. They're all like that. It's this business."

Without even thinking, Lucy jumped up and started running. She was ankle deep in the water, with her shoes still on, when Janice caught up with her and discovered Lucy was sobbing.

"Oh honey, shit." She threw her arm around Lucy, and Lucy let herself lean against her friend, but she couldn't stop crying.

"Come on, Lu, what do I know? I'm strictly a walk-on, remember?"

"It's not that," Lucy stammered.

"What is it then?"

But Lucy couldn't answer because she really didn't know. She wasn't crying about whether Charles loved her. Part of her thought he already did, and all of her was hopeful he would someday. Janice calling her stupid had reminded her of the way her uncle had treated her (though stupid was a mild insult from him), but she wasn't crying about that either.

She cried and cried and her tears weren't for anything she could think of in her present or her past. Which left only the future, but why would she be crying about the future? She was so young; she still had her whole life ahead.

eight

IT WAS THE last week of filming when Lucy heard that the studio executives thought there were "significant" problems with *The Brave Horseman of El Dorado.* No one was questioning the quality—or her own performance, Lucy was relieved to hear—it was the theme itself that worried them. Why would the audience want to watch a story where the main character dies? A story about God of all things? A story about a saint from hundreds of years ago? A Western with a woman as the hero, and an unknown to boot, rather than Clint Eastwood or one of the dozens of well-known men?

The cast was gossiping constantly about whether the movie would even be released. A Charles Keenan movie had never done poorly at the box office, but then he'd never made a movie like this. The only person who refused to worry was Charles himself. He made an announcement on Wednesday that all of this speculation about the future was not only useless, it was counterproductive. "We're here to find the truth of the characters and the story," he said. "It's no concern of ours what some twenty-year-old in the marketing department thinks the public will buy."

Lucy admired this view, though she couldn't totally share it. If the movie failed, it might hurt Charles, but it would probably kill her own chance at a career. She loved acting, and she really loved not being poor. She and Janice had just spent the weekend looking for a new apartment, and there was one she'd fallen in love with that had a dishwasher and a garbage disposal and two bedrooms and two baths.

"Two bedrooms," Janice said, and laughed. "Great. We'll each have our own bedroom for all those nights we bring guys home."

Neither of them had ever brought a guy home: Janice because she just hadn't met anyone she was interested in, and Lucy because the only person she was interested in was Charles. Since the day behind the partition, there hadn't been any real developments, although she felt sure he was looking at her more often. And she had a new theory. What if he felt like he couldn't be involved with her while they were working together? This would explain everything, why he hadn't kissed her or held her hand since they started shooting (and in the weeks before, but Lucy could stretch the theory if necessary). He was obviously a perfectionist, and if they were dating, it might compromise their work on set. The movie came first, and fine, especially since the shooting was finally set to end this Friday.

The last scene to be shot was one of the exterior scenes entirely on horseback. The location was about fifty miles outside the city. By Friday afternoon, Lucy was saddle sore and tired, but she still felt excited when Charles asked if she would come by his office before she headed home. She said yes, but actually she had her driver take her home first, to change into a new shirt and jeans.

As she walked down the hall, she realized she hadn't been in Charles's office since all those months ago, when he first showed her the script for Joan. His office was in the same building as that of the other execs, including Walter, the producer. In fact, Walter was in Charles's office when Lucy walked in. Some blond woman was there too, standing right next to Charles. Her nails were as perfect as any Lucy had ever seen. Lucy noticed them because her hand was resting on Charles's shoulder.

He was sitting behind his desk; Walter was in the chair facing him. But when Walter saw Lucy, he smiled and stood up. "And here's our star now. Take a seat, Lucy." After she did, he said, "Were your ears burning? We were just talking about you."

Before she could answer, the woman said, "Hello, Lucy!" She was smiling too, so broadly that Lucy wanted to look away. "I'm Peggy, and I'll be working on marketing and PR, that's public relations, for the wonderful movie you and Charles have been making."

"I'm sure she knows what 'PR' stands for," Charles said sharply. "Cut to the chase. You wanted Lucy here and she's here. Now will you tell me what all this is about?"

Lucy looked at him. He was frowning in a disgusted way that he never used on set. Peggy moved her hand and even Walter stepped back a little. But Lucy didn't feel anything but sorry for Charles. This frown made his eyes look more uneven. The small one looked smaller, tired.

Walter said he and Peggy were there to talk about the studio's concerns about the marketability of the movie. Charles said he didn't want any of his actors involved in that topic, end of discussion. "Lucy, I'm sorry to drag you over here for nothing. You can go."

She started to stand up, but Peggy said, "Wait, Lucy. This involves you too."

"I want to ask you both what you might term a moral question," Walter said, nodding at Charles. "Suppose you had something you thought the whole world needed to hear. What would you be willing to do to make sure the message got out?"

"Walter—" Charles began.

"It's a good question," Peggy said brightly. "If you don't want to answer, let Lucy give it a shot."

"I would do anything I could to get the message out," Lucy said.

Charles turned to her. "How about lying? Because that's where they're going with this, I guarantee you." He exhaled loudly. "Every movie they try to do this. Anything for press." His voice grew sarcastic. "Got an actor who's Cherokee? How about someone who can handle snakes? Would one of your people be willing to say they were thrown from a horse during taping? How about the leading man and woman pretending they've fallen in love?"

Walter shook his head. "It's different this time. You write a story with a death ending and you can't be surprised if the movie dies. You know that as well as I do." He turned to Lucy. "All we want you to do is help us make sure that your wonderful movie has a chance to be seen. Don't you want your family back in . . ." He looked at Peggy.

"Missouri," she said, reading from notes.

"Missouri, yes. Don't you want your family back in Missouri to see you in such an incredible performance?"

Charles smirked. "You haven't even kept up with the dailies, Walter."

Walter was still smiling at Lucy. "But I trust you and I've seen enough to know you're right. She's given an incredible performance."

"I don't have any family left in Missouri," Lucy said. "But I do want people all over the country to see this. I think the movie has an important message about believing in something so much, you're willing to die for it."

Lucy had heard Charles say this dozens of times, but he was frowning again at Walter. "If you convince this girl to violate her principles in the name of making money—"

"I need money though," Lucy said. "And I want to help the movie get to theaters."

"Of course you do," Peggy said.

"No you don't," Charles said.

"Yes I do."

"Let me handle this," Charles said to her. "You don't understand what they're asking."

"No," Lucy said. She was trying not to be annoyed with him, but he was making it hard. "They're talking to me, and I'm going to answer for myself."

"Good for you, Lucy," Peggy said, still with that syrupy grin. "Director or not, don't let this man push you around. Ever heard of the ERA, Chuck? Women aren't seen and not heard anymore."

"Fine," he said, throwing up his hands. "Can I go then? I don't want to watch this." He stood up and looked straight at Lucy. "Don't say I didn't warn you."

Walter cleared his throat. "Actually, this involves you too."

"How? You already know I haven't ever ridden in the rodeo, handled snakes, buried my mother in Indian ground, fallen—"

"Just listen," Walter said. "Peggy had an idea that I think could work."

Peggy looked at Charles. "As you know, we're pitching Lucy as your big discovery. The complete unknown comes to the director's house and is spotted and becomes a star. Nice but not enough. So we're thinking, what if we add a human interest element to that story?"

Lucy was sitting forward. She was terrified they were going to mention the spoon. But then she realized there was no way they knew. Charles certainly wouldn't have given them that.

"And I'm thinking I don't care," Charles said. "Find the human interest and shove it in your press release. Are we finished?"

Peggy's smile didn't change. "Here's our thought. What if you and Lucy were a little more to each other than director and actor? Can't you see it? The human interest angle would be fabulous."

Charles blinked. "You're not suggesting Lucy and I pretend to be involved?"

"Your first public appearance wouldn't be for months. It really wouldn't be—"

She stopped talking because Charles burst out in a laugh. "This takes the cake, even for you people. No one would believe it in a million years."

Lucy felt her cheeks burn.

"Why the hell not?" Peggy sputtered.

"For one thing, she's nineteen and I'm thirty-five."

"Christ, this is Hollywood. You could be seventy-five and go out with her."

"If I was an amoral bag of filth."

"Keenan, don't be ridiculous." Walter shot him an irritated glance. "Everyone knows you like to date models. Are you saying they're old ladies?"

"It's different with Lucy," he said, looking at the wall.

"Different how?" Walter snapped. "She's an adult, you're an adult. I don't see the problem."

"The problem is, I'm an adult, but Lucy's still a child."

She was already hurt, but then she was furious. How dare he talk about her like that in front of the producer and an exec from PR? How dare he talk about her that way, period? She'd worked so hard during the weeks and weeks they'd been making the movie. Didn't she deserve some respect?

She glared at him and said as harshly as she felt—letting her strongest Southern accent come back as she did—"I am not a child, but you are definitely a jerk!"

Then, before any of them could say a word, she stood up and left the office.

She was halfway down the hall when he grabbed her elbow. "Wait."

"Get away from me."

"I'm sorry I hurt your feelings, but that doesn't mean it's not true."

"It isn't true! I'm not a child and you know it."

"I don't know it, Lucy. If I did, I wouldn't have written a part for you as a fifteen-year-old girl."

She'd never thought of that and she was momentarily confused, but then she put her hands on her hips. "What about that day we filmed the torture scene? Are you telling me you thought of me as a child then?"

He grew visibly paler. "That was wrong. I've thought about it many times since and I think I let my obsession with getting a good scene get in the way of my better judgment."

Two men were coming down the hall. They nodded at Charles, and Lucy waited until they rounded the corner. "All right, what about the day you kissed me?"

He leaned against the wall and put his hand over the right side of his face. Covering the smaller eye. The weaker eye, she thought now.

His answer was a whisper. "That was wrong as well."

"Why did you do it then?"

"Because I was attracted to you, but—"

"So you're usually attracted to children?"

"No," he said, frowning deeply. "Of course not."

"Well then?"

Another group of people was walking toward them. Charles pointed to a door across the hall and asked her to come with him. "I'll try to explain."

It was an empty conference room. Charles sat down by the white board in front; Lucy took the chair next to him. She tapped her fingers to remind him she was waiting, and still angry.

"Remember when you said you'd rather go to jail than have sex with me?" He took a deep breath. "I can't tell you how surprised I was. I almost couldn't believe it."

"Jeez, who do you think you are? I know women throw themselves at you, but come—"

"No. I was surprised because your position was so unusual and admirable. I thought, here is someone who believes in love so strongly she's willing to go to jail rather than accept anything less."

His voice was strangely sad, and Lucy couldn't help but be touched. But then she remembered. "How is that childish?"

"It struck me as very innocent. Beautifully innocent, but still."

"I'm not that innocent," Lucy said, and sighed. "I wish I were."

"You've had a high school boyfriend. Maybe two. But I—I'm not proud of this, and I wish I didn't have to say it to someone like you. I've had dozens and dozens of women over the years. And it was always sex, never the love you're holding out for."

"Well, I've done things I'm not proud of either."

"Like try to steal my spoon?" He smiled a half smile. "That was another reason I knew you were innocent. You thought you could go to jail for that. I think the jails in L.A. have all the business they need from murderers and drug dealers, pimps and prostitutes."

Suddenly she wished that she hadn't followed him in here. Hearing what he thought of her—innocent, admirable, someone who would always hold out for love—made her feel like such a fake. If only she could have been the person he described. If only she'd held on to her innocence.

"I've done other things," she finally said, looking down at the table. "Things a lot worse."

"I don't believe it," he said, and reached over and put his hand under her chin, to lift her face to his. "I'm sure you haven't done anything that bad."

"It was bad." She felt hopeless. "I know you'd think so too."

Most of his movies had at least one prostitute and one good woman, and they were always completely different. The good woman didn't have to be a virgin (some were widows; some had husbands who left them), but she had to have a "pure heart." Lucy remembered in the monologue for *A Silver Dollar and a Gun,* the sheriff had said a pure-hearted person never does anything solely for money. "Better to starve than do something against your principles. Better to lose the world and save your soul."

"I wish I'd saved my soul," Lucy whispered. She was trying not to cry. "Now I've lost everything anyway."

When he asked her what she'd lost, his voice was full of concern; his expression was serious and kind and so wise. It was the same way he looked on set, when he was listening to his cast and crew, like they could admit any weakness, like there was nothing he wouldn't understand.

So she told him. She'd been dying to tell someone anyway, and at least she knew he'd take it seriously. She even told him the parts that made her look like a childish fool. When Smitty had first offered to mark her rent paid and give her fifty dollars if she let him touch her, she thought he meant just that: touching. She was so stupid; she'd never even had a real date before. But then he was on top of her, and she couldn't get away. Afterward, she didn't care. He would come into her apartment and tell her it was time, then throw the money on the floor after he was finished. And she would bend over and pick it up. She never yelled or told him no. She knew it was wrong, and yet she didn't do anything to stop it.

"So see, I'm not innocent at all."

"Lucy, it's not true." He took her hands and pulled her up so she was standing next to him. "That man was evil. He took advantage of your ignorance and your poverty."

"But I let him. It was my fault."

Charles put his finger over her lips. "No, it wasn't. I know you. You have a pure heart, the purest heart of anyone I've ever met. You deserve someone who would protect you from men like that."

A pure heart. She wasn't sure why he thought this, but the relief was so strong it left Lucy exhausted. Even stronger than the relief, though, was her rush of feeling for him.

When he pulled her into his arms, the words were out of her mouth before she could stop herself. "I love you," she said, into his shirt.

"Sweet," he said, so softly that she barely heard it, before he leaned down and gave her another of those gentle kisses, and then pulled her to him so tightly she could feel him trembling before he kissed her again.

They stayed in the conference room, kissing and holding each other, long after Walter and Peggy and nearly everyone who worked in the building had left. Only the janitors were there when Charles asked if she was getting hungry.

They were sitting on the floor, propped against the wall. "I'd rather stay with you," she said, leaning back into him.

"Here's an idea. We could be together *and* eat. It may sound strange, but I've heard it's done all the time."

"Oh," she said, and for a moment, she felt a little stupid, but then he brought her hand to his lips and told her that he was glad she was incapable of sarcasm. "My sweet Lucy," he said, and she beamed. No one had called her "my Lucy" since her mother died.

As distant as Charles had been before, after that day, he was the opposite. Things developed between them so fast that Lucy barely had time to think. He was with her every day: holding her, kissing her, driving her around town in his sports car, wining her, dining her, telling her how beautiful she was, how he was going to take care of her and protect her, how he would be the man she deserved.

The one thing they didn't do was have sex. It was Charles's idea. He said that because of what happened to her in Nashville, he wanted to wait until she felt completely safe. She was so touched she couldn't speak.

Even his mother turned out to be great. Lucy had heard so much about Margaret Keenan, mostly from Janice, who'd read several tabloid stories that portrayed her as a controlling old hag who was always trying to ruin her son's chances for happiness. Supposedly Mrs. Keenan had scared away several of Charles's girlfriends, but once Lucy got to know her, she knew this couldn't be true, though she thought she understood why the rumor had started. Margaret Keenan adored her son, but not in some sick way. It was actually quite beautiful, Lucy thought. The same way Lucy's own mother had loved her.

From the beginning, she treated Lucy like part of the family; she even apologized for taking her to the guest room that first day. "Charles is quite a moralist," his mother said, and sighed. "I was afraid he might be annoyed if I let you take the spoon and just as annoyed if I let you leave before he'd had a chance to talk to you. I was wrong, but I often am when I try to predict his feelings. He told me who cares about a silly spoon?"

She was serving tea to Lucy. Charles was swimming laps in the pool.

"He's always had very strong opinions. I can't tell you what a relief it is for me to know that he finally has someone who cares for him as he is."

"I can't imagine how anyone could meet him and not care for him."

"He said the same thing about you. I can already see why."

Lucy was overwhelmed with happiness. Later that same day, she decided to tell Charles she felt safe.

They spent the weekend at a resort about a hundred miles north of L.A. Even years later, even after everything that happened, Lucy would not be able to convince herself that it was anything other than one of the happiest times in her life. He was gentle and passionate and madly in love with her, and she felt the same. There were no warning bells that would have kept her from saying yes when he asked her to marry him. It was Sunday morning; they were still in bed, finishing their breakfast. When she saw the beautiful ring he'd bought, a delicate, hand-engraved antique with a center diamond that was just small enough it didn't make her nervous, she thought she was just about the luckiest girl in the world.

He knew that she was a little uncomfortable with how rich he was. Or actually, how she would fit in such a wealthy world. She'd never had a massage or been in a sauna or shopped at Saks or owned more than three pairs of shoes. She had a little of her own money from the film, but she would never have spent it the way Charles spent his, without seeming to give it a second thought.

About a month later, when Charles was at the studio working with the editors, Lucy and Margaret were sitting on the couch in the hall, flipping through stationery books, trying to pick the perfect paper for the wedding invitations. The studio had insisted they invite half the town to the ceremony, and Lucy had convinced him not to fight them on it. If it helped the movie release, great. It wasn't like they were lying.

Margaret was excited about such a big wedding. They'd decided to hold it on the east lawn of the house, and she was doing the planning. Lucy had readily admitted she had no real knowledge about any of this.

One of the things she liked about Mrs. Keenan was how willing she was to teach her everything she knew. And Charles's mother never acted like there was something wrong with not knowing already. If anything, Margaret tried to make Lucy feel better. When Lucy seemed shocked by the prices in the stationery book, Mrs. Keenan put the book down on the coffee table and patted her hand.

"You know, Charles did not grow up with this kind of money either. We lived in a small apartment most of his childhood. I think that's why he's always insisted I live with him. He wants me to have a better life too."

"He told me his father was a policeman."

Mrs. Keenan looked surprised, and Lucy realized it wasn't true. Charles hadn't told her; she'd read about it in some sleazy tabloid that Janice unearthed and stuck in her face, claiming it was another weird thing about Charles.

"Director's Father Killed in Shoot-out with Real-life Bank Robbers: Source for Keenan's Westerns Found in Tragic Incident of Childhood."

When Lucy admitted her mistake, his mother nodded. "He never talks about what happened. He was just a boy; who knows why those silly papers would find this interesting. His father was off-duty, and Charlie was the only witness. . . . In some ways, I don't think he ever recovered. I think in his soul he's still that eleven-year-old, wanting to make the good guys win for a change."

"But he's turned it into art," Lucy said. "He's made films that mean something to millions of people."

Mrs. Keenan smiled. "Most people in the business just humor Charles. He's always been aware of this. They have to give him a grudging respect given all the money he makes for them, but they really think he's out of step with the times. But you don't feel this way, do you, Lucy? You really admire his way of looking at things."

"Yes, very much."

"I'm so glad he found you." Margaret put her arm around Lucy and gave her a quick hug. "Oh goodness, you're such a little thing. Who would guess a tiny slip of a girl like you would be the one to save my son?"

Lucy remembered this conversation later that night, when Charles took her to a fancy seafood restaurant in Santa Monica. He was talking about finding a house in this area, so Lucy could wake up every morning and hear the ocean. "Beverly Hills is the wrong place to raise children," he added. "It's far too decadent."

"You're probably right," she said. She loved how Charles talked about their future children like they were a given, though sometimes she worried that he wanted them sooner than she did. Production companies and agencies were sending her projects every day now, and she wanted to give her acting career a chance before they started a family. Of course she couldn't sign on to any movie until she knew if Charles needed her for his next film. She'd rather work with him than anybody else.

"I was talking to your mother today, and she said the strangest thing."

He looked up from his lobster.

"She said I was tiny and—"

"You are." Charles took her wrist between his thumb and index finger. "Your bones are as delicate as a baby bird's." He grinned. "Although there are parts of you I wouldn't call—"

"And," Lucy said.

"Go on. Sorry."

"She said I'd saved you."

"Because you did." He picked up the lobster fork and took another bite.

"That's it? What does it even mean?"

"You are my sweet Lucy. Of course you saved me. You've given my life a purpose: to protect you and make you happy."

She smiled and he reached for her hand across the table.

"I'm thinking a boy and a girl and another boy and another girl.

Keep going until we've made more children than movies." He squeezed her hand and laughed. "Seeing you pregnant will be like seeing a twig that swallowed a bowling ball."

"Maybe not. Maybe I'll get fat everywhere."

"Fine. You could weigh three hundred pounds and you'd still be beautiful to me."

Lucy's smile grew even broader when she realized he actually believed this. How could she have gotten so lucky?

They spent the next few days trudging around the area with Charles's real estate agent. Lucy felt like she was trudging anyway, and she wondered why her energy level was at such an all-time low. She wasn't working; she hadn't really lifted a finger in weeks. Charles's servants did all the cooking and laundry. He even had a servant to bring them tea and the phone and hand them a towel after swimming.

They finally found the perfect house on the north side of Malibu. It was smaller than the Beverly Hills house (which Lucy was glad about), but very private and absolutely gorgeous. Lucy felt like she'd wandered into heaven as the real estate agent took them around the grounds, showing them all the fruit trees: orange and persimmon, fig and pomegranate, lemon and lime, and avocado. There was a guest-house for his mother, and a pool surrounded by the most beautiful garden of lilies, begonias and roses. The main house was set high on top of a hill; nearly every room had a view of the ocean that took Lucy's breath away. Three of the bedrooms had views of the mountains as well, and the master bedroom had both a huge balcony and a rock fireplace. The front hall even had an impressive staircase that reminded Lucy of her mother's favorite movie, *Gone With the Wind*.

There were also six bathrooms, and Lucy felt like she knew them all after she and Charles spent the night there, to make sure they were comfortable before he made an offer. It would have been a romantic night, sleeping on a futon in the empty mansion, except for the fact that Lucy kept throwing up. A few days later, the doctor confirmed what she suspected. She was already pregnant.

When Charles found out, he picked her up and twirled her around until she was dizzy. He was so ecstatically happy that Lucy put aside all her concerns about it being too soon. She just laughed when Janice told her no man was *that* happy about a pregnancy. "Unless he's one of those macho pigs," Janice threw in. "All about knocking up their women, extending their line."

"You know he's not a macho pig," Lucy said into the phone.

Charles was sitting at his desk, sorting through his mail. He looked up. "But I am a pig," he said, and made a silly snorting sound.

Janice heard him. "It must be the end of the world," she said. "Charles Keenan, trying to be funny."

Lucy didn't say anything, but she wasn't that annoyed. Janice disliking Charles was like the smog or the traffic in L.A.—something she was getting used to. The few times she'd gotten them together, Janice gave him dirty looks and sulked, but he treated her in what Lucy thought was a perfectly lovely way. He even offered to help Janice get started in the business, but when he asked her what she wanted to do, she said she didn't know and she didn't feel like discussing it. So Charles dropped the topic, but he stayed pleasant. He told Lucy it was easy to be nice because he knew how nice Janice had been when Lucy first got into town. "Any friend of yours," he said, but then he admitted he was glad she didn't have any other friends who had a grudge against him.

"What time are you coming home?" Janice said. "It's like ten, isn't it?"

Lucy had promised she would stay at their place for the last two weeks before the wedding. Janice wanted her to, and Lucy had told Charles it might be more romantic if they didn't see each other every minute right up until the big day. He'd agreed, but that was before this afternoon, when he discovered she was pregnant. "I don't like you in that Venice dump anyway," he'd said. "It's not safe, especially now, when you're sick and you're a hundred times more vulnerable. I want you here, where I can take care of you."

"I'm not coming home," Lucy told Janice.

"At all?"

"Well, I am getting married in twelve days."

"I know that. I'm your maid of honor, remember? But I thought you were going to stay here until then."

"I was," Lucy said. "But things have changed."

Janice exhaled loudly. "What you really mean is he changed his mind. Jesus, Lucy, what is he, your master?"

"No, of course not," Lucy said evenly. "But he wants to take care of me, and I think it's really nice."

"All right," Janice snapped. "Go back to your Fantasy Island." But then she said more softly, "Wait, don't hang up yet, Lu. I just realized I didn't even say congratulations. I'm glad for you, really. I know you guys will have an adorable baby."

"Thanks," Lucy said. She was honestly touched, which was why Janice's next comment hurt her so badly.

"Wonder if it will have that weird eye."

Lucy slammed down the phone, and ran into the bathroom to vomit again. Charles followed to hold her hair and put a cool washcloth on her forehead. Afterward, when she was lying with her head in his lap, she wondered aloud why Janice had turned mean.

"What did she say this time?"

She looked at him, and his small eye was twitching a little, the way it always did when he was very tired. She reached up and put her hand on his cheek, and he leaned his face into her palm and kissed it.

"I don't want her at our wedding," she said suddenly.

"Wait and see how you feel about it tomorrow."

But the next day, Lucy's feelings were the same. She called Janice and told her if she wouldn't accept Charles, they couldn't be friends anymore. She was hoping Janice would say something to change her mind, but she didn't. She didn't even say good-bye.

nine

ON TUESDAY EVENING, Janice was sitting in traffic on the 405, heading to UCLA Medical Center and gnawing a hole in her cheek, wondering what she was going to say to her old friend. That she would be seeing Lucy in the hospital was part of the problem, but what really made her nervous was that this would be the first time she'd seen Lucy, period, in almost five years.

During that time, Janice's own life had changed dramatically. She'd gone back to college and finished her degree in social work; she'd fallen in love with Peter, a lawyer and activist for the homeless; they'd gotten married and just bought their first house, a fixer-upper in Moorpark. And Lucy's life had changed too. Janice knew this because she'd kept up with Lucy by reading articles in newspapers and magazines. At first, she did it because she couldn't help herself, but after a while, she realized she wanted to do it, even if she didn't really understand why. Of course it wasn't the same as the friendship she used to have with Lucy, but it was something, this connection she felt to all the things that happened to Lucy, the newsworthy ones anyway. Janice had never thought of herself as someone with a good memory, but she could remember exactly where she was when she found out about each big change in Lucy's life. She even remembered more clearly what was going on in her own life during those times, as if Lucy's news shaped Janice's personal history, the way other people remembered things by where they lived or where they worked or who was president or how long it had been before or after a particular earthquake.

Her husband, Peter, knew about this, but Janice had no intention of telling Lucy herself. For one thing, she figured it might seem a little weird, even for a movie star like Lucy, to discover that a former friend had been so interested in your life. And even if she took it the right way—as a sign Janice had never stopped caring about her—it could still lead to trouble if Lucy asked Janice what she'd thought of any of the things she'd read. Not surprisingly, Janice still had her opinions. No matter how much Lucy and Janice had changed, the one thing that hadn't changed was how strongly Janice reacted to certain facts of Lucy's life.

This was how the problem between the two friends had begun: Janice had reacted, and Lucy had called out of the blue and fired her from the wedding. At the time, Janice told herself she didn't care, she'd always hated weddings anyway. She also told herself she would ignore the big day completely, but the morning after the wedding, she found herself irresistibly drawn to the papers and she sat down and read it all, from full articles to brief mentions to everything in between.

It was impossible to avoid the conclusion that it had gone well, from the point of view of the reporters, true, but Lucy and Charles certainly looked happy in the pictures. Too bad nearly every article focused on him. Janice nearly gagged when she flipped to the entertainment section of one Santa Monica newspaper:

"An Old-fashioned Wedding for an Old-fashioned Man: Director Charles Keenan Weds in Front of Hundreds at Home in Beverly Hills."

Where was Lucy Dobbins in this? The third sentence. The third sentence of her own wedding! And another thing. The eighth sentence down, in a quote from the great man himself: "my sweet bride." Why did he have to call Lucy "sweet" every damn chance he had? Wasn't he a writer? Couldn't he come up with "dear" or "darling" or "honey" or something, anything, else?

In the only close-up of Lucy, she did look a little lonely. She had no maid of honor or any bridesmaids at all. She had nobody to give her away either (a stupid tradition, Janice thought, but still). He had his mother and the people from the studio and all the women he'd dated, most of whom were at the wedding, according to Sunday's gossip column. And who did Lucy have? No one.

And whose fault was that? Janice thought. Her own. Why the hell had she said that about Charles's eye? But she had no intention of apologizing. Lucy was off honeymooning on some exotic island, while she was sitting alone in an ugly coffee shop on Wilshire, with her fingers turned so black from newsprint there were smudges on the brick-hard bagel she hadn't been able to finish.

Deep down, Janice felt sure that eventually Lucy would apologize to her. After all, which was worse: making a dumb comment about his weird big eye (which even Lucy herself had joked about once or twice) or dumping your closest friend? How could Lucy live with herself after not even sending a small note when they sent some flunky to pick up Lucy's things and give Janice a check for Lucy's half of the rent until the Venice lease expired? Where was the female loyalty here?

When Lucy returned from her honeymoon, she did call. Janice was right, though the call didn't work out the way Janice hoped. If only Lucy hadn't handed the phone over so quickly to Charles. Janice was both happy and incredibly relieved to hear Lucy's voice, but the next thing she knew, Lucy said, "Hey, Charles has an idea. He wants to introduce you to a friend of his who's starting a production company," and then she was gone. If only Charles hadn't made her so angry with his Great Man routine. Like she would be oh so grateful to have a job working for his producer friend. "Assistant," Keenan called it, but Janice knew that meant glorified secretary. And even if it didn't, what made him think she wanted to be in production? She'd gone to a lot more auditions than Lucy ever had. She'd even taken acting classes for months. The fact that she'd never even had a speaking part and Lucy was about to become a star was just another sign of what she'd always thought: that the world was profoundly unfair.

By the time Lucy got back on the phone, Janice felt so humiliated that she didn't want to talk anymore. When Lucy asked if she wanted to get together, Janice said she'd have to check her work schedule. "Should I call you?" Lucy said, and Janice said no, she'd do the calling. Lucy was moving into her new house, and she gave Janice the number, but somehow Janice managed to misplace it. Later, she couldn't remember if she'd even written it down. It didn't matter since she probably wouldn't have called Lucy anyway. She sensed that this was some kind of mercy meeting, and the last thing she wanted was Lucy's pity. She also didn't want any of the furniture Charles and Lucy were giving away, stuff from his Beverly Hills house that wouldn't fit with the decor of their new place. When Lucy called about that a few weeks later, Janice laughed harshly and reminded Lucy that an eighteen-foot couch wouldn't fit with her decor either, since it wouldn't even fit through the front door. Lucy said the couch was only one of the things they didn't need, but before she could name the rest, Janice said she had to go.

"I'm sorry if I offended you," Lucy said quickly. "I was really just trying to help."

"What makes you think I need your help?" Janice sputtered. "Because you're rich? Or is it that you're married and I don't even have a boyfriend?"

"No," Lucy said softly. "It's not like that." She waited a moment. "I really miss you. It's kind of hard being pregnant and—"

"You know you can come over here any time." Janice's voice was curt, but she was looking at the wedding present, still wrapped and sitting on her kitchen table. It was an enormous vase, intricately cut glass, the kind that splayed light on the walls if you placed it in the sun. Janice had planned on giving it to Lucy before the wedding; she wanted to be alone with Lucy when she opened it because it had a special significance. Whenever the two women had gone shopping together, Lucy had invariably pointed at something like the vase, large and heavy and beautiful, and said she wished she were the kind of person who could own that. Janice would ask her what she meant, and Lucy would mumble something vague about moving too much. Janice bought the vase because she thought she finally got it. Even if she didn't understand anything else about this marriage, she knew it had to be important to Lucy that her days of living on the street were over. She'd have a settled life now, a real house of her own.

"How about if we have lunch tomorrow?" Lucy said, ignoring Janice's comment about coming to their place in Venice. "There's a great new Japanese restaurant in Brentwood. I think you'd—"

"So he still won't let you come over here," Janice snapped. "That's just great. Well, give me a call if you ever decide you're tired of being told what to do. Okay? Now I really do have to go. I have to get to work."

Before Lucy could say anything else, Janice hung up. And a few weeks later, she shipped the vase to her mom in Wisconsin. When she moved out of the Venice house at the end of the month, she wasn't worried that Lucy didn't have her new number. She knew she'd blown her chance; Lucy wouldn't call anymore. And really, maybe it was inevitable since their lives were going in completely different directions, especially now that Lucy's movie had been released.

The film came out on the last Wednesday in February. Janice thought it was so ironic. She'd just walked out of what she'd decided would be her last audition—since it was obvious she didn't get the part; she was blonde and tall but not the big-boob beach type the TV pilot casting director wanted—when she picked up the newspaper and saw the first article about *The Brave Horseman of El Dorado.*

Over the next few weeks, Janice read everything about the movie. Most of the articles still focused on Charles, but it wasn't as irritating as in the wedding pieces. He was the director and writer, after all. He was the big ego, the auteur, the whatever the hell they called it.

Nearly all the reviews were positive. What surprised Janice was how happy she was for her friend—most of the time. Even if the world was unfair, which it obviously was, Lucy deserved this luck as much as anyone.

Of course some of the headlines were easier to take than others.

"Charles Keenan's Latest a Luminous Tale of the 'New' Old West," "Horseman Delivers as Both Adventure and Spiritual Journey," "Keenan's Joan: Bold Portrait of the Hero as Heroine."

Wait a minute here. Keenan's Joan? Excuse me, but wasn't that Lucy's Joan who everyone saw up on the screen saving the poor and bringing justice and slowly walking the gallows to a death that made half the audience break down in audible sobs?

Naturally, Janice had seen the film several times. Actually, her first date with Peter was to *The Brave Horseman*. She liked him immediately when he said he'd never seen a Charles Keenan picture. "Didn't he make *Star Wars*?"

Over drinks at the marina, she told Peter that Lucy had been her roommate. She also told him Lucy was the only good friend she'd ever broken off contact with, though she couldn't help emphasizing how they met, because she wanted him to know that she'd helped Lucy, that a lot of their relationship was based on Lucy needing help since she was young, poor, new to L.A. She wanted to make sure Peter knew there was nothing pathetic about her own position in this failed friendship. Unfortunately that meant she couldn't tell him how bad she felt, a few months later, when she had to rely on a newspaper article to find out that her former friend had become a mother.

James Joseph Keenan was born on July 9, 1978, at 11:27 p.m. at an undisclosed Los Angeles–area hospital. He weighed eight pounds, eleven ounces and was twenty-three inches long. In perfect health, and a beautiful baby, the reports said, though there were no pictures, and never would be if Charles had anything to say about it. "I don't want my son to grow up in the glare of Hollywood," he said, in an interview about four months after the baby was born. "We're a normal family who happens to make movies. Lucy and I spend most of our time together, taking care of our little boy. His grandmother helps, so Lucy and I can have some time to ourselves. It's all very ordinary and quite boring, I'm sure, to an outsider."

There were no pictures of Lucy, either, in any of these baby stories. Janice wondered if she was still rail thin, and suspected she was. Now that Janice had started her social work classes, she was learning more about the kind of poverty Lucy had grown up with. Lucy had always said she couldn't gain weight, but Janice had never wondered if this had anything to do with the fact that Lucy had almost starved when she was a kid. A lot of things hadn't occurred to Janice then: like how attractive it must have been to her friend that Keenan wanted to protect her. Like why Lucy went along with him about having kids so soon, even though she was way too young to be a mother. Lucy's own mother was dead and she'd never even known her father. Charles's weird obsession with having a family probably seemed like a relief to Lucy, after all those years of having no family at all.

Janice thought about sending a baby gift, but she couldn't imagine what Lucy didn't already have. One of the articles had talked about (but not shown) the elaborate furnishings in the nursery *wing* of the house. "When you have a wing," Janice told Peter, "a rattle or blanket just won't cut it."

Peter loved her sarcastic sense of humor. She loved the way he laughed: a big hearty sound that filled her apartment and made her feel like the whole place was smiling with them.

The closer the two of them became, the more she trusted him with everything about herself, including her strange continuing interest in Lucy. She thought it was really sweet when he came to the door one evening holding a stack of papers announcing what she already knew: *The Brave Horseman* had been nominated for eight Academy Awards, including Best Director, Best Picture, and, yes, Best Actress.

It was the first of Keenan's movies to get any nominations, and it helped make a box office smash out of what had already been called a surprise hit. Now, Janice thought, surely she would see her friend—ex-friend—at the awards show. Walking down the red carpet outside, arm and arm with ole Charlie.

How old was he now anyway? Her own boyfriend Peter was her age, twenty-six. Lucy was only twenty-one. But Charles had to be what, thirty-seven, thirty-eight? That old fart, thought Janice.

Her attitude about Sir Charles was apparently never going to change. Especially since she didn't see her friend at the awards show, and she figured it had to be his doing. At least he wasn't there either. She didn't have to see his big eye leering at some model while poor Lucy sat at home with a squalling kid.

Why didn't they go to the Academy Awards though? Did this mean there was trouble in paradise? No, Janice finally discovered, according to the only interviewer that got through to a "representative for the couple":

"Charles and Lucy are very grateful to the Academy for recognizing *The Brave Horseman of El Dorado.* They regret that they were unable to attend due to an illness of their son." (Oh shit, thought Janice, the poor little guy. But no.) "Thankfully, the baby has recovered completely now. The couple sends a hearty congratulation to all the award winners and their families."

Maybe they didn't expect to win anything themselves. Certainly the oddsmakers hadn't expected them to win or even be nominated.

"*Brave Horseman* Takes Oscar for Best Director: Longtime Producer and Friend Walter Urig Accepts Award for Keenan."

The only award the movie received was the big prize for him. Figures, thought Janice, although the truth was she would have been shocked if Charles had lost. Like Peter said, it really was a brilliant movie: probably too odd for best picture, but a shoo-in for director. Lucy did a wonderful job, but Charles had created the entire world. Plus, according to Peter, it was a great example of a truly feminist Western. "He's no feminist," Janice snapped, but when Peter asked what made her so sure, she really didn't have a good answer. Even her insistence that he wouldn't let Lucy work wasn't something she could prove.

Still, wasn't it a little bit strange that all the press in the months after the awards focused on *his* next project? Not to mention how strange that project was.

For reasons that were never made clear (at least in any of the papers Janice read), Charles, having just won an award for a Western, had decided to turn away from them for good. He was casting for his new movie, *The View from Main Street USA,* described as "an ode to fifties family life." The fifties? In 1979? Jesus, Janice thought, leave it to that guy to make an ode to a decade every normal person knew was as empty of real meaning as *The Adventures of Ozzie and Harriet.* The fifties was the time of McCarthyism and *The Man in the Gray Flannel Suit* and miserable women stuck out in the suburbs with a passel of snot-nosed kids. And all those commercials for laundry detergents and floor wax and dust spray. The birth of TV soap operas.

At least Lucy didn't have to clean, Janice thought. And the view from Malibu USA was nothing short of amazing, as she discovered when she picked up a local magazine and saw a feature on Eric Giles, the decorator who had done the Keenans' house. The rooms were painted a muted yellow; the front French windows opened to a view of the ocean that seemed to stretch for miles, while the back looked out on the mountains and the most colorful garden Janice had ever seen. The furnishings themselves were magnificent—and the point of the article—but Janice was so caught up in the views that she didn't pay much attention to the chairs and tables, lamps and rugs. She wondered what it would be like to wake up every morning and see such a lovely world. For a moment, she even considered that Lucy might be really happy there, but then she noticed that Giles never mentioned even one thing Lucy said when he was talking about working with the Keenan family. "Mr. Keenan wanted the decor of the front room to harmonize with the flood of natural light." "Mr. Keenan asked that the screening room wet bar be taken out and replaced with a play area for his son." "Mr. Keenan said his wife's dressing area should have an intimate feeling, and suggested a violet, rose and white color scheme since 'Lucy loves violets.'" Eric Giles said he was "impressed" by the director's "obvious feeling for his wife."

Had Lucy's tongue been removed? Did Charles have her locked in a closet somewhere (a tastefully decorated closet of course)? When she looked at those French windows, did she think of the view, or only of escape? And the most important question of all, put to Janice by Peter: why didn't she just call Lucy and find out if she was okay?

"Because I don't have her number," Janice said irritably. "And it's not like her people will just give it to me if I say I used to be her friend."

"But can't you leave a message for her to call you?"

"What's the point? I still don't like him. Nothing has changed."

It all seemed to fit in a creepy way: Charles and his fabulous fifties family movie, Charles and his fabulous house. Lucy had nothing to do with either, Janice was sure. She told Peter if Keenan offered Lucy a part in his next movie, if he ever let Lucy be in anyone's movie, she'd never say another bad word about the man.

Luckily, Peter didn't hold her to that.

Not only did Charles let Lucy be in a movie, he also encouraged her to do so, according to an interview in *Variety.* The director was a friend of Charles's, Derrick Mabe, and the role was perfect. Lucy would be playing a German violinist who saves dozens of her Jewish pupils from the Nazis. The title of the movie was *The Passion of Helena Lott.*

"When Derrick sent us the script," Charles told the interviewer,

"I read it immediately. I thought it was a brilliant exploration of maintaining personal morality in a time of national evil. I also thought my wife would be a natural for the title role because Lucy is such a principled person and an artist, like Helena."

Dammit, Janice thought, why didn't she do any interviews herself? Wasn't this just a little bit strange for an actress whose career depended on getting herself in front of the public? And what the hell did he even mean when he said Lucy was a "principled person"? The Lucy who Janice knew had smoked an occasional joint and cursed and even tried to steal that spoon just because she liked it. Was he turning her into his clone?

In the last paragraph of the interview, Charles mentioned that Anthony Mills was "eager to work with Lucy again." This time Anthony was playing Lucy's lover rather than her torturer. Wow, thought Janice, what a hunk that guy is. She remembered when he asked Lucy to dinner when they were working together on *Horseman*. Charles knew about that, didn't he? Would he really let his wife pretend to have sex with this guy, and in Germany, no less, because at least part of the film was supposedly being shot on location? And if he did, Peter asked, a little exasperatedly, because he really didn't understand why Janice continued to be so hostile to Charles, would it change Janice's opinion of him?

No, she said, frowning. She was training to be a social worker; she had to trust her instincts, and she just didn't trust Charles Keenan. Never had, never would.

"I'm glad I made it past this infallible instinct radar of yours," Peter said archly, but he smiled. "What if I hadn't?"

"It's completely different," she said, but she smiled back. He'd just asked her to marry him on the flight home from visiting her parents in Milwaukee. Her parents had loved him too. Of course she'd said yes. She'd finally found her own luck.

She was planning the ceremony, looking for a good tailor to make alterations so she could wear her mother's wedding dress, when she found out Lucy's daughter was born. She hadn't even heard Lucy was pregnant, but then she saw the birth announcement in one of the local Beverly Hills papers. The filming of *Helena Lott* must have finished just in time, before Lucy started showing. Janice figured this out by counting backwards from May 7, 1980. She loved the name they gave the little girl. Dorothea Elizabeth Keenan. A tiny thing at just five pounds, but otherwise healthy.

The proud father was quoted in several articles giving his usual spiel about the importance of keeping his family's private life private. No pictures again, not even those caught-on-Rodeo-Drive-type photos the tabloids thrived on.

Janice did send a present this time: an adorable little hat that she found at a funky thrift store on Venice Beach where she and Lucy used to shop. She shipped it in care of Charles's office. But she didn't put her name and phone number on the card. She was afraid Lucy would call again, but even more afraid she wouldn't.

By the fall of 1981, Janice was married and in her senior year of college. She was distracted with her own life, but she still managed to note with some irritation that there were probably five times as many articles about Charles's movie *The View from Main Street USA* as Lucy's *The Passion of Helena Lott*. Apparently, the controversy that erupted over some remarks Charles made at the UCLA film school hadn't hurt his movie at all:

"War of the Directors? Keenan Calls Lucas's *American Graffiti* 'Shallow and Pointless.'"

Peter brought this article to Janice. When she saw that headline, she thought, oh boy, is Charles in hot water now! But then she read the piece and she couldn't help but feel a grudging respect for him.

"'It's all technique, no depth,' Charles Keenan told a group of film students. 'Someone tell me: where is the meaning in this movie? That life is a style? That nostalgia is a substitute for a serious attempt to come to terms with the past?' When asked by phone later if he was only talking about *American Graffiti* because his own movie about roughly the same period was set to debut next month, Keenan barked out, 'Of course. If you'd done your homework, you would know I was answering one of the student's questions about whether I thought another movie about the late fifties and early sixties was necessary, given the success of *American Graffiti*. Because it was a student, I gave the question a fuller answer than it deserved. Obviously I think another movie is necessary. I made one.'"

Say what you will, Janice thought, the man has balls. He was not only making an enemy of George Lucas, but also of the hundreds of industry people who were his supporters, including his mentor, Francis Ford Coppola. But Keenan had never relied on the industry to make his movies work, and even though he was implicitly criticizing the reviewers and the public that had heartily embraced *American Graffiti,* they either didn't know or didn't care because they embraced *The View from Main Street USA* too. Nearly all the reviews were positive and Janice didn't bother reading more than a handful. Lucy was the one she cared about. Charles was only interesting to her up to a point, and she was really getting sick of hearing how wonderful he was. Even Peter had to go on and on about the fabulous *View from Main Street:* how it redefined the period, giving stature to the fifties family, but not ignoring its flaws; how it brilliantly showed the commitment so many people made to giving their children a life they themselves had never even imagined.

The Passion of Helena Lott had a more mixed reception. Most everyone seemed to love Lucy's performance, but the film itself was criticized for being "slow," "quiet," "ponderous" and even "boring." Janice wanted to blame Charles for this (wasn't he the one who said the script was brilliant?), but as Peter ever so helpfully pointed out, a lot of the problem was the lighting (too dark), the soundtrack (too melancholy) and very few jump cuts, which made the story seem slower than it was. Janice told him he was becoming quite the amateur film critic, but then she decided she was glad he took it as a compliment.

For the rest of 1981 and a good part of 1982, there was a flurry of articles about what films Charles and Lucy would do next. They had more freedom than ever to pick their projects after the five

Academy Award nominations for *Main Street* (it only garnered one Oscar, this time for Best Original Screenplay, but that was Charles too, of course), and the nearly universal praise for Lucy in *Helena,* which every commentator agreed was amazing for a newcomer, even though she didn't win any awards. Janice read all the articles she ran across, though she was wondering if she was finally losing interest, maybe even getting ready to stop this weird tracking of Lucy for good. She was out of college now, working as a social worker; Peter had just passed the bar and started his first job. The truth was the whole movie business had started to seem more than a little trivial.

But then Janice found an article that had an effect on her unlike anything else she'd ever read. It was just luck that she came upon this one because it was in a women's magazine and she prided herself on never reading those. If she hadn't been stuck in a long Labor Day line at the grocery store, she would never have opened the slick glossy, and she would never have known that Lucy Dobbins Keenan had finally given her own interview.

The article was billed as an "intimate chat" with the Academy Award–nominated actress, wife and mother, but the first few paragraphs were hardly what Janice would call intimate. All the questions were about the roles Lucy had played (Joan blah blah, Helena blah blah blah), and especially about the movie she had decided to do next: another war picture, this time about Vietnam, with Lucy playing a nurse on the battlefield who takes it upon herself to write letters to the girlfriends and wives and mothers of the men who die in her arms. Called *Tell Laura I Love Her,* it was being directed by one of Keenan's former assistants. "My husband read the script first," Lucy said. (Urgh.) "We both thought it was a beautiful story. It's in preproduction right now, scouting for locations, getting the rest of the cast, hiring the crew. The shooting is set to begin in a few months and I'm eager to begin."

The rest of the interview though really *was* about Lucy's life. And it was three full pages—with pictures. Lucy sitting on the patio in her gorgeous garden. Lucy standing in her gigantic kitchen, with pots on the stove and a spoon in her hand. Lucy in the playroom. Lucy only twenty-four years old and yet the mother of growing children.

The little boy, who they called Jimmy, was four now. The baby girl, Dorothea, was already two. He had Lucy's red hair; hers was brown like Charles's. They both had rosy cheeks and creamy skin and sprinkles of freckles, and Janice thought they were just about the cutest kids she'd ever seen.

In the best picture, Lucy was sitting on a big blue and white love seat in the playroom with the little girl on her lap, and the boy next to her, holding her arm. And there was no denying it any longer: Lucy was happy. She was still as skinny as ever, but the expression on her face was open and radiant and content in a way that Janice had never seen, not in either of her movies and definitely not when they used to live in Venice.

Didn't this have to mean Charles wasn't the ogre Janice had made him out to be? No, Janice thought stubbornly, there must be some other explanation. Maybe he's not home very much. After all, he wasn't in any of the pictures, now, was he? Or maybe he's home, but always shut away in his enormous office—three leather couches and a mahogany desk the size of most people's beds—that Janice remembered from the article about their decorator, Eric Giles. True, Lucy talked about how they shared the task of caring for the kids, how they didn't even have a nanny because they wanted to be there for all the moments of Jimmy's and Dorothea's lives, but Lucy might say that even if she did do ninety percent of the work. Janice had lived with her; she knew Lucy could do all the shopping and cooking and dishes and cleaning and never let on that she thought there was anything unfair about it. Hell, Lucy could get up early on Sunday and walk blocks to get apple donuts she didn't even like. She'd done it nearly every Sunday when she lived with Janice.

At this point, Janice started to feel bad. She was still reading the interview—listening to Lucy talk about why they only had a weekly cleaning service, no servants: "I don't want my children to grow up thinking that they can just drop their socks on the floor and someone else will take care of it"—but she was dying to get out of the grocery store. Wouldn't this stupid line ever move? She thought about deserting her cart, but it wouldn't help: she'd still have to pay for the magazine.

Lucy had really walked all those blocks on Sundays to get Janice's favorite donuts. She'd really done almost all their housework. Whenever Janice tried to thank her, she said it was the least she could do. "You're my friend," Lucy would say. As though that explained everything.

Janice waited until she loaded all the groceries into her and Peter's Datsun before she let herself cry. The worst was remembering the night Lucy told her she was getting married. The guilt was more than Janice could stand.

Lucy had been gone all weekend on her first trip with *him*. She'd confided that it would be their first time in bed too, which Janice thought was really weird, given what a playboy Keenan was rumored to be. Maybe it was some kind of game he played with young girls. Who knew with a guy like him, but Janice was fully prepared for Lucy to come home Sunday night devastated because he'd dumped her. She was ready to sympathize.

Instead Lucy walked in wearing an engagement ring and holding a bunch of pink roses. A big bunch. Four dozen, Lucy said, answering Janice's question about how many.

Janice felt immediately annoyed. It seemed so unfair. Lucy didn't even like roses, and she, Janice, loved them. She loved pink ones best of all.

But then she discovered the flowers were for her. Lucy had bought them.

She was very surprised. "Why?" she said softly, accepting them from Lucy's hands.

"Because of all you've done for me. If it wasn't for you, I might be sleeping on a bench or dead. If it wasn't for you, I wouldn't have gone to the party that day and I wouldn't have met Charles." Lucy put her arm around Janice and whispered, "Thank you for being the best friend I've ever had."

Peter found his wife parked in the driveway of their brand-new fixer-upper, still crying.

"I have to see her. I've been a terrible friend."

Janice had three current girlfriends, but Peter knew immediately she wasn't talking about any of them.

"Good idea," he said. He waited until much later, after they'd had dinner and done some work and Janice had read him most of the article about Lucy and told him lots of memories, good and bad, before he asked if this meant she'd finally changed her mind about Charles Keenan.

"Hell no," she said. "What does that have to do with anything?"

The next morning, she started making phone calls, trying to track down Lucy. It wasn't as easy as she hoped. She was still getting the runaround from publicists more than two weeks later, when she turned on the local news, while she was making dinner, and discovered that Lucy was in the hospital. Something had happened at the Keenan residence, and the police had been called, but other than that, the newscaster didn't have any information. Lucy had been taken to UCLA by helicopter. Her condition wasn't believed to be serious, but "stay tuned."

Peter and Janice spent the next hour speculating what could have happened. A household accident was the most likely thing. The police being called was probably meaningless, especially as this was an upscale place like Malibu. The police would probably rush over if someone broke their foot.

Unless Charles had hit her. There was no evidence that he would, but no evidence that he wouldn't either. As Janice told Peter, the guys who do are often the last guys you'd suspect.

"But you've suspected him forever," Peter said dryly.

Janice shot him a dirty look, but she didn't say anything. She'd just decided that she was going to the hospital to find out for herself. UCLA Med Center would be two hours from their house with traffic, but Peter didn't object when Janice turned off the oven and said she was leaving now. He offered to drive her, but she said she really needed the time alone.

She needed to think about what to say to Lucy. She also needed to work out a way to convince them that she should be allowed to see Lucy, that she wasn't just another fan or well-wisher or nut.

When she got to the hospital, there was a crowd of reporters outside, and she realized that this was going to be tough. No reporters had been let past the front desk of ICU. She overheard one of them complaining about it.

ICU. Lucy was in the ICU? Jesus, Janice thought, and her heart started pounding so hard she could feel it in her fingers.

She knew what floor the ICU was on because she'd had a social work client taken there when her rundown apartment building caught fire. The elevators were flanked by hospital officials, so Janice took the stairs. All the way up, she felt her panic rising. What could have happened to her friend?

She came out of the stairwell right by the ICU nursing desk, where more hospital officials were stationed to keep the curious away from the actress. One of them stopped Janice, but before they could send her back downstairs, she heard a man mumble, "It's all right," and then Charles Keenan himself was standing next to her.

"Janice." His voice was full of agony. "My poor Lucy."

He was swaying with the weight of his grief, but he managed to lead her down the hall to Lucy's room. Neither of them could go inside because the doctors were with her, but they could see her through the glass. Or they could see something: a small human form covered in bandages, tubes coming out everywhere: her arms, her nose, her mouth, her stomach, one that seemed to be attached to her leg.

Charles's hands were flat on the glass; his head was hanging down. When Janice said his name, he turned around and looked at her, and that's when she realized he was crying soundless tears, the tears of someone so heartbroken they have shrunken down and become nothing but their wish that this not be true, because it cannot be true if they are to continue to breathe and live.

Yet they continue to breathe because life is profoundly unfair. That's what Janice thought when she looked at the horrified man in front of her. Of course she took him in her arms.

ten

SEPTEMBER 21, 1982, started as an ordinary day at the Keenan house. Charles's mother, Margaret, was away in Florida, visiting some of her retiree friends, but this wasn't unusual: she took trips like this several times a year. Dorothea woke up ridiculously early, but that wasn't too unusual either, unfortunately.

At 5:14 a.m. Lucy discovered the little girl standing next to the bed, pulling on her arm. "Up, Mommy," Dorothea said, and Lucy pulled her up and deposited her under the blanket, safely nestled between herself and the still sleeping Charles.

"Back to sleep," Lucy whispered, closing her eyes.

Dorothea didn't complain, but Lucy wasn't surprised when she took a peek a minute later and the little girl was looking around. Dorothea never went back to sleep, but sometimes Lucy did. The key was to be very quiet and very, very boring. The key was not to do anything to give the little girl any hope that morning, and playtime, had already arrived.

Lucy was just drifting off again when she heard Dorothea laugh and say, "Daddy!"

He was tickling her foot. At 5:37, according to the big red numbers on the alarm clock.

"Charles," she complained.

"It wasn't me," he said, lifting Dorothea over his head and bringing her back down to give her a tummy kiss. "She was tickling me first. Tell your mommy it's not my fault."

"Not Daddy," Dorothea giggled.

"All right, all right," Lucy said, but she couldn't help smiling a little. "We can't run all over the house though. We don't want to wake up Jimmy. Today is his preschool trip to the firehouse, remember?"

Charles and Dorothea made a *ssh* sound.

"That's right, you two. Now I'm going to get dressed and you lay here and be as quiet as mice."

"Mickey isn't particularly quiet," Charles whispered to Dorothea. "Neither is Minnie. I think we can handle this."

Lucy smiled again before she shut the door behind her and walked into her bathroom suite.

A half hour later, she was showered and dressed and ready to take Dorothea downstairs for breakfast. Charles would have fed her, but Dorothea pitched a fit if Lucy wasn't there in the morning.

"I'll make the coffee," he said, standing and putting on his pants.

She leaned over and kissed him. Then Dorothea had to kiss him too. Her kisses were always accompanied by a wet smacking sound, and he always laughed.

When they got downstairs, Tigger was whimpering to be let out. Charles opened the sunroom door and the dog slowly walked into the bushes. He was a stray Jimmy had spotted limping along PCH, and Lucy had convinced Charles to give in when their son begged them to stop. The vet said the mutt was at least ten years old, but Jimmy named him Tigger anyway, bounce or no bounce.

By seven, the three of them were at the table in the breakfast room and Tigger was back in his basket. Dorothea was tearing up her scrambled eggs and bagel and scooting some into her mouth and some into the river of milk she'd made in the depression of her high-chair tray. Charles was looking at the newspaper, wearing his brand-new glasses. He'd never worn glasses before, but all of a sudden he needed them—and not just for reading, like Walter and some of his other friends, but all the time. The ophthalmologist had explained that in Charles's case, the vision problem wasn't actually new, but the eye muscles had been working hard to accommodate it. Now that he was getting older, the muscles were weakening. "Just chock it up to being over forty," the ophthalmologist had said, trying to reassure both Lucy and Charles that it wasn't anything to worry about and it had nothing to do with the slight dropsy on the right side, a condition Charles had had since childhood, which made that eye sometimes appear smaller. The glasses had thick black frames and an old-fashioned boxy shape. Lucy had convinced him they were the right choice when she said they made him look like a sexy genius.

Lucy herself was drinking her second cup of coffee, watching a gray bird standing in the dewy morning grass, listening to the monitor for signs that Jimmy's cow alarm had mooed and he was up. He wanted to get ready all by himself, but if he was late for preschool, he'd miss the class trip. The teacher had sent home two notes about this. The bus the school had rented was leaving at precisely 8:30, returning at precisely 1:30. If any child wasn't on it, the bus wouldn't be able to wait.

Her little boy was so responsible. He arrived downstairs with his teeth brushed, his hair patted down and pushed out of his eyes (he still wasn't good at figuring out a comb) and his red shorts and red T-shirt and even red socks already on.

Jimmy was wearing red because they were going to the firehouse. He said if the firemen needed someone to help, he wanted to be picked. He was the tallest boy in class anyway.

Charles told him that being the tallest and wearing red *and* having red hair would have to tip the scales in his favor.

"What's 'tip the scales,' Daddy?"

"I'll tell you on the way to school," Charles said. "You need to feed Tigger first. Then come back and have some breakfast. We don't have much time."

After a minute, he put his paper down and looked at Lucy. "I was thinking of driving him to the firehouse."

She told him that the school was going to the fire department headquarters, not the local station. An hour and a half drive, probably more with traffic. "By the time you got back here, you'd have to turn around and get him again."

"I'll wait there then. I don't have that much to do today."

"But why? Jimmy's looking forward to going with his friends. They're all going to have lunch at the big McDonald's. He's told me about it a hundred times."

"He can still have lunch at McDonald's with everyone. I'll drive him there too."

Lucy looked at him. "Is this about the bus?"

He nodded. "I'd rather not have him on it. They don't have seat belts and the drivers are typically undertrained. I think he'll be safer with me in the Mercedes."

Lucy knew better than to argue the point. When it came to safety issues, Charles was implacable, but it was something she loved about him: that taking care of his family was always his top priority, no matter what. God knows he did have things to do today. He had a pile of scripts to read and dozens of phone calls to return from his secretary and his assistants and some budget problem he had to discuss with Walter, et cetera, et cetera. Her husband had an incredibly demanding job. Sometimes he was still working in his office long after she was in bed.

"Do you want me to take the pumpkin with us?" he said, glancing at Dorothea. "You could have the time to yourself. A chance to get some of your work done."

"Yeah!" Dorothea said and clapped her hands, splashing milk all over the tray.

The main thing Lucy needed to do was read the latest script revisions for *Tell Laura I Love Her.* Charles still wasn't happy and was requesting even more changes to enhance Lucy's role. He was very protective of her career, but it wasn't a problem. All the directors and producers she'd worked with so far were people who respected her husband and would listen to him.

The free time sounded wonderful, but Lucy told him it was probably a bad idea. "It's Jimmy's day. Plus, she's going to need her nap or she'll be so cranky by dinner we won't be able to eat."

Jimmy was at the table, pouring his own bowl of cereal. Charles told him to hurry so they could follow right behind the bus. Before he could object, Charles threw in, "You can make faces at your friends and I'll honk at them."

Lucy had already handed Jimmy his little backpack and kissed him good-bye. They were walking out the door when Lucy said to Charles, "I'll miss you."

He put his arms around her and pulled her against him. "I was really looking forward to nap time," he whispered.

"Maybe tonight," she said, but she knew it was doubtful. By the time the kids were in bed, one of them, usually Lucy herself, was always too tired.

"If not, there'll be other naps," he said, kissing her ear.

"As long as you wear your glasses," she said, and he smiled and winked at her. Then he and Jimmy got in the silver car, and she watched them head down the driveway and through the gates and disappear.

By eleven-thirty, Dorothea had already had her nap—an hour, but not nearly long enough from Lucy's point of view—and an early lunch. Lucy had promised her another swimming lesson. When they were both in their matching purple tank suits, they headed out the patio doors to the pool.

Fifteen minutes later, Dorothea was still trying to learn to hold her breath. She loved the idea of going underwater, but she invariably opened her mouth before she came back up. Lucy tried not to laugh at how silly her little girl looked with her cheeks puffed out as far as they would go.

"Look at me, honey," she said, and waited a moment. "I was holding my breath just by keeping my mouth closed. That's all you need to do."

"Try," Dorothea said.

"Okay, we'll try again. Pull down your goggles."

They were in the shallow end, where Dorothea could stand up if she got scared. Lucy was on her knees. They both stuck their heads in, and this time Dorothea got it. She held her mouth just right and gave Lucy a confident look as if to say, *what was the big deal*?

Lucy was laughing when they came back up. Sometimes Dorothea was so much like her father. "You are the coolest kid in—"

The suddenly flat expression on the little girl's face stopped Lucy. She turned around to see what Dorothea was looking at and that's when she saw them. Two men, standing by the deep end of her pool.

Charles had had a lawn care company in last week: pruning bushes, planting a tree to replace one that had died, mulching the flowers. But Lucy immediately understood that these men weren't gardeners. They were dressed in worn jeans and yellowing T-shirts. The taller one had his hands in his pockets and his shoulders thrown back. The shorter one was smoking a cigarette and staring right at her.

Later, she would find out that the lawn care people didn't properly close the back gate. An accident, which normally wouldn't have caused any harm. The neighborhood was hardly a high-crime area. Even the security gates Charles had installed when they moved in were mainly to make him feel calmer about leaving them.

Lucy flashed to a movie she'd seen where someone disappeared through the drain of a swimming pool. If only she and Dorothea could put their heads back under until they disappeared. There was no one to help if she called or yelled her lungs out. Even when she'd hired a band for Charles's birthday party—an outdoor party—the nearest neighbors hadn't heard any noise.

The shorter man walked toward them. "Get out of the pool. Now."

His voice sounded angry. Why was he angry? What response would calm him down?

She tried to think, but her mind was frozen by the man's cold gaze. When he finally told her to get out or he would come in after them, she stood Dorothea up on the side and climbed out herself, then she grabbed their pink terry-cloth robes. She put on Dorothea's, and then belted her own as tightly as it would go.

"Go inside," the man said. Something was flashing in his hand and she realized what it was. The blade of a knife, reflecting in the sun.

She quickly decided that she and Dorothea would be better off making a run for it. She bent down and picked up her daughter, but before she'd taken one step, the taller man was there, holding her arm, pointing at the patio door. "In," he said. "Now."

As she walked into the house, her wet feet made a thwapping sound on the wood floor. Behind her, the short man had already shut the door and locked it; she'd heard the click. The other one had picked up the sunroom phone receiver and was smashing it against the wall.

Dorothea said, "Tewapone," and started to cry.

"It's okay, baby," Lucy whispered, patting her back.

"What's your name?" The short man was standing in front of her now, holding the knife in one hand, and touching her hair with the other.

"Eleanor," Lucy said, because it was the first lie she could think of. She and Charles had checked into hotels as Franklin and Eleanor Eveltroos.

Dorothea tried to swat the man away from Lucy's hair. She was yelling "Daddy" at the top of her lungs.

"My husband will be back any minute," Lucy tried. "He just went to the store."

"Sure he will," the man said, and laughed. He turned to the tall guy. "Check the front door."

"Here's the deal, Eleanor. You gonna tell me what I need to know?"

"Yes," Lucy said. She was trying to keep her voice steady to calm the little girl, who was crying so hard Lucy worried she'd throw up. "Whatever you say."

"That's good," the man said. "Money?"

"Up here," Lucy said, pointing at the stairs.

They all walked up together to Charles's office. The tall man whistled. "Nice place you got," he said, and then laughed like he'd told a joke.

"My husband keeps cash and an extra credit card in the right-hand drawer of the desk. And his checkbook. Take it all."

The tall one walked over to the desk. The short one stayed right next to Lucy. His big meaty hand was resting on Dorothea's arm, and she was squirming to get him off.

"Got it," the tall one said, after he pulled open the drawer. He took the clip off the money and shuffled through it. "Not bad. Two or three grand, looks like. A MasterCard and the checkbook."

"Screw the checks," the short one said. He put his lips close to Lucy's ear. "What else?"

"Jewelry," she said. "It's down the hall. In my . . ." She couldn't bring herself to say the word.

"Take us there."

She led them to the master bedroom. When she saw the bed, she thought about this morning, lying there with Dorothea and Charles, and she felt her whole body start shaking as the fear hit her full force.

Dorothea had stopped crying, but she was still whimpering softly. Lucy held her close and repeated "It's okay," even though she knew her daughter no longer believed it either.

"The jewelry is in the cedar box. Most of it. There's more in the middle drawer."

The tall guy went through it all, pocketing what was small

enough, throwing the rest in a pillowcase he took from the bed. From Charles's pillow.

"Let me see your hand, Eleanor."

Lucy held her hand out to the short man. She was trying not to look at him, but she noticed a thick scar that went all the way around his neck.

"Give me the rings," he said.

Both of them came off easily because her hands were slick with sweat.

"What else?"

"My husband's car," she said, thinking: The getaway car. Thinking: Get away. "It's a black Jaguar. He's had it for years. It's an antique, I think it's very valuable. There's a newer BMW in the garage too."

"We'll take one of them, don't you worry." The short man grinned. "But we ain't leaving yet."

They told her to go back downstairs. She went, gladly. Anything to get away from the bed. The short man had her sit with Dorothea in the front room on the couch and told the tall guy to watch them.

She could hear the short guy going through the breakfast room and the den, the dining room and screening room and playroom. Picking things up, and then the crash as he broke them, maybe intentionally, maybe because he couldn't be bothered to put them back.

Each sound left Lucy more terrified.

The tall man was younger than the other. His voice wasn't as mean. And he seemed to feel a little sorry for Lucy. "If you do what he says, you won't get hurt, Eleanor."

"Her name ain't Eleanor," the short man said. He was holding their VCR and two of the components of the stereo; a garbage bag stuffed with other things was clutched in his fist. "Her name's Lucy Dobbins. She's an actress and her husband is some hotshot director."

"Wow, no shit. She don't look like an actress. No offense, Elea—I mean, Lucy."

The short man put the things down near the table in the front hall. "I saw the posters in that room with the big movie screen." He looked at Lucy. "Kind of stupid to call yourself Eleanor with all that evidence, ain't it?"

She nodded weakly.

"I don't like being lied at. It makes me want to fuck you up."

"I'm sorry," she said.

"We'll see how sorry you are. Ron, take the kid, man."

The tall guy came over and peeled Dorothea from Lucy's arms. The child let out a blood-curdling scream and Lucy screamed too. "No. Please!"

"We ain't gonna hurt her. We're gonna stick her in a closet."

"Oh my God! Why?"

"Why the fuck do you think?" The short man's voice was really angry now. He was so loud that Dorothea's screams turned to frightened sobs. "This is what I hate about you rich bitches. You think nobody like me could give a shit about kids. Guess what, lady? I got kids of my own. Four of 'em, one a baby like your little girl here. I ain't never hurt a kid, and I never will."

"I believe you. Really." Lucy was speaking quickly, but she still didn't understand. "I can tell you wouldn't hurt my daughter. I just don't know why she has to go in the closet. She'll be so scared."

The short man looked straight at Lucy, but he didn't say anything. Finally the taller one, the one named Ron, mumbled, "So she won't see nothin'."

Lucy felt a sensation like falling even though she hadn't moved an inch. The room seemed fuzzy. Her own voice seemed to come to her from inside a tunnel. "All right, but please let me put her in the closet myself. I know which one will be safest for a baby."

The shorter man shrugged. "Rush it along. I ain't got all day."

The only closet that Lucy knew had nothing sharp or dangerous was in Dorothea's own room: Charles had checked it himself when Dorothea went from her crib to her baby bed. Ron went with them, but he let Lucy grab Dorothea's sippy cup full of water from

As long as they left her in the closet.

Before she walked down the stairs, Lucy turned to Ron, who as really only a teenager, she saw now. He still had acne and peach zz on his chin. Just a boy.

She forced her voice to sound friendly. "He has four kids, huh?"

"Yep."

"See them a lot?"

Ron looked at Lucy. No problem. She was smiling and it was so genuine. She was an actress.

"Every weekend. They're his weak spot, that's what Mick says. He calls the moms greedy bitches, but he loves those kids."

"How about you?" Lucy said brightly.

"None so far. But someday. Find me the right woman and I want—"

The short guy, Mick, yelled, "What the hell is taking so lo

"Get down the stairs," Ron said sharply. "Now.

They walked down the staircase and

whe

C

I

the dresser and her fluffy bear from her bed. H
when Lucy asked him to give her a minute with h

Lucy had placed Dorothea on the closet floor. S
in the doorway, holding her frantic daughter firmly
hand, and using the other to stroke the little girl's fa

"Baby, I know you don't want to do this, but yo
here. I'll be back as soon as I can. I want you to lay d
hold on to your fluffy bear. If you get thirsty, you'll hav
Think of it like a game of hide-and-seek that will last
time. You just wait here though, and I'll come and get
you get scared, you can sing, okay? Sing one of the song
taught you."

Lucy pushed back and Ron slammed the door sh
Dorothea could follow. The door had rows of horizontal
Dorothea still started screaming that it was too dark, she w

she could get out though. Even if sh
had quickly wedg

ing out.

There was no way

jump high enough to reach the knob, Ron

dresser in front of the door.

"No, Mommy. No game!"

"It's okay, baby." Her voice was breaking up; she couldn't help it. Dorothea was pounding her little fists on the door.

"Diaper!" Dorothea tried, still crying, but also sounding a little proud, like she'd come up with something the adults would have to care about.

Lucy

ong?

to the back of the house,

Mick was waiting in the sunroom. He was sprawled in Charles's favorite leather chair, with his legs spread apart. The knife, Lucy noticed, was still in his hand.

"She stopped crying," he said, pointing to the wall monitor by the light switch.

Charles had had monitors installed so they could hear the kids' rooms in every room in the house. Mick must have been listening to Dorothea while he waited. It was true, she'd stopped crying. All they could hear was a soft hiccuping sound.

Tigger came in then, wagging his mangy tail, stretching like he'd just woken up from one of his many naps. Lucy winced when Mick bent down, but he only petted the dog before telling Ron to take him outside.

After a minute, Mick walked up to Lucy and pulled on the belt of her robe until it loosened. "Okay, here's the deal, lady movie star. You gonna be nice to me, right?"

He was stocky, but his cheeks were hollowed out and scarred

with pit marks. Yet it was the look on his face that made him seem so ugly. The mean expression and the cold green eyes, especially when he looked at Lucy, though she still didn't understand why.

She took a breath. "I'll give you our car and our money and anything else you want, but—"

"A kiss." He lifted the knife and ran the flat side of the blade along the outline of her face. His voice was low. "That's what I want."

"Just a kiss?" she said. Hopefully. Stupidly.

"That's not all." He laughed harshly and pulled the robe off her shoulders. "But we can skip right to the part where you fuck me. Wanna do that?"

Ron coughed or laughed, Lucy wasn't sure.

The air-conditioner vent was only a foot or so away and she was shivering. Her suit wasn't all the way dry yet, which seemed impossible. It seemed like they'd been in this house for hours.

"No," she said. It was the only word she could think of right then, so she repeated it. "No," she said, and tried to run, but Mick caught up with her before she was halfway to the door. He grabbed her by the hair and pulled her back to face him.

"You're pissing me off again, Lucy. First you lie to me and now you tell me no. Why you wanna make me mad?"

"I don't."

"Then kiss me right now before I beat the crap out of you."

Dorothea's presence had kept Lucy grounded even in her fear, but now she felt something breaking apart in the back of her mind. The knife, his breath, how close he was. What he wanted her to do. So unreal. Was this her house? The room itself looked different. Ron was standing in front of the wall of windows. His tall shadow was making a slash of darkness on the floor. Jimmy had left his Snoopy under the wicker table. They were both white, and Lucy kept thinking the table was melting, only to remember again that the shape she saw was Snoopy's foot.

Better to lose the world and save your soul.

None of Charles's movies had ever had a rape. Sometimes the evil man tried to rape a woman, but she always managed to get away. Or someone saved her. Or she told them no, and they stopped. How could Lucy have forgotten that?

"I won't have sex with you," she finally said. It wasn't her voice. She was gone, and in her place was a sassy, confident heroine. A woman who looked like Belinda Holmes, the actress Charles had used in several of his Westerns: tall and tough with black hair, big brown eyes and a wide jaw, wide hips, muscular arms.

Belinda was the only one of Charles's former girlfriends that Lucy had ever asked him about. "Why didn't it work with her?" Lucy said, out of the blue, during the weepy period she had right after Jimmy was born. They were watching the television premier of *The Last Train*. Charles looked at her and said so gently, "Because she wasn't you."

"She don't mean it, Mick."

"Yes, I do," Lucy said. "I'd rather die."

The first slice opened up her cheek, but it wasn't that bad. The blood felt warm, almost comforting, running down her face.

Mick came closer to her. "Had enough? Ready to kiss me now?"

"No, I'm sorry, I can't." She heard the words come out of her mouth, but she wasn't speaking, neither was Belinda. Someone else was speaking now, someone brave and principled.

Choose, Joan.

"It's against the will of God," Lucy muttered, before she let out a moan as the knife came down again.

This cut was much worse, on the fleshy part of her right arm, a deep gash that burned so badly it brought tears to Lucy's eyes. Why did cuts burn? Lucy remembered the fire that the real Joan had died from. She had faith that could move mountains. Lucy wanted faith, but she was just so scared.

"Throw her down and do her, man," Ron said nervously. "Get it over with so we can get out of here."

"No. She's a rich bitch and I'm gonna teach her a lesson. She needs to learn that all this expensive shit she has doesn't mean she's better than us."

Lucy wanted to say she didn't think she was better than anyone, but her mouth wouldn't form the words. She saw him move the knife from his right hand to his left, and then she watched as his fist came toward her, inch by inch, like the slow-motion violence in a movie she remembered watching with Charles at Walter's house. Charles had told her the guy who directed that film made all his movies with slowed-down violence, but she couldn't remember the reason. Was it to make it more real or less?

The punch felt as real as falling off the jungle gym bars in third grade. The slam of her head against the concrete then was like the slam of his knuckles into her mouth now. Her face exploded in blood, and Lucy lost her balance and fell backward into the wall. She heard the cracking sound her body made—or was it the wall?—and then she was crumpled on the floor.

When Mick told her to get up, she wasn't sure she could.

"I said get up, you bitch!"

She still didn't move, and Mick told Ron to lift her up. He grabbed her under her arms and pulled her to face Mick.

"You gonna kiss me now?"

Her lips were covered in blood; she could feel it running down her chin and taste it dripping into her mouth. And they were already swelling. She could sense the top one brushing against the bottom of her nose.

"Damn," Ron muttered. "You wanna kiss her like that?"

"Fuck no. But she's gotta learn." He grabbed Lucy's ear, twisting the lobe. "You ready to do what I say now, you little whore?"

Choose, Joan.

She saw Charles coming toward her. "I won't do it," she told Charles. "Don't worry." He nodded, but then she realized he was crying. "It doesn't even hurt," she told him, which was such a lie. She'd been thrown to the floor, and now she was curled in a ball. She couldn't see anything, but she could feel the stabs and punches and kicks. There were so many pains now, white-hot places on her stomach, the backs of her knees, the side of her neck. Her throat hurt from screaming, and then she was vomiting and spitting blood and her throat hurt more.

She smelled the smoke and she thought of Dorothea, but then it became only a small point of fire pressing marks into her flesh. Joan had died of fire, but she wasn't brave like Joan. The agony was overwhelming her. She would have to renounce God, unless he heard her screams for help.

And then, just like that, it was over.

Later the doctors would tell Lucy that a violent blow to her head had knocked her unconscious. Charles had found her that way, and it was three days before she came out of it. She tried to tell them it wasn't true, that before Charles came home she had regained consciousness, at least for a minute or two. They humored her, but she could tell they didn't believe it. No matter, Lucy knew it was real. It was one of her most vivid memories: the moment when she'd opened her eyes and discovered that the men had run away, the torture had stopped.

For the rest of her life, she would never forget the peace that came over her then. She was lying on the floor of her house, and she could feel the warmth of the afternoon light as it poured in the windows. She could hear the soft clicking of their dog's paws on the back door, and something else, a sound that would make its way into her dreams for years to come. Of course it was real. It was the sound of her baby girl singing.

PART THREE

Angel Moon

eleven

THOUGH MY FATHER never talked of my mother, I'd grown up knowing that he'd loved her with his whole soul and being. This was why he couldn't bear to see pictures of her, according to my grandmother, who'd told me many times how happy Father had been before Mother died. "I remember the day they got married," Grandma said. "Oh, your father was so delighted! He stood up and told all his guests that he would never again doubt there was a heaven because he'd already found it."

My parents, Grandma said, were every bit as happy together as Jane and Mr. Rochester in *Jane Eyre.* Because I'd read the novel to Grandma so many times, I had many chances to think about this, and to wonder what it would be like to be in love. One sentence in particular seemed curious: "I know no weariness of my Edward's society; he knows none of mine." I tried to imagine never, ever growing weary of someone. It seemed impossible to me, for though I adored Father and Grandma and Jimmy, I couldn't spend more than a few hours with them before I longed to be back in my room with my books and my daydreams.

It seemed impossible, that is, until I found myself passing day after day in my strange new life with Stephen.

Our primary task, of course, was trying to help my brother. Each afternoon we would go to the hospital, and Stephen would sit with me while I gave Jimmy a report of my progress (or lack thereof) in discovering the truth about our family's past, and then we would listen to my brother talk, sometimes for an hour or more, about his own memories and his continuing feelings of guilt that he had been somehow responsible for what happened to our mother. I told him repeatedly it wasn't true, but I didn't tell him that we'd requested her death certificate from California. It was Stephen's idea, as a practical way to make Jimmy feel better. This document would list the cause of death, which, we both felt sure, wouldn't be murder at the hands of a six-year-old.

I hadn't told Jimmy yet because the soonest we could possibly receive the certificate was five days, and this was with the help of the hospital records department, who'd agreed to put in the request after Dr. Baker talked to them. There were a few problems to be overcome, including my lack of knowledge of the exact date of her death, or even of the date she was born. Both of these could be solved, Stephen thought, by contacting my father, but after I explained Father's condition, and how upset he would be by even these simple requests, Stephen talked to the hospital records clerk himself, and the appropriate documents were rushed to California, listing only the year of death, 1984, and other identifying criteria, including Father's name as next of kin.

While we were awaiting the arrival of the certificate, I worked on the task of remembering. Stephen had done what he called a "search" on how to recover childhood memories—using a truly wonderful thing known as a laptop computer. He discovered that most people do remember certain events before age five, and I might be able to do the same if I just tried to talk more about that period of my life. Each night, we would sit at dinner and talk about what kinds of things people typically remembered from their early lives, and what he himself remembered. I loved listening to all this, though it was never enough to jar even the smallest memory loose in my own mind, and I became increasingly desperate to give Jimmy something to hold on to, so he would not lose hope.

Finally, on Tuesday night I realized there was another possible direction I could try, and I started to tell Stephen some of the things Grandma had said about our home. He said it was obvious we'd lived in Southern California, near enough to L.A. to go to movie studios and the pier on Santa Monica. Then I told him Grandma had often mentioned a particular place called Malibu. I asked him if it was near L.A., and he said yes. When I asked him how he'd heard of it, he laughed and said everyone had heard of it. It was home to movie stars and very rich people. It was right on the Pacific Ocean.

We'd just finished having dinner, and he was driving me to a bookstore because I'd told him I would love something to read. He said perhaps I could pick up a book on Malibu while we were there, though if I didn't find anything, it would be all right. "We can always look it up on my laptop when we get home."

The cab was dark; he couldn't see me smile. He'd called it "home." Not "my place" or "my apartment" or "my house" or any of the ways he'd referred to it previously. Just "home." As though it were ours together, which it felt like it was after the six days we'd spent there talking and having breakfast, putting groceries away, doing laundry in the basement of his building, watching movies, which he'd rented from a place called Blockbuster, until the wee hours of the morning.

Not that his apartment was the real attraction. In truth, it had very few of the conveniences of my own home. His bathtub didn't have jets of water shooting from each corner as each of our tubs had. His refrigerator had only one plain door, no ice or water could be obtained without going inside. Parts of his floor were covered with an ugly beige carpet and other parts were exposed, showing a pale wood that was nothing like the gleaming planks of Brazilian cherry wood Father had chosen to cover our floor. He didn't have a baby grand piano, or indeed any piano, and his book collection was really quite awful, containing only a dictionary, an almanac and several forbidding-looking textbooks about medicine, which I guessed was a hobby of his.

But Stephen himself was an entirely different matter, and I loved his apartment for the simple reason that he was in it. I woke up every morning eager to begin another day of just being with him.

Was this my first crush? I did try to convince myself it was that and nothing more. Actually, I spent much of my time alone giving myself stern warnings. Dorothea, how can you be so foolish? You are in no position to judge what you are feeling. Oh please, your whole notion of love has been formed from romantic novels and childish fantasies! And the sensation you have when you see him? This especially means nothing. As he himself said, how many men have you seen in your life? The answer, as you know, is very, very few. For all you can tell, you would have the same response to a thousand other men.

And then my heart would throb—but not race—and I would want to throttle the voice in my head for even daring to suggest that any other man could ever compare to Stephen.

What other man could be as sensitive and intelligent? Taxicab driver though he was, I'd seen into his deeper nature and found that he had the soul of a poet and the mind of a scholar (if not the book collection). Of course he also had that musical voice and such interesting eyebrows and those remarkably perfect teeth.

He was also very kind, not only to Jimmy and me, but to the elderly people he insisted on picking up in his cab, charging them very little or nothing. Some of these people were older than Grandma when she died, but Stephen said they still liked to get out and see their families or go to the store or just sit on a bench in the park. When I asked how he knew their habits, he said he'd been picking them up for months. At first, it seemed odd that Stephen barely spoke to them, and I would turn around from my position in the front, ready to make pleasant conversation, but then I discovered that many of them seemed to want to talk the entire trip, without interruption, and I decided that Stephen was really just being polite by listening.

He was in every way so very appealing. His only flaw was a tendency to limp a little when he was tired, but this only endeared him to me more. So many of my books had heroes with some flaw, often from an injury, sometimes from birth. Of course I couldn't risk asking him the cause in his case, for fear of drawing attention to something I sensed he was sensitive about. Whatever the origin, I admired the way he pushed himself, since it was his weak right foot that he used to drive his taxicab. And even though he'd told me he wasn't driving much now that I was staying with him—only picking up a few of these older people who he knew would have no other ride—still, he had to take me to the hospital and out to dinner and usually at least one more place: the Blockbuster or the mall (for additional modern clothes, which I'd become quite fond of), or the bookstore, where we were headed now.

I was seeking a book about love, though naturally I was a little shy about discussing that fact. The more I'd discovered how little I knew about modern life, the more concerned I'd become that I would not be able to judge what was normal in Stephen's and my situation. Specifically, I wanted to know what was required of a woman. Was it possible that I was supposed to act first, not him?

I was almost certain he'd thought many times of kissing me. During our nightly television or movie, I would often turn to catch him staring at my lips. He watched my movements more closely each day, and when we would brush against each other, the look that would come over him was less embarrassment than expectation, as if he wanted me to do something, as if he couldn't be content until I did. I worried that I was failing him in some essential way, especially after watching a television movie the night before, where the woman not only kissed the man first, but pushed him against a wall and proceeded to pull off his shirt. It was all done with much laughter, and even Stephen laughed, so I knew my failure to find it funny was due to some deficiency of mine. I decided a book must be had.

The store Stephen took me to was three floors tall and so wide, I imagined they had every book that had ever been written in the world. While he was looking in the travel section, I went to the woman behind the counter and whispered what I was interested in. She pointed me to an entire wall of volumes on the topic, but a tall book jumped out at me at once: *Dating and Love for the Clueless.* The title intrigued me, as I already liked the word "clue" from reading mysteries. I found it very cheering that love might be like a mystery, and there would be clues I could discover that would add up to an easy solution of how to act around Stephen.

I managed to buy the book and have it safely installed in a bag before I went to locate him. When he asked what I'd bought, I told him I'd rather not say. Because of his impeccable manners, that was the end of the discussion.

When he showed me the book he was looking at, I felt the breath leave my body, but all at once, rather than gasp by gasp as it did during my attacks. The inscription under the photograph was "Malibu: Paradise on Earth," and it did seem to be exactly that. The sun was setting, and the beach looked orange and pink, the blue water stretched as far as the eye could see. My first thought was that I could not imagine a place more different from where Father had settled us, because Tuma was rocky and brown and as forbidding as Malibu seemed welcoming. My second thought was that I really had seen this before, many, many times. It wasn't that I remembered seeing it, but that I remembered what it felt like to see it. It felt like being embraced.

"I would like to buy this," I said.

"There are other good ones on California." Stephen started to reach for another book.

"Thank you, but no," I said. "This one."

We were back in his cab when he asked if I was all right. I told him yes, and then he started telling me about his own experience in California, a trip taken with two friends when he was in college. He told me he'd learned to surf, and explained what was involved. When I told him I couldn't even swim, he said that if I was from Malibu, I had to be the only native in the history of the place who couldn't surf or swim.

"Not the only native," I said. "My brother would be another one, and surely there are people who are incapable of surfing or swimming due to handicaps or—"

"I'm exaggerating," he said, and smiled. "Remember?"

"Yes, of course. Exaggeration is normal in all but the most serious conversations, and is often used for comic effect." I smiled back. "I remember now."

When we arrived at his apartment, Stephen used the small key to check his mailbox, as always, but then he handed an envelope to me. It was from the California Office of Vital Records. The certificate had finally arrived.

My hands were shaking a little, but I didn't hesitate to open the envelope once we were inside the apartment. It was very thin, which was a good sign, I thought. Not too many women named Helena O'Brien who had been born in Missouri and married to a Charles and had died in 1984.

In fact, they claimed they couldn't find even one.

"How can this be?" I said. "I don't understand."

"Maybe you have the year wrong."

"No, I don't think so."

Stephen sat down on the couch. We were supposed to watch the second half of another movie we'd started late last night: *They Might Be Giants.* I'd been looking forward to it, but now I wanted to talk to my father. Something about that Malibu photograph had made me anxious to talk to him anyway. Now I felt I didn't have a choice.

I couldn't call him (because of our unusual phone that wouldn't ring), but I could call Dr. Humphrey. We'd spoken nearly every day, and Father continued to improve. It was quite a relief, especially as it freed my mind to concentrate on my brother.

I told Dr. Humphrey that it was very important that my father call me. As luck would have it, Dr. Humphrey was already planning to see Father. It was still only eight o'clock in New Mexico. They had arranged to play a game of chess tonight.

"He really is feeling better," I told Stephen. And then I was so happy at the idea of him inviting Dr. Humphrey in for chess that I started twirling around Stephen's kitchen.

He smiled. "Do you still want to watch the movie?"

"Oh, I don't think I can. My father will be calling soon."

"The pause button," he said, raising his eyebrows.

"Yes, right." I smiled. "The pause button for videos, and you don't watch the commercials on TV."

I sat down on the couch and by the time the phone finally rang, I'd nearly forgotten about Father. This movie was so wonderful, easily my favorite of all we'd seen so far.

Stephen told me to answer. As I was walking to the phone, he said, "You might want to leave out the fact that you're staying with your cab driver."

I gave him a new gesture of which I was very fond. I'd learned it from television: the A-Okay. The gesture was made by connecting the thumb and the index finger to form a circle, while holding the other three fingers up. It apparently had many uses, ranging from a simple yes to any approval, general or specific, of something another person had done.

"Dorothea?" He sounded very far away.

"Oh Father! It is you. I'm so happy to hear your voice!"

"Are you all right?"

"Yes, very."

"Where are you? Dr. Humphrey said you located Jimmy in St. Louis. Are you staying in a hotel there?"

He sounded so worried and so loving; I couldn't lie to him. I told him I was staying with a friend. "A new friend," I said, "but very trustworthy. This friend helped me find our Jimmy."

I was careful not to use the male pronoun, but Father guessed. He told me he wanted to speak to "this man."

"Father, I so wish you wouldn't." I was whispering. "Please trust my judgment on this."

"I need to speak to him," he said.

Shit, I thought; my new word, which thankfully I didn't also say. I told Father to wait a moment, and then I asked Stephen if he would mind speaking to him.

"Sure, if you want me to," he said, but his voice sounded very tired. I felt momentarily annoyed with Father, but then I busied myself with trying to interpret what Father was saying from Stephen's responses.

"Stephen Spaulding . . . thirty-one . . . MD . . . internal medicine, pediatrics . . . at the bus station . . . to the hospital . . . widowed . . . of course not, sir." (Sir, I thought. See what fine manners my friend has, Father?)

They went on like this for another five minutes, perhaps more. Some of the subjects were fairly obvious, but I wondered why Stephen mentioned that Father was a widower. Eventually they started talking about Jimmy. "Self-destructive behavior, including self-mutilation . . . initially, but at this point he's considered a voluntary commitment because he doesn't feel ready to leave . . . Dorothea is helping his psychiatrist with his treatment . . . she needs some information from you, sir. Let me put her back on . . . I understand . . . here she is now."

"Father? Are you still there?"

"I'm going to wire you some money to the Western Union office in St. Louis. It should be there tomorrow by noon."

"But I don't really need any. I took quite a bit from—"

"This will ensure you continue to have enough."

"Thank you. Please don't hang up yet."

"I wasn't going to, pumpkin."

I cradled the phone closer to my cheek. Oh, how I missed him then. He rarely called me pumpkin anymore. I was too old for pumpkin, but I still liked the sound of it.

"I hate to ask you this," I began.

"About your mother," he said. Not even a question.

"Yes," I said, amazed. "How did you know?"

"Educated guess," he said quietly.

"The problem is, for Jimmy's sake, I need to know how she died. Of course I completely understand if you can't talk about it, but perhaps you could send me her death certificate?" My voice had become a squeak, and I could feel my heart beating faster. I was surprised how upset I was, suddenly.

"Take a deep breath," Father said.

"I can't," I whispered, because I was already panting with fear. I hadn't had an attack since the first day I arrived in St. Louis. I'd let myself become convinced, foolishly, that I was finished with them for good.

"Put Dr. Spaulding on again. I love you, darling. I'll call you again soon."

It struck me that Stephen had told Father he was a doctor rather than a cab driver, but I couldn't worry about it then. I handed him the phone and stumbled into the bedroom so I could sing with my head between my knees. A minute or so later, when Stephen joined me, I was already feeling better enough to ask him what Father had said.

"He'll send you the information you need about your mother."

"Oh, good." I paused. "Did he mention anything else of interest?"

"Nothing I didn't expect," Stephen said, and exhaled. "Come on, we should go finish our movie."

"It's really wonderful, isn't it?"

"It's cute," he said, heading down the hall.

I was right behind him. "But not just cute. It has an important meaning too."

"What meaning is that?" He sat down on his side of the couch; I sat down on mine.

"That life is as much about what you believe as what seems to be reality."

"Dorothea, Dorothea." He shook his head. "You're way too smart to fall for such New Age hocus-pocus."

I assumed "new age" was the opposite of "old age," but he told me no. Yet the way he explained it, I didn't see the difference between new age and hocus-pocus. Since both were, to him, merely illogical and untrue, why use both?

"I don't agree with you," I finally said. "And I think I can demonstrate why my idea is not this 'new age' thing you clearly don't respect." I stood up. "Would you please follow me to the window?"

The only large window in his apartment straddled the living room and the kitchen. I pulled back the drapes.

He laughed. "If you're about to tell me to wish upon a star . . ."

"Oh, no. I don't believe in wishing on stars myself. I used to do it for years, but it never worked." I pointed. "See the ring around the moon?" I had noticed this earlier, while we were in the cab.

He was standing right behind me, so close I could feel his breath on my hair. "Yes," he said, "I see that." His voice was his usual cello sound, but deeper, more resonant. It made me feel a strange combination of being flushed and wanting to shiver.

I forced myself to concentrate. "There is a scientific reason for the moon appearing this way. I won't bore you with the details because they're not relevant to my point. When Jimmy and I were children, we thought that ring around the moon was a halo. We used to call moons like this angel moons."

I stopped talking there, but my mind suddenly finished the thought: *because this is what our mother called them.*

Had I been told this before? It was possible, and yet, I felt like something more was happening, like I might even be having my first memory, finally. Even in the bookstore, I'd felt that picture of

Malibu starting a churning in my mind. Could this be the result? It was so much better than I'd dared to hope. If I was really remembering something about my mother, how long would it be before I remembered even more? Maybe I would remember her voice saying those two words, "angel moon." Maybe I would even remember what she looked like.

I was so excited that I could no longer think about my point, and I turned around and told Stephen the demonstration would have to wait until another night.

"I'll believe it when I hear it," he said, raising his eyebrows. But then he reached for my hand and placed it securely in his. I was so surprised I burst into a smile, which he returned with one of his own. He held my hand as we walked back to the couch. Too bad it was a journey of only about twelve feet, because as soon as we got to the couch, I foolishly sat down at my usual place, a full cushion away, and he had to let go.

I would have been more miserable if I didn't have my book awaiting me. Tomorrow, I thought, I'll know if it is polite to change seats and move closer to him.

Stephen seemed very tired when the movie ended, and I was too. But I was wide awake again after I retired to his bedroom and began to read. The book continually confused and surprised me, especially the chapter about . . . sex. Here was a word I had never said aloud before, though Jimmy had alluded to it in an argument with Father, calling it "the physical relationship between a boy and a girl" and complaining that he would never experience it because Father was keeping us imprisoned in the "stupid" Sanctuary. He also threw in Father's face that while Father himself may have been dead with respect to women, he, Jimmy, was not. I never felt sorrier for Father than I did that day because I could see in his eyes how lonely he was since he lost Mother. Even in my novels, men would remarry, but Father had never shown the slightest interest in finding someone new. Perhaps we O'Briens love for life, I thought, since Grandma had never remarried after Grandpa died either.

But sex, as I discovered in my book, was no longer even considered an aspect of marriage. The author of *Dating and Love for the Clueless* was very clear that marrying without having sex first was a recipe for disaster. In fact, it was presumed that couples would try sex after as little as four dates! And that wasn't even the most shocking part. If you agree to go into a man's house, the author wrote, you should understand that he will think you want to have sex. No exceptions. Even if you think you are only coming over for a home-cooked meal, the fact of being in the man's house is enough to make him assume you are ready to move the relationship to the next phase.

The next phase. It took me a while to understand that the phase before sex was called "casual dating," about as unromantic-sounding a thing as I could think of, described primarily as the process of trying to decide whether you ever wished to see the person again. (The author also provided advice for choosing the location of the dates, so you could quickly escape if the answer was no.) Serious dating included sex, but it was also moving toward a "committed relationship." By this it was clear the author didn't mean marriage, but she never defined precisely what it did mean. Serious dating could even lead to love.

Though "love" was in the title of the book and half of its ostensible subject, it was barely discussed, which was very disappointing. In the back there was a quiz that promised to help determine if what one felt was love. I tried to take this quiz, but right away I had problems since each answer was restricted to Y or N, no explanations, no wavering.

Q: Do you feel happier when you are with him than when you are thinking about being with him?
A: Very happy with both.
Q: Do you trust him with more of your secrets than your girlfriends?
A: No other friends, girl or boy.
Q: Has he met your family and have you met his?

A: Yes, my brother. No, he never even mentions them and I fear they may be dead.
Q: Do you respect what he does, and does he respect what you do?
A: Yes on the first part, except I would say I respect most who he is, what he thinks and feels, how he seems to care about everything he does, from cooking to driving to talking to Jimmy's doctors. I hope the answer is no on the second part, since I myself have little respect for anyone my age who has lived such a sheltered, ignorant life. Yet I do plan to change, and I would like him to respect me for that. How I will change, I can't say, but I would like him to have faith that I can.
Q: Is your sex life fulfilling, and if not, have you told him so?
A: Nervous, skip.

And on and on for many more questions, nearly all of which I couldn't answer in the strictly yes or no required for the quiz to be scored. By the end I was so confused that I buried the book under the bed. I still had no idea how I should behave around Stephen, though I did want to make him happy. And I wanted him to hold my hand again, and possibly more. Much more if necessary, though it made me very nervous to consider being *that* bold.

I took out my new California book, so I could look again at the picture of the paradise that had apparently once been my home. I thought I would daydream about the past, perhaps even find more memories, but instead I found myself dreaming of Stephen and me in the future, standing on that beach together. He would teach me how to surf and swim, and I would ask Father to give him money so he no longer had to drive a cab with his poor weak foot. (Father would live there too somewhere. Father and Jimmy both. It seemed unlikely, but I would just have to beg and beg until they agreed to do it for my sake.) Stephen and I would be in a "committed relationship" (or even married, such a sweeter word), and he would already be forgetting this ugly apartment where he'd been so sad and alone. Over time, he would go back to smiling easily and often, the way he always had before. I knew this because of the soft smile lines he had, which I took as evidence of his deepest self, the optimistic person he was meant to be, before whatever had happened to hurt him so badly that he'd turned away from the numerous friends he'd once had, friends who never called him or dropped by, but were always part of his stories, whether from childhood or college or even a few years ago.

I envied him his life with so many friends, even as I knew that if he still had them, he might not have found room for a new friend now.

My daydream reminded me of one of the sillier questions in the love quiz.

> Q: Do you know about his past, and does he know about yours?
>
> A: No and no, but then I don't know about my own past either. I don't know the past of my father or mother. I don't know the recent past of my country. I don't know if the past even matters, as long as there is still cause for hope.

Of course if Stephen had had a wife in the attic, like Mr. Rochester had in *Jane Eyre,* that, I thought, would be another matter entirely. But the very idea made me laugh. His building had no attic, and his one small closet couldn't even hold a skeleton. It was too packed with clothes, his and mine.

twelve

IT WAS DURING the seventh day with Dorothea that Stephen finally lost it.

The morning started out with their usual routine. There was the usual awkward moment when he saw her step out of the bathroom after her shower, fully dressed, but with her incredibly long hair soaking wet. They always talked as she sat on the bed and brushed it out, and as always, he tried not to stare. She seemed to love hearing about anything he wanted to tell her, so it was easy to come up with something to say. That morning he told her about the house he'd grown up in, a basic three-bedroom ranch, with a carport and a finished basement, and the thing that fascinated her: no fence of any kind.

"How did you know where your property ended and your neighbor's began?"

"The neighbors on one side had better grass and those on the other side had a line of rosebushes."

He smiled because she was smiling at him in the mirror, but he was wondering if he could offer to brush her hair for her. Then he would have to sit down on the bed too, and they would be on the bed together. He could touch her hair, which was innocent enough, after all. Wasn't it? Jesus, he didn't even know.

"You could cross over to either side whenever you wished?"

"It wasn't a big deal. Most of the kids in the neighborhood were running from backyard to backyard all day. Sometimes they would play baseball games that stretched across four families' yards."

"Amazing," she said.

He closed his eyes for a half second. "You could say that."

When she was finished with her hair, he made her breakfast; that day it was eggs. She always ate whatever mess he set before her, and she always said thank you. Then he went to shower, and she went back to waiting for him. He suspected she'd already spent hours waiting before she'd taken her shower, because she was afraid the sound of water would wake him.

He was still sleeping better than he had since before the accident, though sometimes he wondered if the only thing keeping him asleep was all the dreams he was having about Dorothea. He felt guilty about it, even though there was obviously not a damn thing he could do about what he dreamed.

On the way to the Western Union office, where they were headed before the hospital, they listened to the radio and she asked him about the songs he liked. She said they had plenty of records in New Mexico, but they were mostly from the fifties or before, jazz and classical. Their father didn't want them to have a radio because he worried the news would upset them.

After talking to Charles O'Brien last night, Stephen was in a better position to understand why the man exerted such a pull on both his children. He was very opinionated, but he expressed his opinions with a weird mix of sensitivity that made it difficult to imagine telling him off. In the middle of grilling Stephen, for example, when Stephen had mentioned he was a widower, O'Brien had said, "I'm very sorry to hear that." It was the same thing most people said (except for those assholes who told him he was lucky he was so young, he'd have plenty of time to meet someone else and have more kids), but the difference was O'Brien sounded genuinely sad for him.

If Stephen had been close to liking Dorothea's father, he certainly changed his mind when the man said he would pay a considerable sum if Stephen would guarantee his daughter would be safe while she was in St. Louis. Stephen found the offer insulting, and he told O'Brien that he didn't need to be paid for watching out for Dorothea. What he didn't say, what he wanted to say, was that no matter how close he watched out for her, he couldn't guarantee she'd be safe, and O'Brien was a fool if he thought he could. Even walled off in rancho weirdo, she could have gotten sick or had an accident O'Brien hadn't foreseen. There were dangers everywhere: just ask any doc who has ever done an ER rotation. One of Stephen's friends treated a guy who ultimately died of a mouth infection from puncturing his gums with a tortilla chip.

At the Western Union office, Stephen discovered that Dorothea's father had wired the money to *him*. His first reaction was irritation, but then he realized O'Brien had to wire the money in his name since Dorothea herself had no ID. He wondered if this was why she'd taken a bus to St. Louis, rather than a train or plane, where ID was required to buy a ticket these days.

He'd sent four thousand dollars to his daughter. A ridiculous amount even if Dorothea wasn't living for free. What was she supposed to do with this money, buy more clothes? She had more than enough outfits already, and Stephen was positive O'Brien wouldn't have approved of ninety-nine percent of the things she'd bought. There was nothing wrong with what she liked: shorter skirts, clingier tops, but they were a hell of a lot different from the fifties clothes she'd arrived in. She was even wearing small heels rather than her saddle oxford shoes. Stephen felt sure she didn't notice all the looks guys were giving her now, but that only made it worse. What would she do if he wasn't there? What the hell would have happened to her if he hadn't been at the bus station to begin with? O'Brien really was a fool if he thought he'd somehow protected his kids by giving them zero knowledge of how to handle the real world.

Along with the money, O'Brien had sent Dorothea a long message about contacting some woman named Janice Fowler in California for the information Jimmy needed about their mother. So he wasn't sending the death certificate, but that might have been just as well. What if their mother had been murdered? Not by Jimmy, but by somebody. But why didn't O'Brien just tell Dorothea what happened himself? It was one thing to want to avoid talking about tragedy, but another thing entirely to put your daughter in the position where she has to hear something like this from a stranger. Janice Fowler, whoever she was; Dorothea of course had no idea. When Stephen asked her if she was supposed to call this woman or what, Dorothea sighed and said her father had made a suggestion, but she'd have to talk to him first. She was unusually quiet all the way to the hospital, and Stephen wondered what else O'Brien had put in that message. If he'd told her she had to track down this woman herself, he really was a prick.

As Stephen watched Dorothea sitting with Jimmy, showing him the pictures of Malibu, he found himself thinking how much more mature she seemed than just last week when he'd picked her up in the cab. Part of it was how seriously she obviously took her responsibility to her brother. Stephen heard her tell Jimmy that when he was better, after they went home for a while, the two of them could go visit the West Coast together. It sounded like a good idea, though Stephen personally didn't care much for Southern California. But maybe after she and Jimmy had seen L.A., they could head up to the Bay Area. He knew a dozen restaurants in San Francisco that Dorothea would love.

She was wearing a silky blue dress that Stephen was having a very hard time not being distracted by. When she crossed her long legs, he decided he needed to take a walk, have a smoke.

Ten minutes later, he came back in and found Jimmy sitting in front of the window and Dorothea standing behind him, humming and lightly rubbing his shoulders. She was really good-looking, there was no doubt about that. Especially when she was with her brother because her eyes got even brighter with her affection for Jimmy and she was always more relaxed in her body from the benzodiazepine. She was also one of the nicest people he'd ever met. She never saw a homeless person without rushing over to open her new purse and give them money. True, it wasn't like she'd worked for the money, but then a lot of people hadn't worked for money they had no intention of giving away. She was even nice to Nancy Baker, now that she'd decided Nancy was really trying to help Jimmy. Yesterday, she'd asked to stop at the flower shop so she could bring Nancy a plant. "It's very plain in her office," Dorothea had said. "The entire hospital is very plain, and I'm surprised. How can anyone get better without colors to see?"

Even Ellen would have liked Dorothea. It was a weird realization. His dead wife would have liked the woman who was staying in his apartment, the woman he kept trying not to think about having sex with.

It was off the topic (which was a good thing): he'd just thought of another reason he disliked Dorothea's father. No matter how Dorothea's mother died, he still had his kids. He had no right to let himself go nuts like that. Stephen would have held it together if Lizzie were still here. It would have been hard as hell, but he would have done it because his daughter would have needed more from him with Ellen gone, not less.

Dorothea and Jimmy were winding up when he remembered Dorothea's angel moon last night. He'd been a little disappointed that she hadn't finished showing him why he was wrong. Not that she could have really convinced him, but the idea was certainly agreeable. If only what you believed was as important as what was real, then he could have kept believing that the day he drove Ellen and Lizzie to the amusement park was a great day.

* * *

The restaurant he took Dorothea to that night was a little neighborhood Italian place. The food was good, and it was only two blocks away from his apartment, wedged between a pharmacy and a used-CD store. On the way over, he almost made the mistake of taking her hand again. It was swinging right beside his hand as they walked. He crossed his arms.

During the meal, she kept flashing him those irresistibly genuine smiles. He wondered why she always seemed so happy when they were together. It made him feel very relaxed, and he had to keep reminding himself not to get too comfortable.

When they left the restaurant, she pointed to the pharmacy and asked if she could go in before they walked home. He said sure, but before he could follow her inside, she stopped him.

"I was hoping I could shop privately."

"Not a problem," he said. He figured she needed Tampax, though knowing Dorothea's feelings about privacy, it could be mouthwash or deodorant or even shampoo. He stepped over to the side of the building and leaned against the wall. While he waited, he thought about how Dorothea handled these awkward things. Most people would try to manipulate the situation, but Dorothea just told you in the most straightforward, open way that she wasn't going to be open with you. It was another thing he liked about her.

After she came out of the pharmacy with a small bag, they turned toward the apartment. They walked slowly. She was talking about Jimmy. "I don't know why he's so interested in what Father used to do for a living. Why does it matter?"

"It's part of knowing someone to know about their past."

"Is it?" It was already dark, but he felt her glance at him.

"Sure," he said. "For example, if I told you what I used to do, then you would know me better." It was only a hypothetical, but then he found himself telling her. "I used to be a doctor. I did my residency at the same hospital where Jimmy is."

"Oh," she said. She sounded surprised and he felt bad that he hadn't mentioned this earlier. Anyone else would have known from the things he'd said about working with Jay and Nancy, the med school textbooks he'd kept and probably even the way he talked in general. But Dorothea wasn't like anyone else.

"Did you enjoy the work?" she said.

"Sometimes. Yes, I did."

"Why did you stop then?"

A car down the block was honking. He waited until it quieted down before he said, "Long story."

"Do you miss it?"

"I think I do. I miss so many things, it's hard to know which thing I'm missing now."

She sounded confused. "But you like driving your taxi?"

"I don't know," he admitted. "About half the time, I'm not even sure why I'm doing it."

It was true, but it wasn't the whole story. But how could he explain what he rarely thought about and didn't really understand himself? It was as if one day, the world he knew had been replaced by a world of nothing but accidents: the ones that happened and the ones that were narrowly avoided, which most people didn't even see. Even his medical training became irrelevant compared to the accidents, which could turn everything a doctor could do into *too late.* Sometimes he thought he drove the Checker like bullfighters get back in the ring: not necessarily to prove they're brave, but to stop hiding from their fear. Other times, he thought he drove because it was the only thing he could think of to try. If it didn't make any difference in the long run, what did?

He glanced in Dorothea's direction. "Maybe it has nothing to do with me." He forced his voice to become light, teasing. "Maybe it's for you, part of your charming coincidence."

"It's true that if you hadn't decided to drive the cab, I wouldn't have met you. But it can't be only for my sake. The pattern would have to include us both, or it wouldn't be a pattern, it would be solipsism." She laughed. " 'Solipsism' comes from the Latin *solus,* for 'alone,' and *ipse,* 'self.' I can't imagine a word more unsuited to describe the discovery of a connection."

He laughed too, and a moment later they were at his building. As they walked up the front steps, his forearm brushed against her hair. She'd taken it down when they came back from the hospital. She was wearing it down most of the time now because he'd told her it looked better that way.

They hadn't rented a movie for tonight. Earlier, Dorothea had spotted a deck of cards in one of his kitchen drawers and asked if they could play when they got home. They sat on opposite ends of the couch and used the middle cushion for the deck. Dorothea knew a lot of games, especially variations of poker, which she said her father loved. They played for nearly two hours. It was fun, but the main thing for Stephen was it kept them busy and kept him from getting too close to her. Even last night, in the few minutes at the window, he'd almost kissed her.

When the cards ended, he immediately suggested that they watch TV. One hour of TV, he figured, and the night would be safely over. She said fine, but not five minutes into the program, she gestured to the middle cushion. "Would you mind if I moved here?"

He said he wouldn't mind. How could he really say he did? And the thing is, he wanted her to move closer to him. She'd been sitting with her legs tucked underneath her during the card games, and he thought maybe she would want to stretch them out now, and they might somehow end up in his lap. He could just touch them, which wouldn't have to lead to anything major.

Of course she didn't do this, and he distracted himself as much as he could with whatever they were watching. A half hour went by. Some kind of comedy had come on. Dorothea was laughing more than usual. He thought she had such pretty lips. Maybe they seemed redder because the rest of her face was so pale, but he thought she had just about the prettiest mouth he'd ever seen.

When he leaned forward to kiss her, he wasn't thinking. If she'd pulled away or even acted hesitant, it would have ended right there. But instead she threw her arms around him so tight he had to loosen them a little to breathe. And she kissed him back. It was a little awkward at first, but not awkward enough to stop him. The show came back on, and then ended; he heard the music. Another one started. Still Dorothea had her arms around him, and they kissed and kissed and kissed for what felt like forever.

Any guilt he might have felt about betraying Ellen was obliterated by the strength of his desire. He hadn't had sex for almost two years. Dorothea was a beautiful woman and she was right here, in his house. He wanted her as much as he could ever remember wanting anyone, even in college.

He could have slept with Dorothea right then and he knew it, that was the toughest part. She trusted him so much after the week they'd spent together. If he'd taken her hand and pulled her into his bedroom, she would have gone. If he'd started undressing her, she would have let him.

But instead, he finally did what he thought was the right thing. He pulled away and told her good night.

It was her turn to be on the couch. She'd insisted that they alternate, so she wouldn't have to feel bad about taking his bed. He slumped into his room, and forced himself to read the most boring article in the driest medical journal so he could fall asleep and forget how frustrated he was. He was sound asleep, dreaming about her again, when he suddenly realized he wasn't having a dream at all. She had climbed into bed with him. She was in his bed, next to him—and she'd taken off her clothes.

He already had his hands on her body. He had no idea how long he'd been touching her in his sleep, but long enough that his desire was so obvious, it had to be obvious to her too.

When she realized his eyes were open, she whispered, "I want to do this with you, Stephen. I'm not afraid."

Talk about reminding him she was a virgin. Shit. But she was naked, and he had his hands on her breasts. Her breasts were so soft.

He managed to move his hands away, but then she said, "Have I done something wrong?"

"Not at all," he breathed. "It's just . . . I'm not sure you're ready for this."

"I am ready," she said, and rolled away from him. At first he thought she was upset, but then he realized she was reaching for something on the bedside table. It was the bag she'd bought at the pharmacy, and he couldn't have been more surprised when she opened it and pulled out a box of condoms. She'd obviously put some thought into all this, but how did she even know to get condoms?

When he asked her, she said something vague about educating herself on the "responsibilities of serious dating." Then she said, "May we continue now?"

He would have laughed except he didn't. He moaned instead as she kissed him.

Fifteen minutes later, he'd gotten her to the point where she was moaning too. He really thought he might not make it until they had sex when all of a sudden, she shuddered and he knew she was coming already. He held her close afterward, and tried to calm himself down a little. He owed it to her to make this special. He didn't want to hurt her with how desperate he was for this, for her.

"You okay?" he said.

"Very," she said. He could feel her smiling.

When he tried to touch her again, she giggled. He moved his hand down her thighs, and started over, but this time when she began to moan, he asked if he could make love to her now.

"Yes," she said. Her voice was small, a little nervous, but then she said, "I'd like that."

He put on a condom, climbed on top of her and entered as slowly and carefully as he could manage. He asked her several times if it hurt and she said, "A little," "Not much," and finally "No."

It felt so good to him that he almost didn't want to move because once he moved, it would be closer to being over. If he could have pushed a button right then and made it last the rest of his life, he would have. Once he got going, it wasn't hard to remember to stop every once in a while to kiss and caress her because he was so damned grateful to her for giving him this. When it was over, and his brain could form words again, he told her so.

They were lying next to each other. "You're welcome," she said. "And thank you. I appreciate what you've done for me as well."

He couldn't help laughing a little. "Trust me, you have nothing to thank me for."

"I don't understand," she said, and yawned.

"I just mean it was great."

She didn't say anything, but she patted his arm in a light, almost shy way, especially given what they'd just done.

After she yawned again, he said, "Tired, huh?"

"I'm sorry, but I am so sleepy. Perhaps I'd better get going before I drift off."

"Going?"

"To the couch."

"Dorothea, you don't have to do that."

"But it's my turn," she said, lifting herself up on her elbow. "I've told you, I don't feel comfortable taking your bed each night."

"What if we both sleep here?" He put his arm around her and arranged her head against his chest. "You and me together, just like this."

"Oh," she said softly. "That would be nice."

He kissed the top of her head. He closed his eyes, and when he opened them, it was morning. He woke up still holding her and wanting her all over again.

The next three days passed in a daze of meals and talking and laughing and sex and more sex. They went to see Jimmy every afternoon, as before, but the rest of the day, they spent any way they wanted, mostly in bed. One of their favorite things to do was to stay in bed all morning and read aloud from the newspaper. Stephen loved the way Dorothea talked about the news because it was both smart and weird. Even a simple sentence like "The American people want a new tax plan" would turn into a discussion about the politician who said it, and who was he saying it to, if not the American people, but then why would he be telling the people what they themselves wanted—wouldn't they already know?

After Stephen explained that a lot of these guys lie, not just often but always, he said, "Maybe your dad was right to keep you from the news."

"Poor Father, he was always so worried about everything. He really didn't have a choice in how he acted, I think."

Stephen had no intention of saying anything negative about O'Brien, but he couldn't help asking her something he'd been wondering for days. "What did he say would happen when you grew up? Did he expect you to live with him forever?"

"We never discussed what would happen." Dorothea paused. "I suppose it was a weakness in Father's plan for us."

To put it mildly, Stephen thought.

"But for myself," she said, pulling the blanket up to her chin, "I never doubted that my future would include everything I needed."

"Never?"

"Almost never." She smiled. "I guess I was exaggerating a little, for conversational effect."

He touched her hair. "And what do you need in your future, Dorothea?"

"More books," she said. "Many, many more books. Eventually, a job where I can use whatever talent I have. That's assuming I have a talent, other than reading. Is there a career for that? Perhaps to those who are blind?"

"Not really. But you could always read another article to me." He adjusted the pillow behind him and lay back down. "I'll close my eyes if it'll help."

"You're silly," she said, giggling. "Silly, but beautiful."

He shook his head, but the truth was, it touched him. Who else but Dorothea would ever call him beautiful?

Sometimes he wondered if there was something else he should

be doing for her. He would walk into the bedroom and find her staring at nothing, with an expression on her face he could only call lonely. Yet when she realized he was there, she always broke into a smile. And when he asked if there was anything wrong, she said no.

"If you did need something," he said once, "would you tell me?"

"I think I already have." She gestured around the apartment. "I wouldn't even be here if I hadn't."

He let the topic drop, but then on Friday morning it came up again, when they were sitting on the bed, and she mentioned that she was still reluctant to contact that woman, Janice Fowler.

"Why don't you tell me what you're supposed to do?" he said, lifting up her hair and kissing the back of her neck. "I might be able to make it easier."

"I'm sure you would."

"Then why not use me?" He laughed, then kissed her. "That's what I'm here for."

"I would never use you," she said softly, taking his hand. "I do appreciate the offer, but I don't think it's the right time to ask you for something like this."

He wanted to defend himself, to tell her he'd do anything to help, no matter what it took, but something stopped him before he could say the words. The last few days had been great, but this was hardly a normal relationship. Dorothea called what they were doing "serious dating," and he figured "dating" was as good a term as any for what they were doing, even if in their case it was obviously going to be short lived. He never thought about their future and didn't even know what would happen to them tomorrow. Maybe she'd sensed that he was in no position to make any promises, and maybe she was right.

"Don't you need to get moving on this though?" he said, looking at her. "For your brother's sake?"

She nodded. "I'm going to talk to Father the next time he calls. And you're right; it must be started soon. A few more days at most."

Stephen wondered again what her father had put in those instructions. What could be so hard that Dorothea would be this hesitant? Maybe he should try to talk to the old man about it himself.

But when O'Brien did call later that morning, to see if she got the money he wired and find out how she was, Stephen had other, more important things on his mind. He told Dorothea's father that she would be there in a minute and dropped the receiver on the counter; then he quickly took her down the hall.

"There's something I need to tell you," he said in a low voice. He was running his hands through his hair; she must have known he was nervous. She didn't try to rush him, even though he paused for quite a while, trying to think of a way to explain this. "Okay," he said, "the thing is, for some parents, it can be really upsetting to find out their child is growing up." Talk about a stupid way of putting it. No wonder she looked confused. "What I'm trying to say is, even though there's nothing wrong with what we're doing together—the sex, I mean—you might want to be careful because if you mention this to your father he might . . ."

"Become upset?"

"Yes," he said, exhaling. "I think there's a better than excellent chance."

"I know that." She flashed him a goofy grin. "I wasn't born yesterday."

The last part was a quote from a movie they'd seen. He would have laughed if he hadn't felt so guilty, thinking about when he'd told Dorothea's father he'd look out for her. How the hell had he let this happen?

While she was talking on the phone, Stephen reminded himself that O'Brien was obviously out of touch with reality, and the reality here was that his daughter wasn't a little girl anymore, but a twenty-three-year-old woman. Dorothea had made it very clear that she wanted to have sex, and not only the first night, but every time since. Stephen had asked her over and over if she was all right with what was going on and she'd not only said yes, but she'd made it easy to see that she meant it with how passionately she reacted.

If he needed more justification, all he had to do was look at what happened to Jimmy when he went out into the world. Sure, Dorothea was losing some innocence by being here with him, but she was gaining maturity, and maturity was what she needed. Even though she would go back to rancho weirdo when Jimmy was well enough to leave the hospital, the likelihood that she would stay there was diminishing with each day she was in the city, Stephen could tell. She was talking about a future with a job now. She was talking about a future outside of New Mexico.

And finally, really, the truth was he just couldn't help himself. She was always right there, kissing him, hugging him, sleeping naked with him. Even if he could have backed away now, he would have hurt her feelings.

"Father would like to talk to you," Dorothea said, appearing in the bedroom doorway. "Would you mind?"

As soon as Stephen picked up the kitchen phone and said hello, O'Brien said, "May I ask you a question?"

"Depends on the question," Stephen said cautiously.

"Does my daughter know that your wife passed away?"

He certainly didn't expect this. He turned the other way from Dorothea, who was in the kitchen too, standing in his robe, pouring way too much pepper into the eggs she was whisking.

"No," he said.

"May I ask why?"

Stephen cleared his throat. "I find it hard to talk about."

"I understand. But I think it's very important that she know." O'Brien paused. "I would consider it a personal favor if you would tell her."

If the old man's voice wasn't so strangely kind, Stephen would have thrown it back on him, suggested that O'Brien tell Dorothea how her mother died first.

"I'll see what I can do," Stephen said flatly. "Is that it?"

"Yes. And thank you again for taking care of her." His voice grew quiet. "I can tell she's doing very well there."

When Stephen hung up, he felt a little sorry for O'Brien. The old guy was alone now, and it had to be tough. Especially since Dorothea obviously was doing very well. She hadn't had any breathing attacks and she'd even stopped taking the sedatives to visit her brother.

"No more pepper," he said, turning around to see Dorothea still pouring it in. "No more whisking either," he said, taking her hand and laughing because she'd whisked the eggs so thoroughly they'd transformed into a bubbly foam.

Later, while Stephen was in the shower, he wondered why, if O'Brien thought it was so important for Dorothea to know about Stephen's wife, he hadn't told his daughter himself. And why was it so important? What was Dorothea's father getting at?

Stephen wasn't opposed to telling her about Ellen. If only it had been that simple. The problem was, for Stephen to tell Dorothea about Ellen, he'd have to think about Ellen, and that he was determined not to do.

He'd put the photo of Ellen and Lizzie in a drawer after that first night, so Dorothea wouldn't ask him about them. He didn't intend to put his past away too, but now that it had happened, he wanted to keep it that way.

He knew he couldn't last like this forever, but then Dorothea wouldn't be here forever. This period was a little vacation from his life, and he didn't see why he shouldn't enjoy it as much as possible. As long as he made sure Dorothea enjoyed it too, he didn't see the harm.

thirteen

ON SUNDAY AFTERNOON, Nancy Baker told Dorothea and Stephen that Jimmy had been pacing his room all morning, waiting for his sister to arrive. He'd remembered something important about his father, he said, though he hadn't told Nancy what it was.

"I'll be interested in hearing about this," Nancy whispered to Stephen, on the way down the hall. "Did I tell you the father sent a twenty-thousand-dollar check and called it a 'down payment on the bill'? That has to be a first for this place."

"True," Stephen said, but he was looking at Dorothea, who was walking about ten feet ahead, obviously eager to get to her brother. He glanced at Nancy. "Any talk of releasing him?"

"I don't think he's ready, but if he wanted to go home, we wouldn't stop him. At this point, it's his call."

"Stephen!" Dorothea said, turning back to him and smiling. "Could you please hurry?"

Nancy took a long look at him, but she didn't say anything. He walked faster to catch up with Dorothea.

Jimmy was looking better every day. All of his stitches were out now, and he was healing fast, as fair-skinned people often did. He smelled of oil paints, as usual; he seemed to spend every free moment in art therapy. Nancy was right about how excited he was. He ran over to Dorothea and slipped his arm through hers. They'd barely sat down together when he said he'd been trying all week to remember what their father was like when they lived in California. "It's been driving me crazy," he said, and smiled weakly. "Crazier, at least."

"I can see why this is so important to you," Dorothea said, patting his hand. "Stephen explained this to me. He said learning about someone's past helps you to know them better."

Jimmy shook his head. "I don't want to know Father better. After what I remembered, I don't care if I ever see him again."

Her face crumpled. "You can't possibly mean that."

"I mean it, Thea. If for no other reason, because he still has the fucking gall to talk about honesty and principles."

"But Father does believe in those things."

"No, he's a liar, and now I can prove it."

"Oh," she said, in the smallest voice, barely audible.

Stephen wished he could hold her then, but he knew how she felt about keeping their distance in front of Jimmy. She'd told him she was afraid her brother would feel uncomfortable, even like an outsider, if he knew they were "seriously dating."

He was listening carefully to see if Dorothea was going to have an anxiety attack. She'd already given up breathing through her nose. Her mouth was open, just a little, but he could hear the effort it was taking to fill her lungs.

"Maybe you should wait on this," Stephen said to Jimmy. He nodded at Dorothea.

"Oh, I'm sorry." Jimmy's face went even whiter than usual. "I wasn't thinking about—"

"No," she said. "I want to hear it." She panted for a moment. "Please, just tell me all at once."

"All right. I remembered the way he treated Mom when she had to work."

"Treated her?" she gasped. "What do you mean?"

"He didn't want her to work. I don't know why, but it made him very angry."

"Father never gets angry."

"He used to. I think he even cut her hand once, so she couldn't go." Jimmy looked at the wall. "I keep remembering her walking in with her hand bandaged. She was in her nightgown with the yellow flowers. Father told us she was sick, but I knew he was lying. He didn't say anything to her, even though she looked so scared. I knew he didn't love her. He was lying about that too."

Dorothea didn't move or breathe for what felt like a full minute. Stephen was ready to buzz the nurse for a sedative, but then she was okay.

"I'm sorry, but I know this isn't true." Her voice was kind but firm. "Father is too gentle to cut anyone."

"Why do you always have to defend him?" Jimmy jumped up and walked to the door and back. "Why can't you ever defend me?"

"I do defend you," she said. "I can defend you both, can't I?"

"No. He ruined my life, and you either understand that or you don't!"

Jimmy babbled for a while then, stomping around the room, slapping his hands against his chest, shaking his head so hard his messy red hair kept falling into his eyes. None of the things he was saying made any sense, until suddenly Jimmy said, "He took my mother away from me!"

Stephen looked at Dorothea, but she was still okay. In fact, she was breathing better than before.

"I'm glad you know that you didn't hurt our mother," she said, putting her arm around her brother when he slumped down next to her.

"I didn't say that," he cried. "I was there, but the Liar was there too. I know I didn't do it alone."

Dorothea gave Stephen a look, and it was obvious she didn't believe this. Neither did he, though he was beginning to think something had happened or Jimmy wouldn't cling to this "dream" so tenaciously. He may have had all the details wrong, but there was something he had right. Stephen hoped it wasn't really something Dorothea's father had done to her mother. If he'd killed her, that would certainly explain why he'd taken those kids and disappeared.

"Was I there too?" Dorothea said. She sounded surprised by her own question, as if she'd never thought of it before.

"No." Jimmy sniffed back tears. "I know how foolish this seems, but I keep thinking you were in a dresser drawer."

Dorothea held him for a while until he calmed down. She told him she loved him several times. She showed him pictures from the California book, as she did every day, because it always seemed to make him happier.

"I'm all right," Jimmy finally said to his sister. Then he pointed at the chessboard sitting on the table by the bed. "Are you ready to play?"

Nancy Baker had thought of this as something the two of them could do together, knowing only that Jimmy enjoyed the game. But Jimmy didn't just enjoy it, he was really good at it. Dorothea said he'd always been good at chess and drawing, both of which she said she was terrible at.

But she wasn't terrible, Stephen discovered, when Dorothea talked him into playing with her brother this time, and letting her watch. It usually took Jimmy about an hour to beat Dorothea, but Jimmy had him mated in little more than a dozen moves.

"I'm impressed," Stephen said. He'd played a fair amount of chess in his life, and he'd never run into anyone who could crush him as thoroughly as Jimmy just had. He was just about to ask Jimmy who had taught him to play when he realized how ridiculous that question was.

Before they left, Jimmy whispered something to Dorothea and she nodded. Nancy was with another patient, so they left without giving her any report. They were back in the Checker, heading to his apartment, when Dorothea asked if he thought it could be true that her father hadn't wanted her mother to work.

"Sure, it's possible. This was twenty years ago, but there are still guys like that. Some of them don't think women should work at all."

"Yes, this is what Jimmy wants me to ask Father the next time he calls. Should women be employed." She sighed. "He thinks if I ask that question I will see that Father's view is very different than I think."

"You sound a little reluctant."

"It would be different if I could tell Father why I was asking." She placed her palm on the foggy window. It was raining and the defroster wasn't keeping up. "It feels manipulative, even dishonest."

"Maybe you shouldn't do it then."

"I have to. I told Jimmy I would."

Stephen could hear the sadness in her voice. He knew she felt like she was having to choose between them, and he felt irritated with Jimmy for doing this to her, but then he decided it was really O'Brien's fault. The man could send twenty thousand dollars without blinking, but he'd never bothered to answer basic questions about their past.

He took her hand. "Want to go to the library on the way to dinner?"

He knew Dorothea would say yes: the library was her new favorite place to be. He'd only thought to take her there on Friday, but she immediately fell in love with it. She said someday she was going to live right next door to a library. "That way I can always have another book the minute I finish one." The fact that the books were free amazed her, and Stephen had to admit it was pretty incredible. He didn't have a library card, but he signed up for a temporary one that allowed him to check out two books and they'd each picked one. Stephen hadn't even cracked the cover of his, but somehow, probably while he was sleeping, Dorothea had already finished hers. It was a popular novel about a girl who was murdered and went to heaven, which made Dorothea cry, though she insisted it was actually very happy, since most novels don't have heaven at all. She also loved that the story had what she described as "a charming coincidence involving an icicle." "You don't see that every day," she'd said, and he couldn't disagree.

They had to run by the apartment first, to get the card and the book to return. They'd gone up the stairs and were just rounding the corner—when Stephen saw his parents. They were standing outside his door, arms loaded with groceries. His dad had two bags; his mom had one, and a sack of potatoes clutched in her other hand.

He knew this was his own fault. Whenever his parents didn't hear from him for a while, they inevitably showed up, and always with groceries, as if the only possible reason for his not calling was starvation.

"There you are!" his mother said, but she dropped the potatoes when she noticed Dorothea. The sack burst and the potatoes spilled out onto the floor. His father leaned down to start picking them up and the bread fell out of one of his bags, a can of soup out of another. Dorothea giggled like she always did at slapstick on television. Stephen wished it seemed funnier to him.

He managed to introduce everybody. He cleaned up all the potatoes. He let his parents come inside because he couldn't very well keep them out, even though he knew Dorothea's things were all over the apartment. A pair of her shoes under the coffee table. A sweater draped over the couch. A white belt she'd decided didn't go with her skirt thrown on a chair. One of her bras drying on the shower curtain rod.

It looked like she was living there, which, since they'd never even heard her name before, naturally surprised the hell out of Bob and Lynn Spaulding.

If they'd just been surprised, Stephen could have handled it. But they were just *so glad* about everything. So glad to meet you, Dorothea. So glad you like mushrooms/potatoes/eggs/steak/you name it, and they did name almost every item as they took it out of the grocery bag and displayed it for her approval. So glad you know our boy, Stephen (they actually said "boy"). Where did you two meet again? The bus station. What a nice place.

"It's not nice, Mom. It's a shithole."

"Don't cuss in front of your mother," his dad said, which he hadn't said since Stephen was probably eight. But he was looking at Dorothea, and his real meaning was: Don't cuss around this woman we are so glad to see you with, finally.

"He can cuss around me, Bob," his mom said, also looking at Dorothea, winking. "We don't mind a little salty language, do we?"

Dorothea was sitting on the bar stool, with her legs crossed at the ankles. "Actually, I'm very fond of the word 'shit' since Stephen introduced it to me. I didn't know curses were referred to as 'salty language' though. I love that. So one could say about a person: his talk was *peppered* with *salty* language."

His parents seemed a little confused, but they were still smiling. They sat down at the kitchen table and asked Dorothea the usual questions: where she was from, what her parents did, what schools she went to, where she worked. No matter how bizarre her answers must have sounded to them, they continued to smile. His dad even nodded approvingly when Dorothea said she was looking forward to working someday because she thought it would be "wonderful." This from a man who'd worked forty-four years behind a desk at an insurance company before he retired, a job he'd said he'd hated most of the time.

"Isn't she a pretty girl?" his mother whispered to his father. At least she thought she was whispering, but their hearing wasn't what it used to be. Dorothea let out a nervous giggle.

"How long have you been in St. Louis?" his mom said.

"All right then." Stephen stood up. "Don't you guys need to get going before it gets dark? I know you hate driving in the dark, Dad."

"But we're just getting to know her," his mom said.

"We're in kind of a rush anyway," he said.

"Yes, we're going to the library," Dorothea offered.

His mother said they'd never make it since the library closed early on Sunday. "So we have lots of time to talk," she said, before asking Dorothea again how long she'd been in St. Louis.

When Dorothea answered with the truth, his mom said, "Did you say eleven months?"

"Oh, I wish," Dorothea said. "It's only eleven days, but it feels like much longer." She smiled at Stephen.

"Isn't that interesting, Bob?" his mom said, but her face fell.

"Eleven days?" his dad said, looking at Stephen. His voice was frankly mystified. "And you're already living with her?"

"We're not living together," he said. "It's a long story, but it's not like that."

"No, it's not like that," Dorothea echoed, though Stephen wondered what she thought she was saying.

His mom and dad acted like they both had to go to the bathroom, immediately, together, which could only make things worse—that bra hanging over the bathtub. In the few minutes they were gone, Stephen didn't say anything and neither did Dorothea. When his parents returned, his father said to him, "Before we leave, come downstairs and take a look at the Chrysler. The engine is stalling out again."

"It's raining, Dad. I know next to nothing about engines."

"Come on. It'll just take a minute."

He exhaled. "Mom, why don't you and Dorothea come too?"

"In the rain?" His mother laughed. "We're too sweet, we'll melt."

"All right," he finally said, grabbing his jacket from the back of the chair. "Let's go."

No surprise, they were barely out of the apartment when his father admitted that he just wanted a chance to talk to him. They stood in the hall by the window that faced the street, both men with their hands shoved in their pockets. Father-and-son chats weren't normal in their family. In fact, Stephen couldn't remember ever having one until after the accident, when his parents started worrying that he was throwing away his life.

"Dad, trust me, you don't need to get involved in this," Stephen began. "I know what I'm doing."

He rubbed his beard. "Okay then, what are you doing?"

"She's a nice person. Initially, I was trying to help her." Stephen looked out at the rain. "Her brother's in the psych ward at County. It's a long story, like I told you. She won't be here much longer, a few days, maybe another week, tops."

"But she's been staying with you in this little apartment for eleven days?"

"Yes."

"Have you driven your cab at all? For fares, I mean."

"Not much, but it's up to me when I work. It's not like I need the money."

"That's not what I'm saying. You two have been together solid for eleven days, morning, noon, night? You're sleeping with this woman too?"

"What's your point?"

"I'm just concerned." His father peered into his face. "What's going to happen to you when she leaves?"

"I'll go back to driving. Watching TV, eating, walking. Same as before." It sounded pretty lonely, even to him. He forced a smile. "Coming over to your house for dinner once a week, so you and Mom won't worry so damned much."

"Any chance she'll be coming back to St. Louis?"

"I don't know." He turned to face his father. "Look, what do you want me to say?"

"Well, say you care about her, if you do. Maybe you could talk her into coming back."

"I don't know. I really can't think about it."

"Why not, son?"

"I don't know," he repeated. He took a deep breath. "I just can't."

His father didn't say anything for a while. The rain was coming down harder, and it was getting dark. Stephen felt a gloom coming over him, and he decided he wasn't up to going out to dinner tonight, after all.

"I think you do have feelings for her." His father smiled a half smile. "Your mother told me so, and you know she's never wrong."

"I'll take it under advisement." He nodded in the direction of his apartment. "Can we go back inside?"

His father said yes, but before they made it to the door, he threw in that Dorothea seemed so nice. "It's really too bad. We just want you to be happy."

When they walked back into the apartment, Stephen could tell his mom had been having a heart-to-heart with Dorothea. They were sitting together on the couch, so close their arms were almost touching, but whatever his mother had said didn't seem to have upset her. Both his parents hugged Dorothea good-bye and his mom hugged him, but his dad gave him the customary slap on the back. He tried to give them money for the groceries, but as usual, they protested. Normally, he would have kept pushing them, but this time he let it go.

And then they were gone, and he and Dorothea were alone, just like they'd been for eleven days—except it didn't feel the same at all.

He told her he didn't want to go out to eat, and she said fine. "But I'll cook something," he said. "We have lots of choices, thanks to my parents."

"They're lovely people," she said, following him into the kitchen. "I'm very glad I had a chance to meet them."

He opened the refrigerator. "What did you and my mom talk about?"

"Primarily, the thing we have in common," Dorothea said.

"What's that?" he said distractedly, as he looked around for something he felt like making. He wasn't hungry, even though he knew he should be. They hadn't eaten since this morning.

"Silly—you, of course."

He pulled out ham and cheese and offered to make her a sandwich. "I'm going to wait," he said. "I feel a little off."

"I can make my own sandwich," she said, and smiled. "I'm not completely helpless."

"I didn't say you were."

"I know you didn't," she said slowly, and paused. "Is something wrong?"

"Let's watch TV for a while," he said, knowing he was probably disappointing her. They hadn't watched any television since the first night they had sex. They were too busy talking and reading to each other and just having fun. But now he felt the old need for oblivion. "I'm sure I'll be all right soon," he added, though he wasn't sure, since he didn't know why he wasn't all right now.

He went into the living room and left her making her sandwich. A few minutes later, she joined him and they watched one of the crime shows in Sunday night repeats. Then a movie came on and he told her he wanted to watch that too. She said fine, but she moved closer, and during the commercials, she talked, like they always had. He tried, but he couldn't come up with much to say in response.

The movie was almost over when she said, "I told your mother about my angel moon. She agreed that it was not 'new age hocus-pocus.'"

"Not sure I follow," he said, because he wasn't really paying attention.

"Remember when we were watching that wonderful movie, and I told you that life is about what you believe as much as what seems to be reality?"

He knew the movie she was talking about: an old seventies flick called *They Might Be Giants.* He'd rented it because Dorothea had read the box and told him she'd love to see a movie about Sherlock Holmes. It was only when they started watching that he realized the main character wasn't Sherlock Holmes, but a guy who only thought he was Sherlock Holmes after he went crazy when his wife died. The point of the movie was pretty similar to what Dorothea said: that beliefs can be real if only you believe hard enough—but of course Stephen noticed what Dorothea didn't seem to, that no amount of believing could bring back the crazy man's dead wife.

"I remember," he said, still looking at the screen.

"I told your mother about the angel moon that I was planning to use for demonstration, and how it proved my theory. And she told me it was very true." When he didn't respond, Dorothea said, "Would you like to hear it?"

"All right."

"You have to come to the window."

"Why? There's no moon at all. It's too cloudy."

"All the better," Dorothea said, taking his hand.

Her hand was so soft in his, and yet he wanted to pull away. He didn't want to stand this close to her. He didn't want to smell her hair and the new perfume she'd bought; he didn't want to think about touching her body, how much he always desired her.

"When my brother and I were children, I was very afraid of the dark. I slept with several night-lights and I would ask Father to replace the bulbs every few weeks, for fear that one of them would burn out."

"A normal fear of small kids," he said, giving in and putting his arm around her. The night was pitch-black; there was nothing to see, though Dorothea insisted he keep looking out the window.

"Thank you," she said, "though I was still afraid when I wasn't that small. I was nine when Jimmy finally cured me, as I'm about to tell you." She leaned into him and gave him a kiss on the cheek. Then he kissed her lips until she stepped back, smiling. "Don't you want to hear the rest?"

"Okay," he said, holding up his palms, smiling back. "Hands off until you're finished."

"As I said, when I was nine, there was a bad storm one afternoon that knocked the power out. By night, it still hadn't returned. This had happened before many times, usually from the mountain winds, and Father had a generator, but it only lit part of the downstairs. Normally, Jimmy and I would sleep down there with Father, while Grandma used a candle to get to her room. But on that particular night, I wanted to sleep in my own bed because I had an elaborate pretend game in progress with my dolls and my stuffed animals, and it was very important that I be with them."

"Couldn't you move the dolls and animals downstairs?"

"They were carefully arranged for the game," she said. "Also, as excessive as this must sound, I had over four hundred of them. With some things, Father was overly generous."

"What the hell, he had the money."

"True, but I think his motive was to make up for the many things we couldn't have because he considered them too dangerous." She paused. "But back to that night. When I told Jimmy of my problem, he insisted that I step out onto the porch with him. The storm had passed, and in its place was the unusual moon with the ring, the one we called the angel moon. He asked me to stare into that moon until I saw the angel herself as clearly as I saw her halo."

"And you did," he said. "And then you could go to your room and sleep because an angel was watching out for you."

"No, not at all. I stared at the moon until I saw the angel, yes, but I found her quite frightening. Her face was as blank as death and her eyes seemed to be laughing at me. When I asked Jimmy if she looked this way to him too, he nodded and said the angel in the moon was absolutely hideous."

"What?" Stephen burst out in a laugh. "So now you had the moon and the dark to fear?"

"No again, because Jimmy convinced me that the truly hideous thing about this angel was what he called her 'blinding, boring, arrogant and most of all creepy light.' 'The dark isn't frightening,' Jimmy said, as he stood behind me, covering my eyes with his hands. 'In the dark all you have are the pictures in your mind. And your mind is sweet and innocent, Thea, just like you.'"

She was quiet for a moment before she whispered, "Oh my poor brother." Stephen heard her gulping like she was trying not to cry. "I still can't believe what's happened to him."

"It's okay," he said, pulling her against his chest. He only meant to comfort her, but then she was kissing him. He put his arms around her and she was kissing him with an urgency that he didn't understand, though, admittedly, he didn't spend a lot of time thinking about it.

Within a few minutes, they were stumbling into the bedroom, undressing as they went. She was so incredibly into everything he did to her, this moment, right now: he couldn't remember ever being this excited from the excitement of the woman he was with. It was so intense, the way their bodies moved together, the way she touched him so freely, the way she kept her eyes open this time, those gorgeous eyes shining in the light from the hall, telling him how much she wanted him. It was the best sex they'd ever had, and afterward, he fell back on the bed feeling nothing but calm and satisfied.

They were lying on their backs, holding hands, still a little out of breath, when Dorothea laughed. "I just thought of something. I never finished my story."

"Right," he said. "Tell me the rest."

"The reason we were at the window is that I was going to show you the dark, moonless sky, and ask you if it was a friendly dark or a frightening dark. The idea being that the essence of things is also in the way they appear. It's even more true in life that what you believe is often as important as what's real."

"Maybe so," he said, because he couldn't think of anything to disagree with. Nothing Dorothea said could be disagreeable to him now. "But how did this come up with my mom?"

"Of course I didn't tell her the entire story. We were talking about the eleven days I'd been here. I think she was a bit shocked that it was such a short span of time, especially as she seemed to suspect the thing you advised me not to tell my father about. Which I would not have told your parents about either, and so I pretended not to notice her hints on the matter, remembering your point about parents being upset that their children are growing up."

He laughed. "I don't think that applies to my parents."

"I don't know," Dorothea said seriously. "Your mother seemed very alive to the possibility that I would hurt you, considering I'd only known you eleven days. But I told her I believed it to be much longer, and in fact, I believed I'd known you for many years." Dorothea's voice became shy. "I only realized the reason for this as I was talking to your mother. I didn't tell her this part, but when I was fourteen, I had a daydream about a Civil War soldier who came to my door to ask me to marry him. He was a man in one of my encyclopedias, a very attractive man. He had brown hair and a face very similar to yours. In the daydream, he smiled like you and even had a slight limp as you do."

She squeezed his hand. "I realize how strange it must sound: that we met via one of my daydreams nine years ago. I don't expect you to have shared that daydream. I would imagine you were far too busy in medical school to conjure up the Dorothea O'Brien of your future."

The gloom was creeping back again, but he said something about medical school being difficult. Something that would have been unsatisfying if Dorothea hadn't been chatting so happily she didn't notice.

"Getting back to your mother. She told me she liked my idea about beliefs being as important as reality. She also said—" Dorothea was still talking, but he couldn't concentrate. He was listening to the rain against the window, wondering why his after-sex good mood had already evaporated. It wasn't just in his mind either: his whole body was starting to feel tense. He could feel it across his shoulders and down his arms and in his calves and hamstrings. He could feel it pushing inside his chest, like something had a hold of his heart muscle, even though he knew that was ridiculous.

"She was so intimate with me. It was really very unexpected." Dorothea turned over and put her hands on his face. "She even asked if I would share my thoughts about the future with you. Want to know what I said?"

"Sure," he said, but he was wondering how to get away for a minute without hurting her feelings. If only he could go out driving with the radio blasting or run around the block until he was too exhausted to think. Or just stare at the ceiling until his mind went blank. He knew he could handle whatever this was; he'd handled a hell of a lot worse.

"I couldn't tell her the entire truth because, well, I hadn't told you yet. But I told her I was very happy here and hoped there would be a future, and I think she suspected that I was in love with her son, because she seemed to feel much better then." Dorothea laughed. "Oh, now I have told you. I hope you don't feel you have to reciprocate, although I think you'd better or I may have to tickle you."

"I do," he said, though he honestly wasn't sure what he was agreeing with. He had to get out of here, now, before he lost it.

"I'll be right back," he managed, before he went into the bathroom and crouched down on the floor, trying to calm down, think. But he couldn't think because he kept feeling an incredible urge to break something. He was scared shitless he might cry.

Even her soft knock startled him. No wonder she was at the door. He'd already been in there for what felt like a very long time.

"Are you all right?" she said.

"Yes."

She waited a minute. "Would you like to have some pickles together?"

They'd done this almost every night after sex: sit on the bed and eat from a plate of the several kinds of pickles she'd brought back to his house so far. It was a goofy kind of fun, but now it seemed as ludicrous as if she'd suggested eating pickles at a funeral.

"No thanks."

"Are you sure? I'd be glad to get them ready."

"I said no." His voice was harsh. Shit, he didn't mean for it to come out that way. He told her he was sorry. "It's nothing you did," he threw in, but his tone didn't change.

She continued to wait at the door for a while before she said, "Stephen, please tell me what's wrong. I want to try to help you."

"You can't." He was banging his fist on his forehead because he finally got what was happening, though he didn't understand it at all. It seemed so unfair that this was happening again. Jesus, why had that image of Lizzie's car seat come back into his mind now?

"Oh, I'm sorry," Dorothea said softly.

He couldn't respond.

When the medics had lifted his daughter out, her pacifier was stuck at the bottom of the seat, covered in blood. She was too old for a pacifier, but Ellen had said not to push her, she'd give it up when she was ready. He tried to lunge back into the car to grab it. The police were holding him back, and he was shouting, "She needs that! She won't be able to sleep!"

"Fuck," he yelled, and he heard Dorothea start to cry. But he couldn't do a thing about it because now he was remembering when the car finally skidded to a stop and he'd reached over to touch Ellen. She was already dead, and he knew it, but he couldn't accept it. He wouldn't accept it. He took Ellen's hand and said, "Now this is what I call seriously screwed up." It was something she always said when things went wrong. Like the toilet overflowing. Like the time their Visa got charged twice for their bedroom furniture. Like Lizzie melting a crayon in the radiator.

He was crying too now, but he was also cursing because he was so pissed. He could handle the constant throbbing in his foot and the slivers of glass that still worked their way out of the flesh of his arm, but this was too fucking much. And he'd been so sure it was over. It had been over for months and months. Why had it suddenly come back now? Was this the price of letting himself pretend he was a human being for not even two weeks?

He sniffed hard, stood up and stuck a towel around his waist. He had to get out of this bathroom. He needed a drink.

As he walked, he heard Ellen's voice: "I really think we should go on the highway."

"This will be quicker."

"You always say that, but it never turns out to be true." She turned around and smiled at Lizzie. "Daddy always says, 'I discovered a shortcut.' Discovered, like he's Lewis and Clark."

The accident was only seconds later. There was no choice to torture himself with—different road, different result—because they weren't even to the highway entrance yet. The torture was much simpler. That was the last thing his wife would ever have a chance to say. That was her last smile.

He walked into the kitchen, grabbed a bottle of scotch and drank until he choked. Then he waited until the coughing died down and drank again. He heard Dorothea go into the bathroom, the flushing of the toilet, then the sound of the bedroom door closing behind her. He already knew he would have to make this up to her, but right now, he couldn't deal with it.

He was back on the couch, still crying a little, but at least he was getting drunk too. The pictures were fading, though it was different than it used to be. In the past, when the accident images stopped coming, they were always followed by the usual memories: Christmases and birthdays and ordinary days that were somehow just good. He used to worry that if those normal memories ever left, it would mean he'd stopped caring, but now he knew that wasn't true. This was what he thought about, as he sat on the couch in the dark, watching the shadow of headlights pass across his window. He would never stop caring as long as he fucking lived. He would always, always, always miss his baby girl and his beautiful wife, Ellen, and the family they had been.

He drank until he couldn't hold the bottle anymore. He heard it drop and he knew it was spilling on the rug, but he didn't give a shit. The last thing he remembered thinking was that Dorothea would find him passed out like this, half naked. He wanted to get up and cover himself, but he couldn't move.

When he woke up the next morning, he felt like the back of his head had been nailed to the couch. He closed his eyes, but he could still feel the sun streaming in the window, so he pulled the blanket over his face. And that's when he realized Dorothea had covered him. "She deserves better," he muttered. He tried to think about something really nice he could do for her today, but he couldn't think yet. He had to sleep a while longer.

The next time he woke up it was afternoon; he could tell because the sun wasn't beating on him anymore. He sat up and the headache was still there, but he had to get going. Dorothea would be anxious to get to the hospital to see Jimmy.

He stood up with the blanket around his shoulders and went into the kitchen to get some Tylenol. He'd already swallowed two with a handful of water from the faucet when he turned around and saw the piece of paper sitting on the kitchen table.

He'd never seen her handwriting before, and he just stared at the letters themselves for a moment, thinking that her handwriting was like everything else about her. Elegant, understated, humble, very pretty.

> Dear Stephen,
>
> I am very grateful for your help and your kind attentions. Please do not interpret my leaving as meaning anything about your essential goodness, which I have been the beneficiary of on so many occasions since we met. Even last night, I know that your goodness kept you from telling me that the sentiments I was expressing were making you so very uncomfortable. I don't have words to express how sorry I am. Because of my lack of experience, I'd convinced myself that you felt as I did. It was wishful thinking, the silly dream of an ignorant and often silly person.
>
> I know that to stay for even another day would put you in an unbearably awkward position. This is the one

and only reason I am leaving. Though I would also be embarrassed to face you this morning, I find as I write this that it is far harder to say good-bye.

Your kindness to my brother and myself will never be forgotten.

Dorothea

He sat at the table for a very long time, holding the piece of paper in his hand. Of course he was going to go after her. He would start with the hospital and figure out what to do from there. For one thing, he had to apologize. He also had to make sure she was all right.

It wasn't until he went into the bedroom and discovered that she'd left behind her saddle oxford shoes that he finally accepted the other reason he was going. He sat on the floor and held them to his chest and he felt like he could almost hear Ellen saying it was okay. You're alive, it wasn't your choice. But you're alive, Stephen, so quit being dumb. What else can you do but live?

PART FOUR

The Master of Dreams

fourteen

Lucy had only been out of the ICU for a few days when she asked Charles if he was planning to sell their house. She was afraid she already knew the answer, but she was hoping she could change his mind.

He was sitting in his usual chair by her bed, lightly stroking her face. He didn't say yes; he said they would discuss it later. "We can stay where we are until you're better."

Where they were was The Beverly Hills Hotel, where Charles had taken Dorothea and Jimmy the same night it happened. His mother had flown home from Florida immediately, and she was staying there too, along with a nanny he'd hired.

Talking was difficult for Lucy—she still had the feeding tube down her nose, and her throat was still sore from the tube that had been in her mouth for days—but she tried to explain to Charles that her feelings for the house hadn't changed. The house was where she'd brought her newborn babies home, nursed them and changed them and watched their first steps. It was where she and Charles had danced on the balcony in the moonlight the night when, an hour after nine-month-old Jimmy's fever broke, they learned that Charles had won an Oscar for Joan. It was where her little boy had drawn his first picture and her little girl had sat on phone books to play the first few notes of "Twinkle, Twinkle Little Star."

The skull fracture and contusion hadn't affected her memory; she wanted Charles to know that too. She could do more than pass the neurologist's simple tests. She could remember her life.

He listened but all he said was, "Let's not worry about this now."

Lucy began to cry then. Unfortunately, this wasn't unusual. Since she'd regained consciousness, she'd been crying constantly. She cried because of the pain, because the morphine left her depressed, because she had terrible nightmares, because she was worried about her children. Especially about the children. Charles had been with her nearly every minute she'd been in the hospital, but that meant he was almost never with Jimmy and Dorothea. The new nanny came with excellent credentials, he'd assured Lucy—but so what? Her babies didn't have their mother or their father either. Her babies must be scared to death.

The other problem with Charles always being with her: she still hadn't had a chance to ask the doctors how bad the damage really was. The neurologist had to talk to her to know if she could follow what he was saying, but all of the other doctors only talked to her husband, mostly in the hall outside the room, where Lucy couldn't hear. Whenever she asked Charles what they said, he told her not to worry, everything would be fine. She tried to believe him, even though she overheard him explaining to Ben Zaleski, his former assistant who was directing *Tell Laura I Love Her,* that delaying the filming for months, even a year, wouldn't make any difference. "Lucy can't do this project." Ben must have questioned him, because Charles got angry. "This is the least of my concerns right now," he hissed. "At this point I don't care if she ever makes another movie again." He was facing the window; he didn't notice the tears being squeezed from her tightly closed eyes.

This time he did see her tears, but he told her again not to worry. Even if they did move to a new place, it would all work out.

"But it wasn't the house's fault," she whispered. "The house tried to help."

Lucy knew it sounded ridiculous, but she believed this. The house had protected Dorothea in the closet, and warmed Lucy in the sun when she was so cold from losing all that blood. Most important, it had brought her Dorothea's beautiful voice through the monitor, a sound Lucy still associated with making it through all this. If indeed she was going to make it. Even that she wasn't sure of.

She'd already had two abdominal surgeries. Both arms and her right leg were immobilized in casts. They were planning to start skin grafts on her back tomorrow. Her back was burned, that was all Charles would say about it. She kept hearing something else in his voice, but maybe it was her imagination. Maybe she was going crazy.

"My sweet," Charles said now, and brought his lips down to the fingers poking out of her cast. "Please let me handle all this."

"But—"

"Hey there, Miss Lu Lu."

Janice walked in before Lucy could finish. She'd been by every day. Lucy tried to act happy to see her, but the truth was, she felt as numb about her old friend's visits as she did about the letters of support and flowers and teddy bears that had come from all over the country. Charles, on the other hand, seemed genuinely glad Janice was there. Janice even gave him a quick hug hello before sitting down in the chair at the foot of the bed.

Normally, Janice talked nonstop, obviously trying to distract Lucy, but this time Lucy said she had to ask Janice something.

"You're a social worker," Lucy said slowly. "Would you please tell my husband . . . I don't want him to sell our house."

Lucy knew that under normal circumstances, Charles would

have been annoyed with her for involving anyone in their private business. Of course he didn't feel that way now, or if he did, he didn't show it. His only reaction seemed to be aimed at Janice. The two of them seemed to be communicating something with their eyes.

"I wouldn't even think about this yet," Janice finally said.

"But I am," Lucy said.

"Here's an idea," Janice said, and winked. "Make your husband buy you a new house right on the ocean. Tell him this is what your friends want."

Charles wouldn't consider a beachfront house five years ago. He wanted views of the ocean, for Lucy, but he didn't want to be part of the crowd of industry people in the Malibu Colony. He also worried about their (then future) children drowning. The pool was bad enough.

But this time, he laughed and said it was a good idea.

Lucy didn't know how it happened, but all of a sudden, she heard herself start to scream. The sound seemed to come from her mouth with no more volition than the fluids that pumped in her body through the IVs and the nose tube and out through the catheter that embarrassed her every time Charles sat there and watched while the nurse changed the bag. The only thing she could move freely was her left leg, and she watched as the leg kicked out so hard the lunch tray the nurse had brought for him went flying.

She was every bit as surprised as Janice and Charles, who had jumped out of the way as the private duty nurse burst in, holding a syringe. The nurse had already given Lucy the shot when the orderlies arrived to clean up the mess. Lucy felt bad watching them scrubbing the roast beef and potatoes from the floor and the walls.

Was she really going crazy? Is that why she'd been screaming and kicking like a madwoman? Is that why her husband was whispering about her right now? She couldn't hold her eyes open anymore, but she wasn't asleep. Every time they said "poor Lucy," she heard them. Poor Lucy, poor Lucy, poor Lucy. Janice's voice: " . . . how bad the pain must be." Charles: " . . . doctor about giving her more." Janice: " . . . not long now." Charles: " . . . stand to see her suffer like this." Janice again: " . . . not long now."

From which Lucy concluded she really was about to die.

By the time she realized it wasn't true, it had all become connected in her mind, until losing her house was almost synonymous with dying. Before, she hadn't wanted to move, but she would have done it without hesitating if Charles had insisted. He was her husband and she had never defied him on anything important, much less something he felt as strongly about as this.

He didn't have to tell her what this meant to him. Even as he took out the real estate agent papers for her to sign, she knew how badly she would hurt him if she said no.

She didn't want to hurt him. She still loved him as much as ever. If anything she loved him more now because her love had turned desperate. She'd been in the hospital for almost two months, and even though she no longer feared dying, she didn't know if she would ever be herself again. She still couldn't use her right arm or walk without crutches. She was still having a seemingly endless series of grafts to heal the burns. She didn't even know what she looked like anymore because Charles had had them remove the mirror in her bathroom. And worst of all, she didn't know who she was.

Who did Charles see when he looked at her now? As she watched him walking back and forth, trying to persuade her to sell the house, she thought about that day, when he'd suddenly appeared to her while she was being stabbed and beaten. She couldn't tell him about that because he'd been so relieved when one of the doctors said head-injury victims rarely remember the events that precede their trauma. This was especially true in Lucy's case, the doctor claimed, because she was probably unconscious from very early on.

But still, it hurt Lucy when she discovered that Charles had been assuming she was raped. She'd come into the ICU hemorrhaging, but not from rape, the doctors explained to Charles—after the third abdominal surgery—because her bladder and uterus had both been damaged from the same line of deep stabs that had ripped through two arteries. Charles told Lucy about this because he thought she would feel better knowing she hadn't been sexually assaulted in addition to everything else.

He was wearing the black glasses she loved. The expression on his face was so gentle and kind; yet when he asked her why she was crying, she told him to leave her alone. And when he tried to reach for her anyway, to comfort her, she shrank away from his touch. It was quickly becoming a pattern: the more she ached for him to touch her, the more likely she was to rebuff all his attempts. Sometimes she told him she was in pain from the grafts or the physical therapy, but other times, she didn't offer any explanation. She knew her husband well enough to know he was too proud to ask for one.

When he started to withdraw from her, she focused on the positive effect that at least he was spending more time at the hotel with the children. She still hadn't been able to see Dorothea and Jimmy, but Charles put them on the phone with her every few days and she'd started to live for those calls. Jimmy was much quieter than before and she worried that he was taking her absence even harder than she expected. Dorothea, though, seemed to have a thousand things to say about life in a hotel. They served giant salads in big pink bowls. Grandma let them eat breakfast outside under a big tree. They had the best chocolate cake in the whole world. Daddy wouldn't let her go swimming in the pool. The nanny, Susannah, bought her candy at the little store.

"'Bye, Mommy," she would say, about every third time. The other two she would hang up suddenly because she was giggling or Susannah was calling or a favorite cartoon was starting or any of the hundred things that demanded a two-year-old's attention. It was such a relief to Lucy: her little girl seemed all right.

But now Charles was claiming that Dorothea was one of the reasons Lucy had to agree to move. "Please think about our daughter," he said, trailing off, as he set the papers on the tray and sat down on the chair farthest from Lucy's bed.

He'd already asked Lucy how the little girl would ever be able to go into her closet again. Lucy had reminded him that they were planning to put Dorothea in a bigger bedroom anyway, now that she was out of her crib. He didn't reply because, Lucy felt sure, this wasn't really about Dorothea. This was about his own feeling of powerlessness.

The police still hadn't caught the two men. Charles had said many times that he wanted to kill them for what they did to her. He'd used every contact he had to put pressure on the detectives assigned to the case, but it hadn't made a difference. Nothing he'd done had made any difference.

Buying a new house was something he could do for his family, for her. It was that simple, that urgent. Lucy understood all this, but she also understood that no matter where they moved, they might not be any safer. Plus, going back to Malibu was the only chance she had to have her old life back. A slim chance, she knew, but a chance.

Still, she would have done what Charles wanted if she hadn't let herself become convinced that dying and losing her house were somehow the same. Even as she told him no, she felt her loneliness intensify until she had to put the back of her hand in her mouth to keep from sobbing for him. He'd picked up the papers without saying anything, and now he was walking away. She wanted him to come back to the chair where he used to sit, near the head of her bed. She wanted him to kiss her fingers and stroke her face. Most of all, she wanted him to understand that because of who she was, who she had been, she really would have died for him that day. No matter what she'd become, a pathetic victim that everyone had to keep secrets from, a pitiful woman who cried whenever she was in pain, that day, she'd been a warrior in his cause. If only he understood this, then maybe he could tell her what she really needed to know: if it had been worth it.

fifteen

LUCY NEVER KIDDED herself that Charles could have bought another house without selling their old one. If he'd wanted to, he could have moved the family anywhere in Los Angeles or anywhere in the world. But instead he tried to go along with what she wanted, and so she tried not to mind all the things he'd changed when he moved with the children back to Malibu.

She came home from the rehab hospital to find a strange man standing by the front door. Her heart almost stopped, but then Charles explained that was John, their security guard. She found out later that John was the day-shift guard. There was another man for nights, and still another for weekends. And that was just the beginning of the differences.

An ugly electric fence had been installed between the house and the security gates. Dorothea had been moved to a new room, and her old room had been turned into a storage area. The sunroom was the biggest shock. It hadn't been redone; it had been removed.

Gone completely, and in its place was a continuation of the garden that had surrounded the pool—when they'd had a pool. Now two cypress trees stood where she and Dorothea had been swimming that day.

The monitor system had been enhanced with a whole-house intercom system. Charles had rehired his servant Tom and the cook Krista who'd worked for him in Beverly Hills, before he and Lucy got married. He'd managed to get them back by offering more money, and because they'd always liked him. Now there were four extra people at the house nearly all the time: Tom, Krista, the nanny, Susannah, and one of the security guards.

Everything seemed different, but the biggest shock to Lucy was how different the children were. Lucy had seen them in the hospital, but only for very short periods of time. She didn't know Jimmy was having so many nightmares from seeing her that day that their pediatrician had told Charles he should see a psychiatrist. And she'd never seen Dorothea have one of the breathing episodes that Charles told her often accompanied periods of extremely rapid heartbeat that were so frequent, he was already taking Dorothea to a pediatric cardiologist.

The first time Lucy saw one of these episodes, she wanted to curse her own weakness that she was still using her cane, that her wrist was still so weak. If only she could have grabbed Dorothea and held her tightly in her arms. Her baby was talking so beautifully now, in perfect sentences, with so many new words, but she was gasping between sentences. The longer it went on, the more scared the little girl became. The entire time, she held her hand to her heart, like a tiny Napoleon.

Lucy didn't blame Charles for not telling her about their children's problems before. She knew her doctors had told him the less stress, the quicker her recovery would be. Maybe it was even true that if she had known, she might have healed even more slowly.

She finally understood that Charles hadn't only been withdrawing from her in the hospital. He'd had his hands full taking Jimmy and Dorothea to doctors. He'd been trying to deal with everything as well as he knew how, and she felt bad that she hadn't given him more credit. Even Janice said, "I don't think I've ever seen a man work harder to care for his family. It really got to me, especially when you were in intensive care. I told Peter that if I ever end up in the ICU, he better get down on his knees and pray for me non-stop like Charles did for you."

Lucy had a vague memory of this. She was coming out of her coma, and she saw her husband at the side of her bed. She knew he was praying, and she wasn't surprised. He'd grown up in a traditional Irish Catholic family, and Lucy knew that he still considered himself Catholic, even though the only times they'd been inside a church were when the children were baptized.

The first six months at home for Lucy were spent in a blur of continuing pain and pain pills, doctor visits and daily physical therapy, as she tried to help Charles take care of Dorothea and Jimmy and tried to reconnect with her husband whenever they had time alone. Even after the doctor finally pronounced Lucy physically able to have sex, Charles was so afraid of hurting her that they spent weeks and weeks only holding hands. During one of these nights, he asked Lucy if she would convert to Catholicism and she told him yes. By spring, they were going to church with Margaret and the children, and half the time, Lucy was able to leave her cane at home. But they never went anywhere else, and they never had anyone over.

While Lucy was in the hospital, she'd promised to have Janice and her husband to dinner as soon as she was home. She did invite them several times, but she always ended up canceling. She told Janice that Dorothea was having too many episodes or Jimmy seemed especially stressed, but the truth was, Charles had asked her to reschedule. He thought their family needed more time before they were ready to deal with visitors. He said the same thing to anyone who wanted to see them—not yet.

Walter, who used to spend an evening with them at least every other week, had been over only twice in eight months, and both those visits were less than an hour, up in Charles's office, purely business talk. Ben Zaleski and Charles's other assistants used to drop by for drinks, but they'd given up. Everyone was giving up, including all of Charles's friends and acquaintances from the studio, the actors he had used over the years and stayed friendly with and all the people Lucy had gotten close to during the making of *Helena*.

By summer, even Charles's mother was spending most of her time away from the house, visiting friends in Florida again. Though Margaret wouldn't ever tell her son he was wrong about anything, Lucy knew she'd been missing the social life they used to have, the dinners and parties and going out on the town. Margaret had even seemed sad when Lucy canceled Janice and Peter the last time, though she'd never met them.

It was a Saturday night in early August when, as Janice joked to Lucy, she and Peter were finally allowed into Castle Keenan. They arrived at seven o'clock. The night was hotter than usual because of a thick blanket of humidity that even the ocean breeze hadn't been able to blow away. They couldn't swim because the pool was gone. Charles didn't want to use the pit for barbeque. So they were staying inside, about to have a formal dinner that was being prepared by the cook, Krista.

"How do you afford all this?" Janice whispered. "He hasn't made a movie for what, two years?"

Lucy and Dorothea were giving Janice a tour of the house. They were upstairs, in the hall where Susannah's and the children's rooms were. Jimmy was downstairs watching Charles and Peter play chess.

"He has investments," Lucy said vaguely. Charles had told Lucy about this many times. In 1971, when the first movie hit, he and Walter started buying property all over L.A. They were only planning to set up a fund for future films, but some of the property turned out to be extremely valuable. Charles said he had enough money now to last the rest of their lives, and he might not make any more movies. He was writing scripts because he could do that at home, but he wasn't sure if he'd ever want to make them into films. Maybe he would let Walter attach another director. Maybe he'd throw them into a drawer.

The first priority, as Charles said constantly, was his wife and his children. The family was Lucy's first priority too, but acting had made her feel alive, and she missed it. She missed everything about their life in the business, even the shallow parts like seeing a billboard with her own face or reading the studio's congratulations ads to Charles.

Not that she was complaining. She was a Catholic now, and she knew that the point of life was accepting God's will. Still, she was glad for tonight because it was relaxing being with Janice. Even though they hadn't seen each other since Lucy got out of the hospital, they talked on the phone at least once a week, and Lucy was grateful to have such a good friend.

They were in Dorothea's room, where the little girl was busy feeding her stuffed animals inside her playhouse. Charles had ordered the playhouse from Sweden because they used natural wood, untreated with any chemicals. It was huge, but it fit easily into Dorothea's room, which, as Janice had pointed out, was as big as their entire place in Venice. Lucy hadn't responded. She and Charles had disagreed about whether Dorothea needed such a large room. The playhouse wouldn't fit in a smaller one; it wouldn't even fit easily into the downstairs playroom, but that wasn't a problem to Lucy, who liked the idea of putting it outside, where Dorothea would be getting fresh air and some sun. Charles was afraid she'd hurt herself if she had one of her breathing attacks and lost consciousness. "If she passes out, I want her falling on a rug," he said. Specifically, the very soft rug, several inches thick, that he'd chosen for Dorothea's floor.

"And you?" Janice said. "What about you, glamour girl?"

They were sitting on the window seat, watching Dorothea, sipping wine that Tom had brought up for them.

"What about me?" Lucy said.

"When can I tell all your fans at my job to expect the next Lucy Dobbins picture?"

"All my fans? You told me you work with two people, Janice."

"But those two people loved *The Passion of Helena Lott.*" Janice laughed. "I think it was their favorite movie ever, except maybe *E.T.*"

"E.T. phone home!" Dorothea said, sticking her face out the playhouse window.

"I hope Charles doesn't hear her say that." Lucy giggled. "He thinks that movie having the highest box office gross ever is proof of the decline of civilization."

"He needs to do my job for a day. Then let him talk about the decline of civilization." Janice nodded at Dorothea and lowered her voice. "God, she looks flushed. Does the doctor say that's part of her heart stuff?"

Lucy deflected the question by getting up and taking Dorothea her bunny. She didn't want to tell Janice that they'd changed cardiologists so many times, she had no idea what was really part of the heart-racing problem and what wasn't. Charles was unsatisfied with every doctor they'd found, primarily because the doctors couldn't find anything to make their daughter all right again. He'd done the same thing with psychiatrists for Jimmy, until they'd finally given up on that altogether.

When she sat back down, Janice said, "So really, Lu, when are you going to be in another movie?"

She sighed. "I don't know."

"You are doing something this year, aren't you?"

"This year? No. It's already August, and—"

"But I read somewhere that they still need an actress for that movie you were going to be in. I don't remember the details, but you saw that, right?"

Lucy nodded. She knew all the details by heart. The casting department had found an English stage actress to play the lead in *Tell Laura I Love Her,* but then the actress backed out because of a dispute over the filming schedule. Ben Zaleski had actually called Lucy's agent when Ben couldn't get through to Charles, but Lucy had told her agent it was out of the question.

"Why don't you call them?" Janice paused. "I think it would be good for you to act again. It can't be healthy for you to stay trapped at home all the time, even if you do have one damned fine house."

"It just won't work."

Before Janice could say anything else, Susannah was at the door, ready to help Dorothea get her pajamas on. Both children were going to bed before the adults had dinner, the same way they did every night now.

Susannah was still doing most of the child care. Whenever Lucy asked Charles if the two of them could go back to doing it themselves, he said he wanted to give her more time to heal first. It made Lucy sad, even though she knew he was probably right.

"I'll get her pajamas," Lucy said.

Susannah said she'd get Jimmy then. Janice said she'd better go see if Peter was all right. "He was a little nervous about meeting the Great Man," she told Lucy. "I promised I wouldn't leave him too long without checking in."

Dorothea was already moving her stuffed animals back to the bed.

"What pj's, peanut pie?"

"The pink ones with the footies."

"That will be too hot, honey."

"Mommy!" The little girl rolled her eyes. "Turn up the air conditioner!"

"There's only so much air-conditioning in the world," Lucy began, but then she realized Dorothea was only parroting Charles. He didn't agree when Lucy tried to tell him they should be trying to conserve energy. He said his family being comfortable was all he cared about.

She went to the drawer and got out the pink footie pajamas.

The one thing Lucy always insisted on doing herself was tucking Dorothea into bed. She would have happily tucked in Jimmy too, but he would rarely let her. He was too old, he said, though he was barely five. He didn't even like to be walked to his room.

Dorothea usually asked for a song, and singing to her was the best part of Lucy's day. The little girl didn't like only children's songs, and that night she asked Lucy for "Let It Be." When Lucy was finished, Dorothea clapped and hugged her.

She'd just kissed her daughter when she realized Charles was standing at the door, watching them.

"Good night, sweetie."

"Night, Mommy."

She turned off the light, but it wasn't dark with the three night-lights Dorothea had. They never shut the door either, so Dorothea wouldn't be scared.

Charles told her dinner was ready. They were halfway down the hall when he said, "Janice thinks you want to be talked into doing *Tell Laura I Love Her.* She's asked me to participate."

Lucy looked up at him. "So, are you?"

"Of course not. I know you don't want to do it. I've told Ben that several times."

"Several times? How many times has he asked?"

"I don't know. More than three, less than eight. Several. Why?"

"Recently?"

"A few weeks ago. He said your agent told him no, but he wanted to hear it from me." Charles stopped and looked at her. "Is there a problem?"

"I think I'm getting another headache." It was true. She could feel the back of her head throbbing.

His voice grew soft. "Would you like me to rub it for you?"

"Maybe later," she said, and smiled. He rubbed her head nearly every night, and it helped so much. More than the pain pills Lucy was trying not to take any more of. They made her feel dull and lifeless.

During dinner, they sat together and listened to Peter talk about the rising cost of housing in so many areas of L.A. that was contributing to a sharp increase in homelessness. Lucy wondered what Charles was thinking, since most of his money had been made from this real estate market. Most of their money, she thought, because she was benefiting from the money too. Even this delicious veal and asparagus was a benefit of the money. But she would rather have to cook, herself, which she liked doing, even though she wasn't good at it like Krista, and know she hadn't caused someone else to lose their home.

"I was homeless myself," she said, apropos of nothing. Probably because she'd had another glass of wine. Actually, two more glasses of wine. Her headache was her excuse.

"It's true, you were," Janice said. "Peter knows the story of how we met."

"I mean before," Lucy said. "I was homeless when I was ten years old, until my uncle and aunt took me in. And then I was homeless again in Nashville for a while."

Janice nodded. "You know, I think that's another reason you should do that movie about the Vietnam nurse. A lot of the boys who died in Vietnam were poor, and you could really bring something to the part."

"Interesting," Lucy said, and took another drink.

"Thank you, Tom," Charles said. The servant had just handed him a basket of Italian bread. Charles took a piece and passed it to Lucy, while he explained to Janice why her position, though interesting, was untrue. "Good actors like Lucy don't need to have a common background with the character. In fact, many of the finest actors will tell you a part that is too familiar hinders their creativity."

Lucy was expecting Janice to argue with him, as in the old days. Instead her friend was blushing with embarrassment. "Oh," Janice said. "I guess I showed what I know."

"But some actors don't feel that way," Lucy said quickly. She turned to Charles. "Remember when Anthony told us that his father emigrating from Germany helped him understand Max?"

Max von Durren was Anthony Mills's character in *Helena:* the patriotic German merchant who falls in love with Helena, and ultimately makes a decision to leave Germany to help her save her Jewish pupils.

"Anthony isn't in the same league as you, my sweet. He is a journeyman; you are an artist."

Lucy smiled at her husband, even though she was very surprised by how harsh he sounded about Anthony. Anthony was a good actor, who had nothing but respect for Charles. He was also a friend of theirs, or he had been, before.

"By the way," Peter said to Lucy, "Janice and I both loved *The Passion of Helena Lott.* We thought you were terrific."

"Thanks," Lucy said. Peter seemed nice, and she was happy for Janice. He was such a normal-looking guy, the kind you see everywhere in California: average height, average build, permanent tan, longish blond hair, well-trimmed sideburns and beard, colorful print shirt, blue jeans, sandals. He looked a lot younger than her own husband, and he was: thirty-one to Charles's forty-two.

"Since Lucy is an artist," Janice said, "shouldn't she be making more movies?"

Lucy thought, wow, she is never going to give this up. The thought pleased her more than she would have expected.

"Yes, and she will make more movies," Charles said. "When she's ready."

"Well, she seems ready now," Janice said. "Aren't you ready, Lu? Come on, say yes. Do it for my mom, who loves bragging that her daughter is friends with a real movie star."

"I don't know," Lucy said, but she laughed.

"That's Jimmy," Charles said, nodding at the monitor. He was crying out in his sleep, another nightmare. Susannah had just left for a party with friends.

"I'll go," Lucy said, but Charles was already standing. He put his napkin down and walked out of the room without saying a word.

Janice waited a moment before she whispered, "Did I say something wrong?"

"No," Lucy said, gulping down the rest of her wine. "Don't worry about it."

By the time Charles returned, the three of them were eating dessert, a rich chocolate cake layered with strawberries, and laughing about one of Janice's more bizarre client stories. When Tom asked Charles if he wanted any cake, Charles said no.

He was so quiet for the rest of the evening that Lucy could tell he was upset. So could Janice, but she wasn't worried about him, like Lucy was. Before she and Peter left, she took Lucy aside and told her that she had to confront Charles about his "withdrawing and controlling behavior."

"I thought you liked him now," Lucy said.

"I do, but come on, Lu, you have to work. You have to see people, you have to go out. You and the kids are like prisoners, and I know, he's scared something will happen to you, but that doesn't mean you should accept not having a life."

They were standing over by the piano, whispering. Peter and Charles were already outside. Janice had said she had to run to the bathroom, and dragged Lucy back in with her.

"I have a life, Janice."

"Do you? Or do you have to go along with him or he stops talking? How often does he pull this withdrawal thing? It's one of the ways some guys control women, withdraw—"

"It's not like that," Lucy said.

"Please just think about it, okay? Maybe you guys need counseling. You've been through a lot, but I'm telling you, he isn't getting over this like he should."

Lucy stood up straighter. Janice had never understood Charles, and this didn't seem all that different from the things she used to say. Especially since Lucy knew Charles didn't withdraw to control her, but because he couldn't handle his feelings any other way and remain what he called "civilized." It was very important to him to remain civilized. This was one of the things she'd loved about him from the beginning, that he never yelled or even raised his voice—unlike her uncle.

After Peter and Janice left, Lucy asked Charles if he was all right. He told her yes, but she still knew something was wrong. When they got in bed about a half hour later, she turned toward him to let him know she wouldn't mind having sex. They were back to making love on a regular basis, though they still did it much less frequently than before, and always quickly, in the dark so he wouldn't see her, with as little touching as possible so he wouldn't feel her scars. She told him she couldn't handle it any other way, and he seemed to understand, though she knew he longed for the way they used to be. The strange part was Lucy knew that she was probably being silly, but she couldn't help it. The plastic surgeon had told her that she was healing incredibly well: most of the scars had already become thin white lines, and the few that hadn't were obviously headed in that direction. But Charles had loved her skin so much before, when it was perfect, and she couldn't stand the idea that she wouldn't be as attractive to him now, especially when there was nothing she could do about it.

After they had sex, when they were lying next to each other, he told her he was sorry he'd been so quiet earlier. He had been a little upset—with Janice. "I found it very tiring that she kept returning to the same subject. I know she means well, but she has no idea what you've been through or she wouldn't harp on you doing another picture."

"I would like to work again though," Lucy said slowly. "I realized tonight that I would love to do Ben's movie, if there was any way."

"I understand." He was holding her hand, and he brought it to his lips and kissed it. "But you know how hard production is, and you're just not up to it yet."

"I'm a lot better though. I think I—"

"You still have headaches every day. You have trouble sleeping. Your right leg goes numb if you have to sit still for long periods. Your wrist—"

"I think I could do it, Charles. I really do."

He paused for a moment. "They're shooting in Asia for at least a month. Ben told me. You don't want to be away from home that long, do you?"

"No," she said. Of course she couldn't leave the children, and she couldn't take them out of the country with all the problems they were having. It was out of the question.

But the next morning, Lucy found herself wondering if Ben would be willing to work around this. She wasn't sure it was even possible, but she knew how desperate Ben was to have her. While her husband was in his office, she impulsively picked up the phone and called Ben. And she was glad she did because he agreed immediately to film all her scenes in California. They could shoot the battlefield scenes on location, but have the art department create a field hospital set here for Lucy to work in. Maybe even in Malibu. He said *MASH* had been filmed at Malibu Creek State Park, so why not?

She hung up the phone and went up to Charles's office. His desk was covered with paper, but on top she saw the folder marked "Sept. 21," where he kept a record of all his dealings with the detectives who claimed to be still looking for the two men. He told her he was making notes for a meeting he had tomorrow at the police station.

She sat down on the leather couch across from him. She thought she would wait, but then she couldn't. She had to share her good news. He listened to her whole excited monologue before he said it wasn't going to happen.

"You're not up to doing a film yet, as I said last night. I don't intend to let you find that out by hurting yourself."

Before she could say anything, he picked up thc phone. And right in front of her, he told Ben that Lucy wasn't capable of making a decision like this after what had happened to her. She was already staring at him like he'd lost his mind when he said something that shocked her even more. "If you still insist on casting my wife," Charles said, "now that I've told you the situation, I will ask Walter to pull out of the project."

If Walter pulled out of the project, the studio would pull out, and Charles knew it. Ben was a new director, with no track record other than working as Charles's assistant. But Ben was a friend, and this was his dream. He'd been trying to get this film made for more than four years.

No surprise, Ben concluded that he couldn't use Lucy in the movie, after all.

When Charles hung up, he said, "It may not seem fair, but please try to understand. It's no different from us telling Dorothea that she can't play with the kitchen knives."

"Dorothea?" Lucy was sputtering. "Dorothea is our child."

"And you are my Lucy. No matter what it takes, I will never let anything happen to you again." He stood up. "Shouldn't we be getting ready for mass? It's already eleven."

"I'm not going," she said. "I have to call Pam."

Pam was Lucy's agent. She'd never really gotten her any work because Charles had done that. But Pam could get her work, of course she could. She was a VP at a very prestigious agency.

"You don't want to fight me on this," he said, looking into her eyes. "I promise you, you won't win."

Every time she'd heard him say this before, it turned out to be true. No one ever won against Charles, whether he was up against the president of the studio or the head of a tabloid he was threatening to sue if they wrote a single word about Lucy's attack. It was part of the reason he'd been so successful in a business known for power plays: once he thought he was right, he would never give in.

"I don't want to fight you," she whispered, trying not to cry. "I just want to be an actress again. Can't you understand?"

"I do understand," he said, and his voice was so sincere, she actually thought he did. "For you, it's about working. But for me, it's about my life, my heart, my soul. It's about what I vowed the day I found you half dead, what I promised God I would do if only he let you survive. You are everything to me. You are the only woman I've ever loved, the only woman I ever will love for the rest of my life."

She'd heard this before too: the vow and the promise (which were the same: to protect her) and even the last two romantic lines. He said it when he was explaining why he wanted to accompany her shopping and to the park and to all her doctor visits, why he didn't want her to go anywhere alone or with just the children. He said it when the topic of work first came up in May. He said it when she asked if they would ever go back to a normal life with friends and dinners out and something to live for other than just staying safe.

She never doubted that he believed it, and she didn't doubt it this time either. This was the problem: she knew it was all true, and she even knew how it all added up together. He'd never lost a fight and this was the most important fight of his life. What conclusion was possible, other than that he would win now too?

sixteen

BUT LUCY COULDN'T give up. It wasn't just that she wanted to act again, she *had* to act again, though she couldn't explain why, even to herself. It certainly wasn't about being happy. She'd been much happier before her agent started trying to get her a part—and before she'd found out how completely unimportant she was in this business.

A lot of studio execs seemed very interested in casting Lucy, until they found out that Charles would have nothing to do with the project. Apparently, both her Oscar nomination for *Brave Horseman* and her critical success in *Helena* had been attributed throughout much of the industry to him. In *Brave Horseman,* so the rumor went, he'd not only written a part for Lucy that most actresses would kill for, but he'd used all his talents as a director to make her look good. In *Helena,* though he didn't direct, he'd done extensive script revisions to enhance his wife's role and even strong-armed his friend Derrick Mabe into letting him have input into everything from

Lucy's wardrobe to the angles of her close-ups. Pam told Lucy this was obviously horseshit, but she admitted she'd heard some of it before. Why hadn't Lucy herself ever heard it? Of course Charles must have known, but Lucy didn't blame him for keeping it from her. This was back when he was helping her believe in herself, the opposite of what he was doing to her now.

Even those execs who did want Lucy initially, didn't want her bad enough to alienate Charles and Walter. This was what Pam kept reporting to Lucy, and Lucy knew that Charles had been on the phone again, asking someone not to cast his poor wife, who was still suffering far too much to handle the incredible demands of shooting a film. He didn't have to tell any of them why she was suffering. They all knew about the attack, and most of them knew a lot of the details. Like Pam said, word gets around. Both Pam and Lucy were positive the attack had absolutely nothing to do with why they wouldn't cast her, though of course the studio people comforted themselves by pretending it did. It was all about kissing up to Charles, especially now that he and Walter were planning a brand-new movie that promised to be the biggest-budget film made in 1984.

The movie was called *Master of Dreams.* It was based on a strange sci-fi script that Charles had written, set fifty years in the future, when a group of scientists discover Dream Control, or DC. The idea is that by intense concentration, dreams can be manipulated to any desired outcome. The scientists claim DC will bring on a new utopia, where everyone will have more freedom and more creativity, and also help find solutions to enduring problems like war and cancer. But when DC falls into the hands of a greedy corporation planning to make employees more productive by chaining them to work as they sleep, the scientists have to get help from the only group who knows how to resist DC. Called the Uncons because of their belief in the premodern dreams the unconscious supplies, they will have to save humanity from becoming slaves who have lost their ability to dream.

The tagline for the movie poster was: *Who Will Control Your Dreams?* Walter had a mockup created to show the studio VPs, who went wild over the idea of what they called a "futuristic Western." To Lucy, the truly wild part was that Charles had managed to convince everybody he was making a film, even though he was probably never going to shoot a single frame.

He was very up front about this with her, but only with her, and she could tell he wasn't concerned in the slightest that she would tell anybody. And he was right. She wouldn't publicly turn on her own husband. No matter what he'd done to her, she couldn't bring herself to do that to him. She also hoped that if, by some bizarre chance, he did make this movie, maybe he'd let her act in it.

While Pam was trying to find someone, anyone, who would hire Lucy, Charles was trying to convince Lucy that her "obsession" with her career was hurting their relationship, not what he was doing to prevent her from getting a part she wasn't physically ready for. To prove it, he agreed to go to counseling together, but the counselor he chose was their parish priest. Father Drake was an older man, very conventional, and Lucy wasn't surprised when he said they both needed to put their marriage first, especially as neither of them needed to work to support their family. "The world provides many distractions," Father Drake said. "The lure of money and fame can be very strong, but God tells us that these things will not bring us the peace we desire."

On the wall behind the priest was a gorgeous picture of the Virgin Mary. Lucy had been looking at it since they sat down. Her veil was the richest blue and her halo was so radiant it seemed to catch the sun coming in the window across the room. But it was the expression on her face that really got to Lucy: the sweetness and wisdom and especially the complete serenity. No wonder Catholics prayed to her, Lucy thought. She was a human being who'd lost her only child in the cruelest way imaginable, and yet she still believed.

"I don't want money and fame," Lucy said, because it was true. She wanted serenity like Mary's, but no matter how hard she prayed she still startled awake every morning with a dread that made no sense to her. She looked away from the painting. "I just want a job."

"Have you considered volunteer work? It can be very rewarding, and you could do it for a few hours a week until you're fully recovered."

She'd already had to leave the office to walk around when her right leg went numb. Otherwise, she would have denied she wasn't fully recovered now, the way she had with Pam.

Charles was looking at her, but she still said it. "I'm an actress. That's what I do. If I could volunteer to act, I would."

It was getting harder and harder for Lucy to believe that she'd ever really been an actress. Charles had made her successful, but more than that, he'd given her faith in her own talent. Now she wondered if she'd had any talent in the first place, or if she'd been just like a thousand other starlets, with one big difference. A famous man had fallen in love with her. Maybe he'd only given her the career the same way he'd bought her the house, to make her happy.

"Why is acting so important to you, Lucy?" Father Drake said. "You have two lovely children and a very devoted husband. Your family has suffered a great deal, but you've also been given much joy."

Charles took her hand, and she said, "I like pretending I'm someone else," knowing it would bother her husband. It wasn't even true. She used to like acting because it made her feel everything more, including her own life.

Father Drake looked confused, but he turned to Charles and asked what he thought.

"I wish Lucy could understand that I'm only trying to take care of her." His jaw was tight. "I've made so many more movies than she has, and I know how difficult filming can be in the best of circumstances. If she has a relapse now, it might be years before she is back to being herself."

"But shouldn't that be my decision, Father?"

"I'm sure you've heard 'As God is the head of the church, so the husband is the head of the family.' Sometimes this is taken to mean that the husband has more rights than the wife, but this isn't so. The true meaning is that to a husband is given a great responsibility for the welfare of his wife and children, both physically and spiritually." Father Drake looked at Lucy. "Isn't it heartening that your husband is taking this responsibility very seriously?"

She said yes, but when she and Charles were back in the car, she told him she was finished with Father Drake's marriage counseling. "No wonder you wanted to see him," she snapped. "He's your puppet."

"I'm sorry it didn't work out," he said, and he sounded genuinely sorry. He always did.

"I'm going to a therapist," she said. "Somebody who has some training for a change."

"Fine," he said, "I'll go with you."

"No. I want somebody to hear what I have to say. Just me. Lucy Dobbins nobody, not Charles Keenan's wife."

"You're not nobody, Lucy."

"Sure." She turned on the radio, and cranked up the rock song. She threw her arm out the window, even though it made her feel like a stupid kid.

Janice helped her find a therapist who specialized in women's issues. Of course Charles did go with her because he went everywhere with her, and there was nothing she could do about that. Even her neurologist said she wasn't allowed to drive until she was sure she wouldn't lose feeling in her leg.

He had to wait outside the office though. It was her appointment, so she could tell the psychologist exactly what she thought. She was glad she'd booked two full hours because she had a lot to say. And Tracey, the psychologist, seemed to really understand. She said Lucy's husband was obviously very controlling, and his keeping Lucy from getting any movie roles was both patronizing and aggressive, an act of symbolic violence against Lucy's ability to exercise her own free will. She also said he was using the attack by the two men as an excuse to dominate both her and the children.

Lucy nodded, but she said, "I don't see how he dominates the children exactly."

"He tells them what to do in the name of caring for them. He doesn't let them freely explore their world."

"He does love them though."

"Maybe, but what kind of love? For the controlling personality, everyone in his life is viewed through the lens of his own desire for power."

Lucy looked at the door that opened into the waiting room. She thought about Dorothea giggling this morning when Charles was crawling up to the window of her playhouse, making what were supposed to be elephant noises, but really sounded like a cross between a rooster and a donkey. And last night, when Charles had spent almost two hours sitting with Jimmy because the little boy couldn't sleep. Charles had even written a story for Jimmy about a brave five-year-old with red hair who slays dragons and witches wherever he goes by challenging them to a game of chess and then tricking them into sticking their necks out while playing, so he can chop off their heads. Jimmy loved that story. He was already very good at chess.

Tracey had moved on to another topic. "I assume he also tries to control what happens between you in the bedroom. Tell me, does sex seem unusually important to him?"

"I don't know if it's unusual, but sure, it's important to him." Lucy paused. "It used to be one of the best parts of our relationship."

"Best to him or to you? Did you have orgasms, Lucy?"

"I don't think that's any of your business."

"There's nothing to be ashamed of. You were nineteen when you married, and a woman that age can't even know what she wants, much less know how to ask for it."

"But I did have orgasms. If you must know, I always did, even the first weekend we were together. Now I don't, but that's not his fault. I don't feel very sexy right now."

Tracey nodded. How can she nod? Lucy thought. Didn't I just tell her she was wrong?

"So you still have sex, but no orgasms. Would you say you're only doing it for him?"

"I guess so."

"And he accepts this?"

"I've told him it's the only way I can."

"Do you feel you have to keep him satisfied?"

"I don't feel I have to."

"Are you worried he'll have an affair?"

"No," Lucy said, though it had crossed her mind, but not because of anything Charles had done. It was more because of how damaged she was, not even physically, but in some other essential way that she couldn't put her finger on.

"Why do you think you continue to comply with his sexual demands?"

"I told you, he isn't demanding sex."

"But he does expect sex from you even though he knows you don't enjoy it. He expects you to meet all his needs. This is typical of the controlling personality because their own needs are always more real than the needs of anyone around them."

Lucy wanted to walk out right then, but she was afraid of being rude. She also didn't want to explain to Charles why she hadn't stayed the full two hours.

But a few minutes later, when Tracey suggested that Charles could be dangerous if Lucy ever told him no, Lucy finally said she was finished with the appointment.

"I know it's difficult to face this," Tracey said. Her eyes were sympathetic. "Most women in your position wouldn't have even taken the first step of coming here today."

"The first step?" Lucy said irritably. "And what's the last step, leaving him?"

Tracey said of course she couldn't tell Lucy to leave him, but she did want Lucy to know that she had a responsibility to protect herself and her children. "If a man like that finds his power over the family threatened, he becomes increasingly desperate to regain control." Tracey added that desperate and even dangerous behaviors were often the result, particularly when the man, like Charles, had already shown a propensity for violence.

Lucy wondered what she was talking about, but then she remembered Tracey's point that Charles keeping Lucy from getting any movie roles was some kind of "symbolic violence."

"You know what?" she suddenly said. "I don't think you know a damn thing about violence." Lucy could hear a trace of Southern accent in her own voice for the first time in years. "Violence is when you get your face slapped raw by your uncle while he's yelling that you're a cock-teasing little bitch. Violence is when a guy takes a lighter to your back and then kicks you in the head when you throw up from the smell of your own burning skin. What Charles did, violent? Even if he placed an ad in *Variety* saying I was the worst actress in Hollywood and I never worked again, that would be a walk in the park compared to violence." Lucy stood up and shook her head. "I can't believe you don't have even the tiniest bit of sympathy for him. The man came home and found the woman he loved almost murdered. Can you imagine what that was like?"

Tracey told Lucy that her anger was a normal reaction to having her defenses questioned. Out in the waiting room, Tracey told Charles that the fee was $260 and she would take a check.

On the way to the Mercedes, Lucy impulsively reached out and hugged him.

"What's this for?" he said softly, but he didn't let her go.

"I thought you might need a hug," she said, though now that he had his arms around her, she remembered how safe she used to feel there, and she had to resist pushing him away.

He was so much happier on the drive home that Lucy almost didn't call Pam back. She didn't want to hear any more bad news; she was tired of being angry with Charles. But Tom had written "urgent" next to the message, so Lucy went to the breakfast room and called her agent. And she was glad she did because Pam was calling to report that Lucy was finally being offered a part.

She didn't even have to do a screen test because the director loved her work. The casting people would get Lucy the script tomorrow, but Pam had already read it. She said it was exactly what Lucy wanted: a serious drama that was being filmed entirely in L.A.

The director, Brett Marcus, was someone Lucy had heard Charles complain about before, but she couldn't remember why. But as Pam told Lucy, if her husband was an enemy of this guy, all the better. Then Charles and Walter would have no influence on him.

"You're set, baby," Pam said. "Here we go."

When Lucy hung up, her primary feeling was relief. She decided not to tell Charles right away though. What if she hated the script? Then they would have the argument for nothing. Of course it would be a huge argument because she had won. He would be mad at her for days, but eventually he would get over it.

That night, Lucy felt so much more confident that she decided to risk having sex with Charles the way they used to. She let him look at her naked body and touch her anywhere he wanted, including the scars. He told her she was gorgeous, and she knew he meant it because he was as excited as he had been the first weekend they were together. The next morning, they woke up holding each other and smiling, and they had breakfast on the balcony, just the two of them. It was already December, but it was warm enough that day to be comfortable. Lucy didn't even mind seeing the electric fence. The view was still great. The ocean had never looked more glorious.

The script arrived a little before eleven. Tom brought it to her in the playroom, where Dorothea and Jimmy and Susannah were involved in a game. Charles was in his office talking to Russell Daley, the cinematographer he'd worked with for years, who was also interested in doing *Master of Dreams.* For a movie that was never going to be made, it was proving to be a lot of work in preproduction. She wasn't sure why he was keeping up this pretense, unless it was for Walter's sake. Even though he and Walter had argued plenty over the years, Charles was fiercely loyal to him. It was something she'd always admired about her husband—except when Charles was collaborating with Walter to keep her from working.

As Lucy read the script, she became more and more excited. Pam was right; it was the perfect part for her, playing Adele, the wife of a senator who'd lost his hope after their son drowned. "We still have two daughters who need you," Lucy read aloud, with feeling. She was typecast as a savior, just like Joan and Helena; as the one who would bring the senator back to himself. She could do this role in her sleep.

While the children had lunch, she made acting notes. The difficulty of this part, she wrote, is that Adele has also lost her son. How can she reach through her own damage to help Martin (the senator)? Won't she feel resentment that her pain is so secondary (at least as it's written now) to his?

Lucy shoved the script behind the toaster when she heard Charles coming.

"I have to meet Russell." Charles had his car keys in his hand. "I told him today is the wrong day for this, but it can't be helped." He leaned over and kissed her. "Sorry, my sweet. You know I wouldn't leave you if I didn't have to."

"I understand," Lucy said.

"I'll be home at six-thirty, seven at the latest." He walked over and kissed Jimmy and Dorothea. "Before you two go to bed."

She watched him walk out, and then she picked up the phone to call Pam. She had a feeling Pam would jump at the chance to set up a meeting this afternoon, and she did.

"I have to have lunch with some dickhead producer, but I can make it by two. Will that work?"

"Sure," Lucy said. "But I'll need a ride home, and I have to be back by five-thirty."

"Not a problem," Pam said. "I'll drive you myself."

Krista was leaving for her night off. Lucy asked if she would mind driving out of her way and dropping her at Pam's office in West Hollywood.

"As long as Mr. Keenan doesn't mind," Krista said.

"He doesn't," Lucy said, only feeling a little bad for lying. Krista worked for her too, didn't she?

She hurried upstairs to put on her lucky violet dress. She also had to do her makeup, but she brought most of it with her, to do in the car. They had to rush to get to Pam's.

She made it on time and she and Pam were only a few minutes late for the meeting, which was held over drinks at The Beverly Hills Hotel. The casting director and a guy from marketing were there too, but Brett did most of the talking. What a nice guy, Lucy thought. He praised her talent and told her his vision for the movie. She told him her concerns about the way Adele was written. They talked at length about finding character motivation, what she could bring to each scene and what she might need reworked in the script. Lucy couldn't remember when she'd ever had a better conversation about acting. Probably because Brett had started out as an actor, he brought something different to directing than Charles did.

Different, but not better. Lucy had no bad thoughts about her husband and no reason to feel guilty, though she couldn't help feeling a little bad when they brought the salads and she remembered her little girl's excitement over these pink bowls. She didn't want to think about Charles and the children staying here when she'd been in the hospital, how hard that had been on them—but on her too, of course. She'd suffered plenty. All she was trying to do was move on with her life, was that so wrong?

At four o'clock she told Pam they really had to run. The drive home would take less than an hour and a half, even with traffic, but she wanted to be on the safe side.

All the way back, she and Pam talked about what a fabulous opportunity this was. And how Lucy should approach Charles with the news. "After a blow job," Pam said, smirking. "You'll already be on your knees. He should appreciate that position."

"He's not like that," Lucy said.

"Of course he isn't, kiddo. Didn't mean anything by it." She lit another cigarette. "Let's get back to Brett. Isn't he just a doll?"

Lucy opened the window, though she knew she'd smell like smoke. Everyone at the restaurant had been smoking too; it couldn't be helped. She'd just have to get in the shower right when she walked in the door.

They made it back by 5:10, plenty of time for the shower. Lucy said hello to the security guard, and rushed inside, only to find Charles standing right there, waiting for her.

He hadn't gone to meet Russell. He'd gone into the city, but at the last minute, he'd changed his mind and decided to come home. On the way back, he'd stopped at the jeweler and picked out a present for her: a beautiful milky pearl necklace that was still clutched in his hand, even though he'd been pacing the front hall for two hours.

Before she could say anything to explain, he threw the necklace against the wall with such force that the string broke and the pearls went rolling all over the hall floor.

"Charles, wait—"

"You didn't even leave me a note." His voice wasn't loud, but it was shaking with anger. "I couldn't get through to Krista. I had no idea where you were until I finally thought to call your agent's office about fifteen minutes ago."

"I'm sorry, I didn't think—"

"You didn't think I'd be worried?" He jerked his glasses back and quickly rubbed his eyes. "Oh, of course, it's not as if anything could happen to you. That's impossible."

"Well, it is unlikely."

" 'Unlikely' isn't good enough. 'Unlikely' will drive me insane, and you know that." He paced over to the door and then came up right next to her. He brought his face down to hers. "Are you trying to punish me?" His voice was a hiss. "Is that what this is about?"

"Punish you?"

"For taking Jimmy to the fire station that day. If I hadn't done it,

I would have been home. Don't tell me you haven't thought about that. I've thought about it a thousand times."

"I really haven't," she said.

"Then what are you punishing me for? Being rich? I know you hate having money, and maybe you're right. Maybe if we didn't have all this, you wouldn't have been hurt."

"I don't think that—"

"Do you know what having money means to me? It means never having to do something I don't believe in for money. It means knowing I can always provide for my family, unlike that corrupt bastard James Joseph Keenan."

Charles so rarely mentioned his father that it took Lucy a second to realize he wasn't talking about Jimmy. Whenever Margaret mentioned her husband it was in perfectly glowing terms, calling him a fine man and a good father. But now his son, who had never cursed in the seven years Lucy had known him, was calling his father a corrupt bastard.

Lucy was too surprised to speak, and Charles didn't give her a chance anyway.

"But if it's important to you, I'll give away every dollar we have. Whatever you say. I'll call Peter tonight and tell him I'm donating it all to his homeless project. I can make the money back. The money is nothing to me without you."

"It's not the money."

"Then what is it?" His voice grew quieter. "Please tell me. Why are you determined to break my heart?"

"I don't want to break your heart," she whispered. "It's not your fault what happened to me, it really isn't. But it's not mine either, and I don't see why I shouldn't be able to act anymore."

"Do you have any idea what the last two hours were like? It was absolute torture, imagining you being knifed on Sunset Boulevard or kidnapped and raped if the car broke down on the freeway."

"But here I am, and I'm fine."

He shook his head. "You don't understand what I'm telling you.

I don't know if you can't understand or you won't, but either way, you just don't see that I'm not going to make it through this."

Lucy was trying to think of what to say when the children came downstairs with Susannah, fresh from their baths, already in their pajamas.

"Mommy, you look bootiful."

"Thanks, baby." Lucy reached down and picked up Dorothea. Her daughter was breathing fine. It had been over a month now since she'd had an attack, the longest so far. "What have you been doing, my pumpkin?"

"Playing!"

"How about you, Jimmy?"

"Same old, same old." He smiled then because he knew Lucy would laugh. She always did when he said that. Charles had taught Jimmy the expression, but it sounded so funny coming out of the little boy's mouth.

"What's that?" Jimmy said, pointing at one of the pearls on the floor. Dorothea saw them too and said, "Pretty."

"I guess you're waiting for me to make dinner?" Lucy said. "Since Krista isn't here?"

"Or Daddy could," Jimmy said.

Charles was standing motionless, staring out the front window. He hadn't even looked at the children or said hello.

"I think I should do it," Lucy said. "Come on, you guys, let's find something easy for Mommy to cook."

Lucy sat with Dorothea and Jimmy while they ate their macaroni and cheese. Charles didn't join them. She had no idea what he was doing, but she hoped he wasn't still standing in the front hall.

An hour later, after she put the children to bed, she threw steaks on the broiler for the two of them. She assumed Charles was in his office, but when she looked, he wasn't. She checked their bedroom too, and all of the rooms upstairs. Then she went back downstairs, and flipped the steaks, before looking around for him on the first floor. She was just starting to feel anxious when she saw the glow from the breakfast room patio door. He was sitting outside in the garden, smoking a cigar.

She opened the door and went out to tell him the steaks would be ready soon.

"Thank you," he said.

"What are you doing out here?"

"Thinking about *Master of Dreams.*"

"Oh," Lucy said, sitting down next to him, relieved that this was such a normal topic. "Want to talk about it?"

"So you can talk about whatever project you decided to do today?"

Of course he knew. Why else would she have been at an afternoon meeting with Pam? "I don't have to talk about my movie," she said, "but I'd still like to hear about yours."

"Master of Dreams isn't a movie, I've told you that. The idea came to me when you were in the hospital. It was while you were in the ICU, and I kept having dreams that none of this had happened." He took a puff from his cigar; she watched the end glow bright orange. She wished she had a sweater. The breeze was too cold. "The dreams were all so ordinary. We were feeding Dorothea and playing ball with Jimmy, reading scripts in bed together, driving to the beach. Nothing we hadn't done hundreds of times."

He paused and she tried to see his face, but it was too dark. All she could see was the cigar end and it seemed to be twitching, as though his hand were shaking.

"Each dream was so ordinary that when I first woke up, I didn't understand it was a dream. I thought the dream had to be the nightmare in front of me, with you screaming from a pain I couldn't do anything to stop."

She suddenly realized why he was sitting out here. They were right on top of where the sunroom used to be, maybe even on the very spot where he and Jimmy had found her.

"I have to check the steaks," she said, but before she could move, he grabbed her hand.

"I was wrong, do you know why?"

"Because the hospital was real," she said flatly. "It wasn't a nightmare."

"No. Because all those ordinary things, they were always a dream. Even when we thought we were living them, we were really dreaming. This was why it was so beautiful, don't you see?"

"Please, I can't—"

"This was why it was more beautiful than anything I'd ever written or even imagined. I finally understood. More beautiful than I should have ever thought I had a right to keep."

She didn't respond. She was cold, she was exhausted, and her wrist and leg were both hurting. She'd had a headache for hours. She wished she could go to sleep and not wake up again until all of this was over.

"Too beautiful," he muttered. He waited another minute, maybe more, before he finally dropped her hand, and she rushed away from him, back into the house.

seventeen

THE FILMING FOR *The Senator's Wife* was set to start in the middle of March, but it didn't actually start until the beginning of August. Delays like this weren't uncommon because of the thousand things that could go wrong before production, including losing one of the financial backers, as Brett had, leaving him to scramble for an alternative source of funds. Lucy was eager to get to work, but she was also grateful for the extra time to concentrate on getting her family ready before she had to begin.

She sometimes felt like she was pushing a rock uphill just to watch it roll back down if she relaxed for even a second. Dorothea and Jimmy were unquestionably getting better with every month that went by, but Charles was another story.

After that day when Lucy met with Pam, Charles started sleeping in his office, but he only lasted a few weeks before he was in their bed again. "I can't resist you," he said irritably, "even if you are going to destroy me." Well, hello to you too, Lucy thought, but she didn't object because she desperately wanted things to be better between them. It was the only thing she prayed for anymore because the failure of their marriage was starting to seem less and less impossible. How long could she keep living with a man she couldn't understand? A man whose only consistency was his moodiness? A man who spent hours every week second-guessing the police department, and bothering them, and staying angry that they couldn't focus exclusively on a crime that was more than a year and a half old? A man who, as Janice put it, continued to be obsessed with one day in their lives, as though that one day had ruined everything?

Lucy agreed that the only thing to do was put that day behind her, even though secretly she worried she'd never be the person she used to be. She still had headaches, and she was using her pain pills again since she'd stopped asking Charles to rub her head, knowing he'd only use it against her in the next argument about making her movie. Her right leg still went numb, though she'd denied this to both Charles and her neurologist, and now she was also feeling pain if she walked too far, especially around the shin, where it had been broken in two places. Even her back hurt sometimes, though there was no reason it should, according to the doctor. The grafts had worked so beautifully that Lucy was able to choose a backless gown to wear to the Academy Awards.

Charles was with her when she met with the dress designer, but he was adamant that there was no point in going to the Oscars. He'd never liked industry "VAP festivals," as he called them, where VAP stood for vanity, avarice and pride. He and Lucy had gone to the awards two years ago, when *Helena* was nominated for several technical awards, and the producers asked her to be there, thinking the extra press might help with foreign distribution deals. She enjoyed the whole experience, especially the moment when Charles got Best Screenplay for *Main Street*. He hadn't prepared a speech, but he gave a good one anyway. First he thanked the cast and the crew, the studio and Walter, her and the children—and then he talked about the recent decision by an English judge to throw out a highly publicized obscenity case against a director for the National Theatre. The entire crowd at the Dorothy Chandler Pavilion was expecting a free speech argument, but Charles talked instead about the responsibility artists have to their audiences. "The true obscenity," he said, "is accepting the cynical view of what we're doing. Yes, movies are a business, but movies also represent the chance to communicate with the largest number of people in the history of the world. Rather than be concerned about sexually explicit material, let us be concerned about having something to say that enriches human life."

Parts of the speech had been replayed the next morning on the *Today* show. Lucy remembered holding Dorothea on her lap and laughing when her baby pointed at the screen and said, "Daddy!"

Maybe it was only nostalgia that made Lucy want to go so badly this year. In any case, she had no intention of backing down, and finally, on Monday morning, the day of the ceremony, Charles agreed to go with her.

It actually turned out to be a very good night for them.

They'd hired a limousine, but Charles still complained on the long ride there, especially when they hit the traffic mess around the Music Center, where it took more than an hour to crawl the last mile. Once they arrived though, he was surprisingly pleasant, and Lucy remembered how socially engaging her husband could be. He easily charmed the red carpet reporters by deflecting their questions about *Master of Dreams* with his claim that he was here tonight only as an escort for his beautiful wife, joking that he hoped they wouldn't mar any photos of her by including him. Lucy was so grateful he was there, smoothly guiding her through the crowds of people and blinding flashes of hundreds and hundreds of cameras. It was her first public appearance since the attack, and stupidly, she hadn't thought how it would feel to have so many curious eyes on her, to know that she was being whispered about.

Once they were inside, Charles held court at the bar with Walter and the studio bigwigs, but again he didn't focus on his movie, but instead graciously turned the subject of conversation to the work of whoever was talking to him, especially all the actors and crew he'd worked with over the years, who would beam with pleasure when he mentioned a project they'd done recently, impressed he'd kept up with the progress of their careers. Of course most of the people who came over had some new project to discuss, and Charles listened with interest and responded in a way that made them feel he thought the idea was worth discussing, though he didn't add the usual "call my office tomorrow" encouragement/blow off. Lucy admired him for that. She herself ended up telling a dozen people that they could send Pam scripts, even though most of the parts were completely wrong for her. One producer thought she'd make a good sixty-two-year-old Brazilian nun.

There was one person Charles wasn't pleasant to, but at least he didn't make a scene when Brett Marcus came over to talk to Lucy during one of the commercial breaks. A public scene, that is. Nobody but Lucy heard him whisper, "If anything happens to my wife on your set, I'll kill you."

"Did he forget to call you Godfather?" Lucy quipped, as Brett walked away.

Charles laughed. Lucy couldn't believe it. "I've always liked that movie," he said, with his lips on her ear, "though perhaps it is a little violent."

Even the awards didn't bother him. Rather than be upset with the results he didn't vote for, he concentrated on being glad that Bob Duvall and Horton Foote, a writer he'd always admired, had won for *Tender Mercies.* He didn't even say anything about Gordon Willis not winning cinematography, though Lucy knew how much he respected Gordon and remembered how he'd gone on and on about the fabulous job Gordon did in *Zelig.*

They were invited to the ball and several parties afterward, including a big studio bash in Bel-Air and a smaller party on Melrose with a young crowd of Brett's friends. Charles said they would go wherever she wanted. She was dumbfounded, but she told him she was too tired to go anywhere but home.

Her husband was so much more like his old self that by the next morning, Lucy had come up with a theory. He needed to work again too. *Master of Dreams* should be made.

When she told him this, he surprised her again by saying he agreed. In fact, he said, he'd been thinking the same thing for weeks. The cast had been hired and the dream sets built, and if he didn't commit to start soon, Walter would have to get another director. Charles said if they could work out their filming schedules so the children were taken care of, he would do it.

Lucy thought it was a miracle how much better things seemed after that. For four full months while Charles was working, they almost had their old lives back. Later, she realized she'd been lulled into a false sense of optimism by how perfectly lovely everything was. Dorothea didn't have a single breathing episode. Jimmy was so much like his old self that Charles didn't object when Lucy went to the school and had their son tested so he could start first grade in September, even though he hadn't gone to kindergarten.

And then the loveliest thing of all happened. She found out at the end of July that she was pregnant. She felt like this really was a miracle because, though she'd never admitted it to anyone, she'd been worried ever since the attack that something fundamental had gone wrong with her and she'd never be able to have another baby.

Charles was working on audio, but when she called to tell him, he left his assistant in charge and came home to celebrate. She stopped taking her pain pills and prayed that this pregnancy would be just what they needed to keep them close through the next few months. She would be done with *The Senator's Wife* before she started really showing. It was perfect timing, just like when she got pregnant with Dorothea at the beginning of filming *Helena.*

Unfortunately, it was nothing like when she was pregnant with Dorothea because within days, she was sick as a dog. It was more like being pregnant with Jimmy, and she told Charles it must be another boy.

Knowing she was sick, he was more anxious about her working, but he didn't start any of the old arguments. If anything, he was nicer than before, though he did insist on driving her to and from location, but that wasn't a problem, since he'd finished his own shoot and already had a rough cut in the can. He even coached her a little on the drive, suggesting tiny changes in her lines that Brett usually proclaimed brilliant.

On Monday, the third week of filming, Charles noticed that Lucy was rubbing her neck on the way home. She had a blinding headache, but she told him it wasn't too bad and there was a flu going around the crew. Maybe she'd picked it up.

He seemed to understand. He rubbed her neck and the back of her head for almost an hour that night, while they watched one of his favorite old John Wayne movies.

The next morning she woke up at 10:50 in a panic. She'd set her alarm for five o'clock, the way she always did, to make it on set by six-thirty. How could she have overslept like this? Why hadn't Charles come in to tell her? Why hadn't Dorothea or Jimmy made any noise when they got up? They could never get up without making noise, even when she was desperate to sleep in when she had a day off.

She punched the intercom and yelled for her husband because she was honestly worried that something had happened to them. She was even more scared when she heard him running down the hall and then the loud bang of the door as he pushed it open.

He rushed into the room and over to the bed. "Are you all right?"

The frightened look on his face brought tears to her eyes. "Where's Dorothea? Jimmy? Tell me!"

"They're right downstairs." He sat down and took her hand. "They're fine, my sweet. They're finger-painting a picture for you with Susannah."

"What?"

"A get-well picture," he said gently. "It seems it's already working." He leaned down and kissed her forehead. "You look so much better than you did last night."

"I can't believe I slept through my alarm clock. Why didn't you wake me?"

"I knew you weren't up to working today. You cried out in your sleep at least a dozen times. But don't worry, I called Marcus and explained and he was more decent than I expected. He said they'd shoot around you until—"

Lucy wasn't keeping up. "You called Brett?"

"Yes, but as I said, he was understanding."

She thought for a minute. "When did you call him? What time?"

Charles cleared his throat. "This morning."

"That's not what I asked you," she said, pulling her hand away. "What time?"

When he didn't answer, she knew that he'd called at the beginning of the day: six-thirty, maybe even before. No matter how Charles felt about Brett, he would consider it part of professional ethics to let another director know as early as possible. It was far too costly to sit around and wait for actors.

"You turned my alarm off?" She was reeling with surprise.

"I did." He stood up and closed the bedroom door, as though he expected an argument. But his voice was matter-of-fact. "I've told you many times that I have no intention of letting anything happen to you. Especially now, when it's you and our baby."

She sat quietly for a moment, trying not to feel whatever this meant. "We can talk about this later," she said, standing up. "Right now, I have to get a shower and get to the set."

"There's no point," Charles said. "I told Brett you wouldn't be back today or tomorrow. I'm sure he's already made the appropriate adjustments to his schedule."

Lucy slumped back down on the bed. She knew the last part was probably true, but she also knew what a pain it must have been. Today they were supposed to film the New Year's Eve ballroom scenes where Adele confronts Martin about his self-destructive drinking and a suspected affair. There were hundreds of extras involved, and sure, they could do coverage of the dancing in the ballroom, but they'd still need the extras again to film the master shot for Martin and Adele.

"What did you tell him I had?" she said, when she thought about Charles saying she wouldn't be back tomorrow either. "The flu?"

"No, I told him the truth: that you're having a difficult pregnancy and you're still having headaches from the brain contusion you suffered that put you in a coma."

Lucy hadn't even told Brett she was pregnant. It was none of his business, and she was afraid he'd worry that she'd have trouble meeting the schedule. Of course lots of actresses got pregnant. The brain contusion thing was a million times worse. It was too close to brain damage, which made her sound one step away from a drooling idiot.

She stood up and went to her closet, pulling out her largest suitcase. When he asked what she was doing, she said, "I'm going to take the children and stay in a hotel until the filming is over. I wish I didn't have to, but you've left me no choice."

He walked over next to her. She was still in her bare feet and he was so tall and, she thought, intentionally intimidating. "Lucy, be reasonable."

"Why should I? Was it reasonable for you to turn my alarm off without even asking me? Can you imagine me ever, ever doing this to you? We could have talked about it. I might have even agreed to stay home today, if you were worried. But instead, you had to bully me into doing what you wanted. You had to be the director, except you aren't like this when you are a director. You listen to your actors and your crew because you know it takes collaboration to make a film work. Well, guess what? It takes collaboration to make a marriage work too."

"I only did it because I love you."

"No, you did it because you're afraid."

She set the suitcase on the floor by her middle dresser. She opened up the top drawer and started grabbing underwear and bras, throwing them into the suitcase. Charles was still standing right next to her. Maybe five minutes went by while he watched her pack. She was only taking a few outfits. If she needed more, she could buy something. She wanted to get this over with as quickly as possible.

When he finally spoke, his voice was firm. "You're not going to do this."

"How are you going to stop me? Chain me to the bed?"

"No." He reached into his pocket and pulled out his keys. "But if I have to, I will lock you in this room until you come to your senses."

Their bedroom door could be locked from the outside; Lucy had forgotten that. The lock had been put on years ago, when Charles was worried toddler Jimmy might wander in alone and swallow perfume or walk into the corner of one of the tables.

But she didn't believe he'd really do it, and she told him so. He said he would, she said he wouldn't, and finally she threw up her hands.

"Okay, but just so you know, I won't take it lying down. I'll kick and scream and beg for help until your servants call the police."

"No, you won't," he said, "because our children are downstairs. You won't want to frighten them."

They argued for several more minutes, but it didn't help. She couldn't change his mind; she couldn't even get him to think about what he was doing. He kept saying the same thing, that he was protecting her. The whole time, he made sure he was standing between her and the door. When she tried to move past him, he took her by the arms and told her he didn't want to physically restrain her, but he would if he had to.

"I warned you not to fight me on this. I'm sorry, but I can't let anything happen to you. I can't and I won't."

She turned away from him and wandered over to the rock fireplace, one of the first things she'd loved when she and Charles found this house. She stared at the fireplace for a moment. She didn't plan to bend down and pick up the iron fireplace tool, but once it was in her hand, she turned around and walked toward Charles.

Her aunt and uncle used to lock her in her room whenever she did anything wrong. Once she spent three days in there, eating stale crackers, using a bucket for bodily functions, whimpering, half out of her mind. Of course it was completely different now: their bedroom was beautiful, she had her own bathroom, her husband loved her. So why did she feel this sudden, awful desperation?

"The end of that is sharp," he said. "Give it to me."

The tool gleamed in the sun like a knife. She lifted it level with her face. On the end was a hook; Lucy wasn't sure exactly what it was for. She'd never used it. In the seven years they'd lived here, Charles would never let her start a fire.

"I want you to listen to me." She took her left hand and ran it down the narrow iron until she was inches away from stabbing her palm on the hook. "Will you do that?"

"Be careful," he said, taking a step toward her.

"No," she said. "That's the first thing you have to understand. I can't be careful enough. It didn't make any difference." She dropped her hand down on the hook and shoved hard until it broke the skin. "If you don't listen, I'll push it in all the way."

"Lucy, please—"

"This is what you're afraid of," she said, and pushed the hook in a little deeper. "That I'll be hurt. But what you don't understand is that I no longer feel pain." She laughed, but it sounded hysterical even to herself. "Except sometimes. Most of the time even."

"Stop it," he whispered. "Please."

"No. I can't stop it until you understand. And you don't understand. You haven't understood from the beginning."

The blood was dripping down her wrist and onto the carpet. She watched the drip with a strange fascination. She wouldn't look at Charles.

"I'll try to understand, but first—"

She pushed it in even deeper and groaned softly. "Don't tell me what to do. Just listen."

"Fine." His breath was coming quicker. "I'm listening."

"Okay, once upon a time in America." She laughed again. "What movie is that from?"

"Mr. Keenan?" Susannah was at the door, knocking. "Is everything all right?"

Charles glanced behind him.

"Tell her yes," Lucy said quietly. "Tell her we'll be down in about a half hour." Charles did, and Lucy waited until they heard Susannah's footsteps walking away.

"Anyway, once upon a time, a man made a movie about Joan of Arc." She was starting to feel a little dizzy from watching the blood, so she lifted her head up, but she still wouldn't look at Charles. "The man made the movie because he thought it was so admirable that Joan would rather die than renounce God. And the thing is, there was this girl, this stupid nobody from nowhere, who believed him." Lucy sighed. "Even when she was in the fire herself, she wanted so badly to believe it was burning away everything but her faith in him and her love."

Lucy pushed her hand again until the blood was so thick she couldn't see her palm or the hook. "God, how did we end up here, where we won't die for anything?" Her voice was shaky. "We won't even risk getting too tired or driving late or living in a house without twenty-four-hour armed guards."

"I would die for you. With all my soul, I promise—"

"I know that." She exhaled. "You would die for me, I know." She felt like she was losing her point. Maybe she didn't have one. She was too tired to make any sense. She'd been tired for so long, she couldn't remember the way she was before. "And I would die for you. I was ready to die for you. But it didn't make any difference, don't you see?"

"Please stop," he gasped.

"We don't get to die for each other. I guess that means we're stuck."

She grimaced because the wound was starting to burn. Why had she done this to herself? What was it that she'd been so desperate for Charles to know?

"I wish I could really be brave," she whispered.

"Oh God," he said. His voice was thick. "I can't stand this anymore."

She finally looked up at her husband then, and discovered he was crying.

She'd never seen Charles cry before, and it made her feel like her heart was opening up or breaking, she wasn't sure. Either way, she couldn't bear it. She nodded at her hand and told him he could help her. "I need your help," she said.

He moved his glasses to wipe his eyes and then he was next to her. She let him ease the hook out, and he cleaned up the blood and knelt down beside her to bandage the wound. He thought it would need stitches, but she asked him to wait and see if it stopped. When he said she'd need a tetanus shot, she reminded him she'd had one not that long ago, but she didn't mention the hospital.

When he was finished, he told her to go back to bed, and she did because she was so tired.

"I'm sorry," she whispered, and she was, for everything. She felt like she saw it all at once: him kneeling by her hospital bed, smoking the cigar in the garden, asking her if she was a thief, swimming naked with her in the moonlight. He was confident and brilliant, the way he was on the set of Joan, funny and gentle, the way he was with their babies, and angry and broken, the way he was when he threw the pearls. And through it all, he was crying, she kept seeing him cry, it was burned into her mind, even though he'd stopped as soon as she asked for his help.

Her eyes were closed; he was already out of the room when she said she was glad this was over now. Her hand hurt, but she felt like something had been solved. "I've never stopped loving you," she mouthed into his pillow.

She woke up about an hour later, when Charles and a doctor were standing by the side of the bed. Charles told her the doctor was going to sew up her hand, but it wouldn't hurt because he'd give her a shot first. She was grateful for the shot because her hand was really hurting now. It worked almost immediately, and it must have put her back to sleep because she didn't remember the stitching at all.

When she woke up again, it was already dark, and she realized she'd missed the whole day. She felt bad for the children, thinking about them finger-painting the picture for her, waiting to show it to her. But it wasn't that late yet. Maybe if she hurried she could still sing to Dorothea and tuck her in bed.

She stood up and put her robe on. As she walked to the door, she was thinking how much better she felt. She was even glad Charles had told her to go back to bed, because the sleep was wonderful. But then she reached for the door, and it wouldn't open. Charles had still locked her in this room, after everything they'd said to each other.

She knew it would have made sense to feel hurt or angry or at least surprised, but the only surprise was that she felt nothing. Even as she walked to the balcony, still in her robe and nightgown, with the left sleeve bloodied by her hand, she felt nothing. Getting out of that room wasn't something she wanted to do, it was something she had to do, or she might disappear in all the nothingness.

Once she climbed over the balcony, she would be in the garden and then she would find her baby girl. For the last week or so, every night, she'd been teaching Dorothea another line of "Moondance." Maybe they could sing it together, the same way Lucy had sung with her mother when she was a little girl.

Her mother's name was Dorothy: a pretty name, Lucy thought, though her mother had hated it. "Dorothy is an old lady's name," Lucy's mother would say. "Or a farm girl in the middle of Kansas." When Lucy and Charles were picking out names for a girl, he came up with Dorothea. They agreed it was close enough for Lucy, but far enough away for Lucy's mother, if she'd been there. If only she could have been there. It used to make Lucy feel so bad that she didn't even have a picture of her mother; she hadn't had time to grab one when she ran away from her uncle.

Charles and Lucy's bedroom was on the second floor, but the drop from the balcony wasn't very high because of the grassy hill right underneath. She and Charles had talked about how easy it would be to climb over it, back when they were making their fire evacuation plan, when they first moved into the house. In the plan, he would climb over first, and then she would climb into his arms. She'd always been afraid of even small heights after she fell off the jungle gym bars in third grade.

She was over the balcony wall and trying to use her hands to move down when she realized what she'd forgotten. Her right wrist was weak, and her left hand was completely bandaged. She couldn't hold up her weight even for the few inches it would have taken to get down low enough to jump safely.

And so she just gave up and let herself fall. She fell backward and landed on the ground with a thud, but she sat up immediately, glad she wasn't hurt. Her stitches must have ripped because her hand was bleeding through the bandage, and her legs were scraped, but she could still stand and walk. She could see Dorothea through the breakfast room window, drinking her nightly glass of chocolate milk. She worried she might scare her daughter if she knocked on the patio door, so she headed around to the front.

She got stopped by Martinez, the night security guard, but as soon as he saw who it was, he said, "Good evening, Mrs. Keenan," as though there was nothing strange about her suddenly appearing from the garden in her nightgown and robe.

Inside the front hall, she said, "Hi honey, I'm home," and laughed.

Both Jimmy and Dorothea ran to meet her, and they didn't seem frightened by her scrapes or her hand. They gave her little hugs of comfort while Charles stood a few feet back, silently watching. When she told them she wanted to tuck them in, even six-year-old Jimmy agreed.

After her children were in bed, Lucy asked Tom to bring her some of her things and then she took a shower in the downstairs guest room. She slept there too, with the door locked from the inside, the normal way, after telling Charles there was nothing to discuss. There was a phone in the guest room, and when she called

Brett at home, he was relieved to hear that she'd be back tomorrow. She also scheduled a car service to take her to the set. In the morning, when Charles begged her to let him drive her instead, she turned away from him. "I'll be back tonight," she said, and then she got in the car and left her husband standing in the driveway.

Every day for the rest of the week, it was the same. She took a car to the location, worked until five or six, and came home in time to be with her children for as long as possible before they went to bed. Her head hurt a lot, but she wouldn't take a pain pill because of the baby. She threw up if she tried to eat before noon, but she made sure she ate well the rest of the day and took her prenatal vitamins.

The baby was the one thing Lucy was holding on to. She pushed away all her worries about the future with this one central fact: next April, she would have her infant in her arms. Nothing that had happened to her body or her mind or her soul was irreversible as long as she could still give birth to a brand-new life.

eighteen

PART OF LUCY knew that she was holding on so tightly to the idea of her baby because she feared she'd done something terrible when she fell from the balcony. She'd seen enough movies to know a fall could cause a miscarriage. Her obstetrician told her it wasn't really true, but Lucy thought the doctor was just trying to make her feel better. She was already considered a high-risk pregnancy because she had so much internal scar tissue from the attack.

Charles wasn't with her at the OB's office when she asked about the effects of her fall. It was the next week, on Wednesday, and she'd gone over to Dr. McAffey's during lunch break on set. She figured Charles was angry with her for jumping from the balcony; she didn't want him to know that she was upset about this too. Especially now, when he was being an even better father than usual. Every night when she came home, the children talked nonstop about the stories he told them, the games he played, the funny movies they saw. It made her feel like reaching out for him again, but she couldn't do it yet. She was too confused.

Now that the bandages were off, Jimmy wanted to know what had happened to her hand. Lucy had neglected to have her stitches repaired, and the wound had closed up ugly and raw. Charles said, "She hurt it at work," but she felt terrible, imagining what her little boy would feel if he knew the truth.

Thank God for acting, she thought. Playing Adele, the savior, was so much easier than playing herself.

She had Labor Day weekend off, and she and Charles got Jimmy ready for school. He was so excited, picking out his first notebook and pencil box and new big-kid backpack. When he told Lucy he was worried the other kids wouldn't like him, she knelt down and said, "You are funny and smart, just like your daddy. Everyone will like you. I'll bet you three hugs, two pineapples and a kiss from the sun."

This was Lucy and Jimmy's favorite bet. She'd made it up when he was only a year old, and they were spending a weekend in Hawaii, so Charles could meet with an actor Walter had suggested for *Main Street.* Their suite had a basket of pineapples and coconuts, and Jimmy kept putting the pineapples in bed with them. Lucy thought it was so funny. He even tried to kiss the leaves on top, calling them hair.

Jimmy hugged his mom and said it was a bet before he ran off to play. When Lucy turned around, she saw Charles right behind her, but she walked away without speaking. There was so much to say that she couldn't imagine where to start. Maybe when her filming was done. Maybe when he'd started working with his editors on *Master of Dreams* and he was happy like he'd been before.

On Labor Day night, before she went to bed, she got down on her knees to pray that God wouldn't punish her by taking her baby. She'd been having cramps on and off all weekend, but she kept telling herself that they were from eating too much or exhaustion or both. Cramping wasn't necessarily a sign of anything, especially with only light spotting.

But the next afternoon, the bleeding became heavier. Dr. McAffey was out of the office, but her nurse told Lucy she could go to the ER if she thought she was having a miscarriage. After the nurse admitted that there was really nothing the doctors could do to stop a miscarriage, Lucy went straight home and got in bed.

Charles had already left for some kind of big dinner with Walter. She told Susannah to please take care of the children tonight. The cramps were getting worse and so was the bleeding, but she kept telling herself if she lay very still it might stop.

Around nine-thirty though, she went into the bathroom because she knew it was happening. She sat on the toilet, sweating with agonizing cramps, while she bled and bled, ten times more than the heaviest period of her life. When it was over and she could finally stand up again, she hobbled to the phone.

She called Dr. McAffey's service, but she said the doctor didn't have to call her back. There was nothing to discuss. Then she opened her purse and took out a pain pill. Her head was throbbing and she felt like screaming. She pushed the intercom to the kitchen, but no one answered, so she stumbled out of her room.

She washed the pill down with a glass of wine, figuring it didn't make any difference now. By the time Charles got home, she'd had another pill and three more glasses of wine. She was sitting at the piano, trying to pick out "Lover Man." Charles knew how to play because he'd taken lessons back when he lived in Beverly Hills, when he was single. He used to tell her that she should take lessons, but she was always too busy with the babies.

When he came into the room, he looked so handsome in his Armani suit. He had on her favorite black glasses too. She couldn't help it, she smiled at him and gave a little wave.

He walked toward her. "Have you been drinking?"

"A little." She stood up and stumbled against the piano bench. "Okay, more than a little."

"You're drinking?" His voice was pure condemnation. "You're pregnant and you're drinking?"

"No," she said, looking down at her hands. "The baby's gone." Her eyes filled with tears. "My poor baby." She touched her belly. "I didn't mean to do it; I really didn't."

"Oh, Lucy," Charles said gently, pulling her against him. "It's not your fault. Dr. McAffey told us this might happen. I'm so sorry."

"Yes, it is," Lucy sobbed into his suit jacket. "I killed it."

She felt him stiffen. "What?"

"My poor little baby, he never had a chance."

He took her by the shoulders and pushed her a few feet back, then he held her there, trapped in his gaze. "If you really did this—"

"I told you I didn't mean to," she stammered.

"If you really did this . . ." he repeated. His voice was so angry, it sounded like he hated her. "If you really killed my child, knowing how I feel about abortion . . . I don't know how I'll ever forgive you."

All she had to do was say it wasn't an abortion, but she couldn't make her mouth form the words. Part of it was her guilt for the miscarriage, but the main thing was how stunned she was that he thought she was capable of this. After everything she'd told him about how happy she was about this pregnancy, how badly she wanted this baby. It felt like he'd just stabbed her in the heart.

She twisted until she was free of his grasp, and then she laughed in his face. She laughed and laughed and laughed. If it had been a movie, he would have slapped her. But it wasn't a movie, and he walked away.

She swallowed another glass of wine and then she stumbled to her bed and passed out. She heard the phone ring, but she couldn't move to answer it. She found out the next morning that Dr. McAffey had called, after all, and Charles had talked to her.

His apology was sincere, but too late. "We don't even know each other anymore," she said, and she meant it. She felt like her marriage was over, and so was her life. She would always be in pain; she would never have more children, and her own children were growing up. Now that Jimmy was in first grade, four-year-old Dorothea was trying to keep up with her big brother. She wouldn't let Lucy call her baby anymore; she wouldn't even let Lucy tuck her in. Both the children spent far more time with Susannah than with their own mother. Both of them seemed to prefer playing with Charles.

Dr. McAffey told Lucy it was normal to feel depressed after a miscarriage, and not just from grief, from the sudden change in hormones. But Lucy didn't think she was depressed; she thought she'd finally realized the truth about her life. She couldn't imagine how she could ever again find any hope.

Seeing Charles made it a hundred times worse, and so she tried to avoid him. It wasn't hard. The movie was way behind schedule, mainly because Brett and his assistant weren't as organized as the other directors she'd worked with. Since she was getting out too late to see the children anyway, she started eating dinner with Brett or one of the cast members; sometimes she let them talk her into going along to a party afterward. Everybody at the parties drank and smoked pot and snorted coke; Lucy's own pills seemed harmless in comparison, even though she was taking more now that she could get them without the hassle of going to the doctor. Brett had a friend, Ivan, who gave her as many as she wanted, and Ivan's pills were stronger too, which was good since she could work straight through the schedule, no resting between scenes in her trailer like before. After work, she tried to cut back on the pills, but she always had a few drinks because it made it easier to get past her natural shyness and relax at the parties.

Before long she was walking in the door plastered about half the time. Charles told her over and over that she had to quit this, but she said it was none of his business. And she said a lot of other things too:

"I have to get drunk because I'm a murderer. I murder babies."

"I thought I was not corrupt. Ha-ha."

"I am Joan the brave, fighting to forget my life."

"I remember every damn thing about that day. I remember

exactly what those guys did to me because I wouldn't just screw them and get it over with."

When he told her she was destroying him, she shrugged it off.

"Nobody can destroy the great Charles Keenan."

"A captain should go down with his ship. You're the captain, mister. Come on down."

"I'm already destroyed. So what?"

When he told her she would hurt the children, she got angry.

"I love my children. Don't you ever forget it."

"You hired Susannah because you wanted me to go crazy without my children to take care of. You thought I was too crazy to take care of my own babies."

"I know you blame me for Dorothea's breathing problems. Well, you can just go screw yourself. I did everything I could to keep her from being scared. You weren't there. You have no idea."

"You hired Susannah because you wanted to have sex with her, didn't you? You did it with her while I was in the hospital. You're probably doing it now while I'm at work!"

Lucy would often break down in tears right after saying one of these things. She would cry and apologize, and sometimes she tried to kiss him or sit on his lap. A couple of times, she even convinced him to go to bed with her, but only downstairs in her room, so he couldn't lock her away like a madwoman.

In the mornings, when she woke up with her usual headache, made worse from the hangover, she would swallow two or three pills. What difference did it make, especially as she was still able to act as well as ever? She never forgot her lines and Brett was even more complimentary than before. Of course they were better friends now that they were partying all the time. He'd made it clear he wanted to sleep with her, but she wouldn't do it. "I'm married," she told him, but she laughed when he said, "You're married to an ass."

"Maybe so," she said. "But he's my ass and I love him."

Two days later, a tabloid screamed:

"Brett Marcus and Lucy Dobbins? Not so, says the actress, despite rumors of the two being seen together all over L.A. Of her husband of seven years, director Charles Keenan, she says: 'He's my ass and I love him.'"

Everybody on set thought it was hilarious, but Lucy felt like she wanted to jump off a cliff. That night, she went straight home to face her husband, though she was hoping against hope that he hadn't heard about it.

When she got home it was about nine, and she found him upstairs with Dorothea. She could hear the little girl gasping for air before she even came into the bedroom.

"Mommy," she breathed, when she heard Lucy's hello.

"Oh honey," Lucy said, rushing to her daughter. Dorothea was sitting on her bed with her head between her knees. Charles was next to Dorothea, rubbing her back.

"How long has it been going on?" Lucy asked him.

"She woke up this way." His voice was so cold. He obviously knew about the tabloid. "About ten minutes. Nothing has helped so far."

"I'm scared," Dorothea gasped.

"It's okay," Lucy said, kneeling. She stroked her baby's hair. "I'm going to sing to you. If you want to sing along, you can."

"She can barely speak," Charles snapped.

"Let's do 'Jack and Diane,'" Lucy said. "You like that song, right?"

Dorothea nodded, and Lucy started to sing. For the first verse, it didn't seem to be working. Lucy could feel Charles's disapproval. She wondered if he thought she was drunk.

But then on the chorus, Dorothea joined her, weak at first, but getting stronger with each line. By the time they got to the second verse, they were singing together just like they always did. Dorothea had such a pretty voice, but it sounded funny too, hearing a four-year-old sing a song about holding on to being sixteen. Lucy started laughing, and even Charles laughed with relief.

"I did it!" Dorothea said, clapping her hands.

"You sure did, baby." Lucy hugged her. "Good for you."

They talked for a few minutes and then Charles told her she needed to go back to sleep now.

"I want to sleep with you," she said, pointing at Lucy. And at Charles. Back and forth.

Charles said it wasn't a good idea, but Lucy looked closely at her daughter. Dorothea had never asked to sleep with them since Lucy came home from the hospital. Was it possible the little girl knew what was going on now? Lucy made sure she was always up before the children were. She didn't want them to wonder what it meant that she was sleeping downstairs.

"If it's really important to her," Lucy said, "it's okay with me."

He exhaled. "Fine."

Dorothea was up and running down the hall to their bed before either of them had made it out of her room.

"How unusual to see you at this hour," he said. "And sober." His tone was so angry Lucy flinched.

"I'm going to tuck her in," she said.

She not only tucked in Dorothea, she sang her two more songs, got her a glass of water and listened while her daughter talked and talked and talked. It was probably a half hour before Lucy was finished, and even then, she walked slowly down the stairs, dreading this confrontation.

He was sitting at the dining room table with nothing to drink or eat or read. Just sitting there, at the head of the table. Waiting. Lucy sat down. He folded his hands, but he didn't look at her.

"You have seen your children exactly once in the last twelve days."

"I'm finishing the film; you know how that—"

"You were with them on Sunday night for what, an hour?"

"Come on, this isn't about the children, it's about that stupid tabloid. I hope you know that it was totally out of context. I didn't call you an—"

He slammed his fist on the table so hard that Lucy jumped back like he was going to hit her. "This *is* about the children. Don't even try to delude yourself that it isn't." He looked into Lucy's eyes. "Dorothea dreamed you were dead. That's why she had the attack tonight. She woke up crying because her mother was dead."

Lucy felt horrible, but she swallowed hard and forced herself not to cry.

"Jimmy lost his dog on Monday. When I picked him up from school, he was hysterical. I still can't get him to talk about what happened. The teacher said the children were playing at recess and when recess was over, Tigger was gone."

Lucy covered her face with her hands. She was the one who'd told Jimmy he could take the dog for show-and-tell. Charles had said it was a bad idea, but Lucy had laughed and said to her son, "Ignore him. Your daddy worries too much."

"Did you look for Tigger?" she finally said, lifting her face.

"What do you think?" He frowned deeply. "After I took Jimmy home, I went back to the school and tried to find someone who could tell me what happened, then I spent three hours driving around the area. Susannah said he cried on and off the entire time I was gone."

"Poor Jimmy."

"Yes, that seems a fair assessment. Poor Jimmy. Not only has he lost his dog this week, but tomorrow, it's likely he will come to school and discover that his mother has called his father an ass in a newspaper."

She felt her face get warm. "Those kids don't read tabloids."

"Oh, don't be so naïve. That piece of trash is in the checkout line of every supermarket. Some of those kids have parents who read tabloids, and some of those parents will discuss this at dinner. Particularly those parents who don't like us for a variety of petty reasons, like we have more money, you're beautiful, we're relatively famous and we keep to ourselves. Or I should say, we used to keep to ourselves. You've changed all that, haven't you, Lucy?"

"I didn't mean to."

"But you didn't try hard enough not to. You didn't consider

our children when you decided to get drunk in public with Brett Marcus."

"I didn't do anything with him."

"Don't even bother." He took a deep breath. "Are you leaving me for him? I would appreciate the truth. I think I deserve that."

"Of course not."

"Of course? I don't think that expression is appropriate. There is certainly nothing obvious about your feelings anymore. At this point, I don't even know if you care about the children."

"I love them. They're the only thing I have now."

"A touching sentiment, except for the small fact that you're never with them, that you're neglecting them completely for a career you don't need."

"No one needs a career."

"Ah." He smiled a mean smile. "How far you've come from poverty."

"I meant no one we know." She smirked. "Including you."

"You'll find no argument there. If I was away from home as much as you are, you could try this on me. But I never have been, and you know it. Because I really do love the children, and I know they can't raise themselves."

"When this film is over, I'll—"

"No. That doesn't work anymore. You owe your children, Lucy. You may not owe me anything, but you owe Dorothea and Jimmy because they didn't do anything but love you."

"What are you saying?"

"That I won't allow you to keep doing this. You have to stop hurting them, or you will live to regret it."

"Don't threaten me."

"I'm not, I'm giving you a chance to change. I think I owe you that, no matter how furious I am about you dragging our family into the worst kind of public display."

"And if I don't change?"

"Then this will end in tragedy. And not the kind of tragedy we love in movies, where the heroine wins the affection of everyone even as she loses all she holds dear. I'm talking about the gritty kind of tragedy, where the heroine ends up drunk and alone with no one to blame but herself."

Lucy was nervous, but she said, "I don't care if you divorce me."

"A new twist. Fascinating I'm sure, but irrelevant. You know I will never divorce you."

"Then what are you talking about?"

"Tragedy, as I said, if you don't start honoring your commitment to the children."

He closed his eyes for a moment, and Lucy noticed his face was pale with stress and misery. She remembered when he used to talk tough to the studio suits, how he'd told her he hated it. "I'd much rather be able to be myself," he'd said. "But they'd walk all over me. Most people mistake kindness for weakness. It's an unfortunate fact of human nature."

"Charles," she said quietly. "I wish we could really talk about this."

"There's nothing to talk about. I will not let you hurt them." He stood up. "I will use all my power to prevent that, even if it hurts you, even if it breaks my heart."

Then he walked out of the dining room, leaving Lucy just sitting there, stunned.

Twenty minutes later, when she could finally move, she remembered Dorothea waiting up in Charles's bedroom, their bedroom, for the two of them.

She wanted her pills, but she didn't dare; she needed to stay alert. She could feel that something terrible was about to happen, even though she had no idea what it was. She went into her own room, took off her makeup and put on her nightgown; then she went upstairs and crawled into her old side of the bed next to her sleeping daughter.

When Charles joined them, it was close to two o'clock, but she was still awake. She heard him opening a drawer, saw him in the moonlight taking off his clothes and putting on a pair of drawstring pants. Then she felt the mattress move as he lay down on the other side of Dorothea.

"Good night," she whispered, without thinking how she'd feel when the inevitable silence was the only response.

He was already breathing slower, obviously asleep, when it struck her that the three of them hadn't been together like this since that morning, September 21. They had been in this same bed, in the same positions, and her worst problem then was that Dorothea had woken up too early.

It was November 7, only a little over two years later, and yet her life had been changed so completely she barely recognized it. She was sad all the time now, and as lonely as when she was a kid living with her uncle. And she was always running to keep from facing up to the most shameful thing about herself, the secret she'd kept so well that even she didn't know it.

That night, the fear was so close she could feel it breathing down her neck. But she told herself she was only afraid of Charles, of what he might do to her, and even that didn't really make sense. There was nothing to be afraid of. She was just upset about their argument. If only she could have had a drink or one of her pills, she could have fallen asleep and forgotten about this.

When Dorothea woke up the next morning, Lucy was so relieved to get up that she didn't mind asking Charles to please go get her cane. Her leg had gone numb from lying still for hours, trying not to toss and turn and wake up her daughter.

She took the day off, telling Brett only that she was having a family problem. She helped Jimmy get ready for school, but he still couldn't talk about Tigger without crying. She ate breakfast and lunch with Dorothea and spent all day with her, playing and singing and dressing her dolls. But when Charles took Dorothea with him to pick up Jimmy, Lucy got on the phone with Janice. She needed advice.

Lucy rushed through everything that had happened, and Janice listened to it all. Her first theory was that he was going to divorce Lucy and try to get custody, but Lucy reminded her that Charles took his Catholicism seriously, and also that he'd said he'd never do that. Then Janice thought the answer was obvious. It was an idle threat designed to keep Lucy from finishing the film.

Janice already knew about Charles trying to keep Lucy from getting a part, and even about the locked room. "He's still trying to win," Janice said now. "Christ, he's unbelievable, resorting to using your kids."

When Lucy hung up, she was so angry she wanted to throw something. Of course Janice was right, and the worst part was he'd come very close to getting his way. After all, she was here, wasn't she? She hadn't gone to the set on one of the most important days for the film. They were all important during these last three weeks.

Three weeks was all he had to wait, and yet he was still trying to stop her. This wasn't about Jimmy and Dorothea, this was about his power over Lucy. His controlling personality, as the therapist had called it. His belief that he was always right and he always had to win.

Well, it wasn't going to happen this time.

He was nicer that evening, but of course he was, Lucy thought. He'd gotten his way. He changed his tune completely the next night, when Lucy went to work and stayed until the job was done at nine. She didn't party with the cast; she came straight home, but he was still determined to intimidate her. He came up with a long sob story about Jimmy begging for her, and then he repeated his threat that if she kept neglecting the children, she'd live to regret it.

It was only a few days later when the police had their first and only success in the investigation of Lucy's attack. They never found the two men, partly because the fingerprints the police took didn't match any on file, partly because the two guys didn't steal the Jaguar or the BMW, after all, but mainly because it was three days before Lucy could describe them. The trail was cold, and she had no idea how they even got there. They'd appeared at her pool while she and

Dorothea were swimming—this was all she could tell the detectives. They'd appeared on a perfectly normal day, when she was laughing with her daughter, living a life that seemed so far removed from her past in Missouri and Nashville that it had never crossed her mind she wouldn't be safe here either.

When the police arrested a pawnshop owner for accepting stolen goods, everything in the shop was checked against the item lists taken from the victims of robberies. The Keenans were at the top of the list because their case was high profile, and probably because Charles kept bothering them. The antique engagement ring was unusual enough that it was easy to identify. One of the officers rushed it over that same afternoon.

When Charles opened his palm and showed Lucy her beautiful diamond ring, she was flooded with memories, not only of the day he asked her to marry him, but of the day Jimmy was born, when Charles had held her hand so tightly as she panted and pushed that her rings sliced into her finger. Of course she didn't notice that in the midst of delivering her baby. What she remembered was the security of knowing Charles was there, thinking nothing could go wrong as long as he held her hand.

Now they were standing in the den; Charles had classical music on the stereo. The violin sound was so intense and passionate that she'd felt like she was intruding on him when she came into the room. It was nine-thirty; the children were asleep, but they must have been drawing all evening because there were colorful pictures on every table, most from Jimmy, who loved drawing and did it so well his teacher said he had a gift, but some of Dorothea's scribbles too: a thick brown line with a blob of green at the top for leaves; a giant sun that was smiling as its rays ran off the page.

Lucy felt like she was seeing the way her family was without her. She felt a little scared, as though in some way she couldn't understand, this was already becoming permanent, but then she reminded herself that the film would be over soon, and in the meantime, she was glad that the children were doing well. Of course they were, because Charles was an excellent father, no matter how disappointed he was in her.

"I assume you don't want this," he said flatly, nodding at the ring.

Since the miscarriage, Lucy hadn't been wearing the replacement rings Charles had given her in the hospital. But this one was different. This one reminded her of being happy.

Before she could speak, he said, "It doesn't matter." His hand closed and the diamond disappeared into his fist. "I can save it for Dorothea when she's older."

If he hadn't started in on how upset Jimmy was that Lucy wasn't at dinner tonight, she might have told him she wanted the ring, but probably not. That same morning, in the gossip column of one of the local papers, the tabloid story of Lucy and Brett had been replayed with a quote from a "reliable source" claiming that Charles Keenan, known to be an old-fashioned family man, was "disgusted with the behavior of his young wife." Who knew if it was true, but Lucy convinced herself she didn't care either way after she had a few pills and went into her room.

Every night for the next two weeks, Charles came up with another reason why she'd failed the children, and yet another warning that he was not going to let this go on much longer. She was getting good at letting it go in one ear and out the other, so that by the third week, on Tuesday, when she found out that Brett had come up with enough money to do a few days filming in D.C., she was almost bored listening to Charles tell her why she'd better not go.

He had to know how much better the movie would be with these location shots. They would also have a chance to do retakes for two scenes that had never really worked. It was a great opportunity, and Lucy couldn't turn it down without affecting the entire cast and crew.

"Dorothea had three attacks in the last week. She needs you here."

"Why? You can help her too. So can Susannah."

"But she wants her mother. She's four years old."

"I know how old she is."

He was standing outside of her room, watching her throw what she'd need for the short trip into her tote bag. Two large bottles of pills Ivan had given her were right next to the bag, but she didn't care if Charles saw them. She was under a lot of stress, and he certainly wasn't helping.

"Are you forgetting that Thursday is Thanksgiving?" he said.

They didn't have a choice: they had to shoot over the holiday weekend because the actor playing Marvin, the senator, had another movie starting on Monday. They wouldn't actually film on Thanksgiving (because paying the crew for that day would cost a fortune), but they had to film late on Wednesday night and very early on Friday morning. They had to take every chance they had or they wouldn't finish before they ran out of money again.

Charles knew about the pressure of finishing—when it was his own work. She said something snotty about him playing stupid, but he ignored her and went on with his guilt trip.

"Dorothea and my mother have been making holiday cookies all weekend as a surprise for you."

"That's sweet," Lucy said. "But I'm not going to rearrange my schedule because the great Margaret has decided to come home for a change. And Dorothea doesn't care what date the holiday is on. I'll ask her for some cookies to take on the plane, and we can celebrate when I get back on Monday."

"Lucy, you can't do this. You know Jimmy's class found Tigger's body today, and he's—"

"I already talked to him about Tigger. He seems like he's feeling better."

"He wants you to stay."

"He didn't tell me that."

"Because he knows you're busy. He's trying to be responsible, but he's a little boy."

"Or is it because you don't want me to finish my movie?" She put her finger to her lips. "Mmm. I wonder if that's it."

"If you do this, I'm warning you—"

"Warn away. I love a good warning. It makes working soooo much easier."

"I'm serious."

"I'm sure you are. As serious as you were when you said you'd always love me."

"You can't leave your children again or—"

"Or what?"

"I don't want to threaten you. I just want you to see that they need you. Please." He was banging his hand against the frame of the door, but Lucy didn't look up. "Please, please, put them first for a change."

"This isn't about Dorothea and Jimmy. And you do so want to threaten me. You want to and you're going to. So go ahead, so I can say the same thing I say every day. Or do you want to hear it first? We could reverse the order. I'll go ahead and say, 'I don't believe you and I don't care.'"

"If you do this, you're going to lose everything."

"I don't believe you and I don't care."

"I will leave and you'll never see me again."

"I don't believe you and I don't care." She waited a minute. "Are you finished?"

When he didn't answer, she finally looked up and realized he was gone. Good riddance, she thought, though she wanted to cry, but that was always true. No matter what he did, she still felt this pang about him, which she hoped wasn't love. She didn't want to love a man who obviously hated her.

She kissed the children good-bye before she left. She'd already promised them that when she finished this film, she would be around a lot more. She also told Jimmy that she would be back early on Monday and she would take him to school. When he asked her if she'd really make it, she said of course, that she was driving herself to the airport so her car would be waiting, and she could just jump in and head for home the very second the plane landed.

As always, shooting out of town was hard work. Most of the time, Lucy was in such bad pain that she needed twice her usual pills to get through her scenes, and something to sleep each night. She tried to call home on Thanksgiving, but when they didn't answer, she didn't leave a message. She didn't want to get into it again with Charles. Of course he didn't call her, not once.

They finished up on Sunday evening and the cast and crew hopped on a plane to get home. Everyone was celebrating the wrap-up. Lucy made it out of the airport by 5:30, plenty of time to get home and take Jimmy.

The drive to Malibu took less than an hour, since it was still too early for traffic. PCH was almost deserted too, and Lucy decided to stop at Zuma and take a walk. If she went home now, the children wouldn't be up, but Charles might be. She wasn't in the mood to fight with him. She wanted to savor the end of another film.

Also, she hadn't been to the beach alone in years.

It was cool, but the breeze made her feel more awake and alert. She took off her shoes and rolled up her jeans, and started walking toward the ocean. The sun was just rising and the sea was the deepest blue tipped with white; the rhythm of the waves crashing seemed to match the beat of her own heart. She felt strangely excited and alive, even though she was alone. Because she was alone, and she wasn't afraid.

It was hard walking in the sand though. Difficult to keep her balance. Much more tiring than she remembered. She was just thinking she might have to turn back when, about halfway to the ocean, her leg suddenly gave way. There was nothing to break her fall even if she'd had time to grab for something. The next thing she knew she was sprawled out sideways on the beach.

She wasn't hurt, but she couldn't get up. She tried and tried, but her leg refused to hold her weight, and balancing on one proved impossible. Now she knew how stupid she'd been to come out here, after using up everything she had on the last few days of filming. "You idiot," she said to herself. Yelled it. She looked around and there was no one to help. No one to come even if she screamed.

At some point it hit her how alone she was. Alone and absolutely vulnerable, just like she'd been that day.

She tried to crawl then, but her right leg was still completely numb. She had to drag it along like a dead child, and her progress was pitiful. She kept looking around to make sure no one had come up behind her. After a few minutes of this, she was whimpering, but she kept telling herself she wasn't afraid.

In the distance though, she could see a man. It looked like he was walking toward her. It looked like he was wearing a dingy T-shirt. She tried to crawl faster, but it didn't make any difference. She was back there again and she couldn't get away.

This man had controlled Lucy's dreams for over two years.

She started trembling violently as she thought of his voice telling her what he was going to do to her, the hatred on his face as he stuck the knife into her again and again. The pain had been unbearable. Even at the time, she knew it was breaking her down, changing her forever into someone who knew what it meant to go crazy.

She was sobbing now, so desperate to get to her car and get home, but knowing she'd never make it. She was crawling so slowly that the man in her mind would catch up with her and there was nothing she could do. He had stabbed her and kicked her and burned her in her dreams, night after night after night. Jimmy screamed out his nightmares, but Lucy swallowed back hers, telling herself that if she never spoke of it, never even thought about it, it would have to go away.

But it hadn't gone away. She'd moved back to her house and moved back to her job and even tried to have a baby, but still the man was in her dreams. She'd tried so hard to convince herself that she was a normal person who just wanted to work and have friends and relax. She'd tried to convince herself that her headaches and her weaknesses were the only results of that day she couldn't escape.

But now she was face down in the sand and completely alone. And she was afraid, oh God, she was so afraid she thought she'd die from this much fear. This was what she'd wanted to tell Charles that day when she stabbed her hand. She kept forgetting what she had to tell him, but this was it. I am afraid too. I wanted you to protect me, but you couldn't, you can't. The man will still come after me and hurt me whenever I close my eyes.

"Do you need some help?"

The voice was kind, a woman's voice. Lucy turned her head to see an older lady in a gray sweat suit walking her dog. The dog was sniffing around her, and after a few moments, Lucy managed to calm herself enough to sit up and stroke the dog's soft fur. Finally the woman helped her stand and then helped her to the road so easily that Lucy couldn't believe how hard it had been before. Her leg was stiff, but working again. All the woman had to do was guide her.

Once she was in her car, Lucy reached into her bag and got out the bottle with the strongest pills, the ones she used when she was so wired she couldn't sleep. After she swallowed down two without water, she told herself that she was just having a reaction to how tired she was. Now that the film was over, she'd be fine again. There was nothing wrong with her; she just needed a little rest.

Fifteen minutes later, she pushed the driver's seat back and locked all the doors. She closed her eyes and forced herself to hear nothing but the sound of the ocean and the morning traffic on the highway. She wasn't afraid anymore; she'd never been really afraid. She'd fallen on the beach, big deal. It could happen to anyone with a bad leg.

She was almost asleep when she realized she was forgetting something, but she couldn't remember what it was. She told herself she could deal with it later, once she wasn't so exhausted. There would be plenty of time for everything now. All she had to do was rest here at the beach until she could make her way home.

PART FIVE

Sleepers Awake

nineteen

AFTER TWENTY-THREE years of marriage and twenty-one years as a social worker, raising three kids and burying her parents, Janice felt as though she had learned—almost nothing. Some people are lucky and some people aren't, and really, what else could you say?

Her friend Lucy was one of the horribly unlucky ones. It was hard for Janice to even imagine how Lucy had made it all these years. If there was any justice in this world, Janice thought, Charles Keenan should be sitting in some dive with no money and his balls rotting off. For what he did to her, he deserved to have his butt kicked from sunrise to sundown for the rest of his life. Especially as Keenan wasn't crazy. Let the psychics Lucy used to consult say he was sticking toothpicks under his skin in Maui or eating goat hearts in New Orleans, but Janice always knew he was sitting somewhere in a fancy house, just as normal as he'd ever been. He was power mad, but he wasn't even close to crazy. Not then—and, she discovered, not now.

It was a normal April evening: kids doing homework, Peter working on a brief, Janice trying to clean up after a late dinner, when she picked up the phone and voilà, there he was. She was pretty sure she knew his voice as soon as he said her name.

"Who is this?"

"I'm sorry to disturb you."

"Charles Keenan." She rushed into the dining room, where Peter was at the table. "Charles Keenan," she said again, looking at her husband.

Peter stood up, knowing this was some kind of emergency, but having no idea what to do about it other than stand up.

"You can try to trace this call," Keenan said, "but it won't make any difference. I'm not home, and neither of the children are with me."

"I wouldn't trace it," Janice lied, before looking at Peter, mouthing, *Could we?*

"What I want to know is if you'll talk to my daughter." He paused. "I thought it might be easier on her if you explained the situation. I want to give her your number, if you'll be home for the next week or so."

"We're always home. We have three kids, we can't afford vacations."

"Would you like me to arrange a car to take her to your house?"

Janice was so surprised she shouted, "She's coming to L.A.?"

"Yes. She needs to see her mother, but I'd like you to explain the situation first."

"What situation are you talking about?"

He cleared his throat. "That her mother is still alive."

"You bastard. You told them Lucy was—"

"She'll be flying on a charter plane. I don't know what day yet, but I'll arrange for her to arrive in the evening. Will that be all right?"

Stacy, her seventeen-year-old, was in the room now too, asking Peter what was wrong. As soon as he wrote "Charles Keenan" on a scrap of paper, Stacy said, "Oh my God!"

"I'll pick her up at the airport," Janice said, covering her other ear with her hand. "That would be better than having her come here."

"Thank you."

"But you have to tell me one thing first. Why?"

Janice could hear him breathing. She wanted the answer to this question like other people wanted to know if there was a God. She'd been there from the moment Lucy first saw Charles to the week before he disappeared. She'd seen it all, and she still didn't understand. Calling what happened "unlucky" was really just another way of saying she never would.

When the line went dead, Janice burst into tears.

The domestic counseling center where Lucy volunteered was in downtown L.A., a few blocks up from Chinatown. For eleven years, Lucy had spent every Monday, Wednesday and Friday at the center, answering phones, doing paperwork, and watching out for children while their moms were with the counselors. Lucy had donated the toys for the waiting area, and if a child fell in love with a particular stuffed animal or truck or puzzle, Lucy would smile and insist to the mother that it was all right, the child could take that one home. "Thank you," the mom would say, and pull her son or daughter's hand. "Thank you, Miss Lucy," a small voice would echo, and Lucy would wave good-bye to the child and take one last glance at the toy in his or her arms, hoping she wouldn't forget it, but knowing she probably would. A lot of the toys she'd given the center over the years were things she'd barely known Dorothea and Jimmy had. Charles used to buy them so much stuff she couldn't keep track of it all.

She always got to the center between nine and ten in the morning. It was a volunteer job, but it was still a job, and Lucy took it seriously. The counselors relied on her, and she never missed a day, even if she had to use her cane, as she did on that particular Wednesday. The cane always meant she'd get there closer to ten, because she had to walk several blocks from the parking garage at the building where her husband, Al, worked. Of course Al would have dropped her in front of the center, but it was important to Lucy to walk.

When Lucy came in the door that Wednesday, the only person in the waiting room was Janice. "What a nice surprise," she said, accepting her friend's hug and hugging her back with her free arm. Janice was wearing a navy blue suit and high heels. She was a good five inches taller than Lucy anyway, and now she was so tall Lucy had to look up to smile at her. "Don't you look official."

"I have to testify at a contested adoption. It's a messy case." Janice looked at her watch. "I don't have much time."

"Okay," Lucy said. "What's up?"

"Is there somewhere we can go? Private?"

Lucy led Janice to the office normally occupied by Martha, the head of the center, who was out this week taking care of her granddaughter. The office was at the end of the hall, and Lucy felt bad that she couldn't walk faster. She could sense how anxious Janice was to get there, and she wondered if there was some problem with Janice's son Kevin. Three times now, Kevin had been suspended from high school for smoking pot. The next time they would arrest him, the principal said. Lucy hoped it wasn't that.

Martha's office was a comfortable room with three overstuffed chairs surrounding a brightly painted red coffee table that a client had built for her. On the walls were inspirational posters. I AM SOMEBODY. DARE TO DREAM. CELEBRATE LIFE.

Janice plopped down while Lucy eased herself into her chair. Janice could never hide her feelings well and Lucy knew just by looking at her that she was nervous, but also excited. Now she was thinking that Stacy had heard from Stanford. Or Peter got the court appointment. Or even Janice herself got the raise she obviously deserved.

Then Janice said, "I have some good news for you."

"For me?" Lucy blinked.

Janice reached forward and took Lucy's hand. "It's really good news, Lu. The best kind. You're not going to believe this, but Dorothea is—"

Living in Wyoming. Taking classes at an agricultural college in Georgia. Working at an art gallery in New York. Appearing on an infomercial for an exercise machine.

She'd heard all of these things and many more. Most of the people who wrote Lucy were well-meaning: they remembered the story from years ago, or they read something about her in a "Where are they now?" type piece. "Your daughter Dorothea is my daughter's roommate at Penn State." "Your daughter Dorothea coaches my five-year-old's peewee soccer team." Janice herself had told Lucy she saw a young woman who looked very much like Charles clerking at a bookstore in Santa Monica. They'd rushed over there and the woman didn't look anything like the Charles she remembered. Of course it wasn't her daughter. Lucy tracked down all the leads, but they were never her daughter, any more than the leads to Jimmy were really her son.

"You're not going to believe this, but Dorothea is coming here."

"I don't believe it," Lucy said, and exhaled.

"Lu, he called me." Janice squeezed her hand. "Last night, he called me out of the blue and I almost fainted. That's why I came here, so I could tell you in person. I figured if you heard this on the phone you would keel over."

Lucy swallowed. "He?"

"The prick himself. Charles."

"Charles called you?" she whispered. "Are you sure it was him?"

"Positive. He said she'll be here in the next week or so."

"Charles said Dorothea is coming to L.A. Those were his exact words?"

Janice nodded.

"Did he mention Jimmy?"

"No, but maybe he'll come later."

"But Dorothea is really coming here?"

"Yes, really and truly."

"Will I . . ." Lucy's voice was quivering. "Will I get to see her?"

"Charles said she's coming to see her mother. That's you, honey, last time I heard."

Lucy closed her eyes and opened them, but Janice was still there. The room hadn't changed into a winding staircase leading to doors and more doors with nothing on the other side. There was no long dark hall with a child always running just out of her reach. No sunlit park where Dorothea was hiding behind a bush only to disappear when Lucy saw her pink sneaker peeking out and rushed over to see her daughter, ready to say, "There's my little pumpkin!"

She wasn't sure how much time had passed when Janice said she really had to get going. "Oh," Lucy whispered. She looked at her friend. "Thank you."

"I'll call you later."

When Janice was gone, Lucy wrapped her arms around herself as tightly as she could and leaned the side of her face into the soft chair. Later, she realized that the emptiness in her mind was probably shock, but at that moment, the blankness felt like a reprieve, and she was afraid to move, in case her body reminded her that something was different. If she felt her arms shaking or her knees loosening or her stomach lurching, she would know that it was too late, she'd given herself over again to hope.

She finally moved when she heard a shriek in the waiting area. She made her way into the front of the center and found one boy whacking another over the head with a large blue bunny. The shriek wasn't pain, but laughter. None of the toys were dangerous. Charles had bought them.

Terry, one of the counselors, said, "Great, you're here. I really have to get to work on a grant proposal."

"Sorry," Lucy said. "I'll take over now."

She watched the little boys playing. About five minutes later, when they turned their interest to the tub of plastic blocks, she went over and picked up the blue bunny. It wasn't Dorothea's favorite bunny, that one had been white with a green silk bow, but maybe it was something her daughter would remember. She put it next to her purse, to take home.

By Sunday morning, the waiting had become too much for Lucy, and it took everything she had to get out of bed.

"It's only been five days," her husband said, after reminding her that Charles said sometime in the next week. "I'll bet Dorothea has a good reason for not coming yet."

"Maybe," Lucy said. She'd made it downstairs to the breakfast table, but she had no interest in the crab omelet Al was trying to tempt her with, even though Al was a good cook. They took classes together wherever they traveled. They'd learned to make torts in France, pasta in Italy, tortilla soup in Mexico. The classes weren't fancy or expensive, and Al knew they were for tourists, but he didn't care. "We are tourists," he'd say.

"She could be in grad school taking finals," Al said now, tearing into his own omelet. "She might be studying oceanography or photography or even film, planning to be an actress like her mom used to be."

"Charles was the one who went to film school. You know that."

"Meaning what?" Al looked at her. "Are we back to how much better he is than you?"

Lucy shrugged.

"Let's count the ways then. Number one, he's a criminal. Number two, he's a moralistic jerk. Number three, he deserted his wife. Number four, he—"

"You don't have to do this."

"Neither do you. Dorothea will be here any day and then she'll learn for herself what the real story is."

"The real story is that Charles was a better parent than I was."

"No. The real story is that he was sixteen years older and already successful. He didn't care anymore about working, but you were a kid trying to make something of yourself. How is that bad?"

"Al, you know I was taking pills."

"Because he drove you to it with his insanity."

Lucy knew Al really believed this, even though she didn't and never would. She smiled at her husband, but a minute later, she was pensive again.

She knew how lucky she was that Dorothea wanted to see her. She'd read a bunch of stories on the Internet about fathers who'd kidnapped their children, and if the children weren't located until they were adults, most of them didn't want anything to do with the mothers. Al said this was because the dads had poisoned their minds, but Lucy didn't care about the reason; it was the fact that devastated her. She hated thinking about what Charles might have told Dorothea and Jimmy about her.

"Maybe she isn't here yet because she's spending the weekend with her boyfriend." Al stood up and walked toward the sink, holding his plate. "I'm sure she's in a relationship." He winked at Lucy. "She's your daughter. She has to be."

"What if she's already married?" Lucy said. "She might even have kids. It's possible. I was younger than she is when I had her."

"It's possible, but not likely." Al smiled. "If she did though, I'd get to call you Granny."

Lucy's eyes filled with tears. "I don't think I can handle this."

She got up and left the kitchen. Al found her in the playroom, curled up on the love seat, holding a rainbow-colored blanket that had been Dorothea's.

"What if she won't even let me see her baby?" Lucy whispered.

"If there's a baby, which there probably isn't, she'll let you see it." He sat down and put Lucy's feet in his lap. "Once she gets a look at the spread we have, she'll want to leave the baby with us whenever she goes on vacation."

Lucy looked around the room. "Unless she thinks I'm crazy for keeping all this stuff." She smiled weakly. "Like you and Janice do."

"We never said crazy. We just thought it might help you to pack it up. But like I told you when I first agreed to move out here, whatever makes you happy, that's all I want, babe."

She leaned over and patted his shoulder, but a minute later, she said, "I wonder if I'll recognize her." Lucy wrapped the blanket around herself. "I think I'd have to recognize my own daughter, don't you?"

"You will," Al said.

"I hope she's not disappointed. I'm sure she's seen all of Charles's movies, and she might expect me to look like I did as Joan."

"Didn't you tell me she was always smart?"

"They both were, Jimmy and Dorothea."

"Then she won't expect her mother to look nineteen."

"True," Lucy said, but she was already distracted by her next worry. She told Al about it, and about the next one, and about the one after that.

After almost an hour of this, Lucy said she was going back to sleep for a while. She wanted the time to pass as quickly as possible until she could see her child again. This was nothing new: she'd felt the same way for the past nineteen years. What was new was that it might finally be about to end, and Lucy would be really, fully awake.

twenty

MY FIRST IMPRESSION of Janice Fowler was as someone I shouldn't trust. Though it was Father himself who asked me to come to California and see Mrs. Fowler, I was wary of her from the moment she greeted me at the airport by remarking, with quite obvious relief, that I looked more like my mother than *him*.

Father had told me nothing of what to expect from this woman. When he'd wired me the money on Wednesday, his message said only that Mrs. Fowler would be expecting my call when I arrived on the airplane he'd chartered to take me to Los Angeles. The airplane was prepaid, he said, with a hefty retainer so that I could leave St. Louis any time in the next week, the sooner the better. I'd told him when he called on Friday that I wasn't ready yet, but I didn't tell him that I was waiting until I'd decided whether it was fair to ask Stephen to accompany me on this trip.

It was just this morning when I wrote him a note and left his apartment, very early. I took a plain yellow cab to the hospital and spent a few hours with Jimmy before going to the airport. I finally gave in to the impulse to cry on the plane, but now my tears were spent, and I was sitting in a crowded restaurant in a city I didn't know, with a woman I didn't know, who was forcing a stack of paper into my hands.

She'd asked me what I knew about my parents' lives in California, and I'd admitted the answer was very little. "Your parents were big shots," she said. "Here, see for yourself. I went to the library this morning and made copies of the articles they had."

The waiter brought my orange juice and her margarita. She sipped her drink as I began looking through the papers, reluctantly, fearing what I'd find there.

The articles and photographs convinced me at once of the truth of Mrs. Fowler's claim that Father had been known as Charles Keenan, and I myself as Dorothea Keenan. Mother's name was not Helena, but Lucy. But only a person of no imagination whatsoever would assume that a change of name was in and of itself proof of a deceitful nature, as Mrs. Fowler suggested when she called Father "tricky." My books were filled with people who had to use aliases to protect their very lives. Of course Father must have had a good reason to rename us O'Brien, and I planned to discover the reason, with or without Mrs. Fowler's help.

"Where did you say you're living now, Dorothea?"

"I didn't say." I was still looking at the last article. It wasn't blurry like the others; Mrs. Fowler told me she'd clipped it out of the original magazine and kept it all these years. I was glad she had because inside were color pictures of my mother, and she was more beautiful than I'd ever dreamed. Her hair was just as I remembered, my brother's hair, but much longer and thicker. She was very small, with a heart-shaped face, penetrating blue eyes and a mouth that, all by itself, seemed capable of compassion. She looked straight into the camera with a confidence and zest for life that made me want to break into a smile and sob at the same time. In one picture, Jimmy was standing next to her, and in her arms was a little girl. I was two years old, and this was my mother.

"What are you thinking?" Mrs. Fowler said.

The truth was that I wanted to hold these pictures in my arms and take them home with me. But I couldn't ask for such a thing from a stranger. I told her I was very tired, which was also true.

"It's after nine. I bet you are tired," she said. "Maybe we better make this quick. I already told Al we'd come by the club tonight."

"I'm sorry, who is Al?"

"I'll explain in a minute. Before I start, I want you to take a few deep breaths. I don't want you to pass out, honey."

I looked at her then. She had blond hair, a broad flat face, thin lips, but there was a kindness in her eyes. She'd told me that she knew me when I was a little girl; maybe it was true. Maybe she was there when my anxiety attacks first started.

I would have been worried myself if I hadn't taken the bottle of miracle pills from Stephen's medicine chest before I left this morning. He'd told me that he never used them, and I knew this day would require far more boldness than I possessed.

I told her I would be fine.

"And you're sure you're not hungry? The fries are great here."

"Thank you, but no." I'd never eaten in a restaurant with anyone but Stephen and the idea of doing so now was too sad.

Mrs. Fowler said she had to use the restroom first. As she walked away, I let my gaze wander to the tablecloth. It was blue but without the greenish twinkle of Stephen's eyes. Every time I thought of him waking up alone on the couch, I wondered if I'd made a mistake. I had his phone number written on the back of my poem, and I kept wanting to call to make sure he'd recovered from his terrible sadness last night. But if I was the cause of that sadness, then of course I could do no such thing.

If only I hadn't told him about my feelings, which even my dating and love book had warned me against. But Stephen's mother had given me the impression he would welcome knowing that someone cared for him. "He's been so lonely since the accident," Mrs. Spaulding said. I asked if this accident had caused the weakness in his foot. She said yes, he broke it, but the reason he limped was he'd refused to have it put in a cast. "You are the first good thing that's happened to him in two years. I know you haven't known him very long, but if you just wait a while, you'll see, he can be a real sweetheart. Before the accident, he was the most easygoing boy. Even if he's hard to handle now, he'll get better if you give him a chance." I wasn't exactly sure what she meant, but I told her he was very nice to be with now. Then she asked if I was hoping for a future that included him, and her reaction to my answer was so enthusiastic I assumed his would be the same.

"I guess there's no way to ease into this," Mrs. Fowler said, sitting down. She took a big gulp from her drink. "Your dad kind of stuck it to me when he gave me this job."

I didn't know what she was talking about, but I'd learned from my time in St. Louis that waiting was usually better than asking for an explanation. The meaning almost always became clear soon enough.

"I know Charles told you that Lucy died." Mrs. Fowler was tapping her fingers on the rim of her glass. "Did he tell you how?"

"No. It upset him too much to discuss."

Mrs. Fowler laughed harshly. "I'll bet it did."

"I'd be far more comfortable if you left my father out of this. Perhaps his feelings are funny to you, but not to me."

"Unfortunately, kiddo, your father is the topic here. He's the one who told you Lucy died, but the thing is . . . the thing is, Lucy's still alive."

My response was immediate. "I don't believe you."

"I had a feeling you might not. Hell, I'm not sure I'd believe me if I were you. I told Al, that's Lucy's husband, not to tell her yet that you'd arrived. This way we can go into the club and let you take a look. If you want to meet her tonight, fine. If not, I'll take you to my house and give you a chance to sleep on it and adjust."

"I have to use the ladies' room myself."

"Go on then," she said. "I'll get the check and pay. Meet you at the door."

I forced myself not to run. Once I was in a stall, I put my head between my knees. My heart wasn't racing, but I did feel the strongest urge to vomit, even though I hadn't eaten anything except a yogurt at the airport.

By the time I rejoined Mrs. Fowler, I'd decided that even if it was true, there had to be an explanation. The key, I thought, was this Al person, Lucy's husband. What if Lucy had left Father for Al nineteen years ago? Then he would have been as heartbroken as if she were dead. She might as well have been dead, since she'd never sought out her children during all this time.

Now I wished I hadn't seen the photographs. I felt like I'd fallen in love with her picture only to discover that she hadn't really loved me.

Fifteen minutes later, we were in Mrs. Fowler's automobile, inching our way down a street that was so filled with cars I couldn't imagine where all these people were going, unless they were trying to get to the ocean. I'd been looking around for it ever since I arrived, but I'd seen nothing yet. So far the real California was dirty and crowded and nothing like the beautiful pictures in my book.

"I have all Lucy's movies. Most of your dad's too. Some DVDs, some the old-fashioned kind. I got them out when Charles called, thinking it might be fun for you to watch some of them, but then I realized you'd probably seen them already."

"No. We didn't have a television."

"Jeez, that's different. My kids couldn't live without a TV." She glanced over. "Didn't Charles have a screening room? I remember Lucy telling me the original prints of all his movies were one of the only things he took when he left L.A."

"I don't know what you mean by 'screening room.'"

"Well, I've only seen one myself. It's like a movie theater, but in a house. Your mom and dad had one in Malibu. Lucy and Al turned it into a workshop-type thing instead. Al makes these cute little mailboxes out of wood. They look like miniature houses, with doors and shutters and even chimneys. It's just a hobby; Lucy says it helps him work off the stress from his work at the software company. He gives them away to people at work, friends, thrift stores. He made a two-story mailbox for my family because my daughter gets a lot of mail now that she's applying to colleges. And Kyle, my fourteen-year-old, gets a ton of magazines about cars." She paused. "Where did you go to college, Dorothea?"

"I didn't."

"Really? How about Jimmy?"

"He didn't either."

"I'm surprised. Why not? Your dad could obviously afford it."

"We were taught at home."

"Homeschooled? You can't do that for college, can you?"

"I think I need to rest for a moment," I said, knowing I was being a little rude, but afraid I would become a lot ruder if I continued to try to talk. I closed my eyes and leaned my head against the door of her car, trying to adjust to all this. If our mother was alive, I thought, at least it would help Jimmy. Even if she didn't care enough about us to send one letter in nineteen years, she would have to write to her son now. If I had to, I would tell her about his condition. Surely any mother would feel sorry for a child who was suffering as much as Jimmy.

I wanted to believe this anyway, though I'd read books with mothers who were unfeeling monsters who deserted their children and never looked back. If Mother was like this, no wonder Father couldn't bring himself to tell us the true situation, especially if he was still in love with her, which I never doubted he was. Even in those newspaper articles, Father's love for her shone through in everything he said. "My sweet bride," he'd called her. "My Lucy."

If I could forgive her for neglecting me, I could not forgive her for leaving Father and Jimmy. For the first and only time in my life, I could think of no reason whatsoever for optimism. It was dark now, and the flat, starless Los Angeles sky reflected the lack of any light inside myself, but I couldn't take comfort in the connection. Mrs. Fowler said the sky was almost always like this, due to what she called smog. So it wasn't a pattern. There was no pattern to any of this that I could see.

Mrs. Fowler pulled her car into a parking lot next to what looked to be another restaurant. She told me it was a club though. When I asked what kind of club, she said, "You know, a bar. Let's go in and find Al."

I didn't want to see this Al person, but I had no choice. I stood up very straight and reminded myself that whatever my legal name, I was Dorothea O'Brien, and I had a father and brother who loved me very much.

The club was a dark, smoky place with people standing everywhere in clusters of three and four, like acorns on a tree. Even to make our way to where Al was sitting in the back took several minutes, as we pushed through the small groups drinking and listening to the music, which was very loud but not unpleasant like so many of the songs on Stephen's radio. The music cheered me a little as I knew the piece; it was one of Father's favorite jazz songs, "Don't Get Around Much Anymore." He used to play it on the piano while Grandma and Jimmy and I would sing. Then Father would laugh that it fit us perfectly, since we never left the Sanctuary.

"You made it," Al said, taking my hand before I could stop him, shaking it enthusiastically. He turned to Mrs. Fowler. "I screwed up."

"You told her?" Mrs. Fowler said.

"I had to. She was so low tonight. These last few days have been really hard on her. Sit down, Dorothea," Al said, pointing at the chair next to him. I acted as if I didn't notice and took the other seat, across the table.

Even though it was dark except for the candles flickering on every table, I could see this Al was not a handsome man as Father was. He was younger than Father, but he was short and balding, with a graying beard and a paunch that made the middle of his shirt seem wrinkled. He asked me how I was, how my flight was, what I thought of Los Angeles so far, and I answered as little as politeness would allow. Then I turned my head in the direction of the music and discovered that it wasn't a record, but a live pianist and singer. They were very good, and when the song was over, I clapped heartily.

Mrs. Fowler leaned over and whispered, "Can you guess who that is?"

"Who?" I said, but she didn't hear me, and I didn't repeat the question. The next song was another one I knew from Father, "My Funny Valentine." I turned back to listen.

We were very far from the stage, with lots of people in front of us. I couldn't see the faces of the singer or the piano player, which was why it took me so long to understand. They were up to the fifth tune; Mrs. Fowler and Al were almost finished with their drinks when I realized why I loved this singer's voice. The fifth song was "Moondance."

The effect it had on me was like a starving man discovering a feast is within his grasp. I had no thoughts when I stood up and started moving to the stage, so I could see her. I was almost there when Mrs. Fowler took my arm and told me to wait until the music stopped. But I couldn't wait because now I could see her, and she was just as beautiful as in the pictures, maybe more beautiful because of the sorrow written on her face and in her movements and especially in the way she sang this song that she had taught me, sitting on the side of my bed at night. I couldn't remember her doing this, but I didn't need to. I knew it.

I climbed the steps to the stage like a girl in a trance, unaware of everything but the bright light over my mother, and the sound of her singing the same words that I had sung so many times over the past nineteen years. The expression on her face when she saw me standing in front of her was like looking into a mirror of my own feelings. The sorrow was still there, but it was mixed with a profound confusion; there was happiness, but even more, a desperate kind of relief.

She managed to finish the song, but she sang it to me. Then, after the clapping for the song died down, she said into her microphone, "This is my daughter."

The applause that followed this announcement was very loud, and there was laughter too. The intrusive approval of these strangers seemed very wrong to me, but not as wrong as what Lucy had just said. Though I may have been her daughter in the literal sense, she'd shown no interest in my brother or me for nineteen years. My father was the only person in the world who could claim me as a daughter. The spell was broken, and I knew I didn't belong in this place.

I moved away from her and off the stage. Mrs. Fowler tried to stop me, but I shrugged off her hand and kept going until I'd made my way through the crowd of people and out the front door. The sidewalk was crowded too, and I was so confused I didn't know which way to go. My plan was to find a taxicab and have the cab take me back to the airport, where I would wait until I could contact Dr. Humphrey to ask Father to arrange another plane to take me home. But the street was still thick with cars and I didn't see a cab anywhere. My heart was pounding, though I hoped it was only because I'd been hurrying. I'd taken my miracle pill many hours earlier, but I was afraid to take another one because Stephen had told me only one per day.

I'd just made my way over to a bench a few buildings down from the club, when Mrs. Fowler appeared. "What happened to you?"

I sat down. "I've decided I don't care to know Lucy."

"Good Lord, why?"

I took a deep breath and then another, but still, my heart was getting worse. "She didn't want to know me for most of my life, and I don't want to know her now."

"Wait a minute, kiddo. Lucy had no idea where you were. That father of yours took you and Jimmy while she was working in D.C. She came home and he hadn't even left her a note to tell her what had happened. He vanished on November 28, 1984, and she's been looking for you ever since, all over the country and the world."

"I don't believe you," I said, panting now, suddenly, horribly struggling for air.

"Why do you think Charles changed your last name? Why didn't he put you in school, come to think of it? Why did he tell you Lucy was dead?"

"He must have had a good reason," I whispered. My attack was coming on so quickly it made me even more afraid. My heart was already racing faster than I ever remembered; I thought it would burst and I would die right here, on this dirty street, surrounded only by strangers. I tried to think of Father's face, but it wouldn't come to me. I couldn't hear his voice either. If I died here, I would never see him again.

"Yeah, he had a good reason. So Lucy wouldn't find you and he wouldn't be charged with kidnapping."

"Untrue," I gasped.

"It's a felony. He could have gone to jail for what he did."

No, I wanted to scream, but I couldn't even speak. I dropped my head between my knees as the tears came too fast and hard for me to sing even if I'd wanted to, which I didn't. Singing was a connection to her now.

Mrs. Fowler was cursing herself for not noticing what was happening to me. I held up my hand and waved in her direction, hoping she would go away and leave me alone. But she didn't. I felt the bench move as she sat down next to me, and then slowly began to rub my back. I tried to shrug her off, but she persisted. Her touch was surprisingly gentle, and after a while, I managed to get one breath, and then another, but I was still sobbing.

"My father is a good person," I cried.

"Yes, he is. He's a very good person." Then I realized it hadn't been Mrs. Fowler rubbing my back, for the voice wasn't hers, but Lucy's.

"You shouldn't tell her that," Mrs. Fowler said. "She thinks you—"

"Charles loves you very much," Lucy said firmly. "The day you were born was one of the happiest days of his life."

I sniffed hard and gained control of myself, but Lucy kept rubbing small circles on my back, even when I could sit up again. And she kept talking about my father. She told stories of him playing with Jimmy and me when we were small, and laughing with us, and taking us places, and always, she said, loving us more than anything in the world.

I don't know how long we stayed on the street that way, but it felt like a very long time. I finally broke down and spoke to Lucy after she told me about Father teaching four-year-old Jimmy to play chess, and I couldn't resist mentioning that Jimmy had continued to play chess for all these years. "He's very good at it," I said, turning to face her. "He's also a wonderful painter. He's really a brilliant person."

"I'd love to hear more about him," she said, and smiled a quiet, rather shy smile that made me think of Jimmy. Of course she was his mother. This was all so new, and very difficult to keep in my mind. "But right now," Lucy said, "I think we need to get you some sleep. You look like you've been up for days."

I noticed both Al and Mrs. Fowler were standing only a few feet down from us.

"You have several choices," Lucy said. "We can drive you to whatever hotel you'd like. There are some wonderful hotels in L.A., as your father may have told you. You can stay with Janice, if you'd rather do that. She has a great family, three nice teenagers. Or you can stay with me. Of course I'd like that, but I don't want to pressure you. It's totally up to you."

I had no interest in staying with Mrs. Fowler, and I was still a little afraid of hotels. But I was nervous about staying with Lucy too, especially because I knew her husband, Al, would be there. I did need sleep though. I'd hardly slept at all last night; I'd been so worried about what was happening to Stephen.

"Why don't I give you a moment to think about it?" Lucy said, standing up.

She started in the direction of Al and Mrs. Fowler, but she walked very slowly because she seemed to have something wrong with her right leg. It wasn't a limp; it was more of a stiffness or weakness, and it wasn't her foot, but the leg itself. Still, I knew it was a sign. Here was the charming coincidence, a nearly perfect example. I knew what I needed to do.

I stood up and walked over to them, but I spoke only to Lucy. "Thank you for your offer. I'll stay with you tonight."

twenty-one

LUCY ALWAYS DREAMED of what it would be like to have her daughter back, but it didn't take her long to discover that the reality of being with Dorothea was nothing like her dreams. In Lucy's best fantasy, Dorothea was always glad to be home, thrilled to see Lucy, understanding of all that had happened before—and that was essentially it. What Dorothea herself was like, the person she'd become, Lucy could never imagine, no matter how hard she tried. Whenever she looked at the age-enhanced pictures of Dorothea or Jimmy, it was like looking at a gross distortion of their small child selves and it was both depressing and a little frightening, as if two oddly featureless adults had swallowed up her babies.

The most startling thing about the real Dorothea was that she was so absolutely the same person Lucy had known. She'd grown up, but she was still unmistakably the daughter Lucy had loved for the first four years of her life. There was no distortion, just what Lucy thought of as a completion, and a truly fascinating one.

Of course she didn't look the same, yet there were surprising similarities. Her skin was so white and baby perfect that both Al and Janice noticed it immediately: Janice whispered to Lucy that it looked like Dorothea had been brought up in a cave; Al said more kindly that it was one of many pretty things about her very pretty daughter. Dorothea also had the same hair she'd had before: dark brown, thick and very straight, though it had grown so long she had to move it whenever she sat down, and Lucy wondered why she wore it that way, when it had to be such a hassle to take care of. Her eyes were still large and the brightest blue, still clear and open in a way Al called "absorbing." Al also said Dorothea had Lucy's eyes, but Charles had blue eyes too, though naturally Lucy didn't mention that.

Dorothea had been born tiny, and she was still thin, but she was also very tall. Lucy estimated that she was about five-ten, though it was hard to tell for sure because she didn't slump like most tall women did. Her daughter had great posture, even when she was sitting, and it struck Lucy that this was part of the overall confidence she'd always had from the time she was very little. Al said she had a way of looking everyone directly in the eye, as though no one could intimidate her. "And did you see the way she just marched up on the stage? That's an actress's kid for you."

The other side of the story, of course, was that she'd had a breakdown only a few minutes later. Lucy had felt so sad when she came outside and saw Dorothea doubled over, desperate for air. Her daughter's breathing problems and rapid heartbeat were the one thing she hadn't wanted to stay the same.

Late that night, when Lucy and Al were getting ready for bed, Al told her he agreed with Janice that it was wrong to let Dorothea keep believing her father was a good man. "I know you wanted her to feel better. But you have to set the record straight."

Lucy told him that she would say more, when the time was right. Something was obviously going on with her daughter, and Lucy wanted to figure out what it was before she risked alienating

Dorothea. In the car on the way to their house, Dorothea had answered Al's question about why she'd come to California with a terse, "Because my father told me to." When Al asked how long she planned to stay, she said she'd rather discuss it later, but Lucy heard a sadness in her voice that made her wish she could fold Dorothea in her arms.

What had her daughter's life been like these last nineteen years? Though Lucy was reluctant to ask her directly, knowing Dorothea didn't trust her yet, she had a hunch from the way Dorothea spoke that it had been more than a little unusual. Al noticed it too. He said she sounded a little old-fashioned, but that wasn't really a bad thing. "No kids today say 'thank you' and 'you're welcome' all the time like she does."

The next morning, Lucy had an idea. Janice had already told her that Dorothea had grown up without a TV and had never seen any of Charles's movies. When Dorothea came into the breakfast room, Lucy suggested that she might want to watch *The View from Main Street.* "It's very good. Your father won an award for the screenplay."

"Do you mean now?" Dorothea said. Lucy noticed that her outfit looked a little wrinkled, which wasn't surprising, given that she'd brought her clothes in a large green garbage bag rather than a suitcase. She couldn't imagine Charles letting his daughter travel like that. She wanted to conclude Dorothea didn't live with him anymore, but she had a feeling there was more to the story.

"Why not now?" Lucy said. "Al's at work. We could watch it together and have toast or bagels."

"All right." Dorothea smiled a half smile. "I always enjoy movies. Thank you for suggesting this. Actually, I would love to see a movie Father made."

At nine-thirty, they were settled in the den, each with a bagel and cream cheese and a glass of orange juice. Lucy was steeling herself a little because she hadn't watched this herself since Charles disappeared. The only reason she even owned the DVD was because Walter made sure to always send her every released version of any of

Charles's pictures. He also sent her some of the profits, but she only kept enough for the taxes on the house and for the trips she took trying to find the children. The rest she gave away to charity.

The movie was about an Irish Catholic family in the fifties, the Lanigans, who live in an idyllic little town in Nebraska. Mrs. Lanigan and the four young children are wonderful, but Paul Lanigan doesn't appreciate what he has. He grew up without a father himself; he never wanted a family, but he ended up with one when his girlfriend got pregnant. He's not cruel; he just doesn't care. But then one day, as he's walking his eight-year-old son to the store, Paul Lanigan is almost killed. He's in the middle of complaining about something and he doesn't see a car coming straight for him, but his son does and, at the last minute, he pushes his father out of the way.

The rest of the film charts Paul's transformation as he comes to believe that the only thing that makes his life worth living is caring for his family. The plot itself wasn't why Charles won an Oscar; it was the writing, especially the part of Paul, who the critics said was like the biblical Paul converted on the road to Damascus, except rather than believing in God, Paul Lanigan believes in the fifties dream of giving his children a chance at a better life. The complexity of the movie unfolds as Paul Lanigan has such difficulty defining what that better life would be, and he travels throughout the town, asking questions, trying to understand why his neighbors live as they do. In the end, he realizes that a good life requires being moral and being educated, and he decides to instill those values in his children. The last scene shows those children grown up, and it's clear he's succeeded.

Lucy might have found it hard to watch, with all the focus on the father, if she'd been really paying attention. But she wasn't. She forced herself to look at the screen whenever Dorothea glanced at her, but otherwise she gave in to her desire to stare at her girl. Every few minutes, she was struck again by how amazing it was that the two of them were sitting in the den together on an ordinary Tuesday morning, just as if they hadn't been separated for years.

When the movie was over, Lucy was hoping Dorothea might open up a little about the way Charles had raised her and Jimmy. Instead, the credits had barely begun when Dorothea said that she needed to call her father. "May I please use the phone?"

"Sure," Lucy said, exhaling. She told Dorothea the nearest phone was back in the kitchen, but she didn't follow her.

A minute or two later, Dorothea was back. "I left a message with Dr. Humphrey. I hope he'll get it soon and relay it to Father. I'm so grateful to you for showing me this. It explains so much about Father's love for the fifties. Even the clothes he had me wear were similar to the daughter's outfits in the movie."

"Really?" Lucy said. Dorothea was wearing a short black skirt, a light gray V-neck and black chunky heels.

"I myself am fond of modern clothes."

"Me too." Lucy smiled. This was the first thing Dorothea had said that indicated any distance from her father, and Lucy couldn't help being encouraged.

The movie wasn't long, and it was only a little after eleven. She asked Dorothea if she'd like to see any sights, maybe go out to lunch. "Los Angeles is a great city. There's so much I'd like to show you."

She was just starting to list some possibilities, when Dorothea said, "Thank you, but I really can't stay. I do need to ask you some questions though, before I go back."

Lucy's heart sank. She'd clung to the bulky size of Dorothea's garbage bag as indicating that her daughter would be here for at least a week or two. What if Dorothea was only here because Charles wanted some kind of agreement that she wouldn't prosecute him if he came back to L.A.? This thought had occurred to her when she woke up in the middle of the night last night. One of the cable channels had recently done a retrospective of Charles's work, and there was a lot of interest in what could have happened to him, especially now, when some young director kept mentioning Charles as his primary influence and "spiritual mentor." This guy had even called Lucy to ask her to be in a documentary about Keenan's disappearance. She said no and when he started to argue with her, she'd hung up on him.

"All right," Lucy said to her daughter. "But could I show you the upstairs of the house first?"

Dorothea had slept in the downstairs guest room last night. Lucy and Al lived exclusively downstairs, partly because the first floor was more than enough house for the two of them, partly because it was a hassle for her to walk up all those stairs if her leg was feeling stiff, but mainly because the upstairs was the only part of the house other than the playroom that she had refused to change. For the first year, she couldn't bring herself to change anything, sure that her family would return any day. For several years after that, she was a full-blown addict, and the upstairs was the place she went to wallow in her grief and insanity. Then she met Al, when she rear-ended his car on the freeway. It was just a fender bender, but he insisted on driving her home because he could tell she'd been using, and then he came inside to talk to her about rehab. He'd done it himself, when he was in his early twenties, and he knew what it was about. She told him no, but he kept calling her day after day, and finally, she checked herself in.

Before long, she was off the pills and married again, but still, she couldn't move or change the upstairs of the house. Al agreed to move in, even though he knew he was going to be living side-by-side with Lucy's shrine to her lost family. He said as long as he didn't have to go up there, he was fine with it. Lucy rarely went up there anymore either, but she needed to know she could. Sometimes she thought she clung to all these things because she didn't have anything from her own childhood, not even a picture of her mother; other times, because she was afraid if she forgot any part of the past, she would eventually forget her kids completely. Or maybe she was punishing herself. Or maybe she'd just been waiting for this day, when she could take her daughter into the space of their family's memories.

Seen through her daughter's eyes, the upstairs was entirely innocent. Dorothea didn't remember the bedroom that had been her parents', the fireplace tool that Lucy had used to stab her hand, the balcony where she'd jumped the night she might have killed her last chance to have another baby. To her daughter, the only notable feature of the room was the incredible view of the ocean. "It's just like my book about California," Dorothea said. "Finally!"

Charles's office, which had been pored over by so many detectives for clues, was barely worth a glance, though Dorothea did say it was nice. She said that about all the rooms, more out of politeness, Lucy could tell, than true interest. Probably because the place where she'd grown up was just as nice or nicer. Even her own bedroom didn't seem to impress Dorothea, though she did say it was "very sweet." And she took her shoes off. She said she couldn't resist walking on such a luxurious carpet.

"Your father bought that for you," Lucy said. "It was right after you started having your breathing problems, and he was afraid you'd lose consciousness and fall."

As soon as the words were out of her mouth, Lucy wanted to kick herself for mentioning another positive thing about Charles.

"That sounds like Father." Dorothea smiled, as she stepped around the room in her bare feet. "My room now has a thick carpet also, but nothing compared to this."

"You still live with him then?"

"Up until recently," she said, but her voice was quiet and her face looked so unhappy that Lucy couldn't resist asking if something was wrong. "I'm sorry, but I'd rather not discuss it," she said. She slipped her shoes back on, and Lucy took her to the next room, which had been Jimmy's.

Dorothea walked over to the wall of cork that was covered with drawings and paintings her brother had made. "Oh, look at these adorable pictures!"

Lucy watched as Dorothea moved from one picture to the next, staring intently, as though she was looking for something in particular. Finally she stopped and pointed at a picture of a dog.

"Was this what our own dog looked like? I don't remember the dog myself, but Jimmy has mentioned him."

"Close. There's another one over by the corner that's more like Tigger."

Dorothea walked over and examined that one for a moment. "I just thought of something I do need to see," she said, looking out the back window. "The grounds."

"Good idea. I think you'll like it. It's really beautiful."

They walked around the garden together, with Dorothea stopping to admire the lemon, avocado and fig trees, and touch and sniff nearly every flower she saw. "I love flowers," she kept saying, and Lucy sensed that wherever she'd been living, they didn't have a garden. They'd made it all the way out to the guesthouse and back, when Dorothea said, "But where is the pool?"

Lucy swallowed. "You remember that?"

"No, but Jimmy does."

Lucy pointed to the cypress trees that had grown large over the years. "The pool used to be there. We got rid of it when you were two."

"May I ask why?"

The expression on Dorothea's face was so serious. Lucy wondered what she was thinking. "Yes," Lucy said, "and I'll tell you, but first, I think we need to go inside and have some tea."

Lucy made two cups of herbal tea. They sat down at the breakfast table, and Lucy felt herself becoming nervous. But of course she had to tell her daughter about that day. If Charles had never told her the origin of her breathing problems, Lucy would have to. Dorothea deserved to know.

She kept it as short as possible, and she left out all of the gruesome details. She said they were in the pool, the robbers came, and the robbers put Dorothea in her bedroom closet until they were finished. But it took time, and while Dorothea was in that closet she'd gotten very scared. Afterward, she was afraid of the dark, and her heart started racing. She'd lose consciousness when she couldn't catch her breath, not often, but sometimes.

"A closet," Dorothea said. She seemed lost in thought for a moment. "Was this the same room you showed me with the soft carpet?"

"No. You were only two and you were still in the nursery. It was a smaller room, but still nice."

"In this other room, was the closet next to my dresser?"

Lucy was very surprised, but she forced her voice to stay calm. "No, but the robbers put your dresser in front of the closet door, so you wouldn't get out." She paused and sipped her tea. "You don't remember this, do you?"

"Jimmy said he thought I was inside of a dresser drawer."

"During the robbery?" Lucy was confused. "So you already knew about it?"

When Dorothea didn't answer, Lucy told her to take a deep breath. Her daughter's bright eyes had gone flat, and her mouth had fallen into an expressionless line. "We can stop talking about this now. Why don't you tell me some of the questions you came to ask me?"

"Jimmy also said you were lying on the floor, cut to pieces." Dorothea's voice was hollow. "He said you were dead."

"But I'm not dead, am I?" Lucy said, as brightly as she could manage. "I did get hurt during the robbery, but I got better."

"You were hurt very badly though?" Dorothea looked at her. "You were stabbed many times?"

"Okay, I don't want to lie to you. I did get hurt and I ended up in the hospital for months. I was still hurt for a long time after that. This is why my leg goes out every once in a while. I have a cane for when it gets really bad, but most days I get by just fine."

"So it really happened. Everything Jimmy has been saying. It's really true." Her daughter was talking more to herself than to Lucy, but she sounded devastated, and Lucy wished she understood what this meant to her.

She motioned at Dorothea's cup. "Why don't you drink some of your tea? I could make us some lunch too. You must be getting hungry."

Dorothea didn't answer. She was staring at the patio door. After another minute, she said, "Did Father really get angry when you worked?"

"Yes, but he—"

"Jimmy said he even cut your hand to keep you from working." There were tears standing in Dorothea's eyes, but she was blinking them back. "Is this also true?"

"No," Lucy said quickly. "Jimmy's right that I injured my hand, but your father didn't do it." She felt like she had no choice. She had to defend him, for Dorothea's sake. "He was very upset about it. He was always worried about my safety after the robbery. This was why he didn't want me to work, because he was afraid something would happen to me."

"Because he loved you so much?"

Part of Lucy wanted to scream, No, he didn't love me. Of course he didn't love me. If he'd loved me, he wouldn't have taken my children away. He wouldn't have ruined my life.

Dorothea was staring at her, waiting for the answer.

"I don't know," Lucy finally said. "But it was a long time ago, and I—"

"Please tell me what you really think." Dorothea had regained her composure, but she'd wrapped her arms around herself, as if she were her only comfort. As if, Lucy thought, she was a motherless child, which she'd been, hadn't she? It was something they had in common. A strange, sad connection between herself and her daughter.

"Please," Dorothea repeated. "It's very important."

"In your father's own way, I think he did love me." Lucy inhaled. "But he kept me away from you and Jimmy for all these years. I don't know how someone who ever loved me could do that."

Dorothea sat up even straighter. "Thank you." Her voice was a whisper. "I appreciate your honesty."

Her daughter was quiet then, but her confusion and loneliness were so obvious to Lucy that she couldn't help it, she stood up and went to her. As she leaned down and put her arms around Dorothea, Lucy realized that the part of her fantasy where her daughter understood everything that had happened before was one of the stupidest thoughts she'd ever had. She wished Dorothea didn't have to know about any of this. She wished she could tell her something so wise it would all make sense to her.

It was the first time she'd hugged Dorothea, and Lucy wanted to cry when the girl didn't pull away, but instead, leaned her face against Lucy's neck.

They stayed like that for a minute, maybe more. Finally Dorothea said, "Will you go somewhere with me? It's very important."

"Of course," Lucy said, leaning back, looking at her. "Wherever you want."

"I think we should leave for St. Louis as soon as possible. I don't want him to have to wait any longer."

"We're going to Missouri?" She was very surprised. "That's where I grew up."

"I know. My brother went there to look for your family."

"Jimmy did that?" Lucy's heart was in her throat, thinking about her little boy. That she would get to see him too was like a miracle. This day was changing everything.

Dorothea nodded. "I feel as if I've betrayed him. I don't know why I couldn't listen to what he was so desperate to tell me."

Lucy thought for a moment. "He's the reason you're here though, isn't he?"

"Yes."

"You were trying to help him somehow?"

"Yes."

"Will you be able to help him now?"

"I hope so."

"Well, I think what you've done for Jimmy required a lot of courage. I think he must know that he's very important to you." Lucy waited until she caught Dorothea's eye, until she was sure her daughter would hear this. "I hope your father is proud of the wonderful girl he raised."

twenty-two

ON THAT SAME Tuesday, while Lucy and Dorothea were preparing to go to St. Louis, Stephen was arriving in Tuma, New Mexico.

He'd started his search for Dorothea at the hospital on Monday afternoon. When he asked Jimmy if he'd seen her, Jimmy told him she'd come by that morning to say she was going home for a while. "She said she's going to find out as much as she can about what happened to our mother," Jimmy explained. Then he showed Stephen the California book. "She left this for me, to look at until she returns." He smiled shyly. "She said if I keep looking at it, I'll see what she knows I used to be, just a little boy on the beach."

When Stephen stood up to leave, Jimmy shook his hand and thanked him for everything he'd done for his sister. Stephen felt like a piece of shit, but he said, "You're welcome."

He rushed to the Greyhound station, hoping to catch her, but she was already gone. So he went home, brewed a pot of coffee for his Thermos and hit the road. He still had the address in Tuma from the envelope Dorothea had given him the first day. The town was so small, it wasn't on his U.S. map, but he knew it was in the northern part of the state. The only obvious way to get there was across Missouri and Kansas and then down to the border. When he arrived in New Mexico, he'd buy a state map.

He drove all night and most of the next day without stopping. Finally, when he got into Tuma, he pulled off to the side of the road and let himself sleep for a few hours. It was four o'clock, and he set the alarm on his watch for 8:00. He didn't want to get there too late, but he was also afraid of getting there before she did. He wished he'd thought to get a Greyhound schedule. There wasn't a Greyhound bus station here, and the local bus stop was nothing more than a sign by the side of the road.

He startled awake and realized he had no idea how to get to her house. There were exactly three streets in downtown Tuma, and only one place that was still open: a convenience store/gas station. He went in there, thinking his simple request for directions would get a simple response.

The clerk was an older woman. She was shaking her head before he even finished talking. "You can't go to Charles O'Brien's place. He's a recluse, know what that is?"

"Yes, but—"

"We never tell anybody how to get there. He asked us not to, so we don't."

Stephen suspected she meant *pays us not to.* "Look, I'm a friend of the family. I really need to get there tonight."

"Nah you ain't. That family got no friends."

"I know both of his children."

"You do, do you?" She sat down the box of candy bars she'd been unpacking. "How?"

"I'm his son's doctor. I've been treating him in St. Louis."

She looked him up and down, but her demeanor changed as he

hoped it would. This was what was left of his medical practice: using it to impress people in convenience stores.

After he showed her his AMA member card, she finally gave him directions. Good thing he hadn't thrown it away.

It was twenty miles outside of town, and most of the road wasn't paved. The Checker was designed to take abuse, but neither Stephen nor his cab were used to anything like this. On both sides of the road were steep cliffs. He could hear coyotes howling, and all around, he saw the blinking of what seemed like animal eyes: deer, owls, maybe even mountain lions. He'd never seen a clearer sky. The stars were so bright they looked three times their usual size.

The path to Dorothea's house was even trickier. This was probably intentional, to keep away everyone that the convenience clerk didn't stop first. He felt like he was driving through a war zone because there was a crater-size hole in the path every ten feet or so. But what would O'Brien do if someone got stuck? Unleash a cage full of wild dogs, and then push the car off the cliff?

As he bumped along, he wondered what Dorothea had told her father about why she'd come back. Nothing, he felt sure, but that didn't keep him from hoping he didn't have to deal with O'Brien.

He finally reached the top of the winding path and there was the house. It was even bigger than he'd predicted, but he'd forgotten to factor in that a millionaire out here could afford a lot more house than a millionaire in a city. It was two stories, shaped like an L, with a giant front porch made of stone with a roof supported by wooden beams as thick as tree trunks. There were fourteen windows across the downstairs floor and as many on the second floor. There was one light on in the middle of the upstairs, but the rest of the place was completely dark. He wondered if the light was in Dorothea's room.

The entire time he was driving, he kept thinking that what he'd done to her was really unforgivable. It killed him to imagine how she must have felt, not just Sunday night, but the next morning, quietly packing her clothes (probably into grocery bags, since she didn't have a suitcase and she hadn't taken his), wrapping up her toothbrush, brushing her hair alone. Writing him that letter. Figuring out how to get to the hospital, and then the bus station. Leaving the city that he knew she was starting to love to come back to this place, which seemed as desolate as the surface of the moon.

It was unforgivable, but he had to ask for her forgiveness anyway. He got out of the cab.

There was no doorbell, so he knocked on the heavy wood door. And then he pounded. And pounded again. The side of his hand was hurting when he finally accepted that no one was going to answer.

Shit. If he turned the knob and the door was unlocked, he could just go in, but he wasn't desperate enough yet to risk being shot as a trespasser. He decided to walk around and see if there was another door he could pound on. Maybe they were in the back, and they couldn't hear him. It was possible in a house this size.

He found the back entrance—after walking right into a shrub—but pounding there yielded nothing either. He was just heading back to the front, to think about what to do, when he saw a small building in the middle of a field. He might have thought it was just a storage shed, except he saw a light on. Maybe it was a maid's quarters or the gardener's house.

If it was the maid, she could take him back to the main house and let him in to see Dorothea. If she was reluctant, he'd offer to pay her. It seemed to work well for O'Brien.

He was at the door of the building, an adobe with one or two rooms, tops. When he knocked this time and nobody answered, he decided to see if he could just walk in. The maid wasn't likely to shoot him, and maybe she was asleep.

The adobe was unlocked. "Hello?" he said loudly, as he pushed the door open. He didn't want to startle anybody.

As he walked into the room, he saw a gray-haired man lying on a brown leather couch, covered in several blankets. The man had his back to Stephen, but Stephen could tell he was asleep by the regular sound of his breathing.

He took this in at a glance before he was distracted by the unusual appearance of the rest of the room. One entire wall was covered with photographs of a woman who Stephen knew immediately was Dorothea and Jimmy's mother. The resemblance was unmistakable. She had Dorothea's mouth and nose, Jimmy's red hair and chin. She was also an actress, that was obvious, because another wall had movie posters with the same woman, but her name on the posters was Lucy Dobbins, not Helena O'Brien. Stephen recognized the titles of all the movies, and he was pretty sure he'd seen one or two of them.

There was a large desk in the corner of the room with a computer and a printer and four tall stacks of paper. When Stephen walked closer, he saw that each stack was grouped into ten or fifteen bundles, each bundle fastened with a rubber band. He flipped through several of them until he finally got that they were movie scripts. They had characters' names, stories and the tip-off: notes about camera shots.

The room also had a large rack that held maybe thirty cans of film and on the opposite wall, a flat-screen TV and a DVD player. The floor was covered with an Oriental rug that looked expensive. It was an elegant place, with the exception of a metal shelf in the corner that housed some gardening tools and a serious-looking chain saw.

Stephen turned back to the movie posters. One of them was for *The Brave Horseman of El Dorado,* and he realized he had seen that film. His mom and dad had liked it so much they'd bought the VHS. He'd seen it at their house, his second year of med school, when he was home for Christmas. He remembered that Christmas better than most, probably because it was right before he met Ellen.

He was facing away from the couch, still staring at the poster, when he heard the man say, "Don't turn around, don't even breathe." Then he heard a clicking that sounded like a gun being cocked. "You have five seconds to tell me who you are."

He recognized the voice and he quickly told Dorothea's father who he was. Then, for reasons Stephen couldn't fathom, O'Brien reached over and turned off the lamp before he said, "Why are you here?"

"I came to see Dorothea." Stephen turned around, but he couldn't make out anything. The room was so dark he couldn't see his own hand when he raised it to rub his eyes. "I know she's here. Jimmy told me she left yesterday morning." It struck him as he said this that she had to be here, or her father would have been frantic at the news that Dorothea wasn't in St. Louis with him anymore.

He waited another minute. "Mr. O'Brien?"

"Take a seat," the man said.

He wished he could see O'Brien's face. "Can I turn on the light first?"

"Not yet."

Stephen felt around until he found the desk chair. He carefully sat down and swiveled the chair in the direction of O'Brien's voice, all the while wondering what was going on.

"Do you mind if I smoke?" O'Brien said.

"No," Stephen said, wishing he'd thought to grab his cigarettes from the glove compartment. He thought about asking for one of O'Brien's, but then the man lit a cigar. After only a few puffs, the small room was already thick with smoke.

"I saw you examining my office. I'm curious, did you recognize the beautiful woman?"

"Dorothea and Jimmy's mother."

"Yes," he said, sounding pleased. "Both children look like her, each in their own way."

"Why didn't you ever tell them she was an actress?"

"A fair question. Perhaps you should tell me first what business that is of yours."

"It would have meant a lot to Dorothea to know."

"I doubt that. She and her brother haven't seen movies or television since they were very small."

"Because movies and TV are corrupt. I know, Dorothea told me. But not for you, apparently."

"Does this upset you?" O'Brien asked mildly.

"It seems hypocritical." Stephen was a little annoyed. "The TV you have now is state-of-the-art, but I'm betting you've always had a TV of some kind out here. What did you tell them this was, a storage room?"

"Yes, I told them this was purely storage. I also kept it locked, so they wouldn't wander in here when I wasn't watching them."

"And you don't think there's anything wrong with that?"

"Ah, I think I'm beginning to understand," the old man said, taking another puff. "You don't approve of the way I've raised my children. Do you have any children of your own, Dr. Spaulding?"

"Can we turn on the lamp? This is getting ridiculous."

"Tell me, do you have children? I assume you don't, or you would have some sense of the difficulties—"

"I had a daughter." The man was pissing him off. "She died."

"I'm very sorry." Again, O'Brien sounded like he was genuinely sad for him. "I can understand your self-righteousness, and perhaps you're right that if she'd lived, you wouldn't have made any of the mistakes I have. Perhaps you've never made any mistakes in your life."

Stephen inhaled. "Of course I've made mistakes."

"But nothing that you believe you can't repair, or redeem yourself from by doing better in the future." He snubbed out his cigar, even though he couldn't have finished half of it. "Nothing that condemns you in a fundamental way."

"I hope not."

"I hope not for you." O'Brien's voice was so somber it seemed almost eerie, especially coming from the blackness, disembodied. "The wages of sin are not necessarily death, even when you want them to be."

"Not sure I follow."

"God has forsaken me. He has turned his face from me for my crimes."

Stephen wondered if O'Brien could possibly be serious. It sounded like something from one of those old Bible movies. Then he remembered the pile of scripts on the desk, and it hit him that O'Brien had probably been a screenwriter back in California. Married to an actress. No wonder they could afford Malibu.

Maybe having the room dark was part of some kind of weird scene O'Brien was creating. Maybe the man really was a nut job.

"I hate to interrupt," he said. "But I'd really like to see Dorothea."

"Would you like to hear those crimes?"

Not really, Stephen thought. But the old guy sounded strangely desperate. He exhaled. "If you want to tell me."

"I'm a liar."

"Everybody tells some lies. It's harmless."

"I think very few people would consider my lies harmless. My name isn't Charles O'Brien. Dorothea and Jimmy's mother is still alive. I took the children from her nineteen years ago and came to this place, where I've been hiding ever since."

Stephen leaned back in his chair. "Jesus Christ."

"I thought I was doing the right thing. They had suffered so much. I wanted them to be safe and happy."

O'Brien, or whatever his name was, told Stephen a long story then. It started with the day he met his wife Lucy. He went on and on about how perfect everything was for the first five years. But it all ended on September 21, 1982, when Lucy was assaulted at home during a robbery.

"She was stabbed seventeen times and left for dead. Dorothea was locked in a dark closet for almost two hours while her mother was tortured. When Jimmy and I came back, he ran into the sunroom by himself, while I was looking through the mail. He was so shocked at the way his mother looked that he couldn't even scream. When I finally got there, maybe five minutes later, he'd turned into a painting of a boy, absolutely still, with his mouth stretched open wider than I thought physically possible, but making no sound."

"My God," Stephen mumbled. His eyes were finally adjusting to the dark, but he still couldn't make out anything beyond a form reclining on the couch, next to a tall lamp.

He was already feeling very sorry for Dorothea's father when O'Brien told him what it was like watching Lucy in constant pain, sitting with Jimmy during his nightmares, running to Dorothea before she passed out. Over the next two years, his family fell apart. Lucy drank too much and became dependent on pain pills. She lost a baby, and the doctor told them she might not be able to have another. The children didn't get better. When it started to seem hopeless, he began preparations to leave L.A.

"It was easy to create a new identity and move money into accounts that couldn't be traced. Within a few weeks, I had it all arranged. I left her the house and some money. I would have given her more, but I knew I would need it for Dorothea and Jimmy."

"I don't understand," Stephen said.

"I loved her." His voice grew thick. "I still love her, though I'm sure that's impossible for you to believe."

"For chrissakes, why did you leave then?"

"I didn't feel I had a choice. I thought I had lost her already."

The old man's pain was undeniable; still, what he was saying made absolutely no sense. "But you did have a choice." He thought of Ellen and Lizzie and he felt himself becoming angry again. "You could have stayed. You could have kept your family."

"I loved her too much," O'Brien whispered.

"What the hell does that mean?"

"It became so unbearable. She would get drunk and drive home and I could see exactly what she would look like as she went through the windshield. Every time the phone rang, I thought it would be the police asking me to come in and identify her body." O'Brien groaned as he moved on the couch. "I would dream of her screaming for help, but when I'd wake, she wouldn't let me help her. I wanted her to be safe. I knew if she was attacked again, she might not make it. I wanted to protect her. I was terrified that she would die. I wanted to punish her. I wanted her to stop leaving me."

The old guy's voice was trembling, but Stephen found himself thinking of Dorothea, sitting in the main house now, unaware of what was going on in this dark room, this strange confession. What did O'Brien want from him anyway? Understanding? Forgiveness?

"You had no right to do it," Stephen finally said.

"I made a mistake. It never occurred to me that once I'd done this, it would be very difficult to undo. Lucy initiated divorce proceedings almost immediately, so that the court would rule and give her full custody. She did it on the advice of a lawyer, who told her the police would take the situation more seriously, but it changed the act of taking my own children into a crime. I couldn't bring myself to return Dorothea and Jimmy to the place that had almost killed their mother. That world was too corrupt. When I left, I vowed they would have no part in it."

Stephen knew there was no point in arguing the corruption of L.A. He waited for a while. "Do you even know what happened to her?"

"She made two movies with a no-talent hack who was using her to give credibility to his schlock films. Lucy couldn't save either movie and they flopped." He paused. "Her drug problem got worse. Several times, I tried to help her get treatment. I sent the only person I'd stayed in contact with to see her, to offer to pay for any facility she wished. She didn't know I was behind it, of course. She always refused."

Stephen's voice was harsh. "Maybe she would have stopped doing drugs if you'd told her where her children were."

"I thought of this, but I also thought of the other possibility that I would be charged with kidnapping and the children would be handed over to a woman who was too troubled to properly take care of them."

Stephen knew this might have happened, but he still blamed O'Brien for starting it all. He'd brought this agony and loneliness on himself.

"Did she ever get treatment?"

"Yes. It was around Dorothea's eleventh birthday when I heard Lucy had remarried. I don't know where she met him, but apparently he was the one who talked her into getting help. He works for some company that makes education software. His name struck me as particularly appropriate. Al Goodman, the good man who saved my wife from what I'd done to her."

O'Brien let out a low guttural sound, not quite a moan, not quite a cry. The sound of pure despair, Stephen thought, and sat back in his chair, as if to shield himself from the blast of the old man's feelings.

"I pray to God for forgiveness, but he doesn't answer my prayers."

"Maybe you need to ask your kids to forgive you first." Stephen could already feel what this would mean to Dorothea. Her father was a liar, just like Jimmy said. Her father's entire life was a lie, and so, in a way, her life was too.

"I'm going to see Dorothea," he said, standing up. "I know she's in the house. I have to talk to her."

"She isn't there."

"Where is she then?"

When the old man didn't answer, Stephen decided he'd had it with this game. He walked over and fumbled until he found the switch to turn on the lamp.

"Holy shit." O'Brien was facing him now, without the blankets, and Stephen knew instantly that the doctor who'd been telling Dorothea her father was getting better had been lying through his teeth. The old man had edema of the legs so severe he was only able to wear shorts. Edema of the face, especially on the right side, possibly fever or infection, causing the right eye to seem to recede when compared to the left. Muscle mass loss in the upper torso and arms. Symptoms consistent with starvation, possibly with underlying congestive heart failure, especially as the old man admitted he'd been having chest pains and shortness of breath.

"God has turned his face from me," O'Brien whispered, reaching out and touching Stephen's arm. "I pray for death, but he will not let me die."

"God didn't do this to you," Stephen snapped. But then he said, "All right. Come on." He wrapped O'Brien in the blanket, leaned down and put one arm under his shoulders and the other under his knees. He grunted as he lifted the man and started lugging him to the door.

Once they were outside, Stephen shivered as his sweat turned cold in the night air. He kept going until they got to the back of the house, and he managed to shift O'Brien's weight so he could turn the doorknob. The door wasn't locked, but no one was home. He yelled for Dorothea, for anyone, until he finally gave up and asked O'Brien where the phone was.

"I don't want to be saved," the man said.

"I don't want to save you either. Just tell me where the phone is."

After O'Brien did, Stephen put the old man in a chair and ran upstairs. He dialed 911 and found out how to get to the nearest decent-size hospital, ninety-five miles away, in Pueblo.

When he got downstairs, O'Brien was asleep again. He didn't wake when Stephen picked him up and Stephen realized what an effort it must have been for him to talk for so long, given how weak he was. It wasn't until they were in the Checker, bouncing along the dirt road, that O'Brien woke up and looked around, obviously surprised he wasn't at home, maybe also that he was in a cab. But the only thing he said was he wanted Stephen to explain all this to Dorothea and Jimmy. He wanted them to know he was sorry.

"No way," Stephen said. "You're not getting out of this one. You're going to tell them yourself."

O'Brien coughed, but even the cough sounded hollow.

Stephen was squinting at the road, determined to avoid hitting a pothole. If he got a flat tire now, it could be serious. O'Brien needed to be seen within the next few hours.

"Where is Dorothea?" he said. "I need to know."

"California."

"What?"

O'Brien struggled to sit up. "Last week when she asked for the death certificate." He exhaled. "I sent her instructions about the plane I'd chartered to take her to L.A."

"Last week?"

"She told me when I called that she wasn't ready to go yet." Stephen could feel O'Brien looking at him. "She said she was happy in St. Louis and needed more time."

Stephen didn't say anything. The road was his excuse. He was off O'Brien's property, and he had to watch for cars in the other lane, and make sure he didn't miss the turn to Pueblo.

He thought the old man was asleep when he suddenly said, "You didn't tell her about your wife, did you?"

"No," Stephen admitted.

"Ah," the man said, too knowingly, as if he'd found some kind of connection between them.

He wanted to tell O'Brien to go to hell, but the old guy's eyes were closed again. Even as he slept, his breathing was quicker now, and shallow.

"You're not going to die on me, old man," he muttered. "You're important to her. Whether you deserve it or not, you're getting your ass saved."

twenty-three

IN MY FATHER'S movie, a man's life is changed forever by one moment. If his son hadn't seen the car coming, if the car hadn't been coming, if the man and his son hadn't been on the street that day, presumably Mr. Lanigan would have stayed as he was before, an unhappy man who didn't appreciate what he had in his family. It would have been another kind of movie entirely, the kind I'd heard Stephen call a "dud" because, as he explained it, "nothing happened and everyone stayed just as miserable as they were in the beginning." I asked him if there were duds that worked in the opposite way, where nothing happened but everyone stayed as happy as they were, and he said that wouldn't be a dud, but it would be unrealistic.

I found it strangely cheering to remember this as I rode on the plane with Lucy at sunrise on Wednesday morning—a plane that was owned by an old friend of my father, Lucy said, a man named Walter who owed her a favor. Though I was profoundly confused and miserable, at least my life had become much less unrealistic.

Of course the situation had a positive side. If I no longer understood my father, I now had my mother, and I was already growing fond of her. She was so much like Jimmy. Even her usual expression—friendly but reserved, as though there was something right below the surface that she was both struggling to keep in and wishing to let out—reminded me of my brother, at least the way he used to be.

His reaction to Lucy was nothing like mine had been. As soon as I told him who she was, he embraced her immediately, and then they sat together on the bed, where Jimmy and I usually sat, locked in each other's arms. When she told him about the day of the robbery, he touched her face and said he was sorry for what had happened to her, a reaction that hadn't even occurred to me. I felt so stupid that I almost said, "See, Jimmy, you didn't cut her yourself," which was the only thing I'd been consistently right about, but which was also both irrelevant and self-serving. I refused to stoop that low, especially as I felt Jimmy and Lucy had earned this reunion because each had looked so hard for the other.

Even though Jimmy had thought our mother was dead, he'd not only tried to find her family, but he'd tried to find the truth about her using only his mind and his memories. I greatly admired him for this, even as I regretted that I had not helped him, and in some ways had actively hindered him. Who was it, after all, who'd insisted Father could not have lied about his name? Who'd dismissed so many of Jimmy's very valid questions about our family as merely his rebellion talking?

I owed my brother an apology, and I tried to give him one, but he wouldn't hear of it. He agreed with Lucy that what I'd done for him had required courage. "If you hadn't come looking for me, if you hadn't found Mom, I might have rotted in this place forever." He smiled; they both did. "You're my hero, Thea."

"I didn't actually find her," I said, nodding at Lucy.

"Yes, you did, because it was your questioning that finally forced Charles Keenan to hand over the truth."

Jimmy had been calling him Charles Keenan all morning, as if he were someone neither of us even knew.

"I don't think so," I said softly. "I think Father sent me to California because he was as worried about you as I was."

"No, or the Liar would have told me the dream I was having was something that had really happened. Why couldn't he tell me that? All those times he sat with me after the nightmares, and he never said one fucking word."

Jimmy had a point, but the other side was that Father had sat up with him night after night. Why would he have done this if he wasn't worried? What could this be other than love?

Lucy was looking at me, and her eyes were sympathetic, as though she understood what I was going through. Perhaps she did, but her sympathy, though appreciated, only added to my confusion. The more I liked her, the more I couldn't fathom how Father could have done this.

When Dr. Baker came in to give Jimmy the many release papers he had to sign—because he'd agreed immediately to go home with Lucy; she wanted him to, he wanted to and even Dr. Baker thought it was a good idea as long as he continued his medication and started working with an outpatient psychiatrist—I slipped out of the room, mumbling that I needed some air. I planned to walk until my mind was clearer, but after ten minutes, when it hadn't worked, I found myself standing at the pay phone, holding my poem with Stephen's number written on the back.

I had no plan of what I would say to him, but I knew just hearing his voice might be cheering. Even the way he said my name might be cheering because the word had always seemed so easy in his mouth, not weighted with significance the way it sounded every time Lucy said it.

I dialed the number three times before I could accept that he wasn't home. I assumed he was out driving his cab, and for a fleeting moment, I wanted to run to the entrance of the hospital, thinking the cab might be sitting in the parking lot, as it always was before. Was it possible that I would be in St. Louis and not see him? We would be leaving soon, maybe forever. I might never see or even speak to him again.

My spirits were very low when I finally went back to my brother's room. He was dressed in the clothes Dr. Baker had found for him, which didn't fit well, but were the only option since the clothes he wore to the hospital were so bloodstained they'd had to be discarded. He'd combed his hair too, and he was standing by the window.

"Where is Lucy?" I said.

"She went with Dr. Baker. I think they have to settle the bill and then we can get going." He smiled. "I can't wait to see the house again. Mom said my room has so much natural light that it's perfect for an artist."

I sat down on the bed across from him. "Our house had natural light too."

"But it didn't have any real paints, thanks to Charles Keenan. Paints are poisonous, remember?"

"I wish you wouldn't keep calling him that."

"What do you want me to call him? O'Brien isn't his name."

"Couldn't you call him Father, the way we always have?"

"Why should I?"

"Because he's still our father."

"She's our mother, and you haven't called her anything but Lucy."

"I'm trying, but I don't know her that well yet."

"Whose fault is that, Thea?"

I was silent for a moment. "Do you really believe he had no reason for what he did?"

"No, but I know I don't care what his reason was." Jimmy's voice was emphatic. "What he did was so morally reprehensible that all the reasons in the world wouldn't excuse it."

He sounded so much like Father then that I might have smiled under different circumstances. As it was, I decided not to argue the point any further. I was too confused about my own reaction, and I was afraid of depressing him with my sadness. This was his day.

Both Jimmy and Lucy seemed so happy for the next two hours, as we left the hospital and went to the airport, and then boarded Walter's jet. While we were waiting to take off, I asked Lucy if I could use her small portable phone to call Dr. Humphrey. He hadn't called me back yesterday and neither had Father. When Dr. Humphrey didn't answer again, there was no reason to assume anything was wrong. Both of my calls had been close enough to noon that he could have been at lunch, and I knew there had to be dozens of other possible explanations. Still, I suddenly knew that something was very wrong. I handed the phone back to Lucy and thought for a moment; then I asked her how Mrs. Fowler used to feel about my father.

"It's clear that she doesn't like him now," I said, "but were they ever friends?"

"Where did that come from?" Lucy said.

"It's very important."

"Okay, then no, they weren't friends. I think it's fair to say that Janice never liked Charles. She always had a grudge against him."

I stood up and told Lucy that I had to get off of this plane.

"Now?" she said.

The very loud engine noise had begun. I knew in a few minutes, the plane would be moving. "Please. I have to see my father. It's urgent."

"You're not making sense," Jimmy said. "We already told Mom we'd come with her to California."

"But he needs me. It's very—"

"Mom needs you too. She's been waiting nineteen fucking years for this. You can't do this to her."

My eyes were stinging. I looked at Lucy. "Please don't interpret this as having any meaning about the future you are hoping for. I will come to California, I promise. But first I must go back to New Mexico. I have to—" I felt the plane lurch and looked out the window. "Oh no. Now it's too late."

The tears were coming, but I sat down at the table with Lucy and Jimmy, knowing it wasn't safe to stand during take-off.

"Dorothea, I don't understand," Lucy said.

"He was very ill when I left. That's why I went to St. Louis to find Jimmy."

"Charles is ill?" she said softly, tilting her head. "Is it serious?"

The plane was speeding up.

"No," Jimmy said, and looked at me. "Dr. Humphrey told you he's getting better. You can wait until we get to California and call him again."

"But it's not true." I sniffed, but it didn't help; I couldn't control my emotions. "Dr. Humphrey has been telling me what Father wants me to believe. But he isn't getting better. I think he might be dying."

As the airplane left the ground, Jimmy's face grew paler, but his fear was for Father, I could hear it in his voice. "How do you know this, Thea?"

"This is why he sent me to a person who he knew didn't like him. He wanted me to hear the worst about him, so I would stay in California. He doesn't want to get better. He wants to die."

The sadness was too much for me then. Lucy came over and held me; she also told me to take deep breaths, but my heart wasn't racing. I expected an attack, but instead my heartbeat was as stubbornly normal as though nothing terrible was happening, as though it didn't even know it was breaking.

After a few minutes, she said, "Hold on. Let me speak to the pilot."

She went through a door in the front. A moment later, she was back. "What is the name of the town in New Mexico where your father lives?"

"Tuma," Jimmy and I both said at once.

"Do you know where the nearest airport is?"

Jimmy shook his head. I told her, "I'm sorry, no. Up until Monday, I'd never ridden in an airplane."

She went back through the door. Perhaps five minutes went by before she returned, telling us that the pilot would land at a small airfield in Raton, New Mexico.

Jimmy told her we'd both been to Raton when we left on the Greyhound bus, and it wasn't too far from home. Lucy said she'd call a travel agent and have a car rental arranged. "But one of you should drive," Lucy said, "since I don't know the area."

"Neither of us know how to drive," I said.

"And we don't know the area either," Jimmy said.

"But you do know how to get to your house," Lucy said, blinking. "Right?"

"I don't," I admitted. "I wasn't paying close enough attention as Dr. Humphrey drove me to the bus."

"I think I do," Jimmy said. "But I was walking on the way to the bus stop. The route may look different in the car."

"Wait a minute," Lucy said. "Are you saying that you two never left the house until you took the bus to St. Louis?"

"That's right," Jimmy said. "No school, no grocery store, nothing. The food came to us in trucks; the doctor came for house calls. We didn't even go with Father to bury Grandma. He thought it might upset us."

Lucy's voice was shaking. "No wonder none of the detectives I hired could find you."

"I'm very sorry," I said. "I know it can't be easy for you to stop in New Mexico. It hardly seems fair to put you in this position."

"It's not about fair," she said. She was still sitting by me, and she put her hand on mine.

"I appreciate this so much," I said, and then I leaned over and kissed her on the cheek. It was really the least I could do, and I also wanted to see her smile again.

By the time we arrived at the house it was late in the afternoon. Lucy was a good driver, and she made her way into Tuma without a problem, but the trip to our house was more difficult, primarily because Jimmy kept wavering about which way to turn, and how far to go before turning, and whether we should go back and try another way.

We both told Lucy that she could stay in the car if she wished, but she got out without speaking. Her leg was a little stiff, and Jimmy helped her walk up the front steps and onto the porch. I ran inside and started yelling for Father, but he was nowhere to be found. I went into his study and phoned Dr. Humphrey again, and this time he answered. He also confirmed my suspicion that Father had begged him to tell me that he was getting better, but he couldn't say if he'd really gotten worse, because Father had refused to see him after I left. I asked how Father got my messages, and Dr. Humphrey said he called him each time. When I asked how they made the phone ring, he said he didn't understand the question, and I realized that Father might have been lying about the way our phone worked too.

"He's not here," I said. "But the Land Rover is. Do you think he might have left in an ambulance, the way Grandma did?"

"Maybe," Dr. Humphrey said. "Let me call the hospitals in the area and I'll call you back with what I find."

"Thank you. The nurse isn't here either. It's very disturbing."

"Your father fired her the first day. She told me that he insisted he didn't need her help."

I thanked him again and hung up. I sat at Father's desk with my head down for several minutes until I heard Lucy and Jimmy at the door.

I told them what Dr. Humphrey said, and Jimmy asked her if she wanted to see the house while we were waiting. I didn't hear her answer, but they went on down the hall.

It was at least a half hour before Dr. Humphrey called me back. I was still in the study, and the ringing sound of the phone made me jump. Father was in the hospital in Pueblo, Colorado. He'd checked in last night. His condition was considered critical, but when I asked Dr. Humphrey what that meant, he said it could mean a lot of things. I had a feeling he knew more than he was telling me, but I was too anxious to get to Father to press him for details. I took down the directions for the hospital and told him good-bye.

I left Father's study to find Lucy and Jimmy. I went down each hall, calling them, and finally I went into Grandma's old room to look out the window. They were in the yard, as I suspected, but very far out, almost to Father's shed. Then I noticed the shed seemed to have a light on, and the door was wide open. I thought they'd gone out to shut it, and I found out I was right, when I ran out there to tell them we had to go.

They'd gone out to shut it, but first they'd gone inside to turn the light off, and that's when they discovered that Father's shed wasn't for storage as Jimmy and I had always thought. It wasn't even a shed, but a full room where Father seemed to have been living during the time I was gone, judging from the pillows and blankets on the couch and many cigar stubs in the ashtray. He also had a phone out there, over on the desk, and a small bathroom off the main room. When I saw his glasses on the table in front of the couch, I picked them up and carefully placed them in my purse. I couldn't imagine he'd left his glasses behind unless he was very ill, and I was even more anxious to get to Pueblo.

Lucy seemed shaken by all the pictures Father had of her: an entire wall of them. She stared at them without speaking, and when Jimmy came over and stood next to her, she leaned her head against his shoulder.

I wanted to give them a minute, so I went to the desk to look at Father's computer. I wished I'd known he had this, because I loved Stephen's laptop. Of course I also loved Stephen's television, and Father had a very nice TV as well, though Lucy said later that the only thing he could have watched were movies, since the TV wasn't hooked up to a cable. But his DVD stack was so small, without a Blockbuster I couldn't imagine that he'd used his TV very often. I wondered how much time he'd spent out here over the years, presumably when Jimmy and I were in bed, since I'd never seen him go out here unless he needed a tool.

It must have been quite a lot of time, according to Lucy. A few minutes later, she was answering Jimmy's question about the papers on Father's desk, and she told him they were scripts. "A script is a story for the movies." She picked up one. "This is more like a shooting script because it has camera angles and other production notes telling how the movie should be made." Since Father had written no fewer than forty of these, and maybe as many as sixty or seventy, Lucy estimated, she said he had to be working out here almost constantly whenever he wasn't taking care of us.

"I wonder why he kept writing," she said quietly.

"I really think we should go," I finally said. "Pueblo is quite a distance from here. Dr. Humphrey told me it will take at least an hour and a half."

Lucy and Jimmy agreed, but before we left the shed, Lucy picked up a pile of Father's movie stories to take with us. I didn't understand why, but I felt it wasn't my business to ask.

The drive to Pueblo took closer to three hours; Lucy had to stop twice and walk around because her leg was bothering her again. I told her several times how sorry I was that she had to do this for us, but she said she didn't mind. Otherwise, she didn't talk much and neither did Jimmy and I. I knew my brother was too busy worrying about Father, just as I was.

When we arrived at the hospital, Lucy told us to take our time. "I'll find the cafeteria and wait there," she said. "We'll figure out what to do next once you find out how your father is."

Jimmy and I rushed to the room the clerk told us was Father's. It was on the first floor, but at a distance from the lobby, and by the time we got there I was out of breath.

The first thing I saw was Stephen, sitting on a plastic couch outside the room, with his head cradled in the crook of his arm, and his eyes closed. It occurred to me that he was asleep only after I'd blurted out his name; I was so amazed that he was here.

The first thing he saw was me panting, which must have been why he assumed I was having an attack. He quickly told me to relax;

everything would be all right. He stood up and pointed at the chair. "Here, sit. Lean your head down."

I told him I was fine though. Jimmy asked if he could go in and Stephen said yes. "But he's resting, so you won't be able to talk to him."

"How is he?" I said, when the door closed behind Jimmy.

"They've just upgraded him from critical," Stephen said. "That's a good sign. He's going to recover."

He put his arms around me, and I didn't speak or move for fear it would end.

"I'm so glad to see you," I finally whispered. I leaned back and looked at him. "But why are you here?"

"I came to your house last night and found your father pretty sick. I drove him here, and then this morning, I tried to track you down in L.A. They didn't have a listing for Lucy Dobbins, and the number for Al Goodman was unlisted. I was planning to ask your father how to get a hold of you, once he was more awake."

"You know who Lucy is? Al too?"

He nodded. "Your father told me the whole story."

"Why did you come to my house?"

"I was looking for you. I wanted to tell you that I'm sorry for the other night."

"Please don't apologize. I've been so worried about you."

"I have to talk to you about that night," he said, looking off into the distance. "I have to talk to you about a few things." He paused. "But let's go see your father first."

"Thank you. I'd like that."

As we walked into Father's room, he took my hand in his.

Poor Father, he looked so pale and terribly thin and weak, lying in the middle of the bed, connected by many wires to what Stephen told me were monitors. He was asleep; Stephen said it was partly his illness and partly the medicine they were giving him. "He'll be awake later," he said.

I leaned down and kissed him softly. The wrinkles under his eyes were much more visible without his glasses, and he looked older and so fragile and alone.

Jimmy was sitting on the windowsill, looking out into the dark. When I walked over to him and touched his arm, he muttered, "I don't care what his name is anymore."

"I know."

"I don't care if everything he's ever told me is a lie." His voice was breaking up. "I keep thinking about when I left. I saw his face in the upstairs window. I knew he wasn't spying on me or even thinking I would see him. He just wanted to see me."

I put my arm around my brother.

"God, he's so crazy. When I saw all those pictures of Mom on the wall, I thought, My father is fucking crazy." Jimmy was laughing and crying at the same time. "You know how I felt then, Thea?"

"No," I said.

"I'd never felt closer to him."

twenty-four

LUCY WAS SITTING in the rental car, on her cell phone with Al, trying to explain why she was in Colorado, parked outside of a hospital that was treating her seriously ill ex-husband. She'd already told him what she'd discovered about the bizarre way Charles had raised Jimmy and Dorothea, keeping them away from everything and everyone, as if their house—which was twice the size of their place in Malibu, and as lavishly furnished as the fanciest Hollywood palaces—were some sort of fortress against the world.

"He's all they know," she said. "For nineteen years, he was all they had other than their grandmother, and Margaret could never go against Charles on anything."

"But if he's as sick as you're saying, and he doesn't die, it could be weeks before he gets better." Al's voice was impatient. "Even if they let him out of the hospital, he might not be able to stay alone. What are you and the kids going to do then?"

"I haven't thought that far," she admitted.

"Lucy, you can't let yourself feel sorry for that jerk. He never felt sorry for you, did he? For all he knows, you could have died years ago. You could have jumped off a bridge and he wouldn't have lifted a finger to help."

"I don't feel sorry for Charles. I feel sorry for my children."

"So do I," he said. "That's why I think you should get them away from Keenan as soon as you can."

"Maybe you're right," she said, turning the key to start the engine, so she could turn on the heater. Tomorrow was the first day of May, but here it was still surprisingly cold.

"They should have been with you all this time. Then none of this shit would have happened."

Lucy didn't say anything. Over the years, she'd spent countless hours wondering what it would have been like if Charles and the children had never left. She wanted to believe that she would have stopped the pills and been a good mother, but there was no evidence this was true. She wanted to believe that she wouldn't have driven drunk or high with her children, that she would never have risked their safety—except she knew this wasn't true. She had tried to drive with them, several times, but Charles had always stopped her. She'd even laughed in his face when he'd said it was too dangerous.

Al exhaled. "I hope you're not wearing yourself out, babe."

"I'm not. Really, I'm not even tired."

He paused for a moment. "You said you haven't seen him yet. Are you going to?"

Lucy looked at the fluorescent lights of the hospital, stark against the dark mountain sky. "I don't think I can be in the same room with Charles. Even if Dorothea and Jimmy want me to, I don't think I can."

"Well, I sure could," Al said. "If I got to hit him."

Lucy laughed a little, but when she hung up, she wondered why she didn't want to hit Charles. She'd told Al the truth: she really didn't feel sorry for him. How could she feel sorry for him when he had what she wanted so badly—the affection of her children?

Even Jimmy had changed his tune completely when he heard Charles was sick. Of course she understood, but still it hurt, knowing it was possible, even probable, that they would never feel that way about her. How could she hope to compete with the nineteen years he'd had the children to himself? No matter what she did to make up for the past—and she was determined to do damn near anything—if Charles ever needed them, she could end up stuck in another situation like this, alone in an empty car, with her leg hurting and her stomach growling and her face muscles literally sore from trying not to let on what a strain this was.

The moment when she'd walked into his house was almost more irony than she could bear. After all those years of looking and looking for this place, it was right in front of her, and the door wasn't even locked. As she walked around with Jimmy, her own son, she felt the same sense of being an outsider that she'd had at the party with Janice, the first time she'd gone to Charles's house in Beverly Hills. She'd even stolen something, come to think of it, though she planned to give Charles's scripts back. Not to him, but to Dorothea or Jimmy. She wouldn't want him to know that she was curious, actually more than curious because there was an emotional side to it too. She was hoping the scripts would tell her what Charles had been thinking all these years, and especially why he did this.

She turned on the map light and grabbed the pile from the seat behind her. She needed to eat, but she thought she'd wait to see if Jimmy or Dorothea would come out and want to grab a bite. She had no intention of reading even one script all the way through, but an hour passed, and then another, and she was still turning the pages. Even when she went into the hospital cafeteria, to make sure the kids weren't waiting for her inside, she carried the one she was reading with her, and juggled it on the way out with the large coffee and donut she'd bought.

It was 4:12, according to the clock on the dashboard, when she finally put down the sixth script, finished, and decided to read only the first few pages of the three that remained in her pile. She was pretty sure she knew what they'd be about at this point, and she was right. They were all about the same thing, though Lucy felt sure most people wouldn't realize this. Even if all of the scripts were produced—and they could be because, God knows, they were all really good stories—only a few people who'd been their closest friends would ever see what connected them together. The settings varied from Texas in 1860 to New York in 2002; the characters ranged from coal miners to hotshot executives on Wall Street to people in Hollywood who were an awful lot like people they'd worked with (especially one particularly corrupt director named "Brant Markus"). Even the action was different enough in each script that it had taken Lucy hours to see what was always the same.

The characters always started out happy and then tragedy struck. Once Lucy saw this, she understood why every script had a first scene that was so peaceful and beautiful it seemed like a paradise. The pattern was even more striking because Lucy knew it was the opposite of the kind of movie Charles used to write, especially the Westerns, where the movie opened with a mess and then used the rest of the film to solve it.

Sometimes the characters made it through the tragedy, but usually only one or two were really happy at the end. And always, there was a man who was ruined by it all. Maybe the man was the father of a boy who had leukemia, and even when the boy got well, the father had already lost his job and self-respect. Maybe the man was the cause of the tragedy, as in the only Western in the stack of scripts, about a man who accidentally shot his best friend and was so eaten up with remorse that he became more dangerous than the bad guys.

Lucy thought they were all autobiographical in theme, but the sixth one, the one Lucy stopped after reading, was the only one she knew was actually about Charles's life. The script was called *Sins of the Father,* and it was about an eleven-year-old boy whose father is a policeman. The boy, Frederick (Charles's middle name), adores his dad, Joseph (Charles's father's middle name). But the boy doesn't know that Joe is really a bad cop and a bad man. He spends his nights in bars and strip clubs, and he accepts protection money from half the drug dealers in town. As in *The View from Main Street,* the son tries to save his father, but this time the threat isn't a car, but his own corruption. The boy is in the wrong place at the wrong time and ends up being the only witness to a robbery that his father pretends to stop, but is really part of. His dad is killed during an argument about splitting the money, but not before he tells his son to go home, and when Fred keeps clinging to him, his father elbows him in the face, hitting his right eye and sending him sprawling to the ground.

The person ruined by the tragedy in this script wasn't the father, who started out bad, but his son. Fred starts to change when he lies to everyone and says that his father really did try to stop the robbery and that's how he was killed. He even lies to his mother about his eye, saying one of the bad guys hit him. "Dad was trying to protect me," Fred says. "He died trying to protect me." His mother believes him because she could never think of her husband as anything but perfect. Everyone believes him, but Fred himself starts to go crazy.

Everywhere he goes, he thinks he sees these guys. He's sure they're going to come back and kill him and his mother. Whenever she's late at work, he has visions of her lying on the street, covered in blood, the way his father was. He starts skipping school, and loses all his friends because he can't go to their houses, and he's afraid to have them at his, in case the bad guys come and kill them too. By the end of the script, Fred is grown up, but alone in a dive in downtown L.A., still terrified to be involved with anyone for fear something will happen to them. The last scene is Fred talking to himself. "My father was a good man. A good father tries to protect his children, the way my father protected me."

The impact of this script on Lucy was like everything about this day. On the one hand, she wanted to scream that Charles had never told her about this. Even when the eye doctor asked Charles if his eye had ever been injured, since injuries could cause dropsy like his, he said no, not that he remembered. When Lucy herself asked him how his father died, he said he'd died in the line of duty. "Did you really see it happen?" Lucy said, remembering the tabloid version. "Yes," he answered, "but I can't discuss it. It's something I'd give anything to be able to forget."

On the other hand, Lucy wanted to cry, thinking about him as that eleven-year-old boy, and later too, when he found her on September 21. She wanted to cry thinking about all the times he'd begged the police to try harder to find the two men. She even wanted to cry thinking of the way he'd lived with Jimmy and Dorothea for all these years, as if he were so desperate to protect them that he was willing to give up absolutely everything in his own life, from his work to any friends to even the possibility of love.

Charles's scripts had a compassion for his characters that Lucy hadn't had for either herself or him. This was what she most wanted to cry about. For nineteen years, she'd blamed herself for her addiction and for losing her family and she'd blamed Charles for taking them. But in the scripts, the tragedy just happened. It wasn't anyone's fault. Their reactions were their fault, and eventually their downfall, but first there had to be the terrible event that they couldn't control. The act of fate or God or just bad luck that sent them spinning out of their good lives into something they just couldn't find their way out of.

All this time when Lucy was feeling guilty about her role or angry about Charles's, she'd never thought that the blame had to be at least shared with the man who'd attacked her, whose unbelievable cruelty on that day had started it all. If that day hadn't happened, what would her life have been like? She would never know, but she was sure of one thing. She wouldn't be sitting in this parking lot while her ex-husband, a man she never denied she once loved, was lying in a hospital, seriously ill. She wouldn't just sit there, knowing her children were inside that hospital now, possibly watching their father die.

Lucy got out of the car just as the sky was starting to turn pink over the mountains. She'd been up all night, but she was still wide awake. Even her leg didn't hurt as she walked across the parking lot and inside the door and down the hall to Charles's room.

If she'd had to think about what she would say to him, she would have turned back. If she'd had to think about how she'd explain it to Al later—because of course she would have to tell him about this—she might have decided it was a bad idea, after all. But she didn't think of anything other than the family they'd once been, before that horrible day, when she and Charles had still been living the first scene, the paradise of hope.

Outside the door to his room, Lucy was very surprised to see her daughter and some man asleep in each other's arms on an ugly, waiting-room-style couch. The man was good-looking, but Lucy found herself thinking like a mother, wondering what he was doing touching her little girl. She also wished she could cover Dorothea with a blanket because she had to be cold in that tiny skirt.

Jimmy must be inside with Charles, Lucy thought, trying to stay calm enough to do this. She certainly didn't want to face him alone.

But when she pushed the door open and went inside, her son wasn't there. No one was there but Charles, and he was awake. He saw her as soon as she walked in, but still, she might have run the other way if he hadn't recognized her, if he hadn't said "Lucy" with so much feeling, it sounded like he was seeing a miracle.

She walked over to him and picked up his hand. It was an older person's hand: thinner and more wrinkled, with spots of too much pigment and spots of too little. But it was still his hand, and she remembered what it felt like to hold it, to link their fingers together, to trust that they would have all the time in the world to stay like this.

She asked him if he was all right, and he said he was. Then she sat down in the chair next to his bed, and they started talking, awkwardly at first, but more easily when Lucy moved to the topic of Jimmy and Dorothea. Charles was able to tell her who the man was with their daughter. He also told her that he thought Dorothea was in love with this Stephen Spaulding.

"He's a doctor," Charles said. "A little troubled, but a good man from what I've seen." He paused. "They told me he saved my life when my heart stopped halfway to Pueblo. He used a technique the cardiologists call a precordial thump. It involves strong blows to the chest, to start the heart again. Dr. Spaulding punched me in the chest so hard he broke my sternum." Charles almost smiled. "I don't think he likes me very much."

"She's too inexperienced to be serious about anyone," Lucy said evenly.

"I tend to agree, but it's not up to us."

When Charles coughed, Lucy asked if he wanted some water. He said yes, and she poured him a cup from the blue pitcher on the bedside table, and then held it to his lips so he could drink.

"Do they know what's causing this?" Lucy said, sitting back down, taking his hand again.

"They're still running tests. The doctor said congestive heart failure, but they have to determine the cause to know what can be done."

"Are you in pain?"

"Not now." His voice grew gentle. "Not with you here, sweet."

She thought about pulling away, but then he said, "I know you're married. I'm sorry. I had no right to say that."

She wondered how he knew. She almost said she loved Al very much, but she had a feeling he knew that too. His eyes were so sad, especially the right eye, the smaller, damaged one. She thought of telling him that she'd read the script about his father, but then she remembered he'd never wanted her to know. There was no point in putting him through it now.

They sat in silence for a while, but it wasn't too uncomfortable. Lucy was glad she'd come here, even before he told her that he wished more than anything he could go back and undo the terrible mistake he made when he left her.

She listened while he tried to explain why he'd never returned to California, but all the while she was thinking that no amount of explaining would make those years any easier. Nothing could give her back what she'd already lost.

"I know you'll never be able to forgive me," he finally said. "I'm only saying this so you'll understand that I will never forgive myself."

"Well, maybe you should." Lucy couldn't believe what she'd just said, but the bigger surprise was she really thought this. "Jimmy is having a lot of problems, and I think maybe we have to get past our mistakes, to help him. Dorothea too. She's going to need us to be there for her as she tries to figure out how to live her own life."

Charles didn't respond, but he squeezed her hand.

"I wonder if she really is in love with this doctor. She never mentioned him."

A moment later, Jimmy walked in, looking tousled and sleepy, until he saw Lucy sitting next to Charles. That seemed to wake him right up.

"Is everything all right?" he said, too quickly. Lucy thought he was probably figuring Charles had to be drawing his last breath for her to be there.

She smiled at her son. "Your father and I were just talking about Dorothea. Do you know anything about the man she's seeing?"

"Oh," he said. "You mean Stephen. I know he's nice to Thea." Jimmy yawned and came closer to them. The next thing Lucy knew he was reaching down, hugging his father. "I've missed you," he said hoarsely. "Dammit, I've missed you, old man."

Lucy took this as her cue to leave, but she told Charles she'd see him again later, and she knew it was true. Even if she didn't want to see him, she'd have to see him for their sakes. And maybe it wouldn't be so bad for her either. Maybe the more she saw him, the less powerful he would become, until he was just a man again. Maybe the past would become nothing more than the years that would have gone by anyway, and Dorothea and Jimmy not the babies she'd lost, but the adults they would have inevitably become.

When she left the room, Dorothea and Stephen weren't on the couch anymore. She headed down the hall, thinking she would buy them breakfast and have a chance to get to know this man in Dorothea's life. But when she got to the cafeteria, she found them sitting at a table in the corner, talking so intently that she decided not to interrupt. Before she turned back, she heard Stephen's voice—serious, maybe a little sad, but unmistakably caring—as he took her daughter's hand: "I have to tell you about a day."

acknowledgments

Simon & Schuster continues to be a home for me, and for that I am deeply grateful to four women: Greer Hendricks, Judith Curr, Carolyn Reidy, and my dear friend, the goddess Lisa Keim. Thanks to everyone on the Atria team, especially Suzanne O'Neill, Nancy Tonik, Melissa Quinones, Angela Stamnes, and Justin Lorber. I am also enormously appreciative of the hardworking S&S sales force, with special thanks to all the wonderful people at the warehouse at Riverside, especially Barb Roach, Liz Monaghan, Gail Hitchcock and Karyn Basso; and all those who have graciously hosted me at the trade shows, especially my buddies Terry Warnick, Tim Hepp, and George Keating.

As always, my heartfelt thanks to Megan Underwood Beatie and Lynn Goldberg of Goldberg McDuffie Communications, for their enthusiastic support. To all the booksellers who have championed my novels and all the readers who have written me with their thoughts. To the friends and family who have stood by me during the writing of *Once Upon a Day,* including Sara Gordon, Alix Ravin, Jennifer Ammon, Mary Gay Shipley, Michaela Spampinato, Ed Ward, Elise Juska, Joe Drabyak, Kristin Callaghan, Elly Williams, Jim George, Sue Wanska, Ann Cahall; Jim, Jeff and Jamie Crotinger, and my best girls, Emily and Laurie Ward. To all the Tucker clan, especially Melladi, Patrick, and Leon O'Rourke; Andrea Hensley; Terry Jones, Jamie Freas, and Luke Pruden—I wish I could take care of you in this difficult time. In memoriam, Howard and Minnie Tucker; you will always be missed.

And finally, a huge hug of love and thanks to Melisse Shapiro, Kevin Howell, Marly Rusoff, and Scott and Miles Tucker. You have each meant more to this book and me than (my) words can say.